C000161966

NO SMOKE WI...

ALSO BY CLAIRE S. LEWIS

She's Mine

NO SMOKE
WITHOUT FIRE

Claire S. Lewis

An Aria Book

This edition first published in the United Kingdom in 2020 by Aria, an imprint of Head of Zeus Ltd

A CIP catalogue record for this book is available from the British Library.

ISBN: 9781789541946

Typeset by Siliconchips Services Ltd UK

Cover design: Charlotte Abrams-Simpson

Aria
c/o Head of Zeus
First Floor East
5–8 Hardwick Street
London EC1R 4RG

www.ariafiction.com

For Graham, Christine and Nigel with love

NO SMOKE WITHOUT FIRE

Claire S Lewis

Perhaps in this neglected spot is laid
Some heart once pregnant with celestial fire;
'Elegy Written In A Country Churchyard',
Thomas Gray

Love is a smoke raised with the fume of sighs;
Being purged, a fire sparkling in lovers' eyes;
Being vexed, a sea nourished with loving tears.
What is it else? A madness most discreet,
A choking gall, and a preserving sweet.
'Romeo and Juliet', William Shakespeare

Prologue

The dog strains on the leash, tugging his handler across the wet grass.

Morning sunlight hits the Norman tower, crenellated in black against the shining backdrop of luminous sky. The promise of mid-summer heat shimmers in the air. But the graveyard is still shrouded in the shadow of the church – misty and grey.

A shoe is half buried in a mound of grass cuttings and dead flowers heaped beyond the headstones next to the dry-stone wall. The dog detects it first. He barks and bats his tail before thrusting his muzzle into the steamy, rotting pile and retrieving the shoe in his soft jaws. He's young and eager to please – unfamiliar with the rules.

It's a lightweight ladies' trainer, the top brand, lightly worn, UK size five, in black breathable fabric, still tightly laced and tied in a double bow. But the dog doesn't notice these details. All he cares about is the smell – a smell that promises patting and praise and a tasty reward.

Though glistening with dew and encrusted with blades of grass and faded rose petals, the homely smell of her warm foot lingers in the shoe. It smells of something else too – no less appealing to the dog – salty and sweet.

It smells of blood.

.

PRESENT

I love it when You wear red. God knows, I love You in any colour. But You wore red that night at Heavana – a red dress that slipped off your shoulders and clung to your hips.

Of course, I had seen You before. We were in the same class. But I'd never really looked at You properly. And I didn't know what it meant to be a man until that moment when I watched You sipping Cuban cocktails and laughing with your girlfriends at the bar. You triggered something deep in my core that night. I understood right then that everything had changed.

You've only got yourself to blame. Your profile was so perfect, lit in that red glow. Then You turned. Your eyes were on fire. Your lips were slightly open. You looked right past me at some other man.

And it felt like a stab in the chest.

That's when it started. So now every time I see You, I see red. And every time I see red, I think of You and how I felt

that night – a red sunset, a red rose, a red drop of blood – I
see You and I know You are mine.

'We should do this more often,' said Celeste.

Breathless and damp from dancing, the girls were leaning across the counter, flirting shamelessly with the Australian barman who had just taken their order for mojitos and was giving them all his attention, to the irritation of other customers jostling to be served. The cocktails were outrageously expensive, but Celeste didn't care. She was celebrating her twenty-fourth birthday, the actual date of which had fallen earlier in the week, with her two best girlfriends. Having at first resisted the idea of a big night out at Heavana Republica (dreading the inevitable grim hangover at work the following morning), now that she was here, she was determined to get drunk and have a good time.

It was Anya who had persuaded Celeste to ditch their usual venue for a girls' night – an authentic little Italian restaurant tucked away on one of the quiet streets in the Pimlico grid. Anya had ducked out of a client meeting at her law firm to email a screen shot of Heavana's web page to Celeste.

'Grit and glamour fuse together to create a cool and contemporary Cuban backdrop: enter the club through our rum shop to an eclectic interior shaped by exposed brickwork, graffiti-splashed walls, jazz club ceiling fans and vintage decor. Capture the exuberance and colour of Cuba on the dance floor. If it's a chilled-out vibe you're looking for, relax under the stars at our rooftop bar where you'll discover the finest selection of exotic cocktails and rum this side of Havana!'

The club was holding a red-themed 'night before Valentine's' in place of their usual Thursday DJ club night.

'*Just the thing to shake off your February blues,*' Anya had commented at the bottom of her text, '*#paint-the-town-red.*'

Celeste had put the phone down on the stone worktop to finish tying the roses she'd been preparing for an order when the message had flashed up on her screen. She'd caught her hand on a thorn as she trimmed the stems. She'd licked the droplet of blood from her finger and dipped her face into the blooms to inhale their delicate fragrance before wrapping the bouquet in a length of cellophane, ready for collection by the customer.

Why not? she'd thought. *I deserve a bit of fun.*

From the instant Celeste had escaped into the club, leaving behind a frozen grey townscape on a shabby stretch of the King's Road, she had felt released from the tension of her long day's work at the florist's. She had mingled with the crowd of pulsating bodies on the dance floor, giving up her own body and mind to the hot, intoxicating assault of live Cuban music. Her senses were overcome by the coloured lights that swirled overhead and the pungent waves of cigar smoke, pot, sweat, perfume, aftershave and Havana Club rum as she moved among the dancers.

Now she watched the Australian barman, her eyes drawn irresistibly to the muscles flexing in his upper arms and chest as he flicked the cocktail shaker and expertly scooped crushed ice into tall glasses and sliced the limes into quarters with a sharp knife. It might have been the alcohol she had already consumed but there was something extraordinarily sensual in the way he poured the syrup of brown sugar and rum into her glass, before topping it up with soda water and teasing sprigs of mint to the bottom with a long spoon while at the same time gently lifting the syrup and segments of lime to the surface.

'This one's on the house,' he said sliding it across to Celeste. 'Happy birthday to the lady in red.' She was cashing in on the attention even though it wasn't strictly her birthday. His eyes lingered on the curve of her shoulder.

Two more bartenders got in on the act, pouring out shot glasses, which they distributed riotously to Celeste and her friends before helping themselves and toasting the birthday girl. It was a long time since Celeste had felt so carefree – and sexy. Generally, these days she didn't bother much with cosmetics but she had made a special effort for this evening. She had straightened her dark blonde hair and meticulously applied her make-up, complementing highlighters and bronzers with smoky colours round her eyes to make them pop and dramatic red lipstick to match her dress. She'd ordered a new dress online especially for the occasion. It was fitted and accentuated her cleavage and bare neck. She wore no jewellery except for rows and rows of bracelets that glittered in the spotlights as she raised the glass to her lips. She was bored with the 'ice-maiden' label that her friends teased her with, telling her that guys were intimidated by her reserve and her Disney-princess demeanour. Well tonight she was throwing caution to the wind, putting herself out there as a vamp!

It was true that she hadn't had a boyfriend since she was seventeen years old. And even then, he wasn't a proper boyfriend. God, she'd been single for almost seven years but that didn't mean she was short of admirers. She hadn't exactly shut herself away in an ivory tower. She just hadn't found anyone she could get close to.

'Another year older and still single. It's not as if I haven't put myself out there,' she said.

She'd been out on a couple of dates but nothing serious. In a moment of weakness a few months earlier, she'd even given in to pressure from Jessica who worked in advertising and was into that kind of thing, to sign herself up on Tinder. But she rarely got beyond the first messages, let alone the first date. Anytime anyone got too interested, she shut him down. That was the beauty of online dating – you could press 'delete'.

'You'll never find the man of your dreams if you never give anyone a chance,' lectured Anya.

Celeste didn't care. She wasn't in any hurry to give anyone access to her personal space.

I'd rather be alone than with a loser like Miles, she thought secretly. Anya's new boyfriend was a back-office computer support executive (whatever that meant) whose idea of a good night out was six pints at the local pub followed by a take-away curry. In Celeste's opinion he was definitely punching above his weight. Anya was so intelligent and really quite attractive in her own sophisticated way.

After the third shot, Celeste's head throbbed, and the bar swayed up and down as if she were on a cruise ship in a storm. She stood up and gripped the counter to steady herself. Her friends would write her off as a lightweight for bailing, but she didn't care. Her mood had changed. She'd had enough of all the banter. She decided to go and splash some water on her face to freshen up. The sense of being out of control unnerved her and she didn't like the way the Australian bartender, who by now had introduced himself as 'Brett', was crossing the line, touching her forearm and undressing her with his eyes. She looked away and tugged at the neckline of her dress, which had slipped down revealing an inch or two of black lace.

Turning her back on the bar, by force of habit she scanned the room from left to right, preparing to navigate her way across the dance floor to the cloakrooms. Confronted by the crowd of strangers, she felt trapped. She switched to her default mode of high alert.

As she peered into the tangle of dancers, her face froze. Like an animal, her body reacted, even before her brain processed the thought. She remained fixed to the spot, open-mouthed, while her heart pumped so hard that she could feel the pulse in the veins of her neck. The silhouette of a man across the dance floor had captured her attention. At first, she thought her mind was playing tricks on her. Perhaps the alcohol was messing with her head? But the more she stared the more certain she became. That shadow from her past, but standing taller, and broader – yet with the same brazen swagger, the same easy smile. He was here in this club – only metres away. Her fists tightened and her legs began to shake… How dare he come here! He was supposed to be on the other side of the Atlantic, an ocean away. This was her patch. But it had to be him… right here, escorting a scantily clad waitress through the crowd.

For a fleeting second, she caught his eyes and despite the

changes she had made to her appearance, she saw a flicker of recognition ignite his features before he turned away.

Her cheeks burning, she watched him go, clearing the bodies, chest thrown back, a Champagne glass held high in each hand, the magnum-bearing waitress in tow, until he stopped at a VIP cubicle where a woman with a long sweep of platinum-blonde hair sat facing the brick wall.

PRESENT

2

You think you've given me the slip. But I am too quick for You. I feel sorry for You standing there in the rain, waving your arms above your head like a person drowning. You are so desperate to hail a cab and make your getaway that You don't see me slowly wheeling my motorbike out onto the street. You don't even turn your head when I accelerate past You, riding so close to the kerb that I can almost touch You. In my rear-view mirror, I see You stumble backwards, startled by the spray of water splashing up against your legs.

You should be more careful with your things – and your settings. It takes me all of thirty seconds to find out your name and where You live. I race You home, weaving in and out of the bus lanes to dodge the late-night buses, jumping the lights at the crossroads. By the time the headlights of your taxi come into sight my bike is tucked behind a skip and I am between the hedge and the bins waiting for You.

I watch You handing money to the driver and turning on

your heels. I watch You clicking up the steps and crouching down to rummage through your handbag. You look over your shoulder as you turn the key. You look so sad and lonely.

From now on, You have nothing to fear – I'm your 'someone'.

I'll be watching over you.

Celeste slammed and locked the door of the apartment. She leaned back against the smooth wood, took a deep breath and snapped on all the lights in the hallway. Instead of re-joining her girlfriends at the bar, she had taken one look at her stricken reflection in the toilet mirror, collected her coat and bag from the cloakroom and fled through the emergency exit of the club out to a backstreet where she'd hailed the first passing black cab.

Now home at last her head was spinning and her legs were like putty. She always hated coming home alone to an empty flat. After the shock of seeing him, it was even worse. She pulled off her heels and padded around the flat in her stockinged feet, peering into cupboards and behind doors, turning on the lights in the sitting room and the bathroom, glancing into the shadows of each bedroom before pulling the door firmly shut. Everything was normal. Everything was in its place. Though she knew it was irrational, this was her routine whenever she came home alone. It was impossible to relax until she was certain that no intruder had broken into the flat in her absence. Now the intruder who had stalked her imagination these last seven years was back in flesh and blood.

'Damn him, damn him,' she said bitterly. 'Tonight, of all nights!' She stood in front of the bathroom mirror, gripping the china basin to stop herself smashing her fists against the glass. 'Why did that bastard have to ruin my birthday celebration?' Her rage was as hot and as red as the day after the fire. But it wasn't just anger that flooded her veins and mottled her skin. No. It was shame – a flush of shame and self-hatred that flowed through her entire body like molten lava until she wished she could melt away into the cracks of the bathroom tiles and disappear.

'What's he doing back here?' She wiped away her make-up then ripped off her dress and the bracelets that hid the scars on her wrists and stepped into the steaming jet of water in the shower to scrub away the smell of the club that lingered on her skin and in her hair – the nauseating stench of alcohol, tobacco and weed that after seeing him now rekindled horrific scenes from that night almost seven years ago.

Feeling cleansed at last, wrapped in Jessi's bathrobe, her skin tingling and perfumed with Anya's bath oils, she began to regain control. Now that her head was clearer, she noticed she was starving and had a sudden urge for comfort food to calm her nerves. She'd skipped supper to make herself look super-skinny in her bodycon. She made herself a cup of tea and put a pizza in the oven. She would take a couple of slices. No doubt Jessi and Anya would polish it off when they got back from Heavana later on.

She picked her jacket off the floor and wandered over to the music dock with the intention of plugging in the music from her phone. She was in for another shock. When she reached into her zip-up pockets, they were empty. She tipped the contents of her bag out onto the kitchen table with growing frustration and turned the bag inside out. Not there. She began to panic – she must have dropped it in the cab or left it at the club. This was worse than losing her credit cards or her keys. Her whole life was stored on that phone!

'Calm down and think!' she told herself. She took her tea over to the sofa where she sank into the soft cushions. 'I'll drink this cup of tea and then I'll work out what to do.'

As she sipped the scalding tea, she tried to recall when she last had her phone.

Just before she had walked off to the cloakroom, she remembered Jessi grabbing it out of her hand to take a selfie of the two of them downing shots with Brett. She had a vague recollection of Jessi handing it back to her.

'Damn! I must have left it on the bar,' she said out loud. There was no landline in the flat, so she had no way of calling the club to check if someone had handed it in. She'd just have to wait until the girls came home when she could borrow one of their phones to make the call.

Without her music, every creak and murmur from the building echoed round the flat. The usual domestic noises from the pipework and utilities took on an eerie quality. She thought she heard footsteps on the communal stairs. It didn't help that their money-grabbing landlord had failed to repair the deadlock on the communal entrance, leaving only one flimsy lock on the peeling old front door to prevent anyone from walking in off the street and climbing the shabby staircase.

But when she threw open the door to the landing, of course, there was no one there. Too rattled to go to sleep in her bedroom, Celeste lay back on the sofa unsuccessfully practising her mindfulness techniques and trying to get some rest in preparation for her exceptionally early start at the florist's the next morning for Valentine's Day. All the while she was listening out for her friends' return.

In the darkness, ordinary night-time noises from the residential side street were magnified and menacing. She heard the neighbours' cats fighting, and a rustling below the window, which she imagined must be some creature of the night going about its business. Further down the street a dog started barking, setting Celeste's nerves on edge again. In the distance, the hum of traffic was broken by sirens wailing from the direction of the high street. There were no curtains in the living room since the landlord was dragging out getting replacements for the ghastly rags the girls had taken down when they moved in, so the headlights from the occasional passing car swept through the room like a searchlight.

Eventually she heard the diesel rumble of a taxi approaching. Now fully awake, she sat bolt upright on the sofa, listening to the sound of tyres on wet tarmac as it pulled up outside the house, car doors opening and closing, and Jessi and Anya, their voices loud and shrill, talking to someone on the driveway. As the girls pushed open the communal entrance to the building, Celeste heard someone's footsteps crossing the road, followed by a motorbike engine starting up and then moving away. Right then, she heard the key turning in the lock and at last her friends stumbled through the door, shrieking at Celeste.

'Oh my God! Celeste, thank God you're here. We were worried sick about you. I was going to call the police if you weren't here.' Celeste noticed that they were completely drunk and thought cynically that however worried they had been, it hadn't stopped them enjoying another two hours at Heavana without her.

'Why did you go off like that without telling us? We sent you about a hundred texts. Look…' said Anya, holding out Celeste's mobile phone.

'Oh! Thank God! Thank you, thank you – you found it!' It was Celeste's turn to express relief. 'I thought it was gone for good. It would have been a nightmare to lose my phone.'

'It's not me you should thank,' said Anya. 'Some guy brought it back here for you. He was standing by the doorstep and recognised us from the club.'

'Did he tell you his name? What did he look like?' asked Celeste suspiciously.

'He was wearing a motorcycle helmet so I couldn't see his face properly,' said Anya. 'Don't look so alarmed!' She laughed. 'He seemed nice enough.'

Celeste wasn't reassured. If her 'white knight' had found her phone at the club, then why didn't he just hand it in to the staff or to one of her friends? Most importantly, how did he know where she lived? He must have been through her social media accounts to work that one out. And why did he wait two hours before giving the phone back? She felt violated. Who knows what he had been looking at during all that time? What's more, Anya said he was wearing a motorcycle helmet and Celeste had heard the engine of his motorbike clearly as he rode away. But the odd thing was, she hadn't heard him riding up to the house when he arrived... She had been listening out for ages for Anya and Jessi's return in the taxi and was sure that in her state of hypervigilance she would have heard a motorbike pulling up outside the window. Now, as she threw herself back on the cushions, she had an uncomfortable thought: that rustling outside the window... he must have been hanging about outside for quite some time...

'Average height, a bit lanky, ordinary – not your usual type I would say.' Jessi dropped down on the sofa next to Celeste and ripped a slice off the leftover pizza she had retrieved from the oven.

'So, what is my type exactly?' asked Celeste, trying to shake off her anxiety.

'Why don't you check your Tinder?' said Jessi a little sheepishly. 'When you were busy flirting with Brett, well we had a bit of fun matchmaking for you.'

It turned out that while they were all at the bar drinking shots, Anya and Jessi had sneakily got their hands on to Celeste's mobile and had been through her Tinder account, swiping right and left in a giggling, giddy alcoholic huddle.

'We made some great picks for you,' chipped in Anya. 'Tall, dark and handsome, all local guys, twenty-five to thirty, within a one-mile radius.' She leant over the back of the sofa as Celeste scrolled frantically through the cards of the men the girls had 'right-swipe-liked', and those of new matches who had 'liked' her back.

'I can't believe you did this!' she groaned.

Anya pointed at the faces as Celeste kaleidoscoped through them, her own face set and grim, her fingers hovering above the icons at the bottom of each card, and with lightning speed, tapping the crosses to undo the hearts.

'Look he's hot,' Anya squealed. 'Stop, go back! Don't cross him off.' She carried on pointing and prodding. 'Look, him – dark, a bit rough round the edges. Tap his profile – investment manager, into extreme sports, adventures. Alpha male – that's what you go for isn't it?'

Celeste was too preoccupied to engage. She scrolled through the drop-down menus, getting more and more agitated by the second. It was not as quick and easy to 'un-match' as to undo a 'like'.

Suddenly, while she fumbled through the options, a message popped up on her screen, another match had been made, and he wanted to chat. Speech bubbles... he was typing! She jerked forwards and dropped her mobile to the floor as if it had scalded her fingers. Jessi picked it up and Celeste stared at the image with morbid fascination. It was him, on a beach, somewhere tropical, photographed against the light and with his features shaded by a baseball cap, but unmistakeably him – she recognised the jawline and the set of his lips. The man from the club.

'Give me the phone,' she yelled, snatching for it.

Before she could locate the 'un-match' button, his words appeared on the screen. Just four little words, but enough to send a chill to her bones.

'Hello. I am back.'

PRESENT

3

*I*t doesn't take me long to find out where You work or what You do. Your phone gives it all away without me even having to look through your messages. Your screensaver photo is a close-up of a single red rose lying flat on a work surface made of stone. You must have leant over to point the lens directly into the head of the rose, your body folding – supple and tense.

The image of the rose is my screensaver now too. At its bulbous base, where the flower meets the stem, the petals are velvety smooth and lined with tiny vessels, bulging and soft. At the head, the diminishing circles of rose petals – curling, pulsing and falling away into a black hole – are like an invitation.

Each time I look at my phone, I can almost smell the fragrance of You. Is that what You intended?

Of course, I know that a lot of women have screensaver photos of flowers that have nothing to do with their jobs, but it's your tag that gives it away: #seventhheaven

My first thought is a restaurant or bar. Is this a favourite haunt? – for in my heart of hearts, I know You are too delicate and refined to be a waitress.

It's the work of seconds to google the words 'seventh heaven'. There are lots of entries – but one, in particular, catches my eye – a local business address.

I can guess You cycle to work, because when I paid You a visit last night, I saw a battered bicycle (with your initials scratched into the paintwork) locked up inside the dingy hallway. (As if anyone would want to steal that bike!) So, I reason that your workplace can't be too far away.

It doesn't take me long to click, and link to the @ seventhheaven Instagram account, and then to find a publicity shot of a woman standing at a table, preparing a bouquet of flowers.

It isn't You.

But a quick zoom-in on the shot shows the worktop surface to be identical in texture and hue to the sandstone background I see on your screensaver. Et voilà! QED. Problem solved!

'Seventh Heaven Pimlico – home of exquisite blooms and celestial bouquets.'

The sweetest flower in the shop. That's where You are hiding!

Icy raindrops lashed Celeste's face as she flirted with death cycling through the rush hour traffic to the florist where she worked four days a week in the heart of Pimlico. She was relieved to turn off the busy road and into the side street where Seventh Heaven was located among a small cluster of businesses including an upmarket Italian café and deli, a fashionable shabby chic British restaurant and jazz club, and three quirky boutiques selling lots of fancy things nobody really needed. This bitter February morning the shop's crimson window display provided a welcome splash of vibrant colour against the relentless grey of the pavement. On any other day the street was picturesque and charming with its handsome white stucco terraces made up of residential properties adorned with black wrought-iron balconies and freshly painted front doors. But today under a stormy sky it felt as if the whole of London was in mourning.

Celeste had overslept. Being so distressed and distracted by the chance sighting at the club followed by the message on her phone the previous night, she had forgotten to set her alarm. She'd had no time for breakfast or coffee and due to sleep deprivation and caffeine withdrawal on top of the hangover, a migraine was brewing in her head. She was wrecked.

Celeste knew she was going to be in big trouble when she got to work. She'd promised her boss, Meghan, the owner and manager of Seventh Heaven, that she'd be in by 6am. Meghan had warned her it was going to be hectic. Valentine's Day – one of the busiest days in a florist's calendar. She knew that Meghan was counting on good sales today to make up for the dismal takings since Christmas. Even in the upscale residential area of SW1V, austerity in Britain was biting. Everyone was cutting back on life's little luxuries and flowers were one of the first things to go.

After locking her bike to a nearby lamp post, she glanced at her phone – 8.50am. Only ten minutes to opening time.

'She's going to kill me!' she muttered to herself. 'I wouldn't be surprised if she sacks me on the spot!' It wasn't the first time Celeste had overslept and she knew she must have been at least on her third 'final warning'.

Meghan had her back to Celeste when she slipped in through the back door. Her sleeves were rolled up as she stood over a large china sink full of cold water. She was surrounded by steel buckets filled with red roses. Celeste could tell just by looking at the rigid set of her shoulders and neck and the jerky movements of her hands that she was angry.

'What's your excuse this time?' said Meghan without turning around. She carried on stripping the thorns and snipping and tying the roses into fat red bouquets. Celeste noticed that Meghan's hands were already chapped and raw from the cold water. 'You promised to get in early. You've let me down again.'

Celeste said nothing. Getting drunk with her girlfriends to celebrate her birthday wouldn't cut it as an excuse.

'I'm sorry,' said Celeste as she hung up her coat. She put on her 'Seventh Heaven' apron and reached for one of the steel buckets from the bench. 'I'll work through my lunch break.'

At last Meghan turned to look at her. She seemed to have forgotten the tragic significance of the 14th February date, which for Celeste was anything but a festival of love.

'You've got to stop behaving like a reckless teenager, Celeste.' Her eyes were hard and unforgiving. 'We've all been cutting you slack for the last seven years but it's time you started facing up to your responsibilities. Grow up.

Quit the victim mentality. This is a business, not a charity. I gave you a chance, but I haven't got space for passengers.'

Celeste shrank visibly. Meghan had never spoken to her in such harsh terms before.

Her boss must be really seriously hacked off, to have given her such a dressing-down, on Valentine's Day of all days.

There was no time to mope or feel sorry for herself. Celeste worked straight through the morning, preparing bouquets of roses in the cold room at the back while Meghan resolutely blanked her and remained engrossed in making up the orders for all the more exotic hand-tied creations, dealing with last-minute telephone orders and serving the steady stream of customers coming through the door. Celeste didn't dare break off mid-morning as was her normal routine to get an almond milk latte from the deli next door and when it got to her usual lunchtime, she was faint with hunger and a pounding headache.

When Meghan took a late lunch break in the early afternoon, she called Celeste to come front of shop and serve. Although Celeste had been working flat out in order to prepare enough bouquets for an anticipated surge in customers stopping to buy flowers on their way home from work at the end of the day, so far, the sales had been disappointing. It was so cold and grey that there were fewer people than usual out on the streets – those who didn't have to venture outside were sheltering at home. And as Meghan lamented on her way out the door, it wasn't only the footfall that was down but also the spend. Even the rich were watching their pennies – the more extravagant arrangements remained stubbornly on the shelves.

The flow of customers into the shop had now slowed to a trickle. With Meghan out of the way, at last Celeste was able to make herself a drink. She stood behind the counter sipping her tea, warming her cold, scratched hands on the china mug and staring at the shop window as if hypnotised by the driving rain running down the misted panes. There were only one or two pedestrians passing by – a woman in a long raincoat struggling with shopping bags in one hand and a screaming child in the other; an elderly man walking an elderly dog.

As she stared out vacantly, a young man in leathers approached the shop front and paused for a few seconds on the pavement in front of the Valentine's display. His face was shielded from the rain by a black umbrella. She retreated to the doorway of the cold room. For some reason, his presence outside made her feel vulnerable and exposed. He seemed to hesitate by the door, as if considering coming in to buy one of the bouquets of red roses, before changing his mind and going on his way. A fleeting thought of the mystery biker from the night before crossed her mind before she cast it away.

Suddenly she felt lost and very much alone. The reality of working in a flower shop on Valentine's Day was so much less romantic than people might imagine. It was only mid-afternoon, but she'd been on her feet for hours – prepping the flowers and smiling and exchanging anecdotes with strangers buying gifts for their loved ones. Right now, it seemed like she was the only person in the world forgotten, unlovable and unloved. There was no one to take her out on a date at the end of the day. There was no one waiting for her at home. There was no *one* special person in her life who would be giving her a card, or chocolates, or a single red rose.

All the love had drained from her heart on that Valentine's night seven years ago.

PRESENT

4

*I*know that Friday is your day off work at the florist's
because that's the day you come into college.

I am here early this morning hanging out at the coffee
bar to make sure I don't miss You entering the building.
But You don't turn up. My cappuccino slowly goes cold.
I simply have to see You, so I bunk off my lecture on
computer graphics and head for Seventh Heaven to look
for You there. This time I intend to buy flowers.

That doesn't happen. But it isn't a wasted trip. My luck is
in. As I turn into Camford Street, who should I see pulling
out into the traffic but You – You, behind the wheel of an
ice-blue Fiat 500 cabriolet. I swing the bike into a perilous
U-turn and follow You through the backstreets of West
London and over the Chelsea Bridge and down the A3. You
know where You are going. There's not a second's hesitation
as You come to each junction.

I have to say, Celeste, you're a bad driver!

You smash a wing mirror on someone's parked car as

*you race for the Chelsea Bridge. It's an expensive car too – a
Lamborghini, no less. You don't stop to check the damage.
And, you know, speeding is one thing. But driving at fifty-
five miles per hour in a school zone, when the reception
kids are being marched across the road to get on to a
waiting coach, is another! When I pull up at the crossing,
the teachers are cursing You and whipping out their phones.*

*And I bet that shiny little toy isn't your car. You couldn't
afford it on your salary. The woman who lent it to You
(I know it's a woman – it reeks of femininity – no self-
respecting man would drive that car!) won't be too pleased
when the speeding offences start dropping through the
door... Someone should teach You a lesson...*

Careless with things and careless with feelings.

Careless Celeste – yes, that's who You are.

When she got to the dual carriageway, Celeste felt liberated
– she could breathe freely again. It was wonderful to be on
the open road and to get out of London if only for a day.
After the greyness of yesterday, the weather had cleared and
today the sky was crisp and blue – cold but still – a perfect
day for a drive into the Surrey countryside. This outing was
no pleasure party. But the bright winter sunshine helped to
make her mission a little more bearable.

She put her foot down, paying little heed to the national
speed limit signs and the warnings of speed cameras at
the side of the dual carriageway. She'd managed to lose the
motorbike that had seemed to be tailing her as she drove
across the Chelsea Bridge. Perhaps she was just being
paranoid on account of the chance meeting at Heavana and

the incident with her phone earlier in the week, but every time she checked her rear-view mirror, she caught a glimpse of a biker three or four cars behind her. Surely it wasn't him? Could it be that he was paying someone to spy on her?

She dismissed the idea. It was ridiculous to think that the man she'd been avoiding for the last seven years was chasing her around London. Her fragile equilibrium had been upset by his return – that was all. In any event, now – thank God – the bike was nowhere in sight. She plugged in her phone and tapped on her music. Sound waves from her favourite hits bounced around the capsule of the borrowed Fiat 500, lifting her mood.

Celeste's dated taste in music was a standing joke with her girlfriends. Her playlists were made up of tunes from the previous decade – U2, Oasis, Amy Winehouse, The Killers – she was a child of the noughties and could listen to these all day long.

'You're in a time warp,' said Jessi. 'Lost in the last decade.' Jessi would never understand how truly she spoke.

'I hate myself for being alive,' Celeste had said to her therapist when she eventually agreed to speak to someone about her trauma. 'I carry this dark secret everywhere I go like a millstone round my neck dragging me down into the deep. I was the one who deserved to die. Sometimes I just want to let the waters close above my head.'

'You have suffered enough. Now it's time to stop punishing yourself,' her therapist had replied. 'What you need to understand is that part of *you* died that night too.' It was trite but it was true. Part of her had died that night and she didn't want to move on.

Celeste knew very well that the little Fiat was Meghan's

pride and joy and it was unexpectedly kind of her to have lent it out for the day. Celeste had mentioned in passing when leaving Seventh Heaven the previous evening that she was skipping her Friday classes for a trip down to Surrey. This must have woken Meghan's memory – Valentine's Day was the blackest day in Celeste's calendar.

Celeste had not set out to guilt-trip Meghan. She realised that Meghan had been preoccupied and distracted trying to keep up with the Valentine's Day orders and she didn't hold it against her. But it was clear that Celeste's manager had wanted to make amends for her bad temper earlier in the day. Celeste's compliance had played to her advantage – for not only had she worked through her lunch break, but she had stayed on until 8pm in the evening so that Seventh Heaven could cash in on sales of Valentine's flowers to those who had left it to the last minute, or forgotten, or decided to buy on a whim, as they headed home after work.

In the end, Meghan had been quite pleased with the day's takings and in the mood to be generous. Not all the bouquets of red roses had been sold, but enough to ensure she would make a decent profit. Perhaps Celeste was right, she'd remarked, people were trying to bring some colour and love into the cold, grey day.

As Celeste was gathering her belongings ready to leave, Meghan had held out one of the unsold bouquets of red roses.

'Here, have these. We won't be able to sell them tomorrow. They'll brighten up your flat.' Then on a sudden impulse, perhaps embarrassed by the insufficiency of her gesture, she had got her spare set of car keys from a drawer and pushed them into Celeste's hand. 'Here take my car keys too. You can borrow the Fiat for the day tomorrow. I won't need it. I'll be driving to Covent Garden in the van before the crack of dawn to buy the flower stock for the weekend and I won't be back to the shop until 10am. Sue's opening up for me. But you can come by and collect the car first thing, whenever you like – it'll be in the yard at the back.' She gave Celeste a quick hug. 'Help yourself to more roses. Take as many as you like.'

By the time Celeste pulled off the dual carriageway, old feelings and memories had begun to resurface, triggered by the familiarity of the twists and turns in the route. Muscle memory took over as her mind wandered. Driving along the country lanes she was transported back to her adolescence and her mood became as melancholic as the dark lyrics playing through the speakers...*Now you're killing me with your lies...* Unconsciously she sang along... *I see fire in your eyes* ... Her soft, breathy voice was a shadow of the rich, raspy tones of the troubled, charismatic jazz-pop singer she had idolised in her teens.

Despite her heightened emotions, Celeste was struck, as she always was when visiting the county of her childhood home after living in 'the big smoke', by how vibrantly green everything was. The winter sun was low in the sky, at times blinding her vision as she rounded the bends. Although it was only February, as she drove to her destination, the grass and the fields and the hedgerows of Surrey seemed to encircle her in a tunnel of ever-changing hues of fluorescent green.

When she reached her destination, she pulled into one

of the parking spaces outside the village post office. The village of Shearham looked just as picture-postcard-pretty and sleepy and dull as ever – exactly as it had looked on her last visit. It was really little more than a hamlet. The historic centre consisted of a handful of timber-framed and whitewashed cottages, and, of course, the pub and the church and the village hall, framing the inevitable village green where, true to tradition, they still played cricket matches on long summer evenings. Even without the cricket match in play, it was a quintessentially English scene. There was a red pillar box next to where she had parked her car. On the other side of the green, there was even an old-fashioned red telephone box that had a preservation order on it. She knew it no longer had a working telephone but over the years it had become something of a tourist attraction because it could be glimpsed in several scenes from television and feature films that had been filmed on location in the village.

Celeste walked into the post office and was relieved to find that the gossipy old postmistress was nowhere to be seen and a woman she didn't recognise was serving behind the counter. She bought a small bottle of water and a jumbo-sized packet of jelly babies that she stuffed into the pocket of her coat before turning on her heel, ignoring the woman's attempt to engage in friendly chat by cautioning her lightly not to eat them all at once.

Celeste went back to the car and took her floristry workbox from the boot. Meghan had given her the portable metal box as a Christmas present and was encouraging her to start putting together her own set of floristry tools – scissors, oasis knife, secateurs, deadhead snippers, rose and thorn strippers, binding wire, twine, tape, pins, pin holders, floral adhesives, sponges, cleaning brushes, gloves, pencils and the like – the list went on! – all the items that were required for day-to-day work as a florist.

'I'm building up quite an armoury,' Celeste had joked, when Meghan had checked over the contents of her box.

Celeste put on her sunglasses and pulled up the hood on her jacket to avoid eye contact or further conversation with anyone she should run into and, armed with her workbox on one side and an armful of red roses on the other, she strode purposefully across the village green and up the cobbled lane leading to St Peter's Parish Church. She swung the mossy lych-gate open with her hip and hesitated before making her way up the ancient brick path that skirted the nave of the church to the secluded part of the graveyard behind the vestry where the newer graves were located.

It took her a minute or two to identify the grave, as a number of new headstones had been erected since her last visit. Her eyes were drawn to the site of a very recent burial. It must have taken place only a few days previously because as yet not even a wooden cross had been erected to mark the grave. Instead there was a frozen mound of earth festooned with a blanket of flowers and floral tributes in the shape of teddy bears and hearts with a small plastic angel perched on the top. Hand-written messages, some in childish lettering, were pinned in among the dying flowers.

It was all too painfully familiar. Feeling as if she were intruding on private grief, she bent down to read them. '*I love you Joey.*' The simple message was written in crayon, in big uneven letters on white card. The card was decorated with pink and purple hearts, and childish figure drawings of a girl in a blue dress, holding hands with a little boy wearing bright red shorts. She guessed the drawing was by Joey's big sister. A huge sun, blocked in yellow crayon, was shining in the corner to complete the picture.

A handful of toys had been placed next to the grave – a large blue teddy whose plush fur was already soggy and covered in mud, and an Action Man and a couple of toy cars. Overwhelmed by the pathos of the all-too-relatable scene, Celeste covered her mouth with her hand and stood stock-still staring at the fresh burial site.

Eventually Celeste recovered her composure and was able to locate the grave she was looking for. Like the others in the row, its headstone was made out of silver-grey granite, which was now mouldering and mildewed at the base. What singled it out as she approached was the inscription, carved in italic lettering on the reverse side of the headstone. She had chosen the verse herself, all those years ago, thumbing through the yellowed pages of a family Bible her grandmother had given her a few months before she died. Celeste had never opened the bible until the day after the party...

Blessed are the pure in heart
For they shall see God

Having chosen the words, she had closed the Bible and never opened it again.

PRESENT

5

I *dare not follow You into the churchyard. But a copse of ancient oak trees gives me cover and a good vantage point. It's amazing the detail you can see through the lens of a powerful digital SLR. I wouldn't call it hiding. I have no concern about being seen by dog walkers or joggers. I leave my bulky camera bag close to the path. I set up my tripod slowly and deliberately in full view of any passers-by. I am beyond suspicion or reproof. It would be clear to them – and if anyone were to ask, I have my answer ready – that this spot is the ideal position for taking interesting angled photographs of the architecture of the church, veiled and framed by the branches of the trees.*

I'm sure I'll be pleased with the results. Today You are my black angel crouching down by the grave with the winter sunshine setting your hair aglow. These images will be so much better than the phone shots I stole from You surreptitiously at the club. Now I have time to compose and to frame, to crop and to structure, to sharpen and to soften, to capture your image and to blur the background. You are my subject and there are so many versions of You.

I move away from the camera. But You are just getting started – now on your hands and knees, scrubbing and weeding like a woman possessed.

You reach into your toolbox to take out a knife.

I slide my hand down the front of my jeans.

My eye to the viewfinder, my back to the path, I watch You. Slowly and painstakingly, you scrape the debris from the inscription on the grave, one letter at a time. My lens is angled side-on to the headstone so I can't read the words. But it's plain to see. You loved the person lying there.

I am jealous of that love. I can't watch You any longer and I have to look away.

Finally, You get to your feet and stand with your head bowed and your eyes closed.

And it's all that I can do to stop myself from crashing through the trees and scrambling over the wall and crushing You in my arms.

Celeste walked round to the front of the grave and knelt down on the grass. It was overgrown with brambles and weeds. Dry wilted remnants of flower stalks poked out from the grave vase at the base of the headstone and the surface of the granite was mottled and discoloured where the wind had blown the rotting leaves against it. She opened her floristry kit and pulled out an array of brushes and scrapers and tools. She felt guilty for having stayed away for so long leaving the grave uncared for and unkempt. She was angry too, with her mother, who lived only a short drive away.

She has no excuse for leaving the grave in this state, thought Celeste harshly. Unless being an alcoholic and chronically depressed and living with an intermittently abusive partner absolved her mother from all responsibility.

Celeste got to work on the grave, cutting away the brambles, weeding the grass and clearing the dead leaves and twigs from the grave vase and around the headstone. Then she started on the granite, scrubbing and rubbing where it was soiled and stained until it gleamed like silver, smooth and clean in the morning sunshine. Lastly, she got out her oasis knife, which had a long, hard blade, and carefully scraped off the black spores and debris from the gold lettering of the inscription. To complete her task, she took out a little pot of gold paint and a small paintbrush and meticulously went over the letters to touch up any spots of paintwork that had faded or peeled away.

'There, that's as good as new,' she said out loud, satisfied with a job well done. 'Now for the fun part.' She cut the twine binding the bouquet of flowers and stripped away the thorns. She trimmed the ends with her floristry scissors and arranged them decoratively in the grave vase. She took the giant packet of jelly babies out of her pocket and propped it carefully next to the arrangement of red roses at the base of the headstone. Then she sat back on her heels, took out her phone and photographed the grave.

There was nothing more to do. She got up slowly and stood with her head bowed and her eyes closed. She tried to pray but her mind was a blank. Now that her task was complete, she was filled with a chilling sadness that seemed to rise up from the frost-covered earth, through her feet and her limbs, her pelvis and her heart, all the way up to the top of her head until her whole body and mind were frozen and numb with the tragic futility of it all.

When she opened her eyes, they fell on the date, 14th February 2011 engraved in the stone and yet more deeply in her heart. The passage of the years might dull the intensity of her distress but could not soothe the sickness and misery in her soul. Still, she couldn't find the words for a prayer. The only words she could think of were: 'I'm sorry. I'm sorry. I'm sorry,' which she said out loud over and over again, knowing that there were no words that could ever release her from the relentless pain and remorse.

At a loss what to do next but unable to leave and chilled to the bone, Celeste walked around the churchyard, reading the gravestones and imagining the lives of the people buried below her feet. In an attempt to block out her sadness, she noted with artistic detachment the etchings and carvings that made each memorial unique and special. Most of the graves were in a state of neglect. Almost all the metal vase holders were empty. The older graves were sunken and crooked and covered in lichen and moss. Some of the epitaphs and inscriptions were personalised and evocative, calling to mind the personality of the deceased. Most were generic and ritualistic. The local stone was so soft and friable that on many of the ancient memorials the words had eroded with time and Celeste mused that this gradual erosion was like the slow obliteration of the memory of the person buried beneath the ground. Her difficulty in deciphering the words seemed to symbolise the loss of that person's identity as all living memories of the individual faded into oblivion.

Her gloomy thoughts on mortality were lifted by her observation that the inscriptions on almost all of the headstones began with the words 'In Loving Memory' before naming the dead person. Indeed, on some of the older headstones these three words 'In Loving Memory' were the only words that remained legible – the names had faded away into eternity – only the love endured.

She was reminded of something she had read. A novel she had been given about a high-powered city mum who tries to have it all, until she comes to the realisation when reading the headstones at her friend's funeral that in the final reckoning, loving relationships are all that really matter. In death we are defined not by our job titles or our positions in society, but by what we meant to others. How well we loved our friends and family, and how well they loved us in return. Celeste had found the book funny and sharp but also desperately poignant and moving. She passed from headstone to headstone, reading the inscriptions – 'In Loving Memory' of a father, a daughter, a brother, a son. Now she understood the author's message more clearly. It was loving relationships that gave meaning to the lives of those who had died – not the fact that they were a doctor or a milkmaid or a mechanic or a blacksmith, not the fact that they were rich or poor. These things were not even mentioned on the graves. And it was the memory of the love itself that gave the living, the survivors, the courage and the strength to carry on.

Celeste could be philosophical but she was not forgiving. *Her* loving memory screamed out for atonement – she would never forget. Her love was strong and it was hot. She would never forgive herself and she would never forgive him.

'May this man's soul rest in peace,' she murmured to herself, reading the traditional words off a stranger's headstone as she strode across the uneven grass, 'But as for me? My soul will never rest in peace.'

The churchyard was now overcast and Celeste shivered as the temperature dropped. The morning sunshine had disappeared, and the skies had taken on that heavy leaden texture that promised snow. Celeste zipped her jacket right up to her chin and went back to the first grave to collect her tools. She didn't think the Fiat could cope with heavy snow. She needed to get through the country lanes and head back to London before the road conditions got too bad.

Before leaving she picked up the sweets and sat behind the headstone, leaning back against the cold granite. Her stomach was hollow. An icy rod ran along the length of her spine. She opened the packet and took out a jelly baby – red – those were his favourites. The soothing soft texture and sickly-sweet taste reminded her of happier times from her childhood. A few snowflakes began to fall. She closed her eyes and breathed in the fresh wet smell of snow and let the flakes land on her closed eyelids.

There had been good days. Mostly when her mother had been out of the way. She remembered sledging on the North Downs, hurtling down the steep slopes on a makeshift sleigh, their bodies pressed together as she held him tightly round the waist, then his rosy cheeks as they raced up the hill to go again. One day, they had built a snowman at the very top. She had felt on top of the world that day, looking out over the sweep of the valley and the river below, raised up by his trusting love for her.

She had been in so much trouble later on because she had wound her scarf around the snowman's neck and forgotten to bring it home at the end of the day. She had a memory of being slapped around the face so hard that the next day she could still see the bruise marks of her mother's fingers imprinted on her cheek.

Her eyes were stinging. Snowflakes mingled with her tears. One by one she ate her way through the whole packet of jelly babies, while her legs and the surrounding grass slowly turned white under a light covering of snow. Then she rolled onto her knees, opened her workbox, took out a cutter and pulled up her sleeve to expose her forearm. She made two light cuts in the shape of a cross and, with her head spinning, watched in fascination as the drops of blood slid down the curve of her forearm and dripped onto the snow. She wiped away the blood oozing from her wound with the tips of her fingers, then brought them to her lips before tapping them on the top of the headstone in a bloodied, symbolic parting kiss.

She pulled down her sleeve. Then she screwed up the empty sweet packet and stuffed it in her pocket.

Feeling faint, and sick, and ashamed, she held on to the headstone and levered herself unsteadily to her feet.

It was time to go.

Celeste arrived back in London tired and emotional after her trip to Shearham. It had been a stressful journey back into town with the rush hour traffic made worse by the driving snow and the slushy road surfaces. She turned down an invitation from Anya and Jessi to join them at the local pub. Instead she heated up a microwave meal and decided to spend what was left of the Friday evening working at the kitchen table on the college assignments that she should have handed in that morning.

Celeste was taking a part-time professional diploma in digital marketing at a local college of further education, the Victoria Technology Institute. Having dropped out of school before her A levels, she had missed out on the opportunity to go to art school or university – much to the disappointment of her teachers because she was a talented student. But now she was trying to put her life together and make a fresh start. Ultimately, she wanted to have a business of her own – something like an online graphic design business that would allow her to use her natural creative and artistic skills and yet be her own boss. She couldn't face the idea of going into an office every day.

In the meantime, she needed to earn a living and Meghan's offer of a part-time job at Seventh Heaven (though she was being paid scarcely more than the minimum wage) was perfect. Celeste had a natural flair for flower arranging and Meghan was willing to give her floristry training on the job. While Meghan was strict (and frequently irritated by Celeste's poor punctuality and extravagant wastefulness with flowers and materials) she was also compassionate. She had been friends with Celeste's mother when they were at school. Although they had grown apart years earlier because Celeste's mother had lost her way in alcohol and drug abuse and become insufferable even before her children were born, Meghan knew something of Celeste's dysfunctional childhood and the trauma and troubled times that Celeste had been through recently and was willing to help where she could.

Celeste realised that long term the traditional floristry business was not for her. She couldn't hack getting up every day at the crack of dawn. The cold room where they stored and prepped the flowers gave her coughs and chilblains, and her pale hands were being wrecked by the freezing water and thorns. But her work at the florist's tied in very well with her further education studies. As part of her digital marketing course she was required to do a practical project designing a website and had offered to do this for Meghan free of charge. Until now Meghan had relied almost exclusively on local business and word of mouth. But in these troubled times sales were falling and she needed to 'rethink her business model', as Celeste kept telling her in her newly acquired 'marketing-speak'. The current Seventh Heaven website was basic and crude, in need of a complete revamp.

This week's assignment was on the topic of 'Website Optimisation'. Celeste rubbed her eyes and yawned as she read through the introduction to the course notes:

'This module introduces key concepts underpinning effective website design and the purpose of user-centred design and website optimisation. It will enable you to build and publish a simple, well-designed, and optimised website that is aligned to specific business goals.'

Befuddled by the jargon, she groaned. 'And what does that mean in plain English?'

'Additionally, you will understand design principles and best practices for copy and A/B testing along with exploring User Experience and User Interface as part of user centric design. The Website Optimisation module also covers how to use evaluation tools and metrics to implement monitoring and to capture, track, and measure website activity to develop deeper insights and optimisation best practice.'

'How am I supposed to write a paper on that? How on earth is that going to help me design a website?' Celeste read on through the notes drumming her fingers on the table and getting more and more frustrated and agitated. The marketing jargon was confusing enough but the technical information was beyond her. It was so hard to concentrate. The cuts on her arm were stinging and she was weary from the long drive home. Forty-five minutes and two bars of chocolate later she slammed down the lid of her laptop.

'I give up!'

She changed into a long-sleeved shirt and sent a text to Jessi.

'Get me a G&T. I'm coming down to the pub. This course is doing my head in! I need a drink.'

When she walked through the door of the Devonshire Arms on the corner of the street, Jessi and Anya were both tapping away on their phones sitting at the table furthest from the bar. Jessi looked up and beckoned her over, holding out the extra gin and tonic.

'God, I need this!' said Celeste.

'What's up?' said Anya turning over her phone.

'It's not important,' said Celeste. 'Just this digital marketing course driving me nuts. I'm stuck on the assignment. I'd need a degree in computer programming to be able to understand it! It's for computer geeks!' She glanced over at Anya's phone face down on the table. 'Who were you chatting to?'

'Oh, no one important,' said Anya evasively. 'Just someone from work.' She put the mobile away in her handbag.

When they got back to the flat later that evening, Anya flung her bag down on the sofa as she always did before going off to change into her PJs. While Jessi made the coffee, Celeste sat down on the sofa and switched on the TV. She couldn't help herself. She reached over and found Anya's phone in the bag. She knew Anya's new code. The girls had giggled about it the other evening – the date that she had lost her virginity. Celeste had a good memory for details such as dates. She scrolled through the latest texts, and there it was, a text from one of Anya's old schoolmates that Celeste had met once or twice.

'OMG Ben's back in town!!!! Does she know? He asked me for her number!!!'

PAST

6

She's known him for years, since they were about three years old in fact. They both go to the same fee-paying village primary school on the outskirts of Guildford. Besides meeting at the school gate, their mothers know each other from the local tennis club at Shearham. The women move in the same set of prosperous, middle-class 'homemakers' whose husbands commute into London to work long days in financial institutions in the City, leaving them free to enjoy a privileged existence within the Surrey bubble...

Celeste has many play dates and parties round at Ben's house as a little girl. He has a hot tub, and a swimming pool and his mother always seems happy to host. Her friends never come to hers to play and she wonders why. As she grows older, Celeste becomes aware that there's something wrong with her own mother. It's the whisperings and sudden silences of the other women at the school gate that first make Celeste aware of it. Stacey has become incapable of partaking in the endless round of tennis and lunching and dog walks and yoga and shopping trips with which the Shearham mums fill their time – and they shun her for it.

Celeste becomes more watchful of her mother and resentful of the hours that she spends asleep on the sofa, and embarrassed by her funny, slurred way of talking. Even when her mother is awake Celeste thinks it's like she's not really there. Sometimes Stacey's still in her silk dressing gown when Celeste is dropped home from school by someone else's mum because her mother is incapable of driving or has forgotten to come and pick her up.

Ben's mother is one of Celeste's self-appointed 'guardian angels' who 'rallies round'. Celeste spends hours at his house after school until her father arrives to take her home when he gets off the London train. This might explain why from the time they are in junior school, Ben bosses her around and boasts that he is 'richer', 'stronger', 'braver', 'faster' and 'smarter' than her – and it might also explain why she believes him. Children pick up on the cues of adults.

Ben pretends to hate having a girl around but secretly enjoys the power. In all their imaginary games of murder in the dark or hide-and-seek or zombie warfare, she's the one who gets tied up in cupboards or lost in the woods or blindfolded and shot.

And it's Ben who first gives Celeste a name for her mother's 'sickness' when she is six years old.

'My dad said your mum is a "Alco-Ho-Lick",' he says proudly.

'What's that?' said Celeste.

'It means she's sick in the head,' he says, picking up on the conversations of his parents. And when Celeste is old enough to understand the meaning of the word, she reflects that his explanation wasn't so far off from the truth.

Celeste's father resents Stacey's alcoholism too, and finds his own way of coping, in the shape of a glamorous, possessive, social-climbing younger woman who gets her claws into him, and becomes his mistress then a few years later his wife, after an acrimonious divorce in which he becomes estranged from his children.

When Stacey loses her husband and her luxurious, all-expenses-paid lifestyle, she and the children get ejected from the Shearham social elite. They move to a small, run-down, semi-detached property 'on the wrong side of the tracks'. Stacey can't afford the fees at the tennis club. Her modest maintenance payments evaporate mostly on booze. Celeste gets relegated to the 'B list' for birthday parties and sleepovers.

Things get worse when Stacey is involved in a car accident and injures her back. The accident is her fault – she was driving under the influence, five vodka tonics to the wind, at four in the afternoon and she drove through a red light. Thankfully no one else is injured though her car is a write-off and the person she drove into claims fifteen hundred pounds' worth of damage. She lost her self-respect years ago. Now she loses her licence too.

Stacey's GP prescribes opioid painkillers for the excruciating pain in her back. Stacey succumbs to the cocktail of spirits and tramadol. The painkillers give her short-term relief and euphoria followed by debilitating lethargy and depression. She continues with the pills long after the back pain subsides. So now Stacey's an opioid addict as well as an alcoholic, and whenever she's at home Celeste feels more and more like she's living in one of Ben's zombie apocalypse games.

Celeste still spends some evenings at Ben's. His mother insists on it. 'We must be kind to those less fortunate than ourselves,' she says. It doesn't bother Ben too much because he has discovered his big brother's secret stash of psychological horror gameplay and developed his own addiction. He spends hours lost in awesome dystopian gameworlds – competing with anonymous online players in a compelling mix of survival-horror, and hack-and-slash pornographic fantasy involving freaky scenarios and erotic enemies to be eliminated. Though she is a reluctant player, Ben teaches Celeste the basics of gaming. She doesn't admit it to herself in words, but her instinct is correct: he finds it all the more exciting when she is in the game to crush and destroy.

Because she is intelligent and hardworking, Celeste is awarded a scholarship and a full bursary at the same private grammar school that Ben and all their rich friends are moving up to, but the snubs and the sniping make her feel she is there under sufferance. Having an opioid addict and alcoholic mother shatters Celeste's self-confidence. She spends her life in a state of social anxiety and stress, trying to shield her mother's embarrassing behaviour from the critical eye of her friends and to conceal from them the chaotic existence that she calls home.

Celeste is in fact much smarter than Ben and desperate to be included in the 'friendship group' in which he rules as alpha male. He's her golden ticket to social acceptance and sometimes he remembers that they were once best friends and lets her tag along. Because he can, he uses and abuses her to write his homework and slip him the answers in exams and research his assignments and forge his absence notes. She never says 'no'. She's the butt of his banter and the subject of his memes. Her house, her hair, her make-up, her clothes – nothing is off limits. She pretends not to care. She takes it 'in good sport'. But it's hardly surprising that she struggles with self-image and is borderline anorexic. By the time she's sixteen the psychological damage is done.

He's 'legend of the rugby pitch'... 'a top guy'... 'fittest catch at every party'... Everyone loves him...

She does too. She's loved him for years. Pouncing on each scrap of kindness he slings to her like a hungry stray bitch.

Ben is a player and a bully and Celeste is his victim.

She gets it – everyone needs someone to kick sometimes...

She promises herself that one day she will fight back.

PRESENT

7

It takes me less than an hour to complete the assignment that our tutor set for the weekend. I think I could teach him more than he knows. By lunchtime I am going stir-crazy sitting in my empty room.

It's less than twenty-four hours since our trip to Shearham and already I'm crossing off the days to next Friday's class. I forced myself to stay away from your flat off the King's Road last night. I don't want to be that creep who hangs out on street corners. But this is different.

Almost without thinking I find myself sitting on the pavement on the opposite side of the road from Seventh Heaven. I have come up with the perfect disguise. I'm in my oldest clothes, sitting on an old blanket with my head bowed, my features shielded by a baseball cap and in front of me an empty plastic cup and a cardboard sign that reads:

'I need £10 for a hostel tonight – please help'

No one bothers me. No one wants to catch my eye. Some of the shoppers glance in my direction then quickly look away, with a quickening of the step and tightening of the grip on the straps of handbags and shoulder bags. A few – not many – fumble in pockets or purses and drop a few coins into my cup. Most of them want to pretend I'm invisible, which suits me fine.

But You – You notice. You see me through the foliage and displays that decorate the shop window. I don't know if You recognise a likeness, but You know I'm there. And I can see You in a delicious peep show as You move up and down, in and out of view like a marionette busy with the customers. At one point the shop is empty and You pause right in front of the window, looking straight at me, while You push back your hair. Is it pity or something else that makes You stop and stare?

Late in the afternoon, my patience is rewarded. I hear the gates of Seventh Heaven grinding open on the side street and then I see You at the wheel of the Seventh Heaven van, pulling out into the queue of traffic. Thank God for red lights! Seconds later, I have left my pitch, collected my bike from where I left it parked further up the street and am following in your tracks.

It was unusually quiet in Seventh Heaven for a Saturday morning. Perhaps, after Valentine's Day local residents were tired of romantic gestures and extravagant gifts. Celeste was thankful that Meghan had tasked her with redesigning the window display to remove all the Valentine's motifs and replace them with flowers and decorations looking forward to the spring season and Mother's Day. It was absorbing and creative work, which helped to take her mind off the memories rekindled by her trip to Shearham and the unsettling events of the past few days.

There was an awkward moment when Celeste absent-mindedly took off her cardigan and the Saturday girl caught sight of the cuts on her forearm.

'God what happened to your arm?' she blurted out, without thinking.

Celeste covered the partly healed wounds with her hand. 'It's nothing,' she said hastily. 'I'm so clumsy. I tripped over my workbox yesterday.' She turned her back on her. 'I'll go and put on a plaster.' She went into the bathroom at the rear of the shop and got out the first aid kit. She was angry with the girl for being so tactless – she was sick of having to make excuses, to explain herself to people. But she was even more angry with herself for being such an idiot. She'd been free of this curse for almost two years. She couldn't allow her mind to go back to that dark place. Unconsciously she ran her fingertips softly along the faint scars at her wrists.

'He can't do this to me,' she said grimly. 'He almost killed me once. I won't let him do it again.'

She looked up and couldn't recognise the stranger in the mirror.

You were there in the mirror when I looked at myself. I hated myself and the guilty person that you made me feel I was, that nobody cared about. You were there in my mind each time I took a blade to my body to hurt and cut myself again and again to punish myself for the shameful person I became.

You are here in the mirror.
You are back.
'I refuse to be your victim,' she said out loud.
Her reflected image frightened her, and she had to look away.

Anyone looking through the windowpanes later that afternoon would have been touched by the scene inside Seventh Heaven. It was like the set of a romantic movie. A big delivery had arrived, and Celeste was halfway through unloading and putting the new blooms out on display. She was flushed from the cold air outside and the exertion of helping to carry the boxes into the shop. Although she'd had a bad night, her complexion was naturally clear and luminous, so she looked as delicate and fresh as the blooms all around. She was encircled by a rainbow of petals – scarlets, violets and pinks. Flowers filled the stone counter and cascaded to the floor. Almost the entire floor space was taken up with silver buckets containing single flowers, bunches of spring daffodils and tulips, and varieties of foliage in a hundred shades of green. As she reordered the window display, she worked at conditioning the flowers, placing them in buckets of icy cold water from an outside tap. She went in and out of the backyard. It was snowing again, and the air was so cold that it seemed as if this time it was going to stick.

The Saturday girl had just popped out to get herself a sandwich when the door opened and an elderly gentleman came into the shop to buy fresh spring flowers to celebrate his wife's birthday. Celeste helped him to pick out flowers for the bouquet, asking about his wife's favourite colours and blooms. Now she stood behind the counter making up the hand-tied bouquet. The man was a local resident. She had passed him occasionally walking his dog and had noticed his shuffling, unsteady gait. Today he was without the dog and was walking with the help of a stick. The side of his face was badly bruised. He told her he'd had a fall on the icy pavement. She noticed that a car was pulled up right outside the window with its warning lights on, waiting on the double yellow lines.

Celeste worked quickly and methodically, skilfully placing the blooms in her left hand to distribute pink dragon tulips, gladioli and white roses and structure the bouquet with foliage before binding it with twine, trimming the stems and wrapping it in cellophane.

The man waited in silence, his head tilted forwards stiffly. He was watching her white steady hands with a peculiar intensity as she worked quietly, putting together the bouquet. His own hands shook as he struggled to get a wallet out of his pocket. Celeste guessed he must be suffering from the early stages of Parkinson's disease.

'Would you like to choose a card to write a message for your wife?' said Celeste, nodding towards the card holder that contained a selection of designs. He fumbled with the cards and knocked over the holder.

'Please don't worry,' said Celeste kindly. 'I'll just finish tying this and then I'll help you.'

While the man hesitated, she made polite conversation only half listening to his replies.

'When is her birthday? How long have you been married?'

'Her birthday is today,' he said quietly. 'And we'll have been married fifty years this August.'

Celeste pulled out a card and picked up her pen.

'Now what would you like me to write?' she said. 'What is your lucky lady's name?'

For a moment the man seemed unable to speak. Then he swallowed to clear his throat.

'Marilyn,' he said, 'like the actress. Marilyn Rose.' Celeste wrote the name carefully, in her neatest handwriting. Then she looked up.

'And the message?'

His voice was husky. 'Just something simple... *In Loving Memory...*' he said. '*In Loving Memory of Marilyn Rose, Ever Yours, Ralph.*'

While Ralph was settling up the payment, which seemed to take forever as every movement was difficult and slow, he explained that every year of their marriage, without fail, he had bought flowers for his wife's birthday. She had been his main carer for the past five years of her life as his condition had deteriorated but, sadly, she herself had died the previous September after a short illness. Now he was dependent on the brief daily visits of council carers who came to his home to help him get dressed and prepare his food. He wished he was able to visit the cemetery to place the flowers on his wife's grave, but his carers were not allocated enough time to help him with an outing such as that. The cemetery was more than half an hour's drive away. Instead he would take the flowers home and put them on his kitchen table.

'I can sit and look at them and remember her,' he said philosophically. 'What else can I do? She'll understand.'

As if on cue, the driver in the car outside the shop gave two loud beeps on the horn.

'I better get going,' he said, with a mischievous grin. 'Or I'll be in trouble. She's scared she'll get a ticket.'

Celeste took the man's arm to help him out to the car with the flowers. Touched by his devotion to his dead wife, she had a sudden thought and on impulse she asked him, 'Would you like me to take the flowers for you? Business is slow today. I can leave work early. If you give me the address, I'll find the grave and place them on the headstone for you. If you like, I can take photographs and email them to you or send them to your home address?'

While the woman in the car leant on her horn, Celeste scribbled down the details and promised that before the day was out, the bouquet of fresh spring flowers would be beautifully arranged on Marilyn Rose's grave.

Once Celeste had finished sorting and displaying the new stock, she rummaged in the storeroom cupboard for the key to the van. Meghan had taken the afternoon off to go shopping up in Oxford Street for a date with a new boyfriend that evening. She was recently divorced and was just beginning to dip her toe in the water again. She seemed to be quite dizzy about this new guy – behaving like a twenty-year-old not the mature forty-something businesswoman that she was. It was not like Meghan to take the afternoon off work to buy a dress so she must be pretty keen!

Celeste had been entrusted to set up the new window display and to condition the stock and close up for the day. But she had worked hard and fast and Seventh Heaven was looking, well heavenly, Celeste thought to herself quite proudly. She reasoned there would be no harm in leaving the Saturday girl to hold the fort while she borrowed the company van to drive across to the Brompton Cemetery and deliver the flowers to the grave of Marilyn Rose.

The roads were busy with all the Saturday shoppers. There were a few flakes of snow still dancing in the air, but it was shaping up for a clear night. She put the address into her phone and braved the traffic. Eventually she saw the sign for the Brompton Cemetery and managed to squeeze into a parking space on the Fulham Road before entering on foot through the South Lodge. The light was fading as the pale winter sun sank below the dome of the chapel. The soles of her old trainers scrunched on the frosty paths and the birds were singing an evensong chorus that she had never consciously listened to before.

Celeste had never visited the Brompton Cemetery and had no idea that it was such a vast and imposing historic site. Ralph had given her reference details to find the location of his wife's grave, which turned out to be almost at the opposite end of the cemetery. As she searched for Marilyn's grave, she skirted the chapel, crossed the Great Circle and walked for several minutes along the grand Central Avenue, flanked on each side by rows and rows of elaborate monuments and statues. She felt overwhelmed by the number of memorials to the dead – some 35,000 graves according to the visitor information. So, this was one of the places London hid its dead.

Disconcertingly, she had the same feeling as when looking for her car in one of those vast car parks at big events like football matches or music festivals. Increasingly disorientated she walked up and down the rows until at last, she found the plot she was looking for far away from the Central Avenue in amongst a group of newer graves, memorials to local residents, made up of simpler, modern memorials. In fact, the cemetery was anything but like a car park. On the contrary, it was like a nature reserve in the heart of London – bursting with life – a microcosm of biodiversity of flora and fauna. Perhaps, because it was sheltered by the great city, spring seemed to have come early here – starting with the snowdrops that had sprung up around so many of the headstones like choirs of miniature angels.

It looked as if no one had visited Marilyn's grave for many weeks. The headstone itself was clean and new but overgrown and obscured with weeds. She crouched down and pulled away a few tufts of stray grass and there it was. She read the inscription:

In loving memory of Marilyn Rose Peters
beloved wife of Ralph Edmund Peters

Below the inscription there was a space on the stone, which she understood must have been left blank at Ralph's direction, ready to be engraved when the time came. He had decided he wished to be buried in the same spot as his wife.

By the time Celeste finished weeding the plot and polishing the stone and arranging the flowers it was almost dark. She had set up a torch on her workbox as best she could to give sufficient light for her task. Other visitors to the cemetery had left and she was alone. It was almost closing time. Before leaving she got out her phone to take photographs by flashlight of the spruced-up grave and the arrangement of flowers at the base of the headstone. She was filled with a quiet satisfaction knowing that her kind gesture would give peace of mind to the gentle old man who had come into Seventh Heaven earlier in the day.

Celeste's walk back to her car along the Central Avenue of the cemetery was lit by a vast orange full moon that hung low in the sky. The scene reminded her of the vampire movies that she had watched with her friends as a teenager, with the moonlight sending elongated monstrous shadows of the monuments and graves across the lawns. She heard a rustle behind a row of headstones and saw two eyes glowing yellow in the dark. As she stifled a cry, a fox darted out in front of her – stealthy and lithe as a werewolf. She quickened her pace, anxious that the wardens might have the locked the gate. She didn't want to be trapped here for the night. She doubted she would be strong enough to scale the wall.

Her mood blackened with the night sky. There was menace in the air and her imagination was on fire. She heard footsteps on the path behind her. She saw figures moving between the mausoleums in front of the trees and torches flashing darts of lights among the branches. She jumped at a shadow that loomed ahead of her on the path. Guarding a young child's grave, the vast stone angel to her left had soaring wings and an outstretched arm.

She shuddered.

The angel's shadow on the frozen gravel seemed to be reaching out to catch her by the ankles and trip her up.

PRESENT

8

I sit behind You in class and can scarcely breathe in fear that You will look around. But I shouldn't worry. You're not the kind of girl to turn your head. And even if You did You wouldn't acknowledge me. It's not that you're callous or cruel. It's just that in plain sight, I'm invisible.

Girls like You are blind to boys like me.

It occurs to me that it's only when I'm in disguise or hiding from You that You become aware of my presence. A crack on a floorboard. A rustle in the trees. A fleeting ripple of adrenaline. Then your ears prick, and You raise your head. You have a sixth sense – like an animal – You know You are being tracked.

But I make a pact with myself as I sit here loving the tendrils of hair that play at your nape when You swish your ponytail from one shoulder to the other. I may be invisible, but I know how to grab your attention. You don't know it yet, but You need me. It's time for some straight talking.

Everybody has a price. I'm about to offer myself up to You with a sweetener You simply can't resist!

Celeste was in big trouble when she got back to Seventh Heaven after her outing to the Brompton Cemetery. Meghan was waiting for her at the door with her arms folded. The Saturday girl was pretending to sweep the floor. She couldn't even bring herself to look at Celeste, anticipating what was about to go off.

'What the hell were you thinking of?' said Meghan. 'Going off without telling me and leaving Emily alone in the shop! She doesn't even know how to work the tills.' Meghan followed Celeste into Seventh Heaven and snatched the keys away from her. 'And as for taking the van! I never gave you permission. You're not insured to drive it. It would have been a disaster if you'd had an accident!'

Celeste was on a high and in a defiant mood.

'But I didn't!' she said. 'So, there's no harm done. I'm sorry. I was trying to do someone a good turn.'

But Meghan wouldn't let it go that easily. The takings were down. Celeste wasn't pulling her weight. She was charming with the customers but unreliable and careless with money. She undercharged and gave away flowers for free. She was extravagant with ribbons and wrappings and decorations and her time. She was too slow on the artistic side of the work and too slapdash on the business side.

'I can't fault your creativity or your customer service,' said Meghan. 'Your arrangements are beautiful, and everybody loves you. But I can't trust you. You're irresponsible. I'm going to have to let you go.'

Celeste pleaded for one last chance.

'I've said I'm sorry and I promise I will never leave the shop or touch the van again without asking for your permission. But please hear me out. You want me to earn my wage. Well I've thought of a business idea that might just give Seventh Heaven a whole new lease of life – a "second coming", if you like! It came to me when I was driving back from the Brompton Cemetery.' Celeste's eyes were bright with excitement. 'This digital marketing course that I'm taking, most of it is meaningless jargon. But I've learnt something. If you want to be successful you have to find a gap in the market. I finally understood the meaning of that dreadful word "*optimisation*". You have to find a gap, and then you design your website to "*optimise*" the market opportunity.'

Undaunted by the sceptical look on Meghan's face, Celeste ploughed on. 'This website I'm supposed to be designing for you – instead of just revamping the old one, we could use the new website to launch a whole new online flower delivery venture – like *Interflora* but instead of sending flowers to the living, we'll send flowers to the dead.'

She paused to see how Meghan would react, but her boss said nothing and went over to the kettle to make herself a coffee.

'Think of all the people out there,' continued Celeste, 'the old, the sick, new mums, busy employees, who are unable or haven't got the time to go and visit the graves of their loved ones but would like to mark important festivals and anniversaries with flowers and memorials on their headstones. Well that's where we come in. The service we'll offer will be individualised and unique – we'll personally deliver flowers to the cemetery, tidy and weed the plot, clean the headstone, arrange the flowers, and email photographs to our clients – all this to be available at the click of a button!'

Meghan wouldn't look at Celeste. She seemed to be concentrating on counting up and reconciling the money in the till. Finally, she said quietly, 'Are you sure about this? With all you've been through... I'm not sure it would be good for your mental well-being to spend so much time dwelling on–'

'On the contrary...' cut in Celeste. 'I think it would help me... you know, to use my skills and creativity to honour the dead and do something positive to help others in their time of need...'

'Well, it's an interesting idea,' said Meghan, changing to a business-like and pragmatic tone. 'After all, it's a captive market – we've all got to die! But I don't like your use of the word, *We.*' She locked up the till. '*We* don't have time for this. It's hard enough keeping up with what needs doing on the premises. *If...*' She pointed at Celeste. '*If* I agree to this then *you* are going to have to deal with it all – the website, the deliveries, the grave tending, the photographs, the follow-up. It's your project. It will be hard work.'

Celeste grabbed her hand. 'I promise I won't let you down. I'll put my heart and soul into it.'

'This is your very last chance,' said Meghan. 'You're on six weeks' probation. Any more trouble from you and you're out.'

'There won't be any trouble, cross my heart.' Celeste smiled sweetly. 'I even have a name for it – *CelestialHeadstones. com* – that's what it's called.'

★

Celeste spent the whole of Sunday working on her business plan for CelestialHeadstones.com. She set up an Instagram account, which she planned to link to the website for posting photographs of her work once the orders started coming in. That was the easy bit. The website was more challenging. She made notes and drawings for the website design. Death was not the easiest topic to market and advertise. She wanted CelestialHeadstones.com to look beautiful and uplifting, not morbid and depressing. She needed to explain the service being offered but more importantly she wanted to showcase her creativity and floral designs.

She planned to include photo galleries showing images of all the different kinds of floral tributes and memorials that were available to choose from – sprays, wreaths and cushions and garlands – as well as offering a bespoke service for customers wanting an original design. There were so many varieties of foliage and flowers she wished to experiment with instead of the usual funeral staples such as lilies, carnations and the garish chrysanthemums that she abhorred. She didn't want to be cynical, but she knew that Meghan would expect her to maximise profits, so the website would also need to entice 'upsells' with add-ons such as cards, balloons and soft toys to decorate the graves.

More mundanely, she would need online forms, enabling customers to fill out their details, as well as the address and coordinates of the grave and the name of the deceased. Then she needed a fees schedule, for same-day, next-day and specified-day deliveries, and delivery charges based on driving distance from London with a sixty-mile cut-off.

On the payments side, the website would need to process online orders via a secure shopping cart and transfer payments directly into the Seventh Heaven bank account.

Celeste was confident she could deal with the artistic side including the photographs and the blurb, but the technical bit was beyond her. She would have to seek help at college. In the meantime, she decided she needed to buy herself a decent SLR camera. She would have to raid her savings as her Seventh Heaven salary barely covered her share of the rent and she was continually overdrawn. But she could look on it as an investment, a business expense. Her clients would expect to receive professional quality prints showing her beautiful arrangements on the graves. She expected that her older clients would not be satisfied with digital images alone.

She snapped closed the lid of her laptop and grabbed her bag. A few minutes later she was herself dicing with death, pedalling at top speed across town on her shaky old bicycle to the nearest camera superstore. Armed with her new toy, she spent the rest of the afternoon wheeling the bike through Green Park and Hyde Park capturing the flora and the fauna and the wildlife. And for perhaps the first time in the last seven years, she was truly at peace.

Friday morning, she was back in college, having submitted her paper on 'Website Optimisation' (written as best she could) and now fired up with enthusiasm to get started on the website design for CelestialHeadstones.com. The first half of the morning was taken up with each of the students giving a five-minute presentation on the business model for the website they were proposing to design as part of the course. Most of them had business ideas relating to computer games or fashion or cosmetics or the music industry. Along with Celeste, a couple of the students had more original plans. One was intending to set up a pet dating and mating agency, which raised a few laughs.

'That'll be a money spinner,' said the tutor, 'and I really mean it! People care more for their pets than their kids in this country!'

Another was obsessed with gaming. He was in the process of designing his own virtual reality platform – something to do with a fight for survival in a post-apocalyptic world – where gamers could register and take sides and fight out their post-apocalyptic fantasies.

Celeste's project got a fairly cool reception. 'That's sick,' said one of the girls – and she didn't mean it in a good way. But then her website was all about 'finding your colour wheel' and choosing clothes to match personality, which Celeste thought rather lame.

When they got on to the technical part of the session, Celeste listened attentively, taking copious notes and trying to understand the software features that her teacher was expounding. By the end of the lesson her head was aching with the effort of concentration. She was lost. It was like a foreign language to her. Her brain just didn't work that way. She felt hopeless. Her business venture would fall at the first hurdle, if she couldn't get her website up and running.

Celeste ate her sandwich quickly and alone in the canteen. Although it was her day off, she couldn't wait to get started on her website. She wanted to cycle over to Seventh Heaven in time to take photographs of the front of the shop for the website while the sun was still out and high in the sky. She walked out of college to the street and crossed over to the railings where she had chained her bike. Someone had used her bicycle basket as a waste bin to dump a half-empty packet of jelly babies and a sheet of paper torn from a notebook. She took the litter out crossly before placing her rucksack into the basket. However, when she looked more closely at the paper, she noticed that there were words written on it. She flattened it out on her knee and read the note, written in capital letters in black biro.

STOP BLOCKING ME. WE NEED TO TALK. TEXT ME.

She wasn't sure if the message was meant for her. She looked around uncertainly at the faces of the students going up and down the pavement on either side of the road as they came and went from their classes.

Was anybody watching her?

She remembered the message she had seen on Anya's mobile…

It had to be him. He was trying to contact her – hounding her. That girl could have told him where she was studying, thought Celeste. He might have waited for her outside college and seen her arriving. Or, he could have seen her bike. She'd had it for years – they'd been on bike rides together as teenagers and her initials were scratched on the frame.

Her hand clenched into a fist around the sweet packet and she shuddered as something sticky oozed onto her fingers before she let it drop to the pavement in disgust. She rubbed her fingers frantically on her jeans.

'It's no use running away,' she said to herself. 'I've got to stand up to this manipulative bully once and for all. He can't control me now. I need to confront him and tell him to get out of my life forever...' There was a mobile number scribbled below the message. She pushed the note into her rucksack. Her hands were trembling. She couldn't think straight.

Without so much as a backwards glance, she bumped her bike off the kerb into the traffic and pedalled away furiously up the street.

PAST

9

Tom is about four years old – that age when little children enjoy sandpits and digging and grubbing about in the mud with toy watering cans and spades. She's almost twelve years old, and more and more she has to act as his surrogate mother.

There's a commotion going on in the kitchen – the usual soundtrack for a Saturday morning – swear words and sniping, raised voices, building to a full-blown row, with shouting and screaming and then a crescendo of shattered glass.

She goes into Tom's bedroom. He's hiding under the bed sheet, his face pinched and pale. 'Come on, let's get out of here!' She helps him find his clothes and get dressed and they creep down the stairs. She glances into the kitchen as they go out the back door. Stacey is sitting hunched over her black coffee, her forehead resting on one hand and a cigarette in the other.

Her father is standing with his back to the sink, holding a

large piece of broken glass – the jagged base of a gin bottle. He glares at her. A stream of red runs from his palm and drips onto the floor.

He has a well-paid job in the city. Though not as grand as Ben's with its pool and sloping wooded grounds and boating lake, they live in a big detached house with a big garden like all the other prosperous, privileged, middle-class families in the neighbourhood. Not one of her friends knows the full extent of the chaos that reigns behind its high, dark green hedges.

Stacey used to be a keen gardener with a flair for garden design until drink got the better of her. Celeste's happiest memories date from early childhood. She can remember helping her mother to prick out seedlings in the springtime even before she could see over the top of the potting bench. And she recalls misty autumn mornings when she knelt beside her mother on the damp grass digging holes with her little trowel to plant spring bulbs. Stacey showed her the pictures on the packets and taught her the names: narcissus, snowdrops, crocus, tulips, alliums and bluebells.

And then there was the excitement of seeing the flowers poking their bright green shoots up out of the grass the following March. Her mother would tell her they were making magic with the flower fairies – turning the wrinkly brown bulbs into beautiful creations in all the dancing colours of the rainbow. She gave the best hugs then. And she had the softest lips to kiss things better.

Celeste takes Tom down to the potting shed, now tangled in weeds and shrouded in cobwebs but still a place of refuge. She remembers that there is a dusty sack of spring bulbs abandoned in a corner under the bench. She finds the old toolbox and takes out her mother's big trowel and her own little trowel. Both are rusty from lack of use.

She hands Tom the little trowel. 'We're going to make some magic,' she says, and he follows her to the overgrown border near the apple orchard at the bottom of the garden. While she clears and weeds the plot, he potters around with his trowel. Then together they dig holes in the black crumbly soil and bury the bulbs in the earth. Celeste tells Tom that in the springtime the flower fairies will come and make the pretty flowers grow, and the shouting will stop, and everything will be sunny and bright out in the garden and inside the four walls of the house.

But Tom doesn't care. 'NeeNaw, NeeNaw, NeeNaw.' His noisy refrain gets on her nerves as she wanders off to return the trowels to the potting shed. Fairies are not part of his imaginary universe.

No.

He's a firefighter, racing up and down with his red plastic watering can, putting out the flames.

PRESENT

10

I'm so anxious and agitated that I can't sleep. You do this to me. I toss and turn in my bed and all I can see in my black hellhole is You in a red dress, standing over me laughing.

In the dark, I hold my breath waiting for the phone to ring. I reach out to see the screen, which I've been checking obsessively for new texts every five minutes since yesterday lunchtime. You haven't responded. But the spyware app I activated on your mobile when I found it at Heavana enables me to track your location at the tap of a finger. So, I know that You are at home. But are You alone? I imagine You in your bed and that man from the club doing horrible things to You.

I get up and switch on my computer. Two hours of U-Porn later and I emerge from the swamp feeling even worse. I still can't sleep and now I imagine myself in your bed doing to You all those revolting, unspeakable things I have been watching on my screen.

I hate You for making me feel this way. It's 3am in the

morning but there's no point lying here torturing myself. I get up and start on my college work. It takes me less than an hour to complete the assignment that our tutor set for the weekend. I should be teaching him.

By the first glimmers of dawn, I have to get out of my empty flat. Almost without thinking, I find myself standing on the pavement in the freezing rain on the opposite side of the road to where You live, looking up at your window, my eyes fixed on the gap in your curtains. From this angle, all I can see is a strip of darkness. But it's enough to know that You are there.

As the city begins to stir, my watch is interrupted only by the occasional taxi, speeding down the slippery tarmac, its grey-skinned occupant craning his neck to gape at me.

Like a mariner scanning for icebergs... I keep my eyes ahead... don't flinch a muscle... Nobody can arrest me for standing here quietly minding my own business... keeping watch while You sleep.

Looking isn't a crime.

Anya's boyfriend was out with his mates for the evening watching football at the pub, so she had offered to cook a seafood linguine for Celeste and Jessi to be followed by a girls' night for the three of them watching a movie at the flat. Celeste hadn't decided what to do about the hand-written note left in the basket of her bicycle. Coming after the text message that she'd seen on Anya's phone, it was the combination of the sweets and the note that made her sure it must be Ben. After all, he was the only person who could know about her childhood love of jelly babies.

Celeste had spent about twenty minutes washing her hands obsessively at the bathroom sink when she got back to the flat. She was distracted throughout the meal. She kept checking her phone for messages and peered anxiously over the other girls' screens whenever she heard them pinging.

In the end, Celeste decided to speak to her friends about it.

'I'm scared,' she said. 'He's trying to make contact with me again. He won't back off. First, he found me at the club, next he tried to match with me on Tinder, then he tried to get hold of my phone number, and now he's following me to college and leaving weird stuff in my bike basket.'

'Don't be daft!' said Anya. 'Stop being paranoid. Your imagination's running riot.'

'How do you know they're from Ben?' said Jessi. 'Could be from Steve or another one of your new mates?'

'I'm sure it's him.' Celeste continued obsessing about it. 'He's the only one who knows I was addicted to jelly babies when I was a little girl. He's bloody stalking me. It's freaking me out.'

'So, he left you some sweets. Big deal! Do you think he poisoned them?' Anya laughed sarcastically. 'You need to chill out.'

'I think it's cute,' chipped in Jessi. 'He wanted to leave you a little gift as a peace offering. Probably some joker ate half the packet.'

The bike rack was right near the bus stop. It was true there were always students hanging around who could have helped themselves.

'*The Mystery of the Missing Jelly Babies...*' Anya teased.

'I wish you would stop gaslighting me!' snapped Celeste.

'I'm sorry,' said Anya. 'I didn't mean to make light of it. I thought you were getting over him now. You've been so preoccupied with your new business venture and out socialising with your new college friends. You've seemed so much more positive and confident recently. Like a new person.'

'Look, I didn't imagine this,' said Celeste. She held out the crumpled sheet of paper. 'I don't want anything to do with him. That girl who sent you a text, Louise, or whatever her name is, she must have told him I've gone back to college.' Anya would know she'd been snooping on her phone but Celeste didn't care. 'For God's sake don't give that girl my number.'

Anya took the note and read it silently while Jessi looked over her shoulder. Celeste caught the two women exchanging a glance.

'No – this is not my illness coming back,' snapped Celeste. 'I'm over that now. I'm not deluding myself. This note is from him. I'm sure of it.'

Celeste understood only too well the meaning of that look. Anya and Jessi were a little younger than her and had been in the year below her at school, so they hadn't been close to her or to Ben at the time of the tragedy. She had connected with them at a party in London some five years later and once their friendship was firmly established, Anya and Jessi had offered Celeste the spare room in their rented flat when their former flatmate moved out.

Because Celeste spoke very little about what she had been through, it was mostly by hearsay and idle gossip that Jessi and Anya were aware that the trauma Celeste had suffered had plunged her into mental illness requiring strong medications and successive long stays in a specialist clinic. Celeste tried to keep secret the fact that spikes in her anxiety when she was particularly stressed could trigger a resurgence of her depression and mania. She was largely over this roller coaster of ups and downs and seemed to be getting her life back on an even keel. But whenever she was overwhelmed by anxiety the delusions and other mental health issues returned.

Anya read the note out loud. '*Stop blocking me... We need to talk...* Well, it's not exactly a death threat is it? There's nothing sinister in that. If this is from him, I guess he's reaching out for some kind of reconciliation now that he's back in the country.'

It was perhaps not surprising that Anya and Jessi found it hard to empathise with the angst, foreboding and distress that Ben's return to London had aroused in Celeste. Being in the year below, they knew Ben mainly by reputation – a popular guy that all the girls fancied and all the boys (as well as most of the male sports teachers) hero-worshipped. Anya and Jessi had had nothing in the way of intimate contact with Ben, nor had they ever witnessed or been on the receiving end of his bullying and intimidation. Moreover, Celeste had never confided in them about the way in which Ben had abused her on the night of the party. She couldn't blame them for thinking she was being pathetic. Ben had always been brilliant at hiding the cruel and despotic side of his character beneath a social veneer of confidence, good humour and charm.

It was also clear that nothing Anya and Jessi had heard coming out of the evidence given at the inquest would have given them cause to change their opinion of Ben. If he hadn't emerged from it blameless, he didn't come out of it looking like a monster. Word on the street was that Ben was a foolish and reckless kid caught up in a tragic accident. He had suffered too. Let's face it – his childhood had gone up in smoke.

Close to tears, Celeste stared at her friends. 'I know you think this is just a big joke but it's freaking me out. I never want to set eyes on the bastard again. I don't want a reconciliation. As far as I'm concerned, he's out of my life forever. But it looks like he's already found out where I go to college and where I leave my bike. Next thing, he'll be following me home, or following me to work.' She snatched back the note, screwed it into a ball and threw it in the recycling bin.

As Celeste continued to fret, Anya grew impatient while the supper she had prepared was getting cold. She had seen the results of her friend's wild imaginings over the last two years and she knew that despite her protestations, Celeste was still vulnerable to anxiety attacks that clouded her judgement and sense of reality.

'If it's bothering you that much, you should notify the police,' said Jessi gently.

'What would I tell them?' said Celeste. 'I don't even have any proof.'

'Well there's a very easy way to find out if this really is him,' said Anya. 'Just call the number.'

'That'll encourage him,' said Celeste. 'I don't want him to have my number or he'll never stop calling me.'

'Well, give me the number and I'll call it then from my mobile,' said Anya briskly, nodding towards the bin.

'No way,' said Celeste. 'I don't want you getting involved.'

Ever practical but unconcerned about money, Anya said, 'OK – so buy another cheap phone, pay-as-you-go, then you can call the number and find out who it is – and he won't be able to trace you.'

'Or I could ignore it,' said Celeste. 'Why should I throw money away on buying a second phone?'

'Make your mind up,' said Anya, who was rapidly losing interest in the subject as the dinner got cold. 'Now, more importantly, what film are we going to watch?' She banged the plates of pasta that she had been dishing up on to the table. 'Don't let this spoil our evening. Forget about it. Let's sit down and eat.'

Although her first impulse had been to reject Anya's suggestion, the very next day, Celeste stopped at her local phone shop on her bike ride to work and bought the cheapest phone she could find and a pay-as-you-go SIM card. During her lunch break, she went to sit on a park bench in one of the nearby garden squares. She unscrewed the ball of paper she had retrieved from the recycling bin before going to bed and she called the number. The voice on the other end of the phone was unexpected yet strangely familiar.

'Who is this?' she said.

PRESENT

11

I know it's a good sign when I check the notice board on my way into class for the weekly contact hours list. The sessions take place in pairs and every week, I've been living in hope. At last. There it is – written in black and white. Our names almost touching on the same line of ink. We're sharing a slot in the timetable with our tutor today.

This clinches the deal I brokered last week. You sealed our fate when You made that call. You can't ignore me any longer. We're meant to be together.

By the end of the tutor contact session, gushing with enthusiasm, you've revealed all the 'must haves' of your marketing project and I understand all the system requirements needed to make it work. This is my opportunity to make myself useful, indispensable even! For me it's so simple. It's not your fault you're incapable of getting to grips with any of the technicalities to get the website up and running. It's the way your female brain is wired. And it's obvious to us both that our tutor is less than interested in teaching You the mysteries of keychains, encryption and algorithms and more interested in getting his hand up your skirt! He's just some jumped-up dude with an MSc in digital marketing. I'm the computer expert here.

We'll be a perfect team – You can deal with the flowery bit and I can make the software work!

So, we walk out of class together and go for a coffee. And I'm so nervous, that I almost spill the coffee when I put it down in front of You. And I try hard to listen to what you're telling me, and I try not to stare when You lick the foam of your caffè latte (almond milk and two brown sugars – I won't need to ask You next time) from the corners of your mouth.

Now we are Facebook friends and we have made a date to meet in college to talk about me helping You to build your website. And if I play my cards right, soon we will be real friends and every link in the keychain that powers your website will be copied to my own devices.

Celeste leapt up in excitement the next Saturday morning when she got into Seventh Heaven and switched on the computer. There it was on the CelestialHeadstones.com website – new message. She squealed when she opened the client inbox and called out to Meghan.

'Meghan, come and see this. We've got our first order!'

The website wasn't perfect yet. She still needed to expand the galleries and refine the options on the ordering system and streamline the links and add the final touches to the eye-catching homepage. But the key thing was it was up and running and the incredible thing was that she was staring at her first order. She scarcely dared to open the message in case it should disappear into the ether, but once Meghan had strolled over with her morning fix of strong black coffee and was looking over her shoulder, she clicked, and the words came up on the screen.

The message had come in overnight from the US – all the way from Mrs Barbara Garcia in Santa Fe, New Mexico. She had sent a long message and attached a further document with information about her father, a lieutenant in the United States Army Air Corps, Navigator Eugene Jack Ashford from Sacramento, California, who had been killed in March 1945 when his aircraft, a B-17(G) Flying Fortress bomber crashed into a hillside on the North Downs as the crew were returning to their base in Northamptonshire after an operation near the German–Czech border.

'Wow! This is fascinating,' said Celeste as she read through the email. Even Meghan who was usually so pragmatic and business-like seemed interested.

Celeste read out loud from the message. 'I was three years old when my father, Eugene Ashford was tragically killed on 19th March 1945 in a crash in the Surrey Hills just two weeks after his twenty-seventh birthday. Before he joined up, my father was a reporter for the Sacramento Chronicle newspaper where he met my mother who was a typist. They had a whirlwind romance followed some weeks later by a shotgun wedding and I was born a short eight months later.

'My childhood memories are so fragmented, and I can't be sure anymore what is memory and what is imagination, but I carry a childhood picture in my head of the man who was my daddy and my hero – so tall and so handsome and so strong – the only man in the whole wide world as far as I was concerned! When I wasn't clinging to his knees to stop him walking out the door, I was up on his shoulders, clinging to his neck with my little legs and patting his glossy black hair – and I can still relive that feeling, of being on top of the world, looking down from my daddy's shoulders. If I close my eyes and sit very still, I can smell the musky scent of the gel that he used to slick back his cowl. I remember him swinging me round above his head and I remember him leaning over my bed like a gentle smiling giant and calling me his "little angel" and soothing me to sleep as he stroked my hair with his big, soft hands.'

Celeste felt a kind of wistful and jealous admiration for these expressions of love. She had never had such feelings for her own father. In contrast, Meghan bridled at the sentimental message. 'Well she's certainly got a good memory!' she said tersely, when Celeste looked up at her triumphantly.

Below the text, there were two pictures of Eugene.

'She's right,' said Celeste. 'He was a handsome man.' The first photograph, sober and posed, must have been taken by a professional photographer soon after Eugene was mobilised. He was in characteristic US air force military uniform, standing upright and confident, his fleece-lined leather bomber jacket zipped to the chin, as dashing as a Hollywood actor. His sombre eyes stared directly at Celeste from beneath the gleaming black visor of his cap that he wore tilted a little to one side, perhaps revealing a defiant and rebellious side to his character. His features were strong with firm lips, straight nose and dark eyes, well suited to the determined expression that still shone out from the image, surviving the passage of the years.

The second picture was a family snapshot taken in a

city park – Sacramento City Park – according to the title beneath it. Although, the picture was, of course, in black and white, Celeste could tell that the sun was shining on that day in 1945 – the play of shadows and light was sharp and bright. Eugene was wearing a short-sleeved cotton shirt and his face was lit up with sunlight and laughter as he squinted at the lens. And the tiny girl up on his shoulders was presumably, Barbara, in a pinafore dress, cherub-like, with a mop of light curly hair. He was holding one of her chubby legs in one hand and reaching up with the other to hold her hand in his. Barbara was beaming and her mouth was smothered in ice cream. With her free hand she seemed to be waving a cone of melting ice cream like a flag while it dripped down her little fist onto her daddy's head.

'This photograph must have been taken just a few weeks before Eugene died,' said Celeste.

Mrs Barbara Garcia's email went on to explain that this year would be the one hundredth anniversary of her father's birth and that she had been hoping to commemorate his life and his tragic loss by coming to England to visit his grave at the American military cemetery near to Cambridge. Unfortunately, she was prevented from travelling by ill health. Having almost resigned herself to marking the anniversary privately in her own home, she was blessed to have come across CelestialHeadstones.com while browsing for a florist local to Cambridge. She had felt as if she had been touched by something mystical and divine. CelestialHeadstones.com was offering exactly the service Barbara Garcia was looking for.

'My prayers have been answered,' she concluded.

Celeste clapped her hands.

'Isn't it wonderful?' she said. 'To think that a sweet little old lady on the other side of the Atlantic in Santa Fe, New Mexico, is able to connect with us and that we can be the answer to her prayers!'

Meghan was more hard-headed.

'She isn't that old,' she said. 'By my calculations she must be seventy-six – and she isn't that helpless! She's certainly internet savvy – look, she signed up for your free delivery promotion, which means that if you honour her order we'll be paying for the diesel between here and Cambridge, which must be at least a 150-mile round trip – not to mention your travel time!'

But Celeste was passionate. 'I can't turn this down. Look on it as a *loss-leader*. It's Sunday tomorrow. I've got nothing planned. I'll come in at 6am to prepare the flowers and I'll do the delivery in my own time. I'll take lots of photographs myself and I'll ask Barbara if we can post her photographs and feature her father's story on the website. It'll be great publicity – a brilliant way to launch the website.'

The next morning Celeste arrived at Seventh Heaven at the crack of dawn. She let herself in through the back door. The shop was eerily quiet. In the stillness, the smell of flowers and foliage was overpowering, almost intoxicating. For a moment she allowed her guard to fall. She closed her eyes and breathed deeply.

Now she was in a different room, white and clinical. There was soft music playing, and crosses on the walls and a shape in the middle of the room that she couldn't look at – a black hole that she would tumble into if she reached out or stepped any closer. She screwed up her eyes and bowed her head, sick and faint with the smell of decomposing flowers. She couldn't even cry.

A tap had been left dripping in the cold room at Seventh Heaven and the sound of water hitting the china basin struck like small hammer blows in her head. Celeste opened her eyes and made a conscious effort to wrench the waking nightmare from her brain. She ran to the tap and screwed it up tightly. Then she took her workbox from the shelf and opened her laptop. She opened up Barbara Garcia's order and went through to the cold room to select the blooms.

Barbara had chosen the 'Misty Mornings' arrangement as featured on the website. Celeste had described this as a sympathy tribute in 'a very nuanced and soft style' made up of 'heavenly pale and pastel vendela roses, cloud-pink peonies, pure white lilies, purple-dawn lisianthus and a mix of striking and delicate foliage in shades of green from dark to fresh lime'. It was one of the most expensive arrangements in the CelestialHeadstones.com offering, listed in the 'luxury' category. Celeste had created the design with femininity in mind and understood that in picking this one out Barbara had been thinking less about the character and attributes of her father (or whether this arrangement was fitting for a soldier's grave) and more about her own sense of loss and longing that she had carried in her heart since losing her father when she was a little girl. No doubt Barbara had fallen for 'Misty Mornings' because it spoke to her own romantic yearnings and memories. Perhaps she had been swayed by the lyricism of Celeste's marketing prose.

'If this could be delivered with the morning dew found on misty mornings, a sweet chorus of birdsong, and the faint shimmer of dawn, we could capture the celestial beauty of nature in this exquisite floral tribute.' Barbara's choice revealed more about Barbara, than her father. But that was the whole point, reflected Celeste as she paced around the cold room from one steel bucket to another, selecting the foliage and blooms that she needed to create the arrangement.

In her business model, the giving of sympathy flowers was all about making the person who gave them feel good. Her clients might not be able to visit the graves in person. It was possible that the only person to see and enjoy the floral tributes would be Celeste. But it was the act of giving that mattered. And Celeste would send her clients photographs and feature the graves on her website, and they would know that any casual passer-by and any visitor to the website would see that their loved one was still remembered and cherished. The flowers delivered by CelestialHeadstones. com would be a celebration of that loving memory in the real, the spiritual and the virtual world!

Celeste was soon absorbed in her work – preparing the pottery vase that she would leave on the grave, laying out and then trimming the stems at an angle, snipping some of the blooms to shorter lengths to give visual impact and statement to the flowers, criss-crossing the woody Pitto greenery in an 'X' shape to give a sturdy base before filling the gaps with the delicate green foliage and finally pushing in and arranging the blooms to create a display that was eye-catching and gorgeous from every angle. It came naturally to her. As Meghan had told her, she had a gift. Her artistry went beyond what Meghan herself could teach her apprentice about the trade and the craft of floristry.

Celeste could see beyond sentimentality. She understood the meaning of suffering. And she had an instinct for turning it into something beautiful.

PRESENT

12

*J*ust *when I get my lucky break, now here's another setback. Your social life is taking off.*

I used to be able to spend my evenings loitering in your street, rewarded by fleeting images of You moving round the flat or warmed by the amber glow of your bedside lamp shining through the gap in the curtains. But now You are out almost every night. Tuesday night it was bowling, Wednesday night it was the pub, Thursday night it was a late-night shopping trip and tonight it's the cinema.

These days You are never alone – always surrounded by your new gaggle of college friends. I don't get it. Are You looking for safety in numbers? Are You trying to freeze me out?

The faces change from one night to the next – all except for one that crops up too often. I've never seen him at college.

Here he comes, bearing popcorn and Cokes. He muscles his way past the other girls in your group to sit next to

You in the row. I slip in as the lights are dimming and find a seat to the side at the back. I don't see much of the film (some puerile comedy about a foursome of sex-craved pre-menopausal women) but I have a perfect view of the back of your head. I can't see your profile very well because his thick neck and big head keep getting in the way. Thank God he doesn't try to kiss You, but it's only a matter of time. You are sharing his popcorn.

I can't bear the way he leans in to touch your arm or catch your eyes whenever some inane scene raises a laugh. Soon you'll be sharing his bed.

Tomorrow, it will be blissful to have You to myself at last.

Celeste was already beginning to feel light-headed by the time she turned off the Madingley Road to the entrance of the American Military Cemetery and Memorial on the outskirts of Cambridge. True to her word, Meghan had lent Celeste the Seventh Heaven van for the day. The roads had been clear and at 9am she was bang on opening time and the first visitor to arrive in the car park. As she turned off the engine, Celeste remembered that she hadn't eaten or drunk anything since the popcorn and Diet Coke that had passed for supper at the cinema the night before. She'd been so absorbed in arranging the flowers at first light in Seventh Heaven that she hadn't even bothered to make herself a coffee.

She hauled out her floristry bag, her camera and her tripod, all of which she managed to carry on one side of her body. Then she wedged the ceramic pot containing the 'Misty Mornings' arrangement between the crook of her arm and her hip, on the other. She set off in the direction of the visitor centre in the hope of getting a drink before figuring out the location of Eugene's grave.

The cemetery was a vast, sloping site framed by woodland, extending over thirty acres, (as she found out later from the information boards in the visitor centre) and designed with military precision and geometric sensitivity. She paused beneath the flagpole that rose up from a platform overlooking the site. Turning her face upwards, she could see stars and stripes from the partly unfurled American flag as it fluttered in the breeze beneath the soaring golden eagle at the top of the flagpole, and beyond that, a clear pale blue sky extending to infinity.

She was struck by the great ocean of mortality spread out before her eyes. Beyond the Great Mall with its reflecting pools bordered by beds of blood-red roses, the burial area was laid out in concentric waves of headstones sweeping over the lawns like the ridges on a shell. Each untimely death was marked in the curving swathes of white crosses and Stars of David that sparkled against the backdrop of green grass and from a distance reminded Celeste of foamy crests of waves surging into shore.

Like everything else, the visitor centre was on a grand and formal scale but Celeste was disappointed to find that there was no café. As it was still empty, she was able to ask a member of staff to keep an eye on her things while she spent a few minutes looking at the exhibits, photographs and interactive displays, many of which disclosed poignant personal stories about members of the US military who had lost their lives in World War II.

Celeste's knowledge of military history was sketchy at best. Reading the information boards, she felt overwhelmed by the huge number of deaths and scarcely able to comprehend the immensity of the personal tragedy and loss laid to rest within metres of where she stood. These young men, many of them still in their teens, had given their lives for her country and for people like her.

She learnt that the cemetery contained the remains of 3,811 American war dead and that the Walls of the Missing recorded 5,127 names of those who had been listed as 'missing in action'. Most of the fallen had died in the Battle of the Atlantic or in the strategic air bombardment of north-west Europe.

She understood these references a little better now and began to form a picture in her mind of the conflict that Eugene Ashford and so many others like him had been caught up in. She knew they had died as heroes and were lovingly remembered as such by their families and friends. And yet, she couldn't help but reflect that for every name engraved on a monument or headstone within this cemetery, there were other names engraved in other cemeteries on other shores in loving memory of those who had died on account of their actions. These included innocent children and babies – victims of Allied bombardments.

She wandered through the Memorial Building, constructed of the famous British Portland Stone that was used for the construction of war memorials thanks to its exceptional hard and durable qualities, and on into an elegant anteroom whose ceiling was covered by an extraordinary mosaic, predominantly blue in colour, through which ghostly aircraft were depicted making their final flights. Perhaps more than any photograph, this evocative work of art made her feel for herself the pathos and tragic waste of life of these high-flying young men sacrificed in the war.

Celeste unfolded the copy of Barbara's email that she had printed off and went over to find the helpful old gentleman, who was looking after her stuff. Barbara appeared to be a very efficient lady. She had provided Celeste with details of Eugene's full name, rank, dates of birth and death as well as his memorial ID and the burial plot coordinates needed to find his headstone. When Arthur (she'd read his name on his lapel badge), picked up Celeste's workbox and tripod and offered to accompany her to the plot, she was happy to accept his help. It wasn't long before she was following him along the neat strip of grass separating two concentric curves of grave markers laid out in parade-ground precision, each one gleaming pristine white in the morning sunshine.

I won't be needing to scrub the stone, thought Celeste happily. It was all so clinically well kept. The grass was as perfectly mown as a croquet lawn. She could hear the mowers going up and down in the distance already even though it was a Sunday in March. Most of the graves were bare though a few of them were adorned with small flags – the Stars and Stripes and The Union Jack – and occasionally a small posy of spring flowers or a black-and-white photograph were propped up against the headstone.

After a couple of hundred metres, Arthur stopped, checked the piece of paper Celeste had handed to him and pointed to the marker.

'This is the one' he said. '*Eugene J Ashford.*'

Celeste hung her head, saddened to see how little

information was given on the headstone. With stark simplicity the inscription read.

EUGENE J ASHFORD
351 BOMBER SQUADRON
CALIFORNIA 19 MAR 1945

She crouched down to place the pot of flowers in front of the headstone and ran her fingers gently along the grooves of the inscription. Was this all that remained? For a life given in sacrifice, a few clinical words carved out on a stone cross? There was so little space on the cross – no room to add a date of birth (which was perhaps a blessing since so many of the dead soldiers were so painfully young), or for the family to add a comforting thought or endearment or message in memory of their loved one.

Once Arthur had left, it didn't take Celeste long to tend to Eugene's grave since she had accomplished most of the work arranging the flowers at Seventh Heaven that morning. She completed the final touches – a few tall statement stems that she had kept to one side for fear they would be damaged in transit, a purple ribbon to go around the rim of the clay pot. She had also brought copies of the two photographs sent through online by Barbara, which she had laminated at her college and attached with clips to plastic plant-markers taken from the shop supplies. She pushed the markers firmly into the turf so that the photographs were displayed in front of the headstone.

Eugene's eyes seemed to follow her – dark and serious in the first photograph, mischievous and twinkling in the second. There he was, frozen in time in the shallows of life's great adventure, unaware he had so few days left to live when he posed for the camera. She felt a connection with him and sat very still on the grass gazing at the two images of his face.

There was one more laminated card to display. The CelestialHeadstones.com website included an optional box where clients could type in a message to be displayed with the flowers on the grave. Celeste read over Barbara's message, which she had carefully transcribed from the screen onto a handwritten card. Although, it was rare for her to put pen to paper these days (since all communications seemed to take place via a screen), Celeste's handwriting was clear and neat in the copperplate style that she had perfected as a schoolgirl.

Barbara's message read like that of a little girl to her daddy and Celeste could understand this only too well – Eugene's death must have stopped the clock for Barbara, somehow arrested her emotional development – her love for her father was crystallised in those cherished memories of early childhood.

To my darling Daddy,
Lieutenant Eugene Jack Ashford of the US Army Air
Corps
Navigator of the skies.
I was your little angel.
Then you flew your airplane all the way up to heaven.
Now you are my guardian angel watching over me
from the stars.
You were so strong, so gentle and so brave.
Not a day goes by without me missing you. You are
always in my heart.

Forever your little girl,
Baby x

Barbara had also included a quote from the English First World War poet, Rupert Brooke. Celeste knew a little about Brooke's poetry as she had studied the First World War poets for her English literature exams at school. She knew that Brooke had connections with Cambridge having been an undergraduate at The King's College and having lived for some time only a stone's throw from where she now knelt, in the little village of Grantchester, which was the namesake and setting for one of his most famous poems. Of course, Celeste was also familiar with the poem 'The Soldier' (*If I should die, think only this of me/That there's some corner of a foreign field/That is for ever England...*) But she had never come across the poem 'The Great Lover', from which Barbara had chosen a hauntingly beautiful and fitting quote:

> *My night shall be remembered for a star*
> *That outshone all the suns of all men's days.*

As Celeste attached Barbara's message to the headstone, she reflected that Brooke's sentiment expressed in this verse was prophetic. The poet himself had been a young man of great beauty and precocious talent who had met an untimely death in 1915 from sepsis on an army hospital ship moored in a sheltered, sunlit bay off the Greek island of Skyros. He had been hastily buried on a hillside among olive groves with only a painted wooden cross to mark his grave. But thanks to his entrancing and luminous poetry, Brooke's humble grave marker had been replaced with an ornate stone monument and had become a place of pilgrimage dappled with sunlight through olive branches, for lovers of his poetry. So, the prophecy in this verse had come to pass. His star continued to shine on down the generations whilst the lives of others who had survived him were soon forgotten.

In meditative mood, Celeste took photographs of the grave from every angle and set up her tripod to include a picture of herself, kneeling to one side of the memorial flowers. As she balanced on her haunches, focused on the shots, she began to feel strangely on edge. She glanced over her shoulder, overcome with a creeping electric sensation that she was not alone. She shrugged it off. This was a graveyard after all. It was easy to start imagining things. She stood up to take a video sequence showing the 360-degree views from the spot where Barbara's father was buried.

It was as she turned towards the trees that she froze mid-circuit. Her hand began to shake as the video continued to roll. She could see a figure, there in the woods, watching her, half-hidden in the shadows. When she looked up from the viewfinder, the low winter sun was dazzling. But shielding her eyes she could make out the dark shape of a man, very upright and still. His silhouette against the trees fitted the photographs of the airmen she had seen inside the visitor centre clothed in loose trousers and boots and bomber jackets. The shape didn't move but seemed to shimmer as the breeze stirred the new spring leaves and sunlight filtered down through the branches.

She couldn't tell how long they stood there, eyeing each other, senses connected and alert, like predator and prey on an African savannah. From nowhere, an icy gust of wind crossed the cemetery, toppling the pot of flowers and blowing her hair across her face. Once she had righted the pot and swept her hair away from her eyes, the figure was gone, and its trailing black shadow seemed to dissolve into the trees. She put out a hand to steady herself on the stone cross. As she gripped the cold white marble, she felt the blood draining from her head and her legs began to buckle.

PAST

13

She's at her father's house. It's his weekend. It used to be her house and she still has her bedroom here but now she thinks of it as his – ever since he moved in his new bimbo Natasha. It's such a tired old tale. Natasha is his former secretary – more than twenty years his junior. Celeste supposes older men would find her attractive – good figure, bottle-blonde hair and striking features if you can ignore the pocked skin that she cakes in foundation. Celeste has no idea what Natasha sees in her father – with his grey, thinning hair and his flaccid belly and his self-important arrogance – apart from his money of course and his position – money and power – so many young women will settle for that over a full head of hair and toned muscles and sex appeal… He's her meal ticket to a comfortable life.

As for her life, she and Tom moved out of their luxury five-bedroom home with their mother after the divorce to live in a small semi in the next village rented from a social housing association. By rights, Stacey should have kept the house, since she kept the children, but she was so out of her head with alcohol at the time of the divorce that she hadn't the sense or the money to take advice or engage a decent lawyer. She just wanted out. He fleeced her. He's supposed to pay the rent of their 'so-called' affordable housing but somehow, they always seem to be in arrears each month, even though he has no trouble affording the costs of Christmas holidays in Barbados or skiing in the Swiss Alps to keep The Bimbo happy.

Stacey doesn't earn a penny so she relies on her ex's child support payments and alimony to put food on the table and clothes in the cupboard for her children except when she blows it on booze.

Tom is with Stacey. Their father usually has them both on alternate weekends, but he asked for some 'one-to-one quality time' with Celeste. He feels they are growing apart. She's getting out of hand. He wants to talk some sense into her. She would much prefer to have gone with Tom and Stacey to Alton Towers. (Stacey made her father buy the theme park tickets in exchange for 'bagging' Celeste.) Instead, her brother got to take a friend, and she got to make up a threesome for the weekend with her father and Natasha.

She's already in her father's bad books again and she only just arrived – late as usual. Natasha cooked a special meal in her honour – paella with chicken and king prawns, followed by chocolate soufflé. To be fair, Natasha is a good cook and according to Celeste's father she spent most of the day, planning and shopping and cooking the meal. She's trying to ingratiate herself. But Celeste has recently decided to go vegetarian and gluten free, so she point-blank refuses the paella and eats only two or three spoonsful of the chocolate soufflé (under duress, even though it's delicious).

Natasha puts a brave face on it. 'It's no problem,' she simpers. 'It's my fault. I should have asked.'

Her father is furious, but Celeste doesn't care. She doesn't want to eat supper anyway because she's planning to go to a party later (someone's eighteenth from the year above) and she doesn't want to 'look fat' in her size XS skin-tight mini dress.

He has a go at her in front of The Bimbo, and she swears at him and leaves the table in 'disgrace' (disgust) and goes up to her room and shuts the door and sits on the bed and gets out her laptop intending to do a couple of hours' homework before getting ready for the party. He steams up after her and marches in, yelling his head off. He calls her a 'selfish little bitch', and she calls him a 'lame bastard'. He keeps on at her until she shouts at him to 'leave me in peace to work' and 'go back downstairs to your two-faced, money-grabbing, vile little whore'.

And that's when he loses it. He lunges across the room to the bedside and slaps the side of her face with all his force. She puts up her hands to protect herself. Her ear is ringing, and he jolted her neck and her cheekbone hurts so badly she thinks he might have cracked it.

'You asked for that,' he says grimly, as he walks out and slams the door. Through the door, she hears him shouting his parting shot. 'If you think you're going to that party, you can forget it. You're grounded.'

She's too angry and shocked to cry. She looks at her face in the mirror. The marks of his fingers are still on her cheek. Her mouth tastes salty. She pulls down her lip to see. The inside of her lower lip is bleeding where it knocked against her teeth and already beginning to swell up. She fingers her cheekbone carefully. Bruised but not broken, she thinks. But she wouldn't be surprised if she has a black eye tomorrow.

He's never hurt her physically before even though she knows he has a vicious temper. There was always a lot of shouting and screaming in the house, but it was usually between her mum and dad. She never actually saw him hit her mother – and, God, let's be honest, Stacey gave him a lot of provocation with the way she behaved. But now she comes to think of it, there were mornings when her mother came down to breakfast with bruises on her arms or her forehead or her chin, which Celeste always put down to drunken falls after one gin (or several) too many.

But maybe it was him leaving his marks on her?

Stacey will never tell. She's too proud.

So, Celeste will never know.

PRESENT

14

Y*ou.*
You are even more beautiful from behind.

As I follow You round the cloisters and backstreets of Cambridge, I would know You in a crowd of a thousand people.

You walk fast for a girl. Sometimes it's hard to keep up.

I know the way You hold your head and the way your hips swing from side to side and the way your hair bounces as You walk and the length of your stride and the way your left shoulder is always slightly in front of the right, as if you are hurrying to get ahead of yourself.

I want to walk in your footsteps – on grey pavements or chipped cobbles or crushed blades of grass.

I would die to hide in your sunlight or shine in your shade.

I have become a part of You.

I am your ghost.

Thinking she was about to faint, Celeste sat down on the ground in front of Eugene's headstone and put her head between her knees.

'Stop being an idiot,' she said to herself. 'You're just low on blood sugar. You need something to eat and drink.' She decided the best plan would be to drive into Cambridge (a city she'd never visited) to get some lunch and have a look around before setting off on the long drive back to Pimlico. She gave herself a minute or two to recover her composure, sitting quietly with her eyes shut, listening to the birds singing in the trees. Just as her breathing was beginning to slow, she felt a sudden drop in the light intensity and temperature as if she were in someone else's shade. But when she opened her eyes, there was no one there. She shivered and stood up. Seconds later the peace was broken by the revving and then rumbling engine of a motorbike starting up from the direction of the wood and moving away into the distance.

She opened her eyes then stood stock-still, listening to the sounds in the landscape. It didn't make sense. The cemetery was surrounded by fields beyond the treeline. There couldn't be a road... a track through the woods at most... What was a motorbike doing down there? This was too weird! She'd had enough of this place, surrounded by the dead. It was messing with her head. She had to get away.

She retraced her steps to the entrance, stopping briefly like a tourist to search for the names of Joseph Kennedy and Glenn Miller in the 'Tablets of the Missing' inscribed on the vast Portland stone memorial wall. She had learnt in the visitor centre that Lieutenant Joseph P Kennedy

Jr (the oldest of the Kennedy brothers), in the US Navy Reserve, was flying a B-24 Liberator aircraft loaded with high explosives on a secret mission against a German V2 rocket site on 12 August 1944, when his aircraft exploded. And also, that Major Alton G Miller (better known to all as the famous jazz musician and band leader Glenn Miller), was flying to Paris from a small airfield near Bedford on 15 December 1944, to make arrangements for a Christmas broadcast, when his plane disappeared over the English Channel. They were never found. Like the airmen depicted in the mosaic they had passed from this world into another heavenly sphere – vanished into thin air, vaporised.

Walking on, Celeste's eyes fell on the towering stone airman statue positioned in front of the memorial. The airman statue was standing tall, eyes directly ahead, next to a machine gun on its right and holding an unopened parachute in its left. The statue was sporting a fleece-lined helmet, fleece-lined bomber jacket and fleece-lined boots. Celeste stopped abruptly as if she herself had been turned to stone, struck by the resemblance in the stance and attire of the statue to the apparition that had confronted her from a distance in the woods.

It was time to go...

When Celeste drove into Cambridge, her spirits rose. After the austere formality of the cemetery, where the flowers and lawns were tamed and controlled with military rigour, it was a relief to park her car and stroll up a tree-lined path to the riverbank, where the natural world was bursting into life untamed on this beautiful spring day. The daffodils and crocuses were now in full bloom, colouring the meadows with splashes of yellow and blue. The cherry blossoms were at their best, kissing the branches in delicate shades of white and the palest of pinks. The scene was like an impressionist painting. The contrast with the American cemetery couldn't have been greater.

It struck her that death was stark and hard-lined and geometric whereas life was filled with colours and curves and blurred edges and softness and light. Everywhere she looked was buzzing with insects and birds and students walking arm-in-arm, and young families with children and babies in pushchairs and tourists clicking cameras. They were all out and about bathed in the soothing midday sun.

She was overwhelmed by the loveliness of this stretch of the River Cam, known affectionately as 'The Backs' because of the university colleges whose green lawns and flower-filled courts backed onto it. To stave off her hunger she stopped to eat an ice cream bought from a mobile tricycle stall, then wandered along the riverbank, snapping photographs of the college buildings and gardens and bridges, and smiling at the antics of the undergraduates and tourists crashing their punts on the water.

Though she didn't know much about history or design, she was awestruck by the soaring architecture of the Kings College Chapel and all the visually stunning and imposing colleges she passed on her walk. Their names sounded as romantic and poetic as the shipping forecast when she recited them to herself – Clare, Kings, Magdalen, Trinity and St John's.

Although she hadn't planned this as a tourist outing,

eventually she gave in to the advances of a pushy tour guide and jumped into one of the ten-seater wooden boats being punted up and down the river by students dressed in straw boaters and cream flannels. It was relaxing to sit back and listen to the young man reciting from his memorised script the potted history of Cambridge and its colleges. She used the boat trip as an opportunity to get some 'Instagrammable' photographs for the CelestialHeadstones. com account and to find the perfect 'thank-you-for-your-business' message image to send to Barbara in New Mexico to accompany the photographs she had taken of the Cambridge American Cemetery and Eugene's grave.

They punted down as far as the Bridge of Sighs, aptly named after the Bridge of Sighs in Venice. It was here that she captured the perfect archetypal image of Cambridge on her camera as she photographed the smaller punts passing beneath the bridge. The dappled reflection of the ornate stone arch with its crenellated-covered passageway shimmered in the dark ripples. The vivid green of the oak tree on the riverbank beyond the bridge was visible through its latticed arch-shaped window openings. The bridge was framed by the walls of the courts of St John's College on either side of the River Cam. Patches of sunlight and shade highlighted the architectural lines and features of the ancient buildings.

After the punting tour Celeste wandered through the ancient courts of Clare College and along a winding cobbled alleyway into the centre of town. The tour guide had mentioned 'Fitzbillies' cake shop and café on Trumpington Street, a popular spot with students and tourists alike, which had been around for over 150 years. Apparently, it served an excellent brunch as well as being famous for its traditional Chelsea buns.

Celeste was charmed by the place. It was so Cambridge! The name 'Fitzbillies' was emblazoned in large gold lettering on the timber frontage. There were bicycles propped up against the glass window displays of tiered wedding cakes and iced buns and jars of traditional marmalades and preserves. She took her place at a corner table across the room from two undergraduates just a few years younger than her who were wearing black scholars' gowns over their T-shirts and jeans. She felt as if she had strayed on to the set of a Harry Potter movie. They were chatting and laughing about nothing in particular and the boy kept leaning across the table to touch the girl's hand. He'd placed a book on the table next to him, and she glanced over to check the title:

Marcel Proust, *À La Recherche du Temps Perdu.*

Her first thought was *how pretentious!* But then she thought she should cut him some slack. He was probably a modern languages undergraduate so it was perhaps natural that he would read Proust in the original and bring him to brunch.

In Search of Lost Time…

She had read the novel herself in translation and now the book lying there seemed imbued with significance. Watching the young couple sitting there flirting and lost in each other's company made her sad and nostalgic for things that could have been. She was lost… just lost… and alone. She pushed away her plate, nauseated by the smell of the full English breakfast. Her stomach was in knots. She had been a star pupil in her senior school, having gained straight A's in her GCSEs aged sixteen and then having been predicted the highest grades for her final end-of-school exams. Once upon a time, this happy gilded life or something similar at another university had been within her grasp, not an impossible dream. But it had all been wrenched away from her so very brutally, that fateful night in February, seven years ago.

If only I hadn't let him order me around... If only I hadn't gone with him... If only I hadn't let him ply me with drink... If only I hadn't smoked that cigarette... If only I hadn't locked the door... If only I had said No! No! No!

There were too many *If onlys* to torment herself with.

She stood up to leave, despising herself. She was not worthy of self-pity or compassion.

My loss is nothing compared to...

This moment of self-indulgence in Fitzbillies, in search of lost time for things that might have been, tortured her with guilt, making her feel all the more wretched and broken and irredeemable...

And for that, she hated him all the more.

PAST

15

When she stops shaking, she stoops down to pick up her laptop and check that it's still working. It fell to the floor in all the commotion. She powers it up. It works thank goodness – she would be distraught to lose all her A-level notes. She puts in her headphones then opens the document she was working on when her dad barged in, and tries to concentrate on her homework – an essay question from a Philosophy A-level past paper: 'How might a utilitarian attempt to justify preventative imprisonment (imprisoning someone to prevent them from committing a crime, rather than because they have already committed a crime)?'

Her head was buzzing with ideas when she first started making notes on this topic, but now she can't do it. Utilitarian arguments about calculating the good of the many versus the good of the few get tangled up in her head with ideas about absolute ethical values and natural justice.

All she can think about is the punishment that her father has unjustifiably subjected her to. At this very moment she would like to kill him. Should she be imprisoned? Would that be justified to prevent her carrying out the crime?

What an absurd essay title! she thinks. *How can you be sure who will commit a crime and when? Every one of us is capable of committing a crime if we are pushed too far.* Instead of feeling cowed and chastened by her father she is bursting with defiance. Right now, the devil is in her. She sees red. She would like to burn the house down and everyone in it. *We are all fallen angels*, she reflects. *Given sufficient provocation, the most peace-loving of individuals may unleash his or her anger and turn to violence...* And she types that, as the first line of her essay.

Her cheekbone throbs and her fingers stumble over the keys. Message bubbles pop up in the notifications corner of her screen. She saves her document and closes it. Her homework will have to wait until tomorrow. She can't concentrate anyway. She clicks on the texts.

The messages are from Lucie and Harry – they're in a new thing together. Lucie's message says:

'Get your ass over here – we're pre-ing at Ben's.'

Lucie is Celeste's new best friend. Celeste has always been on the fringes of the 'popular group' – her parents' divorce and her mother's alcoholism (these kids are narrow-minded snobs underneath it all), and her reputation for being something of a swot, keep her out of the inner circle. But in the past few months, her NHS braces have come off, and she's become a fitness fanatic, and started wearing black eyeliner to school, and she's highlighted her hair and lifted her hemline and suddenly the boys have agreed 'she has good tits and a great pair of legs', and Ben has let it be known that in his estimation she's gone up from a 'seven out of ten' to a 'nine out of ten' and the girls have started to respect her and decided it's better to have her as a friend than a rival.

Harry is Ben's 'wingman' – not as tall or as good-looking or as strong, but the girls like him because he's funny and doesn't take himself too seriously. She reads Harry's message:

'Ben says bring the vodka.'

That's as close to a 'come-on' as she's had from Ben.

She scrabbles around in the bottom of her suitcase and pulls out a bottle of vodka. This is the other asset that's raised her net worth in the popularity stakes recently – she can always be relied upon to bring the booze. Her mother has so many bottles of spirits stashed away in hiding places around the house that she doesn't notice when one of them goes missing. And even if she did notice, she would be too embarrassed about her own secret drinking habits to challenge her teenage daughter. Celeste finds a shot glass (stolen from the local pub) in amongst her underwear and pours herself a measure. If the pre-lash is already happening at Ben's house, she's gonna have to 'pre' the 'pre'!

Having knocked back the vodka and pulled on her bodycon, she immediately feels more confident and up for the party. She grabs her make-up bag and heads for the bathroom.

And that's when her anger explodes... Her bedroom door is locked. She yanks at the handle and hammers frantically on the door with her hairbrush. Unlike the flimsy doors at her new place, it's made of solid wood – though she's mad with rage, there's no chance of breaking it down.

She gets no response from downstairs. Through the oak she can hear the TV turned to full volume as usual. She rattles the handle again. Her father seems to be going deaf. The lovebirds must be watching a movie so there's no knowing when they'll come up. Ironically, she's the one who insisted on having a lock fitted to her door. It's still her bedroom. She's got to have one place of refuge in the old family home. And now that Natasha is squatting here, there's absolutely no way she's going to give that snake the opportunity of nosing through her stuff when she's away.

She opens her bedroom window. In this high-ceilinged house, it's a long drop to the gravel driveway below. She's not that crazy. Thank God, she has her phone. She calls her father's number. It goes to voicemail. Of course, he's switched it to silent. He's probably otherwise engaged, slavering over Natasha.

The claustrophobia of being trapped in her room begins to creep up on her. It's too melodramatic and mortifying to let anyone on her social media chats know that her father locked her in. Instead, she messages the chats to say she can't make it, and she pours herself another vodka, and another, and another to keep the panic in check and spends the evening on her phone, stalking her friends on Facebook, torturing herself by poring over their inane, drunken posts from the party, gutted with that perverse feeling of anxiety, frustration, misery and self-pity, that in this infancy of social media already has its own acronym – FOMO – fear of missing out. And this FOMO – or, could it more accurately be described as COMO? – certainty of missing out – fires her anger against her father until she really and truly believes that she could kill him.

PRESENT

16

*I*t's been a good day.

I get back to my accommodation late in the evening, pleased to find that my Amazon package is waiting for me in the hallway. I get out my penknife and cut strips through the cardboard. With a guilty frisson, I lift my purchase carefully out of the box and break away the polystyrene with a pleasing crunch and snap.

I may be old-fashioned to seek out print, but this will give me hours of fun.

Ten laminated photographs later, I dine on toast and marmalade washed down with Horlicks. I stick the photographs to the wall next to my bed and turn out the light.

No more bare walls. You are my poster girl. Exhausted but content, I sleep like a baby for the first time in weeks.

★

Celeste cycled into work bright and early on Monday morning and had a spring in her step when she walked through the door of Seventh Heaven.

'How did it go?' called Meghan from the back of the shop.

'It was brilliant,' said Celeste. 'Thank you so much for lending me the van. I'll show you the pictures later.'

The morning was taken up with dealing with deliveries of new stock and fulfilling the orders for regular trade customers such as local restaurants and businesses who bought flowers from Seventh Heaven on a weekly basis to add a touch of colour and poetry to their prosaic premises. Although she was rushed off her feet, Celeste was in a good mood. Meghan had let her plug in her music to the speaker, and she sang along to her favourite tunes while she worked on the flowers. Finally, at three o'clock in the afternoon, all the regular jobs were done, and she was able to sit down in front of the computer with a cup of coffee to go through the photographs that she had downloaded from her camera the night before.

The pictures of Eugene's grave had come out perfectly and she was spoilt for choice in deciding which to send to Barbara. She also had some nice shots of the surroundings in the American cemetery, which she was planning to send over as she knew that it would be more moving and meaningful for Barbara to see pictures of the setting taken on the anniversary date that Celeste had placed the flowers on her father's grave, rather than simply looking up images that she could find online.

It was when she got to the photographs of the Bridge of Sighs in Cambridge that Celeste was in for a shock. She had shot a sequence from different viewpoints as her punt approached the bridge. The stonework on the bridge could be seen in all its intricate detail. But it was something behind the stonework that caught her attention. Through one of the stone openings, the head and torso of a figure could be seen, standing sideways on, partly obscured by the shadows, gazing down at the water below. There was nothing unusual in this. The bridge was a magnet for tourists and was used by them and members of the university alike as a walkway between the courts of St John's that straddled the River Cam. But what floored her, when she zoomed in and blew up the shot to its maximum size, was the uncanny resemblance between the image in the photograph, (the facial features were masked by shadows but the outlines were the same) and the person or apparition (she no longer knew what to think!) that she had spotted watching her from under the branches of the trees, at the Cambridge American Cemetery.

At that moment, Meghan strolled over with her sandwich.

'Come on then, are you going to show me?'

With some instinct to keep her reflections private, Celeste quickly clicked on the cross to close the magnified image of the bridge and scrolled back through the other pictures.

'It's very beautiful,' said Meghan. 'You did a wonderful job. I'm sure she'll be delighted.'

When she got back to the flat that evening, Celeste opened her laptop and looked again at her photographs of the Bridge of Sighs. She was agitated and on edge and couldn't decide whether to talk about it with Anya and Jessi who were camped on the sofa scrolling through their social media while pretending to watch the latest popular series on Netflix, some ridiculous teenage coming-of-age story featuring a sequence of unbelievable paranormal events and a two-dimensional cast.

She glanced over at the TV monitor. Sinister music was playing, signifying the scene was leading up to yet another 'jump-out-of-your-skin' cheap thrill.

'Do you believe in ghosts?' she asked directly. She had to say it twice before the girls looked up from their phones.

'Not sure I believe in ghosts,' said Anya absently. She was in the middle of putting together an Instagram post and was more concerned with applying the right filter to set off her pose than in engaging in existential questions.

'Why do you ask?' said Jessi. 'Is all this business delivering flowers to the dead getting to you? You've been hanging round graveyards a bit too much recently!'

'I had a funny turn at the cemetery in Cambridge,' said Celeste, without rising to it. 'I thought I saw a man watching me from a copse of trees on the edge of the cemetery. I must have been seeing things, but it seemed so real – and yet so unreal at the same time. It gave me a scare. He looked just like the picture of the World War II pilot whose grave I was putting flowers on, just like the statue of the airman I walked past in the grounds of the American cemetery.'

'Could be your guardian angel,' muttered Anya. She pressed 'share' on her Instagram post and put down her phone.

Jessi and Anya were not as quick to laugh Celeste out of court as she had expected. But then, they loved a bit of drama and were fans of the supernatural and the sensational. Celeste remembered that Anya, who had an interest in researching family ancestry, had even been taken to some weird séance by a friend of hers to try and make contact with her great-great-grandmother who had 'disgraced' the family by eloping with her lover aged sixteen.

They quizzed Celeste about her experience in the cemetery – What did he look like? How did it feel? How long was he there? What made her think he was a ghost?

'Well there wasn't any spooky music playing, if that's what you're suggesting,' said Celeste disdainfully, grabbing the remote to turn down the volume on the TV. 'There was nothing malevolent in the presence. But it was such a strange atmosphere. Deeply unsettling. Everything was shimmering, and my ears were ringing, and yet it was so still, like I'd stepped out of ordinary time.'

'It was probably just that you were feeling faint, low on blood sugar,' said Jessi, when Celeste told them how she hadn't eaten, and had been feeling so weak. 'It can do strange things to your brain.'

'I would have dismissed it as just my mind playing tricks on me,' said Celeste, 'but look – here's another photograph that I took in Cambridge.' Celeste passed across her laptop to show them the picture of the Bridge of Sighs. 'There it is again – that's the figure I saw. I'm sure it was the same person or apparition or whatever it was.'

'I'm not sure,' said Anya, magnifying the screen to scrutinise the photograph with her forensic legal eyes. 'It looks like the shape of a man, but you can't see his face.' She handed back the laptop. 'And if it is a man or the ghost of a man, I agree that it looks like he's wearing a leather bomber jacket, but you can't really be sure. It could just be the play of light and shadows from the bridge.' She turned up the volume on the TV again dismissively. 'Perhaps the ghost is stalking you.' She laughed unkindly. Then taken aback by the look of genuine fear on Celeste's face, said, 'Joke! I'm sorry, it was a joke.' She smiled at Celeste reassuringly. 'Anyway, I love the photograph. Looks like a great place and I like the idea of punting. I must get Miles to take me there.'

But Celeste was not finished and didn't appreciate Anya making light of her confusion and disquiet. The events of the weekend had jolted her fragile mental equilibrium.

'There's another strange thing,' she said. 'And this definitely wasn't a trick of the light. Just as I was leaving Eugene's grave to walk back to my car, I heard a motorbike revving up and then driving away. It sounded like one of those old-fashioned bikes from the war movies. It was coming from the direction of the trees. But there wasn't a road there – it was just a copse of trees with fields all around.'

Jessi looked at Celeste with concern in her eyes.

'You were exhausted from the early start and the long drive, you were low on blood sugar, you were emotional and upset. You said so yourself! You thought you had a funny turn. If you imagined a man, you could have imagined the noise of a motorbike engine.'

Celeste snapped her laptop shut and went to her bedroom, slamming the door. She understood that look on Jessi's face. Only four years previously she had been mired in depression and prone to episodes of paranoia and delusions triggered by post-traumatic stress disorder. Her flat mates had heard the rumours. She knew they were always vigilant, always on the lookout for a recurrence. But this was for real.

'They're gaslighting me again,' she muttered to herself. It was infuriating to have her best friends making her doubt her own sanity just because she had a history of depression. Not everything in the universe could be explained by low blood sugar levels and neurons misfiring in the brain!

She sat up on the bed and wrote a long email to Barbara, enclosing the photographs she had selected of Eugene's grave, the surroundings at the American cemetery and the enchanting views of The Backs and the bridges over the River Cam. She wrote that she had been 'honoured' to decorate the grave of United States Army Air Corps Navigator Lieutenant Eugene Jack Ashford, and that she had felt a strong connection to Barbara's father when she had sat quietly at his graveside.

'I sat there very still,' she wrote, 'reciting to myself the words of *High Flight*, a poem that you must know by the Canadian poet John Gillespie Magee, Jr.' Celeste had learnt this by heart some years previously in preparation for the paper on war poetry that she had taken as part of her GCSE exam in English literature. 'While I sat there saying the words in my head, and keeping perfectly still, I felt very close to your father. I could feel the sun moving and his aircraft circling above the clouds. I heard his laughter coming down from the heavens as he *'danced the skies on laughter-silvered wings...'* and flew towards the sun *'Up, up the long, delirious, burning blue...'* She knew that she was straying into sentimentality, using phrases her English teacher would have highlighted with imperious red lines and exclamation marks but she didn't care. 'And he told me that he died loving you and doing the thing that made him happy.' She wasn't sure if she really remembered feeling this or if she had created the memory in the act of writing to Barbara – but as she typed the words, they felt sincere.

Just before she pressed 'Send', on impulse she added a postscript to her message.

'Do you happen to know if your father drove a motorbike while he was stationed in England during the war?'

PAST

17

As the night goes on, Celeste finds a way of getting back at her father even though she's locked up in her old bedroom as his prisoner. In fact, you could say he's to blame for what happens next. Her father thinks he can stop her having fun. But he's too old to know that the power of social media transcends physical boundaries. The party she is missing out on ends early when the host's mother walks in on a pair of partygoers popping pills and making out in her en-suite shower, after which Ben invites Harry, Lucie and a few others back to his place – his parents are more chilled. Soon there are more Facebook shots in his games room for Celeste to torture herself with of Ben and Harry and Lucie (in various compromising combinations), slow dancing and drinking and kissing, in gradual stages of undress.

Suddenly, a private message pops up on her phone. It's Ben.

'come over'

She replies:

'grown dead sorry'

She's had so much neat vodka that she can't remember how to spell 'grounded', but the predictive spelling makes it look like a Freudian slip. Ten minutes later he sends another text.

'hey can you send me a pic'

That's a first for her. Any other time, she would have deleted his text. Sending nudes is not her thing. 'Demeaning,' her mother would say. But tonight, she is tempted – if only as a small victory to spite her dad. He smashed up her face but he can't stop her having a bit of fun. She hesitates.

'you first'

He sends back a photo – something dark and shapeless – it could be anyone or anything, but she gets his drift. It comes with a message:

'your turn'

She giggles but also feels vaguely ashamed.
She ignores it for a few more minutes. Another text comes through from Ben.

'want to be my girlfriend?'

He must be soooo drunk, she thinks cynically...

Just typical that tonight of all nights when Ben's got the hots for her, she's locked in her bedroom. She looks at her face in the mirror. The tender spot below her eye is now puffy and bruised and her mouth is distorted by her swollen lower lip.

'I look like a freak,' she says to herself. 'Even if the sick bastard hadn't locked me in, I wouldn't be seen dead at the party looking like this.'

But Ben's not interested in receiving pictures of her face. Defiantly, she adjusts the neckline on her dress to make it more revealing, stretches out her arm, takes a shot of her nascent cleavage and pings it across.

'c'mon,'

he texts back, remarkably lucid all of a sudden.

'get serious! wanted to get with you tonight. Luce coming on to me all night. I fought her off. you owe me.'

Whoever said romance is dead? It's the longest text she's ever had from him and it's all the encouragement she needs. She strips off her dress, lies back on the bed, takes six photos in quick succession of herself in various poses, uploads without reviewing, and presses 'send'.

He comes back with one word – *NICE* – and lots of exclamation marks.

Celeste curls up under the sheet and smiles to herself – empowered and exhilarated. At last she's got Ben's attention

– and more importantly she has the secret satisfaction of getting 'one over' on her overbearing father who thought he could control her and spoil all her fun.

As she lies back on the pillow triumphantly, another text comes through from Ben.

'Ten out of ten'

PRESENT

18

You're seeing another man. Is it that dolt You were with at the cinema? Is he your boyfriend now? Or is it the man from the club? I can sense there is history there.

What do I care who it is? He means nothing. All that matters, is that it isn't me!

Right when I think you're about to turn around and open your eyes—

You betray me.

I follow You into the tube. I make an exception. I conquer my fears despite my phobia of being underground in confined spaces.

You are swinging a bottle of red wine in one hand as You skip down the escalator – that is proof You are cheating on me.

You stand looking out of the window at the black wall of the tunnel spooling by. The carriage is crowded so I'm able to come close without drawing attention to myself... close enough to smell your fragrance – Flowerbomb (of course!)

by Viktor&Rolf – I've done my research – I saw it in your bag… close enough to shuffle towards You with my back turned and to position my mobile below the hemline of your dress.

'Up-skirting' I think they call it. I'm not proud but I'm not sorry. You can call it deferred payment for services rendered, if You like. I can't help myself. You make me angry… giving yourself to another man… when I've offered myself up to You for free!

When we get to your stop, I follow You out of the tube and along the streets. You have to put the address into your phone. That cheers me up a little. This is your first time here. Maybe it's not too late. I hang back at the corners of each street, and when You reach your destination, I retreat between two parked cars, watching You waiting for the door to open. You take a mirror from your bag to check your face and retouch your lipstick and run a brush through your hair. Damn! You care!

You're taking me for granted. It's time to teach You a lesson. I know what I need to do. I could fix this in a matter of minutes once I put my mind to it.

Any day now the website of CelestialHeadstones.com will become inaccessible to users due to a catastrophic error in the web server software. Then for sure you'll come crying back to me! But I won't make it too easy for You. I'll make you wait for your fix. This time we'll do it on my terms.

'You've got a text,' squealed Anya. She put down the chopping knife and peered at the message that popped up on Celeste's mobile, left lying face up on the kitchen table. 'Come and see.

It's from Steve. That's the guy you went to the cinema with, isn't it?' Celeste was lying down on a rubber mat, following a YouTube exercise video on her laptop that was open on the floor. She sighed, put down her hand weights, pressed pause on the video and wandered over.

'God, anyone would think you were on *Love Island*!' said Celeste, affecting indifference. 'Calm down.'

'He's asking you for a date, wants to see you again this weekend!' Anya was virtually jumping up and down in her excitement. Celeste helped herself to a raw carrot that Anya had just finished peeling, ignoring Anya's complaint. 'Hey! That's my supper. Make your own food.'

She picked up her phone and read the message. Steve was one of the guys she had hooked up with in a very casual way on Tinder. He was the best of the bunch she had matched with after that night out clubbing at Heavana. They were in a 'thing'. He made her laugh and didn't take himself too seriously and he got on well with her new college friends. He wasn't one of those self-important losers who claimed in their profiles to be 'polyamorous' as an excuse for sleeping around and their pathetic failure to commit. He wasn't too pushy. And for now, he seemed happy just to be friends. He hadn't tried to grope her yet. He hadn't even held her hand. He was obviously playing the long game.

As far as she was concerned, it was just nice to have someone around to meet at the pub or for a trip to the cinema or a tour round an art gallery or a walk in the park. If she was honest with herself, she wanted a companion, not a lover.

This sounded a bit more intense though. He was inviting her for dinner at his place on Saturday night. She didn't reply straight away and instead went back to her exercise mat to finish the routine. She didn't want to appear too keen. So far, she'd been careful not to lead him on or give him false hopes. Was he planning to make his move? Was he going to ask her officially to be his girlfriend? Dinner at his place seemed to be taking it to another level – out of her comfort zone. On the other hand, she knew that Anya was going away for the weekend with Miles, and Jessi had a reunion that had been planned with some of her old uni friends weeks ago. She'd be facing another Saturday night on her own in the flat, listening to the creaking floorboards and gurgling pipes, if she didn't accept.

In the end, egged on by Jessi and Anya, who nagged her all evening, she replied to his message.

'Sure, sounds great. What shall I bring?'

Celeste was irritable and stressed for the rest of the week. Though she didn't say anything to them, she felt annoyed with Anya and Jessi for having talked her into accepting this date. Now she felt trapped. As she caught the tube over to Steve's flat in Putney, she couldn't wait for the evening to be over. To avoid any misunderstanding, she had already booked her Uber home with pick-up from his place at 11pm.

Steve lived on his own, in a neat, functional one-bedroom flat in a new development just over the river in Putney designed with single professionals in mind. Celeste knew he had recently qualified as a chartered accountant with one of the big London accountancy firms – she couldn't remember the name. But she'd decided not to hold his profession against him. 'He's not as boring as that makes him sound,' she had told the girls. In fact, he actually did have the proverbial 'GSOH' that every man seemed to lay claim to in his Tinder ads. He was also quite good-looking in a conventional way and worked out regularly in the gym. He liked the cinema and he liked to travel. That was pretty much all she knew about him so far. And when he buzzed her in through the door, her first impression of his dwelling place, uncluttered and stylish in a predictable kind of way, suggested that he enjoyed an ordered and uncomplicated existence. That was a plus.

Steve handed her a gin and tonic. He'd taken care over preparing it – served in a highball glass, with ice and lemon.

'It's slimline tonic,' he said. 'I know that's what you like.' And coming from Steve, she knew that wasn't meant to be an insensitive comment (even though she was always hyper-sensitive about her weight despite being on the thin side). On the contrary, he was considerate and attentive to her preferences – unlike most of the guys she had known in the past.

Dinner was surprisingly un-awkward. He'd made a tasty chicken-in-wine casserole, one of his mother's recipes, with steamed vegetables. He hadn't been as clichéd as to put out candles, but he'd dimmed the lights, and put on a CD of greatest hits from the previous decade that he'd come across when having a clear-out of his CD collection.

'I saved this one for you,' he said. It included the songs of her favourite pop artists from when they were both in their teens. He'd taken note of her taste in music in their earlier conversations. 'It's a throwback to the time we were students. I've got a weakness as well for the music we were listening to then – all those parties in the college bar.' He wasn't to know that Celeste had missed out on going to university. She'd never spoken of it to him. And because he knew she'd been to such an academic school and seemed so interested in literature and history of art, so all-round educated, he'd made an assumption – wrongly.

They chatted about this and that. There was a new exhibition at the Royal Academy that he thought might interest her. He told her about a film he had seen. He asked her how CelestialHeadstones.com was going, and her eyes shone as she replied that it was really taking off, she was receiving lots of new orders and finding it so interesting discovering new places and learning about people's lives.

'I love it,' she said. 'I love designing the website, taking photographs and learning about recent history and exchanging poems all round the world with my clients. I've learnt so much about the Second World War since I started it.'

Celeste told him about her trip to Cambridge, and how it was such a beautiful city and how she'd like to go there again.

'Perhaps we could go there together one weekend,' he said. 'I'd love to take you.' He was a good listener, showing a real interest in her floristry work, with helpful suggestions about how she could grow the grave-tending business. As she sipped her red wine, she began to feel relaxed and opened up to him, telling him about her strange experiences at the cemetery and the Bridge of Sighs. And he didn't laugh at her or explain it away as a trick of the mind.

'There are some things that go beyond the realm of

reason,' he said seriously. 'Sometimes we just have to live with that. Even in accountancy, sometimes the columns just don't add up.'

And at that moment, in the soft lighting, her senses pleasantly numbed by the conversation, and the food and the wine, and the nostalgic melodies filling the room with sound, she thought maybe, just maybe, she could begin to let it go and start over. She was the one to hold out her hand and take his.

'I don't believe in ghosts, but I do believe in angels,' he said, gazing deeply into her eyes. She couldn't deny that it was an unusually good chat-up line, especially coming from an accountant. She felt herself melting. It was time to move on from the shame and the pain. She was ready to take her chance – to reach out and choose happiness.

It was Steve who pulled away first. 'I'm forgetting the pudding,' he said. He stood up to turn on the oven. 'I decided we'd go for comfort food tonight. And I remembered you said you loved your gran's blackberry crumble.' On their last date, Celeste had told him how she used to love blackberrying along the lanes in the Surrey Hills with her little brother. 'I had to use frozen berries at this time of year but hey! It'll be a taste of late summer.' Celeste was touched. He was the first man she had dated who would admit to baking crumble!

Now they had moved to the sofa – and still she was OK with it – comfortable. One of the big romantic anthems popular when she was 'sweet sixteen' was playing on the CD. His hand was gently rubbing up and down her stockinged thigh in time to the music and he was kissing her, and his mouth was wet and warm, and he smelt nice and there were stirrings deep inside her that she hadn't experienced in a long time. It was unexpected and it was good. Her body at one with the rhythm of the melody, she was kissing him back and breathing in his aftershave and wanting to touch him in ways that were new to her. She had lost track of time – and it seemed so had he.

And then the music changed...

The rap section came to an end and now it was Roxhanna's beautiful, resonant voice coming in with the heart-rending refrain about burning and hurting and crying and lies. Celeste shoved him off and moved away from him on the sofa. Her heart was racing, and her breathing came in shallow gasps.

'Something's burning!' she shouted. 'I can smell smoke. Something's burning.' The hateful lyrics seared through her brain. Here they came again, relentless, pounding, suffocating.

She leapt up, covering her ears with her hands. 'Turn it off, turn the bloody music off...I'm choking...That song...'

Steve didn't move for a second. He sat there confused, watching her in amazement. She grabbed the speaker and threw it to the floor. The music kept playing.

He stood up, spun her round and held her firmly in his arms. 'Stop! What did I do wrong? What the hell's got into you?' He shook her hard.

She stared at him with terror in her eyes. His face had changed. He'd become someone else. Not the placid man she knew as Steve. His features had morphed into those of a monster.

'Get off me,' she screamed. 'Let me go.'

At that moment, a shrill alarm rang out, drowning out the pop song with its deafening insistent bell. Steve loosened his grip and turned his head to look at the smoke coming out of the oven. 'Shit, I forgot the crumble.'

While he turned to look at the oven she struggled out of his arms, her arms flailing and punching wildly at his chest. A sharp blow from her elbow caught his cheekbone and he pushed her away roughly, sending her stumbling back against the wall.

'What the fuck!'

She grabbed her bag and shoes and ran for the door, which Steve being security-conscious, had double-locked on the inside. She grappled wildly with the key, yanking the handle and trying to force the lock. At last, the key turned, and she flew down the stairs like a bat out of hell.

PRESENT

19

*A*t least *You* don't stay the night.

I can't face going back to my room, so I go to buy a takeaway and then return to his address and spend the next two hours roaming up and down his street like a stray dog.

It's bitterly cold in London tonight and I blame *You* for my frozen hands and feet. It will be your fault if I get sick.

Less than two hours later, *You* are throwing yourself out of his doorway like a woman possessed. I stop feeling sorry for myself.

What did he do to *You*? Your hair is a mess and your shirt is undone and *You* come down the steps in black-stockinged feet and *You* left your coat behind even though it is now minus three degrees with a cold easterly breeze.

Did he rape *You*?

I'm torn between battering down his door and beating him to a pulp or racing after *You* and bundling *You* into a taxi and taking *You* home.

I hesitate for too long. When I emerge from my hiding place behind the bins, the pavement is empty.

You are gone.

It was a bad start to the week. Celeste was feeling fragile and depressed after her disastrous date on Saturday evening. After a sleepless night, she had stayed in her bedroom all day on Sunday with the door shut, still in her pyjamas. She'd been too agitated to work or even to read. She'd switched off her phone and all her social media (she couldn't face seeing messages from Steve), and passed the day dozing and watching mindless movies on her laptop. She'd pulled herself together sufficiently to cycle into work on Monday morning but couldn't disguise the fact from Meghan that something was wrong. She was deathly pale, with dark circles under her eyes and that absent, closed look, familiar to Meghan from the early days after the tragedy.

Celeste wasn't in a fit state to welcome customers or deal with the regular weekly stock deliveries of fresh flowers and floristry supplies, so Meghan sent her into the office to sort out some of the admin and check for any new online orders. Celeste started with the Seventh Heaven website (still in need of upgrading), which had a basic online ordering service for home and office deliveries of floral bouquets as well as weddings and funeral flowers. There were only a few orders – a glitzy restaurant on the Kings Road wanting themed flowers for a private event at the end of the week, three orders for hand-tied birthday bouquets to be delivered to office premises in Victoria on Tuesday and Wednesday, a late order for christening flowers for the following Sunday at St Gabriel's Anglo-Catholic church in Pimlico, and an enquiry about wedding flowers for a marriage ceremony at the end of May to be held at the fashionable Chelsea Register Office.

It was easy enough to process the orders, check supplies for the arrangements, diarise the deliveries, and respond to the queries. It was when she turned on her laptop and clicked to open CelestialHeadstones.com that the trouble started. It was impossible to get into the website. It had crashed. All she could see was a message on her screen with the words:

'Sorry, the website CelestialHeadstones.com cannot be found...'

and then, below that, those two infuriating words: 'Server error', followed by a series of unintelligible letters and symbols. However many times she refreshed the screen or switched her laptop on and off in growing frustration, it was hopeless. It was impossible to get the website up and running.

Although she hated having to ask for his help – again! – there was nothing for it. That kid in her class at college had practically designed the whole website for her. She didn't have a clue where to start. He would be the best person to fix it. And what's more, it was his responsibility to fix it. If the website had crashed, the most likely explanation was that something had gone wrong with his software.

'Now, what was his name?' she said to herself. She switched on her mobile to scroll through her contacts and send him a text. It had been switched off since Saturday and when she powered it up, it started to ping, as nine texts from Steve loaded onto the screen. Barely glancing down, she deleted them all. She didn't want anything more to do with him. Now she was focused on the task in hand. '*Theo* – that's the one,' she said to herself with satisfaction as she got to the 'T's'. His number was saved in her contacts.

Over the course of the next two hours, she sent Theo seven texts, increasingly demanding and insistent, when he failed to respond immediately. Eventually a message came through as she was on her way to the deli to buy a vegan wrap for her lunch.

'Sorry to hear about your technical issues. I'm out of town until Friday but I can see you after class. Bring your laptop. I'll run some diagnostics on the system. I'll need access to my desktop to check the software so come to my student accommodation – Flat 9, Staircase 3, the Cavendish Building. See you there, 2pm.'

The days seemed to drag by. Celeste was impatient to get CelestialHeadstones.com back up and running again, disappointed to think that she would be losing clients just when the business was beginning to grow wings. She was desperate for the distraction of being busy with work. She tried to block the memory of Saturday night from her consciousness. She was embarrassed but she was also angry. It wasn't Steve's fault, but the unlucky coincidence of the song and the situation had opened the Pandora's box of bad feelings that tormented her – sorrow and shame and guilt – and (though she knew it went against all the received tenets of psychotherapy that urged everyone to 'get in touch with your feelings'), the only way she could cope was to seal them up again inside a box in the back of her brain.

There was only one problem. In her panic to leave his flat on the Saturday night, she had run out without taking her coat that Steve, who was so tidy and organised, had carefully hung up for her in the hallway cupboard. It was the only smart coat she owned, designer label, three-quarter-length, in a black wool-cashmere mix. She wore it very rarely. She couldn't understand what had possessed her to wear it for the date. But she had to have it back. Her father had given it to her for her seventeenth birthday – but that was of no importance – another one of his extravagant, guilt-laden presents. She had worn it to her brother's funeral service – that in fact being the first and last time she had worn it, until the date with Steve. That was why she had to have it back.

Steve wouldn't stop texting and tweeting and FB messaging. So, she had decided to ghost him. Before she did so, she sent him one last text, asking him to drop off her coat at Anya's place of work, a law firm near London Bridge. By Thursday morning, she decided ghosting wasn't good enough – he wouldn't give up and leave her alone. She blocked him on all her social media platforms and deleted him from her contacts. From now on he was a non-person, she decided with satisfaction. Her foray into romance had turned sour. She would stay happily single or stick to soulless one-night stands from now on. She had no intention of allowing anyone to get emotionally intimate with her again.

Steve had other ideas. He was genuinely shocked and disturbed by what had happened and wanted an explanation.

It was three o'clock in the afternoon on the Thursday and Celeste was standing behind the counter, making up a hand-tied arrangement for one of their regular customers, when she heard the doorbell jangle and looked up to see Steve walking into the florist's, holding her black coat folded over his arm. He stood there, quietly watching, while Celeste put together the flowers and tied them with twine. Her hands were shaking so much that it took her three tries to tie the bow and she dropped the scissors as she trimmed the bottom of the stems. But there was nothing she could do. He was a silent witness to her discomfort. She couldn't run away or tell him to leave, with the customer standing right next to him.

'I thought I should return this to its rightful owner in person,' he said when the door finally closed on the customer. They were alone in the shop as Meghan was delivering flowers to the hospital. He held out the coat.

Celeste couldn't look at him as she took it. 'Aren't you supposed to be at work?' she said.

'Why didn't you return my messages?' said Steve.

'I've been busy,' said Celeste.

'Come on! I sent you a hundred messages. It would have taken twenty seconds. And now you've blocked me, without a word of explanation. Why? What have I done wrong?' He raised his voice in exasperation.

She looked up and noticed dark shadows below his eye on one side – he was recovering from a black eye. Celeste heard Meghan coming in through the back entrance and moving around in the cold room. She didn't want her to hear the conversation.

'Look, all I know is one minute we're having a great time and the next minute you're whacking me in the head and running for the door.' He gestured to his eye. 'Look what you did to me. What happened? This isn't you, Celeste.'

'Please,' said Celeste. 'Leave me alone. I don't want to talk about it.'

'I don't deserve to be blanked out of your life without knowing why. I don't understand. Did I come on too strong? I thought you were feeling it too.'

'Well I wasn't. And I don't want anything more to do with you.' She turned away to return some unused stems to the steel buckets. 'Thank you for bringing my coat. Please go away now. I need to get on.'

For a full minute Steve stood watching her in silence. Celeste could sense Meghan hovering in the doorway behind her.

'Actually, I'd like to buy some flowers please,' he said. 'To brighten up the flat.'

PRESENT

20

I go back to the address in Putney at the crack of dawn on Sunday and install myself in a nearby café in the hope of intercepting your aggressor. I sit at a table by the window checking every passer-by. In the course of the morning I consume six espressos and the 'Mega All-Day Breakfast Combo'. I get nothing for my efforts apart from indigestion and a searing headache. I can't be sure who You met last night though the apartment building looks rather modest and functional for someone who drives a red Ferrari.

I repeat the exercise every morning the following week with no success. I have to know. By Saturday I am cranky and tired and two kilograms heavier. I feel like I'm wasting my time.

It turns out I'm not wasting my time though, because just as I am settling my bill, here comes that man from the cinema approaching along the pavement dressed in a suit and dragging a small black suitcase. So, your new man is *not the driver of the red Ferrari. Cinema man looks tired and worn at the edges today. Has he been away on business? Come in on a transatlantic red-eye? Or was he thrown out of some other woman's bed? It comes as no surprise to find out that it's him You were running away from. I never did like the look of that dude.*

Celeste didn't want to make a scene while Meghan was working in the cold room, within easy hearing range.

'What would you like?' she said with icy calm.

'You choose,' he replied. 'You're the expert.'

He watched her intently as she selected foliage and stems in dark greens, purples and blues to complement the neutral colour scheme of his flat.

'I could have reported you to the police, you know… for assault,' he said. Celeste kept her eyes down as she placed the flowers in an aesthetically pleasing bouquet in her left hand. Steve spoke very quietly as she worked in silence. He seemed to be captivated by the graceful movements of her fingers and the enticing fragrance of the blooms. It created an intensity between them. He didn't seem to want to embarrass her either. 'If this was anyone else, I'd delete her number and move on – but it's not someone else. It's you. I can't just turn my feelings off. I like you. Even after the way you behaved on Saturday night. I can't walk away. I thought we had a good thing.'

Celeste snipped the ends of the cord and placed the flowers on the counter.

'No, we didn't,' she said. 'It's not going to work, Steve. Trust me. I can't be with you.'

'Why? Why? How can you be so cold?' he said passionately. 'What made you panic? I've been going over and over it in my head. Did I say or do something to offend you?'

'What do you want from me?' said Celeste in exasperation.

'The truth,' replied Steve. 'What are you hiding? Is there someone else?'

Suddenly she'd had enough. She didn't owe this man any explanations. If she had to hurt his feelings to get rid of him, so be it. Forgetting about Meghan, she raised her voice.

'Yes, there is someone else,' said Celeste. 'There always has been and there always will be. Whatever happens, whatever I do, he'll always be here inside my head.' She tapped her fingertips against her temple. 'Do you understand? Now, can you leave me in peace?'

'I understand perfectly,' he said grimly. 'Perhaps you should have thought of that before you put your profile up on Tinder.'

He slapped a twenty-pound note down on to the counter, picked up the flowers and opened the door.

'Keep the change,' he said.

There was a metal wastepaper bin screwed to a lamppost a little further along the pavement. Through the glass frontage of the shop, Celeste watched him shove the bouquet into it as he walked briskly away.

'What's going on?' said Meghan as she came into the shop front carrying a bucket full of closed daffodils that she had divided up into bunches of ten. 'Wasn't that the guy you've been dating?'

'It's over,' said Celeste.

She had thought she didn't care but suddenly she was choking back her tears.

'I'm sorry,' said Meghan.

'It's OK,' said Celeste. 'It never really started.'

Tears were streaming down her face.

Meghan walked over to the door, turned the lock and flipped the sign to read 'CLOSED'.

'You need a break,' she said. 'I'm going to make you a cup of tea.'

'Do you want to talk about it?' said Meghan. Celeste had calmed herself down and they were sitting together in the office sipping mugs of tea.

'It was like I was there, Meghan, a waking nightmare, the old PTSD coming back. I was OK with what we were doing, until that damn song started playing... then I was back there, down in the mud, with "him" on top of me, and smoke and flames all around, burning, burning... and I was fighting to get free and suffocating and screaming to break away.'

Meghan looked at her with concern. 'Did he put you under pressure...' She nodded towards the shop front. 'Try to force you?'

'No,' said Celeste ruefully. 'Steve was a perfect gentleman. I was the one who was out of order. Oh God, Meghan, I just can't do it. It was good... and then it wasn't... His hands on me felt... I can't be with another man... He's still here... that bastard... He's still in my hair, in my skin, in my hands, in my head. I can see him... I can taste him. I can't get rid of him. How am I ever supposed to be with someone else? Just that song, playing on his CD, and suddenly I'm shaking and gagging and fighting to get away.'

'It's not going to be easy,' said Meghan, clearly not wanting to say too much. 'After what you lived through... the trauma you have suffered... You're going to find it hard to trust someone ever again. But if you take it slowly... one step at a time...'

'No,' said Celeste. 'I'll never get over it because I don't want to get over it. I can never forgive myself for what happened that night. It is my fault. I was so weak; I always gave in to that bully. His word was my command. I should never have gone to the party. I should never have let him ply me with alcohol and drugs. I should never have let him treat me like a whore.'

'It wasn't your fault,' said Meghan. 'You are not to blame. You were a child... Just seventeen years old. It was a tragic accident.'

'I was the one who locked the door, Meghan!' cried Celeste. 'I was the one who turned the key... How can I ever forgive myself for that?'

'Things don't happen in a vacuum. Let's call this out. That boy subjected you to mental abuse. There's a term for it now – coercive control – months and years of it when you were both teenagers and at a time when you were particularly vulnerable and impressionable because, let's face it, you were living in a broken home. If anyone is to blame, it's Ben. Why should you suffer all your life for what happened that night? You shouldn't be torturing yourself like this.'

Meghan took Celeste's hands and looked into her eyes.

'Ben's the one who deserves to be punished!'

PAST

21

Although she resents having to babysit her little brother on a Saturday night, things are so much calmer when their alcoholic mother is out of the house, so it's a relief to be just the two of them together. There's always some kind of drama kicking off when Stacey's at home – if she's not fighting in the kitchen with her sleazy new partner Mike, she's slumped on the sofa watching TV with a bottle of red by her side, and a bottomless wine glass in her hand. In her mother's world 'wine o'clock' seems to be at any time of the day! Celeste feels like she has to babysit her mother too.

Stacey's round at Mike's tonight, thank God, so she won't be back at least until after lunch on Sunday. Celeste's been left to hold the fort with a long list of chores, cooking the supper (the first time all week they'll be eating a proper meal instead of the microwave meals that her mother serves up when she remembers and can be bothered), washing the school uniforms and sports kits, supervising Tom's homework and monitoring his screen time. Her mother's good at issuing orders if nothing else!

She's got her own homework to catch up with now. The sixth form workload is heavy, and she's got exams coming up in two weeks. This evening, the chores done, she breathes a sigh of relief to have a break from her mother and the toxic atmosphere that hangs over all their interactions.

Now Tom and Celeste are happy in each other's company, sitting together at the kitchen table. She's got an essay to write this evening for her English A level on Tennessee Williams' play *A Streetcar Named Desire*. 'How far is Stanley's rape of Blanche DuBois a premeditated attack and how far was it precipitated by her own behaviour? To what extent can she be described as a victim?' It occurs to Celeste that there is inbuilt bias in the framing of these questions. She bets they were written by a man. She's fully engrossed on her laptop planning out her arguments and Tom's fully engaged on his Nintendo lost in some alien universe survival game, when a text comes through on her phone. Her pulse races even before she opens it.

'Fr'ouse at mine tonight. Come over'

She types back:

'Sorry babysitting'

followed by a sad face.
He types back:

148

'Don't be wet!'

She types back:

'Sorry, Mum's out all night. I can't leave Tom home alone!'

He types back:

'Got to see you. Driving over to get you now. Tom can come too'

And that's it. He ignores the rest of her texts. She knows he won't take no for an answer. She knows his plan. His parents are away. He's got a free house for the night and he's throwing a party. And tonight, she's the one he's got in his sights. He's a player. He's played around with every other girl in their friendship group. After the nudes, he's got the hots for her. And now that he's finally decided to pay her some attention, he expects her to drop everything for him. It's her turn tonight.

She's stressed out of her head. Her hair could do with a wash. There's no time for a shower. Thank God she shaved her legs yesterday. She runs upstairs, rips off her sweatshirt and jeans and puts on the red dress that her mother says makes her look slutty – she's a fine one to talk! Then she puts on her make-up – foundation, black mascara and the brightest red lipstick in her drawer. She goes into her mother's bedroom and grabs the tallest pair of heels from the jumble of shoes in the bottom of her cupboard and squirts herself liberally with Stacey's Chanel No 5. She stands awkwardly in front of the full-length mirror fixed to the back of the wardrobe door.

That'll have to do.

Coming down the stairs, she sees his car lights in the distance through the kitchen window. She hands Tom his coat and a can of Coke from the fridge and grabs a half-empty bottle of vodka from behind the breadbin (one of many hidden bottles stashed away by her mother).

'I'll make it up to you,' she says.

But Tom doesn't care. He hero-worships the older boy. He's beyond excited to be getting a ride in his car. And he can't wait to tell his mates at school on Monday that he went to Ben's party! It's sick!

Celeste watches the car pull into her driveway. He's driving his dad's vintage MG. His dad would go insane! He doesn't bother to cut the engine or come to the door. He just leans on the horn. *WTF* will the neighbours think?

PRESENT

22

*T*his should be my moment of triumph. I taught that man a lesson and if You only knew what I have done, it could change everything. I waited, You see. I waited around the corner while he shaved and took a shower, changed into his chinos and navy polo neck, and came out of the flat again carrying your black coat. I knew where he'd be going because he had your coat. I was in no hurry to follow.

When he turned the corner of the street, I broke into his flat with the help of a rusty spanner that some careless builder had conveniently left behind in a neighbour's skip. It didn't take me long to trash his place. An 'economy size' five-litre bottle of bleach from under his kitchen sink and one of the sharp little vegetable knives from his kitchen block were all it took. First, I walked around the flat starting with his neatly made bed, slashing his clean white duvet cover, his feather pillows and his one hundred per cent Egyptian cotton sheets. Then, I moved on to his brown leather sofa and his all his matching cushions. After that, I walked around once more, trailing the open bottle of bleach over the grey woollen carpets of his open-plan living room, spelling out the word 'RAPIST'.

I think that will deter him from going to the police. I suspect that Steve (yes, I found out his name) isn't the sort of guy who would risk tarnishing his reputation or damaging his career. No smoke without fire. He won't want to get into a conversation with a detective about what happened in his bed or on the floor. Even if he does report my crime, I calculate that the police won't be too thorough in investigating a simple break-in when they've got more than enough in the way of teenage knife crime and counter-terrorism raids to keep them busy on the streets.

I put the rusty spanner, the empty bleach bottle and the knife in my rucksack and leave, disposing of my tools in the skip before making my way to Seventh Heaven just in time to see him coming out the door of the shop. Your flowers are like his parting gift. I retrieve them from the bin and take them back to my place and arrange them in an old beer mug on the shelf above my bed so that I can smell You when I go to sleep.

This afternoon You are here and suddenly I don't know what to do with You. All I can think about is that the dried-up bunch of flowers You sold to Steve, is now in my wastepaper bin under the desk, and I am terrified that any minute You are going to want to throw your chewing gum away.

You are here in my bedroom.

You are sitting on my bed and without even looking I know You are beautiful.

I could turn around and touch You.

You set me on fire… and turn me to stone. Both.
You are strong and I am broken.
I thought I was in control, but You have taken me apart.

Theo was sitting at his usual place in class when she took her seat the next day for the Friday session. She smiled at him, but he didn't say hello. He wasn't a bad-looking guy, yet so painfully shy and socially awkward that it was hard to notice. Now that she looked at him properly, she could see that he had smartened himself up recently with new jeans, a sharp haircut and a pair of trendy black-rimmed glasses. It was perhaps because she was a few years older than him that he was so intimidated. The lesson dragged. Celeste struggled to keep her eyes open. She'd had a bad night. The confrontation with Steve had stirred up so many painful memories. And she couldn't get Meghan's words out of her head. *Ben's the one who deserves to be punished.* She had lain there, looking up at the black ceiling, and hearing Meghan's words over and over again… *deserves to be punished…* an insistent refrain burning into her brain that unsettled her as if she had unfinished business.

As they filed out of class two hours later, Theo hung back. She heard footsteps behind her as she walked down the corridor. When she turned around, he was there, almost in her shadow. He couldn't meet her gaze.

'Two pm. You've got the address.'

She smiled briefly. He nodded then he turned off to the library.

'I'll see you later,' she called after him.

She wasn't sure why he didn't take her straight back to

his room after the lesson. He'd mumbled something about needing to spend a couple of hours working on his weekend assignment. She wasn't in the mood for academic work, so she bought herself a coffee and a sandwich at the college bar and went to a nearby garden square to have her lunch. She sat down on a park bench. The spring sunshine was warm and she closed her eyes, feeling the soft glow of sunlight on her eyelids and listening to the sounds of birds, and leaves rustling in the breeze and the cries and laughter of little children coming from a nursery bordering the square, and beyond this the sounds of this great capital city that were never silenced – the traffic and the builders' drills and the planes passing overhead.

Theo's flat was just a short cycle ride away. His student accommodation was in an ugly concrete block newly clad with bright orange panels. It was an eyesore standing out against the attractive Regency architecture of the other buildings on the street – one of the incongruous post-war structures built on the site of bomb craters created by the Blitz. She could see from the list of names posted on the communal entrance that he shared his flat with three other male students. He buzzed her up and opened the door. The accommodation was dingy and functional. Four doors led off from a dark hallway to the bedrooms.

She glanced into the shared bathroom, and a sitting-dining area fitted out with basic kitchen equipment, table and chairs and a small sofa. The place was a mess. There were used breakfast mugs and plates and food debris on the table. The kitchen surfaces were piled high with clutter and packets of food that no one had bothered to put away.

'My flatmates live like pigs,' he said. 'This is me,' he opened the door to his bedroom.

It was in the style of a shoebox with nothing but a single bed and a desk and a chair and storage cupboards. Unlike, his flatmates, Theo appeared to live like a monk, thought Celeste. His pinboard was empty. Though dotted with discarded Blue Tack, there was not a poster or a picture on the walls. He had a few files lined up on his desk and his desktop was covered with expensive-looking IT equipment – computer, printer, laminator and headphones. Clearly, he didn't skimp on that!

Theo powered up his computer while she sat down on his bed, opened her own laptop and put in her password.

'You can leave it here, if you like,' he said. He couldn't make eye contact with her. 'It's going to take me a while to run some tests.'

'No, I'll stay,' she replied, reluctant to let the laptop out of her sight for too long. 'I might learn something.'

Theo went to fetch another chair from the kitchen and motioned to Celeste for her to sit beside him at the desk.

The room was claustrophobic and disconcertingly quiet. At least she didn't have to worry about what was on his playlist. He didn't seem the type to listen to music while he worked. She sat down next to him. Due to the shoebox-sized proportions of the room, she felt uncomfortably close to him. Her thigh was inches away from his. She could see the stubble on his chin and a patch of pimples on his lower cheek where his skin had been irritated by shaving.

It was airless in the room. Theo was sweating. There was a patch of darker blue at the armpit of his denim shirt and though not offensive, his pungent male odour permeated the room as he punched at the keyboard. It couldn't always be easy being a teenage boy. It crossed her mind that Theo could not be much older than Ben had been at the time of the calamitous party – but they were very different animals. And Tom would now have been almost exactly the same age as Theo... if only... but she couldn't dwell on that. Irrationally, these thoughts made her rage against Theo. *That way lies madness*, she reflected, calling to mind some Shakespearean quote or other she remembered from school as she struggled to contain her anger.

'Can I open the window?' she said. 'It's so muggy in here.'

She reached up to undo the catch for the window, the stretch exposing her flat stomach and pulling her blouse taut across her chest. She could feel Theo's eyes on her. When she sat down beside him, he squirmed awkwardly and pulled his chair in closer to the table. His discomfort was palpable. He started tapping away jerkily on the keyboard. She noticed his fingers shaking, causing him to miss-hit the keys. It was curiously thrilling and unexpected to realise that her presence could exert such a power. She had always cast herself in the role of victim in her dealings with the opposite sex. This new thing opened up a world of possibilities that she wasn't quite sure what to do with as yet. His features were rigid as if he were holding back some intense emotion, on the verge of tears.

She would put him out of his misery... for now.

She stood up.

'I'm going to make myself a cup of tea,' she said. 'Is that OK? Would you like something too?'

★

Most of the shelves in the kitchen unit were either bare, or stacked with a jumble of tins, jars and sauces. But the top shelf was neatly ordered and marked with a label, printed and taped proprietorially to the laminated edge: 'THEODORE PETWICK.' She stepped up on the rung of a chair to look for teabags and coffee. As she moved the jars around, another label caught her eye. It was a jar of marmalade, pushed to the back of the cupboard. It was the logo that had captured her attention, and the words:

Fitzbillies
Organic Seville Orange
Marmalade
Thick Cut

She stared at the jar. Strange coincidence? There was a loaf of sliced bread in the cupboard too. Suddenly she felt hungry. She put two slices of bread in the toaster and boiled the kettle. Two minutes later, she headed back to Theo's room, his coffee in one hand, and in the other, her mug of tea with her toast (slathered with Fitzbillies marmalade), balanced precariously across the rim. If nothing else, it would be interesting to see his reaction.

When she crossed the hallway of the communal flat, she was in for another reality-check. She hadn't noticed on her way in – perhaps because her eyes hadn't adjusted to the gloomy interior after the brightness outdoors or perhaps because this section of the wall would have been hidden by the open door. But she saw it now, a row of pegs screwed into the wall, and hanging from one of them, a brown leather jacket, and on the floor below, a motorbike helmet and a pair of leather bikers' boots.

The smoke was beginning to clear. Could the kid have followed her to Cambridge? Should she confront him? CelestialHeadstones.com would be dead if the website crashed again. She wanted his help to ensure the continued success of her business but not at any cost.

She pushed open the door to Theo's room with her foot. His eyes were glued to the screen of her laptop.

'How's it going?' she said.

Her words didn't break through Theo's concentration. He tapped 'Return' three times without taking his eyes off the screen. He seemed to be fully engrossed in restoring her system to life.

As she reached out to place his coffee on the table, the slices of toast balanced on her mug of tea fell to the floor, marmalade-side down.

'Bad luck,' he said automatically, without even turning his head. She bent down to throw the toast in the wastepaper bin and was struck by the sight of a bunch of withered blooms, almost certainly her own arrangement, rammed inside it. Still more disturbingly, poking up between the dry stems, she saw the corner of a laminated photograph, that if she wasn't mistaken, was a profile view of herself, taken in the back yard of Seventh Heaven.

At that moment, Celeste was distracted by a tiny red dot of light winking at her from between two filing boxes on the top of the wardrobe. She froze. As her eyes focused on the spot, she saw the reflection of a black circular lens. What the fuck was the kid playing at? This was freaky. She understood now why he hadn't asked her to come straight back with him from college – he wanted time to clear his room and set up the webcam before she arrived. Was he some kind of stalker or pervert – offering his services to fix her computer but secretly pursuing his own agenda to lure her to his room and film her covertly? It was pathetic – and sad.

Her first impulse was to give vent to her outrage and escape but in a split-second decision she stifled the urge to shout and scream, grab her computer and run from the room, and chose instead to pretend that she had seen nothing.

Theo was besotted with her – that much was now blindingly obvious. But however uncomfortable that made her feel, she wasn't afraid of this dysfunctional teenager. In a way she felt sorry for him, her ghostly apparition. A plan was beginning to form in her head. She needed time to think it through and work out how she could turn Theo's obsession to her own advantage.

PAST

23

Even before they get to his house where the party is in full swing, she's swigging from the vodka bottle to get in the mood. Tonight, she's his girl. The chosen one. Ben installs Tom in his bedroom in front of his gaming console and she loses herself in the cavern of gyrating bodies, and exposed flesh, and loud music, and shrieking teenage girls, and zombie-eyed testosterone-fuelled teenage boys, that his living room has become. But he comes to find her in the throng, holding out a big glass of red wine (sprinkled with something else she doesn't know about) that she gulps down much too fast, and they dance, and she's bouncing off the walls and she's falling into his arms, and it's never felt so good until he goes off in search of a beer – and doesn't come back.

The beams seem to buckle and tilt as she makes her way to where he's entrenched in the kitchen with his pack. Unopposed pack leader – he has a Budweiser in one hand and a roll-up in the other. Seated on the granite breakfast bar, he's man-splaying – if that can be a thing for a teenage boy? But he looks like a man. Broad-chested, ripped with muscles, at least six feet tall. Flanker in the rugby scrum and fastest kid on the pitch. All-round sixth form hero. His mood has changed – and his manner – now that he has an audience. He beckons her over – proprietorial, coercive, he who must be obeyed! That is, unless she wants to risk becoming the school pariah, a social outcast... He doesn't take kindly to losing face!

Despite her best efforts with the make-up (vampire eyes and glossy red lipstick – now smudged from the kissing on the dance floor), next to him she looks like a child. Even in her ridiculously high heels, she only comes up to his shoulder and she's so slender that she seems breakable.

'Come here, I saved this for you!' He hands her the joint. She inhales deeply and everything goes hazy.

She goes over on one ankle and falls heavily against his chest. He puts his arms around her and half-carries her up the spiral stairs to his bedroom. It's easy – she feels light – and his bulk is rock solid from training for the rugby team.

He puts her down outside his bedroom. The door is shut. Tom is in there. He forgot.

'Where's Tom?' she says, slurring her words. Then more frantically as she comes to her senses and he blocks her way, 'What are you playing at?' She bursts into tears. 'Let me past. I want to check he's OK.' She beats his solid chest with her small fists.

'Stop worrying! Relax!' he says calmly, not moving an inch. He looks down into her anxious blue eyes circled with black stains. 'He's got my whole Xbox collection to keep him occupied. He'll be fine. No one will disturb him here.'

He doesn't like being made to wait. Her tousled agitation makes him horny as hell. He manhandles her along the corridor to the bathroom door. It's also locked. He knocks on the door and rolls himself another joint. He shoves her back against the wall, holding her upright with one arm and exploring down the front of her top with his free hand. Her lips are blow-job-red. He takes the joint from his mouth and places it between them before bending down to kiss her breasts. God – he hadn't expected to want her this way, but her skin feels so soft and she smells so good! He flicks the lighted joint from her lips to the floorboards, presses his mouth against hers and hungrily forces his tongue to the back of her throat until their teeth clash.

He's so hard inside his jeans that it hurts.

Still kissing her deeply, he raps loudly on the bathroom door. There's no answer, just a stomach-heaving noise that sounds like someone throwing up into the toilet bowl.

She gags. The combination of spirits and red wine and pot and his curry breath and searching tongue and the pressure on her belly and the noises off have done their work. He's not too drunk to pick up on her disgust and pulls away abruptly. She sways and slides down the wall to her knees so that her face is level with his hips.

Like the lead in his own porno clip, he grabs her thick long hair at the nape and pushes her head forwards while he plucks at his belt. He feels the weight of her skull in his palm as her head lolls. She is literally 'off her head'. His fingers work at his buckle. Inside the bathroom, someone flushes the toilet. He hesitates. Behind the door, the retching noise begins again. And then he changes tack.

'Come on you need some fresh air,' he says, dragging her up roughly by the arm. 'Let's get out of here.'

PRESENT

24

*I*t didn't take me long to get your website fixed – simply a case of neutralising the virus I'd introduced into the software. And before I logged out from your laptop, I introduced a system upgrade, developed by me, especially for You.

You asked for it. You wanted anti-virus software to improve the security of your website. I gave You a copy of my own – specially modified, of course. I could make money out of this one day – I'm good and there must be a market for it – at least on the Dark Web. But for now, it's for my own personal use. Anti-virus software with an additional modification – my own brand of spyware. With it, I can access a mirror image of your screens 24/7, real-time, at the click of a button. For as long as You want to make a success of your business venture, I hold all the cards. CelestialHeadstones.com is nothing without a website.

The other day You put me in my place. Made me feel like

an awkward, adolescent boy when you came to my room.
You're better than that. We're better than that.
   I'll forgive You – just this once.

The young woman was flipping through the florist's
Wedding Portfolios when Celeste came into the Bridal
Room at Seventh Heaven. She looked up and gave a big
smile. She had a confident and open face with perfectly
straight, whitened toothpaste-ad teeth, big trusting puppy-
dog eyes, and stunning blonde hair. Although it was only
ten o'clock on a Wednesday morning, she was wearing a
full face of make-up with false eyelashes and glossy pink
lipstick. Celeste groaned inwardly but immediately checked
her instinctive dislike – it wasn't fair to judge her before
she'd even opened her mouth to speak. Perhaps she felt
under pressure to look this way? Perhaps it wasn't her fault
that she looked like a Barbie doll?

When the bride-to-be introduced herself, Celeste was
relieved to hear her American accent. So, she wasn't one of
the *Made In Chelsea* set – they were always so demanding –
for those women always had such set ideas and impossible
ideals of perfection. Meghan had told Celeste that the bride-
to-be had come in for an initial consultation – but it soon
became clear that she had already decided to use Seventh
Heaven as her wedding florist and that the wedding date
was imminent – there was no time to lose.

Celeste happily spent more than two hours with the new
client explaining all the options and running through the
albums and online galleries that Meghan had put together
showcasing previous weddings and illustrations of designs

for the bridal bouquet, bridesmaids' flowers, buttonholes for the groom and best man, flower headbands and corsages for the ladies in the wedding party, flowers for the ceremony and flowers for the reception. As Meghan had said, it was good for her to be working on flowers for a joyful event for a change – she realised now that all the time she spent working in graveyards had been making her morbid and depressed.

Celeste had to admit that Mia seemed very nice, if a little dumb. Moreover, she, along with her fiancé, appeared to be minted (judging by the gold Cartier bangle on her wrist) and not afraid of flashing it around (starting with the huge stone glinting on her engagement finger). This made her an attractive client as far as Meghan was concerned. It came as no surprise to Celeste that Mia was tempted by the *Heavenly Platinum Opulence* wedding package, which was the most prestigious offered by Seventh Heaven. It turned out that no expense was to be spared for the wedding, even though the event was apparently going to be small and exclusive.

Mia told Celeste that all the guests at the wedding would be on the groom's side other than her dearest friend who had been working in Paris for the last two years and was flying over to be her chief and only bridesmaid. She confided that the wedding was being held at short notice and without the knowledge of her family who were all based in the north-eastern United States, mostly in New York City and Long Island – she gave a nervous giggle and tapped her stomach.

'Nine weeks,' she whispered. 'I haven't told anyone from home about the baby or the wedding, except for my best friend and she's sworn to secrecy. They don't like him – my new fiancé, you see. It's not really fair but my family blame him for the break-up of my previous relationship. They think I'm here on holiday but I'm not going back.'

Perhaps because of all the secrecy, Mia seemed bursting to share and very soon Celeste knew every detail. Mia Madison said she came from a family of old-school Catholics – one of those dynastic Democratic clans that pass for minor royalty in America. She claimed her ancestors had rubbed shoulders with the Kennedys and acknowledged she had grown up in a closed and privileged social sphere. Since high school she'd been in a relationship with a boy from a similar background – in fact, Mia understood that they shared the same bloodlines – were fourth or fifth cousins removed or something of the kind. Mia's parents had always assumed she would marry her teenage sweetheart (though she herself had suspected for some time that deep down he might be gay, because he didn't seem able to commit). Whatever!

Mia had met her new English fiancé while working as a celebrity events planner in New York, and well, he'd come on strong and she'd fallen for him hard, and he'd proposed to her after a whirlwind romance when she discovered she was pregnant, and had brought her back to London to get married away from her family, where they could not exert pressure on her to think again or castigate her with scandalised pronouncements about the 'impropriety and sin' of her unmarried pregnancy.

'My future husband has forbidden me from having any communication with my family,' she blurted out, twisting her engagement ring nervously.

Really? thought Celeste but she kept her mouth shut.

'So here I am,' Mia gushed on. 'The wedding is booked

for May 21st at The Chelsea Register office. That gives me just over six weeks to make all the arrangements.'

Of course, they had chosen The Chelsea Register Office in Chelsea Old Town Hall. It was the obvious local iconic venue if you didn't want a church wedding. Celeste knew that many famous couples had tied the knot there – Patsy Kensit married second husband rock singer Jim Kerr in 1992, Judy Garland wedded Mickey Deans in 1969, only months before the singer's tragic death, and Bessie Wallis Warfield married her second husband, Ernest Simpson, in 1928, becoming Mrs Wallis Simpson. So many of these marriages had dramatic or traumatic associations. Yet in spite of this (or perhaps because of...) it was still the most fashionable place to get married within the Royal Borough of Kensington and Chelsea.

'An elopement! How exciting!' said Celeste, her tone half-joking and half-ironic. 'I thought that was a thing of the past.' She wondered at the rush.

'You haven't met my father... or my brother...' said Mia only half-joking. 'It would be a shotgun wedding, or a contract killing if they knew about it!'

'What about your fiancé?' said Celeste. 'Isn't he going to help with all the wedding preparations?'

'He's left it all to me,' she said. 'He says he's got too much going on at work, and I'm the events planner anyway, so he's told me to sort it all out. He says he doesn't care what I choose as long as it's "absolutely fabulous" and I "do him proud!"' She attempted a comical imitation of the bridegroom's upper-class English accent.

'Well, you've come to the right place for the flowers,' said

Celeste briskly, thinking privately that the man's attitude was an easy cop-out. He sounded like a jerk – piling on the pressure with his wedding proposal, forcing her to uproot and emigrate at short notice, cutting her off from her family and then leaving his pregnant bride to do all the work at a time when she should be getting as much rest and relaxation as possible.

Celeste was touched by Mia's trusting naïveté in pouring out her story to a complete stranger.

'How did you find us, by the way?' she asked as Mia was preparing to leave.

'Oh, that was easy. I just googled "most beautiful wedding flowers London" on my fiancé's laptop. Seventh Heaven came up immediately – top of the list.' Celeste cheered inwardly. That must have been thanks to Theo's computer algorithms. He had been helping her to expand the profile and boost the sales of Seventh Heaven. He knew all the tricks of the trade when it came to 'optimisation of the digital presence'.

Celeste put down her notebook, gave her fullest smile and leant across the table to take both Mia's hands in hers. She felt sorry for the sweet young woman, about the same age as herself, so innocent and so eager to please with her guileless American charm.

'Well I'm so glad you found us,' she said. 'Don't worry. You're in good hands. We're going to make sure your wedding day is exquisitely beautiful – truly out of this world.'

PAST

25

He leads her down the stairs, out of the back door and across the lawns. Her stilettos sink into the soft turf so she takes them off and walks barefoot, singing to herself tunelessly and throwing back her head to look up at the stars in the black sky. She knows the way down to the lake. They used to come and play here as kids. He carries her the last bit along the overgrown path that leads down through the trees to the boathouse, swinging her up into his arms like a child or a new bride. At one point he trips on a tree root and she clings on round his neck even tighter and giggles as he swears and lurches forwards before recovering his balance.

The boathouse is padlocked but that doesn't stop him. Still carrying her across his chest, he kicks down the door, with one hard kick. It seems that no one's been inside for some time. The air is musty and dank. 'Boathouse' is a grand name for it – more like a broken-down old shed. There's no light inside but part of the roof is missing. Sounds from the party reverberate on the air – pounding music, high-pitched laughter and the occasional echoing shout. In the moonlight shadows the shapes are sinister and menacing. As her eyes adjust, she makes out an old rowing boat raised up on trestles on one side (*that brings back memories...*) and on the other a jumble of rusty implements, and dried-up brushes, pots of wood stain and paint, some fishing rods and a broken deck chair. Most of the floorboards have rotted away, exposing the bare earth, icy cold beneath the soles of her feet.

'Nobody will bother us here,' he says.

The cold night air has sobered her up a bit and she begins to fear what she has let herself in for. She hasn't been down to the lake for years. 'I used to have sleepovers here with the boys when I was a kid,' he says. He opens a wicker trunk and pulls out a couple of tattered blankets – mildewed and rank.

She tries to keep him talking. 'I remember coming here when we were little kids too. Remember that time you tried to drown me?' She gives a nervous laugh. 'I was scared of the water... before I could swim. You made me get in the rowing boat and rowed us out to the middle of the lake. Then you dropped the oars and swam back to the shore leaving me stranded on the boat.'

He throws a dirty blanket to the floor then pushes her onto the damp ground with one hand as he pulls off his belt with the other. 'You're remembering it all wrong,' he says. 'You dropped the oars. I swam back to get help.' Even in her drunken state, Celeste knows he's lying. In the end it was Ben's mother who had found them at the lake, swum out and rescued her by towing in the boat. Of course, Ben had blamed Celeste. His mother had been so angry that she had spanked them both for disobeying her orders to keep away from the lake.

'You always did try to make me your "fall guy" didn't you?' she says.

He lies down next to her then pulls her close and makes another ardent 'learner driver' attempt at French kissing. His mouth tastes of beer and cigarettes.

'I'm your fall guy tonight. I've fallen for you – hard.'

That's the most romantic thing he's ever said to her. She nuzzles into his chest and wipes the saliva he left all round her lips into his cotton shirt. And that's where the romance begins and ends…

The earth is cold and the blanket scratchy against her hips and bare legs as he pulls at her dress. The grit digs into her spine and scalp as he rolls on top and hunkers down, pinning her body to the ground. There's nothing erotic about this. The clumsy groping of a teenage boy in a man's body. Instinctively, her body tightens and stiffens and the more she resists him the rougher he gets. Her fingernails claw at the soil while his clumsy fingers explore between her legs.

Is this it? she thinks. *Is this what I've been waiting for?* You could say his rucking and mauling is more suited to the rugby scrum than a night of passion. Where is the rapture, that she used to read about in those romance novels sneaked from her mother's bedside pile when she was a little girl?

The worst part is the kissing. She can detach her mind more easily from the rest. But he's not interested in kissing her anymore. His ardour has cooled, giving way to something more selfish and prosaic. He's not even looking at her. His eyes are fixed on something in the corner of the boathouse, about a ruler's length above her head. Disconcertingly the look in his eyes calls to mind her father's when he's in a rage.

His breathing is shallow and raspy like he's sprinting in a race. She knows he's lost all interest in her as his 'girlfriend'. All he cares about now is his own pleasure. He doesn't flinch when her face suddenly contorts. Lovemaking. What a joke! This is sordid. She tries to concentrate on the dull beat of the bass from the disco in the barn as he grinds and moans on top of her.

She too feels disconnected from him – strangely disembodied. Maybe it's the alcohol and God knows what else was in that roll-up. It's nothing like what she imagined from the rom-com movies that she loves to watch with her girlfriends. His expression makes her want to run away or laugh out loud – she's not sure which. She turns her head to one side and keeps her eyes on the stars and the moon visible through the gap in the roof.

Did she consent to this? She wants to tell him to stop but she's lost her voice. She's scared that will make him angry. He's so used to getting his own way. Now she just wants it over with. The smiley face of the teacher who taught the sex education lessons they sniggered at in school, comes into her head. Would her teacher say this counts as rape? If she lies back, docile but hating him, is that consent? If she struggles and fights, does that make it rape? She's so confused.

All she knows is that the thrusting continues... like a near-death experience the seconds expand to forever... on and on... Will it never end?

And for her, the ground hasn't moved.

PRESENT

26

Y*ou weren't in college yesterday. Our tutor had a strop about people missing classes and sending in lame apology notes, and how everyone needed to commit, or we wouldn't get through our exams. But I know You have been busy at the florist's. That woman with the long blonde hair came in to see You three times this week. She won't leave You in peace. If she weren't getting married, I would think she had a crush on You.*

There's one advantage in it for me. She comes in the evenings, after dark, when the other florists are gone. I have found a new vantage point where I can watch You undisturbed for hours. From the backyard of Seventh Heaven, if I stand on some discarded packing crates, I can see into the Bridal Room through a small high window. Here I'm hidden from the street behind the shed. And the sofa where You sit knee to knee is positioned away from the window and You and she are both so absorbed in your intense conversations and in poring over the albums and the laptop, that You scarcely look up.

Mostly, I get to see the top of your heads. Hers is sleek and blonde and static – of no interest. Yours is the one that fascinates me. You never stay still. You tilt and You twist, and You bob, and without seeing your face, I can imagine your eyes sparking, and your smile uncovering your teeth, and your lips moving as You speak and your mouth opening and closing – and the pictures in my mind move me more than the most erotic silent movie ever made.

But it's been over a week since I smelt your perfume or felt your breath on my arm. So even though my mother died almost six years ago, I think this would be a good day to buy her a bunch of flowers. Visiting cemeteries is becoming something of a habit. Why not? Tomorrow, I shall visit her grave.

Seventh Heaven was buzzing – Saturdays were always busy but today even more so since it was the day before Mothering Sunday. Celeste had arrived at 5am to help Meghan prepare the flower arrangements for the special orders of the day. The new Saturday girl arrived at the usual opening time to help with prepping the flowers and serving in the shop while Meghan went out in the van to deal with the deliveries. Celeste remained in the cold room, making up bouquets and leaving Emily who was always bright and friendly to deal with the customers face to face. She herself felt dishevelled and already exhausted as she had been up most of the night and hadn't had time to wash her hair or do her make-up. She wasn't in the mood to be gracious or make small talk.

Friday had been a big night out. Jessi, who seemed to know all the right people, had got the three of them onto a free VIP guest list for a new private club in Mayfair called Chimerical. Being on the VIP guest list meant they could get free entry and free drinks and they had spent a wild night dancing, drinking and having a cracking time across the five glitzy bars of Chimerical, without having to take out a credit card once. Admittedly it was a meat market in there, and they'd all had to fight off the unwanted attentions of self-important young men from the City with more money than sex appeal who seemed to think the VIP guest list (which, of course, they'd subsidised) was their ticket to ride. Even so, the girls had stuck together and had fun.

Celeste was paying for it now though, with a cracking headache and the shakes. She wasn't in the best frame of mind to cope with Mother's Day, a family celebration she would dearly have loved to ignore. It was unfortunate for her that in the floristry business this was such a huge day in the marketing calendar. She'd been dreading the commercial jamboree for weeks because her own relationship with her mother was so difficult and toxic and the deluge of sentimental gifts and cards that filled the shops simply served as a heart-rending reminder of all they had lost.

So, on this sad and poignant day, Celeste was in the cold room trying to lose herself in mindfulness techniques. She focused all her attention on the cool touch of the stems and leaves, the sweet, woody, damp smells of woodland and spring mornings, and the glow of sunlight reflecting off translucent petals. She was working on one of her own designs, a fresh springtime mix of lisianthus, freesias, snapdragons and miniature rainbow lilies, that featured on the Seventh Heaven website as their signature Mother's Day bouquet. She was so much in the zone and so absorbed in the moment that it was only after the Saturday girl had put her head round the door and called her name for the second time that she looked up.

'Someone is asking for you,' she said. Celeste's first thought was that it would be one of the losers from the club. 'Enrico' had been particularly difficult to shake off at the end of the night (he'd more or less tried to clamber into their taxi home) and she remembered that over their first drink she'd made the rookie error of telling him she worked for a florist in Pimlico. 'He says he's an old friend of yours.'

Phew! Not him.

Celeste's next thought was Steve. Not him again surely!

Emily grinned manically. 'He's really fit!'

Celeste immediately got a bad feeling. Her fist closed tightly round the stems of her arrangement. If Meghan had been serving in the shop, she would have had the sense to be discreet, but the clueless girl had probably already confirmed to her caller that she worked at the florist's. Celeste threw down the flowers and grabbed her coat.

'Tell him I'm not here,' she said. 'Tell him I must have gone out to get some lunch. Get rid of him.'

'I can't.' She pulled a face. 'He came in to buy some flowers for his mum.'

Celeste hovered in the doorway to the backyard, hidden from view, listening intently, as Emily returned to the shop front. She could just make out the conversation. Yes, it was him. She could hear the girl's nervous laughter. So, he still knew how to turn on the charm. She remembered that voice – confident and entitled. There was something different about it though. For a minute or so she couldn't work it out. Then, she caught on – of course, the accent. He'd been living in the United States for the past seven years – first as a student at Yale University, then working at a financial 'hedge fund' in the city of New York. (Stacey insisted on giving her updates from the Shearham mums' network that she engaged with sporadically when she surfaced from her addictions.) Understandably, his voice had taken on a slight mid-Atlantic twang.

Ben's parents had dealt with the 'situation' all those years ago in the way that so many rich and privileged families deal with such things – by sending their beloved, delinquent son away – far away from the heartache, devastation and broken lives that he had left in his wake. But it had not been a hardship posting. On the contrary. He had been rewarded with a place to study Business and Economics at a top Ivy League university, the perfect launch pad for a successful and prestigious career in international finance. In contrast, Celeste had been engulfed in profound depression, dropped out of her A levels, and abandoned all hope of qualifying for her offer of a highly sought-after place on an Art and Design Foundation course at the University of Leeds.

His life had expanded. Hers had shrunk.

'I'm happy to wait,' she heard him say. 'I'd really like

to speak to her.' She couldn't make out Emily's words but guessed she was making Celeste's excuses. Then she heard him again. 'Can I write down my phone number on this?' There was a pause. 'And please can you pass on this message. I need to speak to her urgently. She knows why. Ask her to meet me at the Cricketers Arms this evening at seven. It's her local. She'll know where I mean.' She heard the doorbell as the door opened. 'Cricketers Arms, tonight at seven,' he called out to the girl one last time. Then thankfully the door closed behind him.

Celeste waited outside the back door for ten minutes then crept back into the cold room. The coast was clear. He was well on his way. The Saturday girl put her head around the door again.

'He wasn't really bothered about the flowers for his mum. He told me just to wrap up the most expensive bouquet. But he was very keen to see you – 7pm Cricketers Arms tonight. Made me promise to give you the message. Lucky you! He seems such a nice guy.'

Celeste ignored her suggestive grin. What could be so urgent? Could it be something to do with the comments she'd been posting anonymously about him online since that night at Heavana when he reappeared back on the London scene?

'Oh, and he wrote down his number.' The girl nodded towards the little card she'd left on the worktop beside the half-finished arrangement abandoned by Celeste. 'Sounds very mysterious!' said the girl, wheedling for details. Celeste picked up the card and looked at the mobile number pensively. It was one of those cards for writing names and short messages that florists attach to bouquets. She turned it over. The words 'In Sympathy' were printed on the back.

'He always was a tactless moron,' she said to herself bitterly.

Then she put the card into the back pocket of her jeans.

PAST

27

She stares up at the jagged expanse of night sky visible through the broken rafters of the boathouse. There's a change in the atmosphere of the night. Even before she sees it, she senses it – an electric menace in the air. It feels as if a storm is about to break. The sky flashes and glows. She imagines the bursts of light must be coming from lightning in the distance. Then she becomes aware of a change in the soundscape. That dull beat of the bass, which was the accompaniment to his grinding, has stopped. The drunken laughter is gone too. Now all she can hear is panic-stricken shouts and screams.

He seems oblivious, all his attention channelled in one direction. She tries to sit up, but his hands are pushing down firmly on her shoulders fixing her to the ground. She struggles to push him off. His weight is immovable.

She can't bear it any longer. At last she finds her voice. 'Get off me,' she shouts. 'Let me go. Stop. Get off me.' As she shouts, his grip stiffens, and his fingers dig into the base of her neck. She wants to stand up and listen to the noises of the night. And she's scared. The more she fights, the more he bears down on her. Fear rises in her throat.

She hears more screams and now she's screaming too. His thrusting becomes more urgent and he puts his hand across her mouth to silence her. His fingers smell of some other girl – but she's past caring. All she wants is to break free. He presses harder against her face, crushing her lips against her teeth. She can't breathe and she thinks he's accidentally going to kill her. She kicks and writhes like a stray cat caught in a bag but he's too strong for her – crushing her whole body now. It's not for nothing that he just got selected to play county rugby for the under twenties league.

Despite the pounding in her ears, she becomes aware of a new sound – sirens, more than one, getting louder as the vehicles approach. In desperation she sinks her teeth into his hand – as hard as she can – until she tastes blood.

He howls like an animal and his chest springs up. He's about to strike her full in the face but his hand stops in mid-air.

'Fucking bitch,' he yells. He rolls off her and onto his knees, cradling his gashed, throbbing hand against his bare stomach and crotch. 'Fucking cock tease.'

She leaps to her feet and flings open the shed door. The smell of burning sears her nostrils. There are sparks flying in the air. The barn is hidden behind crest of the hill. Above the line of the treetops a red mountain of fire lights up the night sky.

Adrenaline pumps through her limbs as she races up the path through the trees, each footfall pounding out his name:

Tom, Tom, Tom.

PRESENT

28

It takes me more than two hours to get ready before I go to buy the bunch of flowers. First, I have to wash and dry my only pair of smart black jeans and my best dark green cotton shirt in the communal student laundry down in the basement. Then I shave and shower and wash my hair and iron my outfit – the first time I've ironed anything this term – and then I'm off. I decide to go by bus because I usually enjoy listening in to other people's conversations. It's a mistake. Today there is no one with anything interesting to say on the bus. The journey is painfully slow in the Saturday afternoon traffic.

When I finally get to Seventh Heaven, I'm in for a disappointment. Through the shop window I see not You, but another girl serving at the counter, and another man who got here first – the man from the club. That throws me. Is he an old boyfriend? Are You hooking up again?

I wait out of view on the other side of the road, expecting You to appear but ten minutes later You are still not there, and he is walking out the door holding a bunch of flowers. Perhaps You are out of town for the weekend or left work early to go and visit your mother? It is Mothering Sunday tomorrow after all. Unlike me, most other people have a family life.

I decide I have nothing to lose by tracing his steps. He might lead me to You and even if You are not around, I've got nothing better to do. I follow him down the street, pausing to look in shop windows and check my phone when he goes into a shop or stops to grab a coffee. Twenty minutes later he turns into a smart garden square on the borders of Chelsea. The light is beginning to fade and I'm able to position myself on the edge of the square where I am shielded by a tree and camouflaged by the greenery.

A light goes on in the hallway as he goes up the steps and the door opens. In a theatrical gesture, he holds out the flowers, lifts the woman off her feet and carries her effortlessly into the house. It isn't You but even from a distance I recognise her. Her hair is like a beacon. And I know her name because I helped You to redesign the Wedding Portfolio Client File linked to the Seventh Heaven website. It's Mia Madison, your American bride. And if I'm not mistaken, the man she is marrying is the man you ran away from at Heavana Republica that night when I fell in love with You.

Witnessing this scene leaves me feeling deliciously empowered and weirdly aroused as if by discovering the identity of the mystery bridegroom, I have 'got one over on You'. The curtains are drawn but my mind fills with images of what will happen next as he throws her on to the sofa or the bed. It's only when the front door slams shut in a gust of wind leaving me out here alone in the cold that I remember – I never bought that bunch of flowers for my mother's grave. I walk home briskly. I have work to do.

Things were going well with CelestialHeadstones.com. The business was really taking off. Now that her website was functioning again (thanks to Theo's latest intervention in neutralising the virus with which, unbeknown to Celeste, he had previously infected it!), Celeste had redoubled her marketing efforts and was getting an average of ten to fifteen hits, and three to five orders a week. She had fulfilled three orders for headstone flowers for Mothering Sunday, and in addition to a steady stream of enquiries relating to anniversaries of birth and death dates, she already had five orders in her schedule for Easter Sunday.

Although the business model worked on a very low profit margin, Meghan was happy to let Celeste indulge this 'hobby' as long as she continued to pull her weight in the shop with all the traditional floristry work – the weddings and christenings and office contracts that were the bread and butter of the business. Celeste was fine with this. She was desperate to be busy. Losing herself in her work was the best way she knew to keep the demons at bay.

Celeste had deleted her Tinder dating app. Knowing that Ben was back in town had disrupted her precarious mental equilibrium. It was no use pretending otherwise. That excruciatingly embarrassing incident with Steve had made it clear to her. She was not in the right frame of mind for dating or romance. In fact, in the past week Celeste had deleted all her personal social media accounts (except for the ones that were not in her real name). It was bad enough being stalked in real life without having people stalking her in cyberspace. Just about everyone was a stalker these days when you stopped to think about it – herself included. Until the recent upset, Celeste had enjoyed many a hilarious, drunken evening with Anya and Jessi, the three of them 'stalking' some guy that they agreed was fit, through his Facebook page or Instagram account.

From now on, as far as her own social life was concerned, she would stick to texting and WhatsApp. If it wasn't a direct message, she wasn't interested, she had decided. Her privacy was more important to her than boosting her capital in the social media popularity stakes by growing the numbers of her followers and 'likes'. However, the fact Celeste had deleted her own personal social media accounts did not mean that she was no longer active online. On the contrary, she was more invested than ever with her fake (or as she preferred to call them, 'pseudo') social media accounts.

Celeste had bailed on meeting Ben at the pub that Saturday night. She had intended to go. She'd even dressed up for the evening – all in black – black polo neck, black jeans and black thigh-length heeled suede boots. She'd got as far as walking round from her flat to the pub entrance, repeating the mantra, 'I am strong, I am free, I can do this. He has no power over me anymore'. But when she pushed open the door of the Cricketers Arms and saw him sitting there, scowling fiercely at the screen of his mobile phone, she lost her nerve.

God he must be so angry with me, she thought. His glaring eyes and furrowed brow said it all. He must have seen the tweets she'd been sending out on a daily basis since that night at Heavana when he crashed back into her consciousness on his return to London. She had set up a fake Twitter account called FeministFlowerPower (@ FemFloPow) in which she interspersed tweets and retweets of floral designs and arrangements that pleased her with anonymous posts related to the #MeToo movement and her own survivor's story and reflections. She had come to the conclusion that the best defence was offence at least where her mental well-being was concerned. Calling out on these platforms made her feel empowered and emboldened. With every tweet she sent out relating to predatory behaviour or sexual abuse she made sure to put him in the frame by adding the hashtags #survivor #Ibelieve #predator and #MeToo alongside the hashtag #BenJohnson. He was at liberty to block @FemFloPow from following him but he couldn't do anything about the hashtags that linked his name to predatory behaviour and sexual abuse.

So that explained why he was so desperate to meet her, Celeste concluded. He was trying to save his reputation. Celeste guessed that he had worked out she was behind the fake Twitter account she'd set up to taunt him, since her tweets were peppered with intimate and embarrassing details from their past that only she could know. Having been on the receiving end of his temper as a child, it made her scared to think how he might try to punish her if ever he was able to get her on her own. But she was fired up by what was going on all around her in the media and determined not to back down.

She'd only caught a glimpse of him under the coloured

lights that night at Heavana and hadn't dared to put her head round the door when he came to Seventh Heaven, and she knew you could never trust social media photos, so now, standing in the doorway of the pub, she took a long, hard look. He was as handsome as ever, with a full head of brown hair dropping across his brow and a firm, arrogant jawline. His profile picture on Tinder was a fair representation. He had always been the pack leader at school as much for his dominant personality as for his clean-cut good looks marred only at the time by teenage acne. His complexion had cleared up and his face had matured: any gawkiness now morphed into intense, rugged features – he could pass for a male model, with the kind of face and torso used to advertise razors or aftershave – the essence of masculine, the breed of man many a woman in her twenties would like to wake up to in her bed.

Before heading out to the pub, she'd had a drink with Jessi and Anya at the flat. Anya had made her a Tom Collins 'for Dutch courage' and because it gave her an excuse to have one herself. They'd looked up Ben's social media accounts to check on his latest posts.

'Oh my God, you're cyberstalking him.' Anya laughed as she glanced over Celeste's screen at her fake Twitter accounts. In addition to @FemFloPow she had opened three other Twitter accounts that (if Ben bothered to check) would look like innocuous accounts forming part of his extensive fan club of followers (five thousand plus) and would arouse no suspicion.

'I'm not prying,' said Celeste defensively while she searched up his account and scrolled down through his tweets. 'I mean, it's not as if he's hiding anything. He wants us all to know exactly how important he's become, and how much money he's made and what a great guy he is!'

Anya reached for her own phone and searched for 'Ben Johnson'.

'Looks as though he's been making himself unpopular recently,' said Anya. 'There's a whole #MeToo Twitter storm against him, calling him out as a bully and a sexist.' Celeste said nothing, preferring to keep her connection to @ FemFloPow a secret.

When Anya had finished looking through the torrent of online abuse, whipped up anonymously by Celeste, she looked at Ben's own Twitter feed. Ben's recent tweets revealed his promotion to the position of 'Vice President' at the London office of the private hedge fund he had worked for in New York since graduating from Yale, and splashed pictures of his newly acquired company car – a red Ferrari coupé – clearly the biggest perk of his new job and the one that made his heart sing.

'That beast must be worth more than a quarter of a million pounds!' squealed Anya who was pretty clued up on such things.

'That's disgusting!' said Celeste.

'Car porn,' said Jessi.

'Better than sex!' said Anya in admiration. 'Not bad for a welcome handshake to the London office.'

'If you've got it, flaunt it!' chipped in Jessi.

'I've got to meet him,' said Anya, undeterred by the negative posts. 'Can you give me an intro?'

'Don't go there,' said Celeste grimly. 'Anyway, I think he's seeing someone. He was with some woman at Heavana that night.'

★

Celeste didn't envy his success. She couldn't imagine anything worse than 'selling your soul' to a financial institution. Learning the skills of floristry had unleashed a creative passion in her own soul, and she could feel herself gradually unfurling like a tight spring bud coming into bloom. She was now an attractive and confident young woman – or at least, she had learnt how to wear that mask. The years of therapy had helped to some extent. She couldn't escape the legacy of the past, but she refused to be Ben's victim any longer. In recent months, all the media coverage of the #MeToo movement had given her a new sense of purpose and self-worth. Though she had never had her day in court, there were other ways. His return to the UK was a pivotal moment. She had been steeling herself to confront him tonight at the Cricketers Arms, to start the conversation that should have been had seven years ago.

'He wants to talk… so let's talk,' she said to herself. 'It is long overdue.' For too many years they had been locked in an unspoken, shameful pact of silence.

And yet, at the last second, she couldn't face it. Before he had a chance to look up and see her standing there, she turned tail and fled…

In those dreadful black weeks after the party, she had imagined taking her own life and had made several abortive plans. She had wanted to hide in the dark, better still to disintegrate and disappear. The last thing she could contemplate was opening up to her mother or to the police about what Ben had done to her. She believed that whatever she had suffered down in the woods was nothing more than she deserved. She hated herself and she hated Ben.

Now seven years older and wiser, she despised herself for her cowardice in being the one to flee the premises of the pub. There was no logic to it. With the passage of time, she understood that he was the one who should be hanging his head in shame. Nothing could exonerate him for what had happened in the woods that night. Ben had never said he was sorry or made atonement for that crime. He was her aggressor. Perhaps she had been a willing party when he led her down to the woods – but she hadn't been in a fit state to give her consent to what had happened on the bare earthen floor of the boathouse. She was drunk. She was high on weed and God knows what else that he had spiked her drink with. He had used brute force to pin her to the ground.

By force of concentration and reflection, Celeste had recovered certain memories from the night. Now she could remember that he had been the one to ply her with drinks on the dance floor. He had painted a very different picture of her at the inquest. But in truth he was the one who had made her drunk and high. It made her uneasy to wonder what else he could have lied about.

She still struggled with her inability to remember. There was no amount of mindfulness that could break through the fog of uncertainty shrouding what had taken place. But yet there were certain scenes in the boathouse that she could now recall vividly. Flat on her back, she had fought him to escape, and he had held her down. He should have been prosecuted. He had raped her – it was as simple as that.

With this new lucidity, she could see that her own

weakness and stupidity that night did not excuse his crime. Her punishment had been her suffering. It wasn't right that Ben should pursue his carefree life of privilege and power scot-free, unpunished for the wrongs he had committed in the past. He had not been prosecuted. But did that mean he should never be punished? It was not too late.

Those words, she'd heard Anya say in jest on more than one occasion in response to some spat with her friends, came into her head as she turned on her heel:

Revenge is a dish best served cold.

Crossing the road, an expensive-looking low-slung red sports car caught her eye, parked on the other side of the street. She approached the car to be certain. Of course, it was his red Ferrari, parked on double yellow lines.

'Typical,' she said out loud. *If your car's worth a quarter of a million pounds, I guess you don't worry about parking tickets*, she thought bitterly.

She was about to walk on, when she noticed the number plate.

'BJ 696'

To her mind, there was nothing more cringey than a personalised number plate. Obviously, it was 'BJ' for Benedict Johnson. But then there was the crass double entendre clearly intended and coupled with the sexual connotations of the numbers on the plate. It felt like a punch in the face. So, he was still the same old Ben she remembered from their school days – the old joke – putting himself out there as deserving of sexual favours from girls. He hadn't learnt a thing.

That is just so Ben and so beyond pathetic, she thought. *How much did he have to pay for that absurd, pretentious number plate?* Clearly, the message of the #MeToo movement had passed him by. Suddenly, she felt empowered and incandescent with rage. The red mist came down. It was a good feeling.

She was holding her house keys in the palm of her hand inside the pocket of her coat as she always did when walking home alone late at night. She always planned ahead – it made her nervous standing at the front door with her back to the street fumbling in her bag. Now, on impulse, she took her hand out of her pocket, glanced behind to make sure no one was following, then braced her arm to scrape her house key along the full length of his car as she marched off briskly in the direction of the flat.

When Celeste got back, Anya and Jessi had already gone to bed. She made herself a cup of tea and remembered that she hadn't eaten supper. She took an apple from the fruit bowl and a sharp knife from the drawer. She held the blade up and watched the light glinting off the metal. For a fleeting second, she held the knife against her arm where the faint lines of old scars were visible on her skin. Then she smiled to herself and cut the red apple into quarters. She put the knife out of the way and ran her fingertips gently, almost lovingly along the scars. The apple was sweet, crunchy and cleansing. It was a simple pleasure that made her feel like a normal person once again. It was good to feel calm and in control – free of the old compulsion. Defacing his car with a deep, metallic gash had been so much more satisfying than the painful and bloody act of seeking to relieve the anger and angst etched into her brain through self-harm.

That night she slept better than she had slept in weeks. It was as if her act of vandalism had lanced a boil. She woke at dawn, refreshed and full of optimism, looking forward to her Sunday outings in the van driving around London delivering flowers to the dead. But before that, she was going for a run. It was time to get fit.

With a new sense of focus and determination, Celeste ripped open the Amazon package that had arrived for her the previous day and took out a pair of black Nike running shoes. She couldn't wait to try them on. She tied the laces in a double bow. They fitted perfectly.

PRESENT

29

I've seen off Steve, now that man from the club is on your *tracks. There's something about You, some vulnerability that drives men crazy. They just can't leave You alone.*

I wasn't counting on company when I placed the order on CelestialHeadstones.com. It cost me a whole week's food allowance on my student budget, so You can imagine that I was disappointed when he turned up at the church. I was hoping for the chance to speak to You alone.

Men harry You like wild dogs circling a wounded gazelle. It's hard loving You.

Being so sentimental, I had a hunch You wouldn't turn this order down. I found some news items about the ten-year anniversary of this girl's death. It seemed fitting somehow. I knew her story would touch You.

Even so, I almost thought You were going to disappoint me when I saw You taking off across the park in your new black trainers at the crack of dawn. I was in my usual place behind the bins when You came out of the front door. I could see that one of the laces was loose and it bothered me to think You might trip and tumble down the steps. But You noticed, and You turned away from me to tie your laces. And I was rewarded with a symphony of black Lycra, bending and stretching, that set my heart pumping and made my eyes water as I watched You tie each trainer in a double knot.

Anxiously I watched You jogging down the pavement. You looked so lost and lonely on that empty street. I would have followed You into the park, but there's not much in the way of trees and vegetation close to the paths – just wide, open grass. And, anyway I'm not in training. I don't want to make a fool of myself, puffing and panting after You.

He was watching You too. Later. He was there when you chained up your bicycle outside Seventh Heaven after your run and your breakfast and your shower. He was parked in a side road, waiting. He must have seen You going into Seventh Heaven, and he must have seen You later getting into the company van and then followed You here. Sick bastard. Does he think he can turn your head with a fancy set of wheels?

He isn't right for You. He doesn't know You like I do...

Just when You were sitting comfortably on the bench... just when I had You in my sights... just when I was working up the courage to break cover and declare myself... right then, he had to rock up and spoil everything.

He got what he deserved.

Perhaps those hammer blows will teach him not to chase after You in his flashy red car.

★

Meghan had allowed Celeste to take the Tuesday off shop duties and to borrow the van for the whole day because she had a CelestialHeadstones.com order that involved a two-hour drive from Pimlico to the Oxfordshire village of Astridge. The village lay on the western boundary of the county, closer to Birmingham than Oxford. This was beyond her usual cut-off distance for accepting orders, but she didn't want to turn this one down. She knew from the notes in the booking that the grave was that of a teenage girl whose life had been cut short in unspecified circumstances and that Tuesday was the tenth anniversary of the month of her death. She was moved and disturbed by the story and it felt right to be facilitating a gesture to cherish and honour the memory of the young girl's life.

What had first caught Celeste's attention when the order popped up on her screen was that the girl had died aged only seventeen, the same age at which her own life had been devastated. This added poignancy to her task.

It was almost noon by the time Celeste arrived at the church. When she found the grave, she read the inscription and shivered to see that the time of death engraved on the headstone was simply given as 'April 2008' – the actual date must have been unknown, suggesting that the poor girl's life had ended in appalling circumstances.

In Loving Memory
Susan Alison Slade
21st March 1991 – April 2008

The granite headstone was cut in a simple design that stood out from the others in the historic parish church of St Mary's, Astridge, which were mostly ancient, weather-beaten and tangled in ivy. Usually on her visits to remote country churchyards, Celeste arrived to find the grave bare and neglected. But she was surprised to see that the plot and the headstone were clean and tidy and already adorned with several floral tributes and memorials sparkling in the spring sunshine.

There were poignant handwritten messages from family members. Celeste bent down to read a note written in a childish script that was pinned to a red velvet heart, hand-stitched with silver sequins and beads:

> *My lovely sister Susie*
> *Always in my heart*
> *Forever sleeping in paradise.*

As well as these personal messages, there were others that were more formal in nature. A classic arrangement of white and pink carnations caught her eye, marked with the message:

> *Susan Alison Slade*
> *May Your Soul Rest in Peace*
> *Remembered with sympathy and respect*
> *the family of DC Alan Paine*
> *Oxfordshire Constabulary*

The involvement of the Oxfordshire Constabulary suggested that there must have been something sinister or tragic about the girl's death. She was clearly a victim. Celeste began to feel anxious and looked around the graveyard nervously while she arranged her own bouquet in amongst the other tributes.

There was something 'off' about this booking. It was more impersonal than most. Clients of Celestial Headstones.com were usually quite specific in their choice of flowers and messages. For this order, however, the least expensive option had been selected. The bouquet featured on the website was called 'Loving Memories' and was a simple arrangement of white roses and miniature lilies in a hand-tied bouquet. It had taken Celeste less than twenty minutes to design. And, whoever had placed the order had written the shortest of messages to go with the flowers:

With best wishes

The phrase was oddly inappropriate for a memorial tribute. Perhaps, the sender had difficulties with social communication?

After Celeste had finished tending the grave, placing the bouquet and taking photographs to email to her client, she began to feel hungry. She had picked up a lunch box from the deli before driving out of London. She sat down on a memorial bench thoughtfully placed in a sunny and sheltered spot behind the south-facing wall of the nave of the church, overlooking the graveyard. She smiled at the dedication on the brass plaque nailed to the top rail of the bench:

Thomas Handley of this Parish 1933–2014
His legs gave out but not his heart

As she bit into her chicken and avocado wrap, she reflected that Thomas must have been blessed with a GSOH (as per the dating ads) as well as a positive outlook on life to have inspired such a quote. If only descriptions on dating sites were so authentic and so revealing! She amused herself with the absurd thought that dating the dead on the basis of their memorial dedications would be so much more straightforward than trying to pick the perfect match from profiles on Tinder...

She closed her eyes and tilted back her head, enjoying the glow of sunlight warming her eyelids. The churchyard was peaceful but not silent. With her eyes closed she became aware of the orchestra of sounds filling the air – birdsong, rustling leaves, a distant helicopter and the relentless hum of traffic from the motorway that dissected the countryside a few miles to the north of the village.

All at once the soundscape changed. A peal of bells rang out from the tower – she guessed it must be the weekly bell-ringing practice. The sound of chimes filled her with nostalgia for times when as a little girl she would occasionally accompany her grandfather to the bell-ringing practice in the village church and every once in a while, as a special treat she would be given the chance to ring one of the bells. She remembered the scratchy feel of the rope burning against the soft palm of her hand. It required concentration to keep up with the sequence of the bells in the chime. And it required so much more strength than she had imagined tugging down on the rope to swing that heavy bell. She would throw her whole body into the movement as if she were on a seesaw or a fairground ride.

She opened her eyes and was for a moment dazzled by

the brightness of the idyllic English country scene. The cherry trees growing next to the dry-stone wall were at their best – in full blossom at that point in the season where the slightest breeze would cause them to shed their petals like pastel flakes of snow. For now, the sunlight on the petals clinging to the branches made them shimmer with light.

Celeste began to wonder about the life of the young girl whose grave she had been tending. There were so many tributes on her grave, from members of the public as well as her family and friends – but somehow an aura of sadness seemed to cast a shadow over the headstone. She took out her phone and googled the name. The search pulled up a number of entries including recent items commemorating the tenth anniversary of the girl's death and some old press reports. The *Birmingham Post* and the *Birmingham Advertiser* had both run the story. 'Susie' Slade was a murder victim.

It was uncanny but Celeste had sensed the bad vibes surrounding this grave. Suddenly the breeze in the cemetery seemed chill and Celeste shuddered as she bit into her apple. All was quiet now. The bells had stopped ringing and she had heard the parishioners leaving the church, calling out cheery goodbyes as they headed off home. Now she was alone in the graveyard. She put on her sweatshirt and began reading obsessively through all the information she could find online about the girl.

The press reports from the trial of Mark Packham, the nineteen-year-old charged with her murder, were distressing. The girl in the press photographs was slim and attractive, with fine features, light hair cut into a bob, and a wide smile – not unlike her own appearance at the same age. Celeste learnt that Susie's body had been found on 23rd April 2008 buried in a shallow grave in an area of scrubland along a remote stretch of the Grand Union Canal between Birmingham and Oxford. The victim had been found with severe bruising around her neck, suggesting that she had been strangled. An autopsy of the body had revealed that she had been three months pregnant.

According to the prosecution case at the trial, Susan's superficially sunny appearance and disposition hid a troubled life in and out of care. She had first met and entered into an abusive and coercive relationship with Mark Packham when she was fifteen years old during one of her stays in a care home. Packham was two years older than her and had been a long-term resident of the care home. While in residence she became a drug addict under the influence of Packham on whom she depended for her supply of crack cocaine and other substances. Packham was said to be 'controlling to an obsessive and excessive degree'. A witness from the care home testified that he was verbally and physically abusive towards her:

'Packham used to hit her all the time. He was always ordering her about and swearing at her. She was scared of him. The care staff turned a blind eye. They didn't want to have to call in the police.'

The prosecution case was that eighteen months later when they were both living out in the community, she had met another man, Angus Bridstock, an 'associate' of Packham's. She had entered into a new abusive relationship with Bridstock (also a convicted drug dealer) and become pregnant. Bridstock had proposed to her. Accompanied by Bridstock, she had then arranged to meet Packham in a pub in the suburbs of Birmingham to end the relationship with him once and for all. But when Packham found out about the pregnancy there had been a fight between him and Bridstock and he had subsequently strangled Susie in a fit of jealous rage.

The police evidence included CCTV images of Susie following Packham out of the pub after the fight. This was the last reported sighting of Susie who had been reported missing by her sister at 09.34 GMT the next morning. Forensic evidence matching Susie's DNA had been found in the back of a truck belonging to Packham's father who was the owner of a scaffolding company.

The prosecution concluded that seventeen-year-old Susan Slade had been killed by her violent ex-boyfriend sometime between 18.53 GMT on 15th April, when she was last seen on CCTV camera outside the Charrington Arms and 06.25 GMT on 22nd April, when he was caught on a speed camera driving his father's truck on an approach road to the Grand Union canal. During that one-week interval, the police had launched a 'missing person' inquiry but according to evidence given by the family at the trial, the police had been slow to mobilise their full resources for a murder inquiry because the disordered background of the young girl in care led them to believe that she would probably turn up within a few days of her own accord.

In the event, Susie's mutilated body had been discovered by a dog walker on 25th April 2008 when the murder inquiry had been launched. The prosecution case was that Packham had killed Susie sometime between 15th and 22nd April before he transported her body in his father's truck and buried it in a shallow grave in woodland near to the stretch of the canal where he used to go fishing with his dad when he was a small boy. It had not been possible to establish the exact moment of death.

'So that explains the absence of the date of death on the headstone.' Celeste sat there on the bench, shocked at the harrowing details she had just been reading. There seemed so little connection between this idyllic spot and the violent end of Susie's life. Her flowery grave in this peaceful country graveyard was a painful contrast to the life that the troubled teenager had lived and the careless brutality she had been subjected to at the hands of two aggressive young men, which had ended with her untimely tragic death. She felt overwhelmed with a sense of sisterhood, solidarity and empathy towards the girl who lay buried just a few feet away from where she sat.

Celeste began to wonder who had placed the order on the CelestialHeadstones.com website and what that person's connection had been to the young murder victim. She took out her phone again and went on to her website to check the order details. The payment had been made by bank transfer, which was unusual as most users simply gave their credit card details or used PayPal. She sent a text to Meghan at Seventh Heaven and asked her to look up the details online in the company bank account.

Fifteen minutes or so later, Meghan sent through a screen shot of the online business bank statement including the relevant entry for the order. She scanned down the image. There it was:

FASTER PAYMENT RECEIPT ON 2018 04-13, REFERENCE B. WARE: £38.50

'REFERENCE B. WARE' – was this a genuine reference or was it supposed to be a sinister joke? If so, it wasn't even remotely funny. Was someone mocking her? Was someone trying to warn her or more likely to frighten her? Was it someone who knew about the trauma and tragedy she had lived through herself? Among her new friends and acquaintances, not many people were aware of the dreadful events that had engulfed her aged seventeen, the same age as the murder victim at whose headstone she had knelt arranging the 'Loving Memories' bouquet. Celeste had done her best to keep her past hidden. But it seemed as if someone was trying to intimidate her, and whoever it was, had to be someone who knew her well. She stood up and glanced around the graveyard.

Suddenly she had that prickly feeling she was being watched.

As if on cue, she heard the throaty engine purr of an expensive car approaching up the single-track lane leading to the parking area behind the church. Her eyes were drawn to the sound and she watched a patch of red moving behind the trees. Even before the car pulled in to view and parked up next to the Seventh Heaven van, she knew who it was.

Of course, it had to be him! she thought bitterly. *Ben must have placed the order. He wants to have it out with me for what I did to his car the other night... What an idiot, to have fallen into his trap.*

She grabbed her things from the bench and entered the church through the west porch. The heavy oak door closed behind her with a loud scraping of wood against the stone flagstones and a clanking of hand-forged ironmongery. She ran down the nave of the church past the rows of ornately carved box pews, beyond the pulpit and into the chancel in search of a place to hide. Lit only by small stained-glass windows, the interior of the church was dark after the brightness outdoors and it took time for her eyes to adjust to the gloom. Short of trying to conceal herself beneath the benches of the pews or behind the curtain of the altar, there was nowhere to hide away in the main body of the church.

She spied a door behind the pulpit. She tried the latch. It opened into the vestry – a small side room containing a desk and chairs (used during marriage, and other ceremonies, no doubt, for the signing of the registers) at one end of the room, and at the other, a large slatted built-in cupboard running the full length of the wall where the choristers and the clergy hung the robes and vestments used in the services. It was big enough for her to step inside and flatten herself against the back wall behind the long red and white robes.

Straining to hear, she made out the muffled sound of the solid oak of the church door creaking on its hinges, then scraping the flagstones as it closed with a clunk. The tapping of footsteps on stone neared the vestry door. She shuffled along the back of the cupboard behind the clerical garments that smelt of musty linen, lavender and mothballs. Her foot clattered against a large metal box. In the dim light from the slats she made out an assortment of cleaning materials and tools – hammers and screwdrivers and the like, for use by the church caretaker, she supposed – as well familiar floristry items that she assumed must belong to the flower arrangers in the church.

She heard the latch of the vestry door releasing and sank down silently to the floor, huddling in amongst the cleaning fluids and mops. Without thinking she took a hammer from the box and crouched there gripping it tightly and praying that her pursuer wouldn't see her through the gaps or rifle along the whole length of the cupboard.

Feeling as if her lungs must burst, at last she heard the latch of the vestry door closing followed by retreating footsteps. She waited a few more minutes before sliding back the cupboard door and creeping out. Cautiously she ventured out of the church, scanning the churchyard before making her way back across the grass to collect her floristry workbox, which she had left behind Susan Slade's headstone. Heading for the van, she saw a man crossing the village green in the direction of the shops and the pub. She recognised his silhouette and upright gait. He must be going in search of her. She watched him disappear into a café. Maybe he thought she'd gone to the village to pick up some lunch.

The red car was still parked beside the van. The scratch was gone. Had she imagined the scene the other night? Or had the paintwork already been repaired? If only it were as easy to paint over the scars that disfigured her soul and her skin! The empathetic anger roused by Celeste's research into Susie's life story seemed to explode as the Ferrari's deafening alarm screeched out across the village. Any second now, he would come running to check on the commotion. She flung open the door of the van and threw in her workbox before jumping in behind the wheel. She dared not turn her head. But the car's windscreen was clearly visible in her rear-view mirror as she accelerated down the lane.

The bright spring sunshine set the windscreen gleaming with three sparkling starbursts of shattered glass that called up in Celeste's agitated state of mind an image of celebrations and popping Champagne corks and spraying bubbles.

As she drove along the country lanes back to the motorway, she was overtaken by a strange, reckless euphoria like a delinquent schoolgirl bunking off classes. She hurtled round the bends at speed, her foot almost flat on the accelerator.

'This is better than cocaine! I could get hooked on this feeling!'

Halfway back to London she had to pull off the road to fill up the van with diesel. It was only when she reached into her workbox for her purse that she realised she had acquired a new tool.

She must have forgotten to leave behind the hammer when she legged it out of the church...

In addition to her credit card, she took out the little cardboard sympathy card that Ben had left for her at Seventh Heaven.

Before she set off again, she punched out the number scribbled on the back of the card and typed out the message:

For Susie and all the women in the world who suffer abuse at the hands of men.

And #MeToo

PRESENT

30

*Something's changed. You don't speak to me anymore.
Not a smile or a nod when you pass me in a corridor –
I might as well not exist. After all the work I did for you,
setting up your stupid website, your behaviour is not just
unfriendly, it's fucking uncivilised!*

You've only got yourself to blame for what I'm doing.

*Out of sight but not out of mind. That's the only way I
can get close to you.*

*You look far too happy when you're going about your
business without me.*

You need to learn some respect.

*My father kept a Rottweiler and this is what he liked to
say as he kicked the dog into submission.*

*'Make them love you or fear you. It doesn't matter which.
Either will learn them to respect you.'*

'Love or fear?'

*He used the same method with me. Kicked me into
submission. In the end, I gave him my respect.*

'Love or fear?'
I'm coming out of the shadows.
It's your choice.

Celeste was sitting at the kitchen table with her laptop open. Anya leaned over and plonked a large glass of gin and tonic down on the table in front of her.

'Got a lot on this week? You've been working late every night.'

'Yes, I'm preparing for a big wedding at The Chelsea Register Office in two weeks' time. It's a last-minute job, American bride, she's very sweet but such a pain. She won't leave me alone, and she wants the best of everything. Meghan's made me drop all my other work – just to focus on this wedding.' She flipped through her notebook to show Anya her pages and pages of copious notes about the order. 'Look, that's just from my meeting with her yesterday.'

Anya sat down beside her. 'Well it's good to see you're back in the land of the living for a change,' said Anya. 'I was beginning to think you were *ghosting* us – all that time disappearing off to graveyards.' She smirked at Celeste.

'Ha, ha... very witty. Well, you'll be pleased to know, Meghan's banned me from any new orders on *CelestialHeadstones.com* for a while. She was furious because I pranged the van and picked up another speeding ticket on my way back from Astridge.'

'Oh my God! Celeste,' said Anya. 'You need to slow down. Or we'll be the ones putting flowers on your grave.' Celeste knew Anya's fears for her welfare were not too deep even though both she and Jessica had been voicing their concerns about her mood swings the past few weeks – one minute she was hyper, verging on mania, the next she was down in the dumps, scarcely able to speak.

'It's like you're on speed,' Anya had said to her the other day. Now Anya was more interested in looking at Celeste's wedding plan than worrying about her flatmate's state of mind. Celeste was happy to indulge her friend – she knew Anya was fascinated by all things extravagant and glamorous and enjoyed fantasising about her own lavish wedding in the not too distant future.

'She's gone for our most expensive package, *Platinum Heavenly Opulence*. To go with her hair, I guess – she's a natural platinum blonde,' said Celeste drily. Anya read the description of the package:

A beautiful mix of all the freshest, most delicate and stylish flowers really captures the essence of a heavenly wedding that exudes romance and sophistication. Choose our Platinum Heavenly Opulence wedding package and we will create stunning flowers for you and your wedding party, the ceremony and reception – everything you need for your perfect 'out of this world' experience on your wedding day.

In the course of her consultation with Celeste, the bride had been tempted into adding a number of other arrangements to the already extensive package.

'Look at this,' said Celeste, 'She's gone completely nuts – taken virtually every single extra option available. I've just finished amending the description of her proposal. Does she think it's a royal wedding? She's not marrying the future king.'

Celeste read out the final draft of the wedding proposal to Anya.

Featuring an exquisite personalised bridal bouquet, two bridesmaids' bouquets, a flower girl's basket, six buttonholes, six corsages, a bridal headdress, two bridesmaids' headdresses, three flower adornments for handbags, festive garlands for the bride and groom, three magnificent ceremony arrangements, a floral arch for the entrance to the ceremony and a matching floral arch for the entrance to the reception, one stunning flower wall backdrop for photographs, two elegant pedestal arrangements, a full-length table top display, a table top display for the Registrar's table, a foliage garland, waterfall cake-flowers, place-setting mini bouquets and five hand-tied thank you bouquets, all beautifully coordinated and individualised for your special day.

'God, I never knew there were so many different categories of wedding flowers! How much will all that cost?' said Anya.

'I haven't drawn up the final budget yet,' said Celeste. 'It depends on what flowers she chooses. But it'll be north of ten thousand. It seems that money is no object…'

'Did you write this?' said Anya laughing, pointing at the final paragraph of the proposal.

We promise to give you guidance in your choice of colours and flowers and to use our expertise and attention to all the finer details to ensure that your wedding flowers fit perfectly with your chosen theme and are just what you imagined, reflecting your personality, vision, dreams and desires.

Celeste nodded. 'What's so funny? What's wrong with it?' she said.

'Well, it certainly sounds as if you've given her the hard sell!' said Anya. 'You're making me want to get married.'

'I'm still working on the draft function sheet. That's a huge task. It's fifteen pages long.'

'Poor thing!' said Anya. 'I feel sorry for her. For something that's supposed to be an exclusive and private wedding what you've talked her into sounds pretty excessive. Maybe she thinks that's the way we do things over here? All she's seen of English weddings is Lady Di, and Kate and Will on her screens.'

'That's what she wanted. It's her *vision*. I think she's trying to impress her husband-to be. To be honest I think she's trying a bit too hard!' said Celeste, leaning on the final words to emphasise her point. 'I'm beginning to question her objectivity.'

Anya chuckled. 'Is that a polite way of saying you think she's crazy?'

'Let's just say I'm concerned for her mental well-being,' said Celeste diplomatically. 'She seems so stressed and anxious about it all.'

'Who is this husband-to-be anyway – that she's trying so hard to impress?' said Anya.

'To be perfectly honest, I don't know his name. During

all our consultations she's never once mentioned it. She just refers to him as her fiancé.'

'Well, I hope she loves him! More importantly, I hope he loves her – and that he isn't just marrying her for her money,' said Anya.

'I get the impression he's loaded too,' said Celeste.

The next morning Celeste sat down in the Bridal Room at Seventh Heaven with Meghan to run through the function sheet for the Madison wedding before they began calling suppliers to check on availability of the various blooms that Mia had requested for the bouquets and arrangements.

'The delivery and set-up is going to take hours,' said Celeste. 'We're going to need extra help.'

'You don't need to worry about that,' said Meghan. 'I made it clear to the bride when she contacted me last week that we could only offer to her help out at such short notice if she made her own arrangements for delivery and installation of the flowers. As you know, we've already got two weddings the same weekend that were booked in months ago. You'll be rushed off your feet dealing with those. She was OK with it. Apparently her chief bridesmaid is going to organise a wedding planner who'll take responsibility for collecting all the wedding flowers from Seventh Heaven on the Friday afternoon.' Meghan explained that the wedding planner would also supervise the set-up of the wedding flowers at The Chelsea Register Office. 'You just need to make sure all the wedding flowers are ready for collection by 3pm on Friday.'

Celeste shrugged off Meghan's use of the word 'just'. They both knew that this was already a big ask.

When they'd finished with the business, Meghan turned to Celeste and said, 'I'm worried about you. Are you OK? Smashing up the van last week, and the speeding ticket – that's really not acceptable. Any other manager would have shown you the door! And then, you've been looking so tired and stressed the last few weeks. I didn't want to say anything. But when I heard on the grapevine, that Ben's been seen back in town, I wondered if that's what's sending you off the rails.'

Celeste got to her feet. 'For God's sake don't mention his name.' She went over to the sink and began obsessively washing her hands. 'He means nothing to me now.'

Five minutes later, Meghan stood up, went over to the sink and turned off the tap. 'That's enough. Stop it. So, if it's not that, what's up?'

Celeste's face was pale and drawn. She was determined to divert Meghan's attention away from the subject of Ben. She blurted out defiantly, 'If you must know, I am feeling anxious and stressed but it's nothing to do with him. It's a student at college. He won't leave me alone. I think he's stalking me.'

Meghan looked shocked. 'What's he doing?' she asked.

'He always sits behind me in class – I can feel his eyes on the back of my head. Then he waits for me outside class in the corridors, and sometimes follows me home, and I've noticed him lurking around near here once or twice and look...' Celeste opened up the screen for the Seventh Heaven bank account. 'This order last week – B. Ware. It was a fake order, I'm sure of it. I think it was him, this student; for some reason he wants to intimidate me. I made the mistake of letting him help me set up the website and now he seems to think I owe him something. I think he placed the order and followed me there.'

'Are you sure? *B. Ware* – that's so immature! But following you to the graveyard – that's creepy! This is outrageous, completely unacceptable behaviour,' said Meghan. 'You should have told me sooner. We should get the police onto him. I'm not putting up with someone threatening my staff.'

But Celeste was adamant she didn't want the police involved, if only because of what had happened to Ben's car at the churchyard.

'This is why I didn't tell you. I knew you would want to steam in...' she said. 'I can't bear the thought of having police officers coming around and interviewing me and asking all sorts of questions and having to give formal evidence. You can understand that can't you... after what happened?' Celeste glared at Meghan. 'The sound of a police siren is enough to give me a panic attack,' she said quietly. 'If you want me to be open with you, you've got to promise that you won't ever do anything behind my back like going to the police. You know very well I have absolutely no trust in them. I was treated so badly last time...'

'I'm sorry,' said Meghan, taken aback by Celeste's passion. 'OK I promise. But you need to take care. You're an attractive young woman. You're bound to get some unwanted attention from men, but this is out of order.'

'Meghan, he's only a kid! Seventeen or eighteen years old. I must have given him some encouragement without meaning to. He's completely harmless. He's got a teenage crush on me. I can deal with it.'

Meghan picked up a carton of roses and carried them through to the cold room.

'OK, if you're sure you feel safe. But from now on, no more trips on your own to graveyards in the middle of nowhere. In the future, you can do the trips on a Saturday and go with Emily or one of the other Saturday girls. Any more trouble from that kid, and I'll come with you myself to drag him out from under his bush and give him a piece of my mind. He needs to grow up.'

PRESENT

31

You spend so much time with that woman that I'm dying to know why she's got such a hold on You. I know you're planning her wedding flowers (I've watched all the orders going through the Seventh Heaven online ledgers and accounts) but that doesn't explain all the time You spend together, all the private conversations and whisperings and hugs. It's making me jealous.

One rainy night in April, I'm in my usual spot, precariously balanced on the packing crates peering into the Bridal Room, when finally, I get proof that something strange is going on. A wedding should be a happy thing, right? But Mia is not happy tonight. She's been agitated and distracted all through the consultation. Though I can't see her face, her hand gestures say it all. Out of the blue, she stands up, unbuttons and pulls off her blouse, then hunches over as if she's going to cry.

You stand up and caress her back gently. Then You walk round in front of her and run your fingertips across her *chest. You take a step back and look her up and down before reaching for your iPhone to take photographs. Finally, You draw her in towards You until her head is resting against your shoulder. I can see from the juddering of her back that Mia is crying inconsolably while You stroke her hair. But it's the expression on your face that captivates me.*

It's not love or compassion. You have morphed into another person. If looks could kill...

The next couple of weeks were really busy. Celeste had several more meetings with Mia in Seventh Heaven to finalise her choice of flowers and designs for each of the arrangements. Hours were spent sourcing the blooms, which included unusual variants of classic wedding flowers such as peonies, lilies, orchids and wild roses. These were seasonal flowers that should have been readily available for a late spring wedding, but Mia turned out to be unexpectedly specific and sensitive when it came to colour tones and scents. To keep Mia happy, Celeste ordered in single stems of three varieties of oriental lilies 'Casablanca', 'Le Reve' and 'Stargazer' – known for their 'heady and intense fragrance' – and spent a whole morning with her 'sampling' the scents until she finally opted for 'Le Reve' as 'the most sensual and escapist'. It was the same for every bloom in every bouquet.

'I'm just so thankful I'm not dealing with her make-up and hair,' said Celeste to Meghan, when she finally got Mia out the shop.

Mia had also fixated on certain 'out of season' items that were difficult to source through Seventh Heaven's usual suppliers. She insisted on including mimosa because its light, lemony fragrance 'made her want to swoon' and reminded her of balmy summer evenings on childhood holidays to the Mediterranean. Orange blossom was another 'must-have'. Its sweet citrus-fragranced flowers reminded her of the Californian orange groves that she had so loved when living on the West Coast of the US as a student at UC Berkeley. Celeste tried to keep reminding her client that they were designing wedding flowers not creating a new perfume, or sensory distillation of her life so far. Mia was very sweet, but it seemed the anxious young woman was taking perfectionism to extremes.

The bridal bouquet was a whole saga in itself. Mia had chosen an elegant bridal bouquet known as the 'Composite Flower Bouquet' or the 'Carmen Rose' that looked deceptively simple in design but was fiendishly difficult and fiddly to create. This bouquet was constructed from hundreds of individual rose petals wired together to look like one gigantic flower. Meghan tried to talk Mia out of it.

'I know it looks simple to a casual observer – and that's the beauty of it – a single, perfect, giant rose. But this is one of the most sophisticated types of bouquet – it's the most expensive option, if only because of the hours of work that go into it.'

Mia was not to be put off.

'I don't mind the expense. I've set my heart on it,' she said. 'The sophistication and simplicity of the single rose will contrast beautifully with the romantic opulence of all the other arrangements.'

Well there is that, thought Celeste ironically. It seemed that Mia had taken on board the language of floristry marketing – Meghan would be offering her a job soon if she spent much longer on their premises!

To keep her client happy, Celeste agreed to take on the challenge of creating the 'Carmen Rose Bouquet' for Mia. Of course, first, they had a long discussion about the varieties of roses to include – as Mia desired a certain effect in terms of tonal and textural graduation, and the mix of floral scents. When this was finally agreed, then there was the small problem that Celeste had never created a bouquet in this design before. She knew she would need a few trial attempts to perfect the technique before doing the real thing so she looked up floristry tutorials on YouTube as well as the official floristry websites that Seventh Heaven subscribed to, and took instructions and advice from Meghan (who had once made a Carmen Rose bouquet for another fancy wedding).

In the end, Celeste made a special trip up to the New Covent Garden Flower Market to bulk buy three wraps of pink roses (managing to charm the wholesaler into selling them to her at a discount when they remained unsold at the end of the morning) and then spent the whole of that afternoon experimenting on threading and wiring her trial Carmen Bouquet, using up bucketsful of rose petals in the process.

'They won't go to waste,' said Meghan, ever practical and business-like. 'Save all the petals. We can put them out in the garage to dry and make them into rose petal confetti for the wedding. She'll like that. Just add the invoice to her bill.' Meghan went back to her accounts, then added as an afterthought, 'Oh and don't forget to keep a record of all your hours and add them to Mia's account too. We're not running a charity here.'

Eventually it was all sorted. The flowers were sourced and ordered, and the function sheet was finalised. Mia was prompt with her payment. She had no problem with the Seventh Heaven policy of getting everything paid for up-front for weddings. She had paid her fifty per cent deposit fifteen days in advance of the wedding date in cash. Given the sums involved, Meghan was taken aback when Celeste handed her the large wodge of fifty-pound notes. But she didn't object. Cash payments were always welcome in her eyes, leaving some scope for a little creative accounting that helped to balance the books and didn't hurt anyone. The balance was due two days before the date of the wedding.

Celeste had a new spring in her step. This was the first wedding on which she had taken the lead and she was enjoying the responsibility and autonomy of the role. In their lengthy 'consultations', she had begun to feel close to Mia. She had learnt a lot about her background and her outlook on life. Mia was a chatterbox – prone to gushing enthusiastically about everything and nothing in that guileless American way. Everything was 'awesome' or 'so cool'. It made a change from the irony and cynicism of her English friends. The only topic on which she was secretive was the identity of her fiancé.

Celeste became very protective of 'her client'. She kept Meghan, with her judgemental acerbic English wit, at arm's length – only involving her when absolutely necessary. She took every call and dealt with every matter herself. She gave Mia her private mobile phone number (which was against Seventh Heaven staff policy as laid down by Meghan) so that Mia could contact her out of her shop hours, or indeed at any time of the day or night, if she had any ideas or concerns.

'What on earth are you talking about? All those hours… closeted in the Bridal Room…?' said Meghan. 'I don't think you've served more than ten customers in the past week.'

'Oh, you know,' said Celeste defensively, 'she doesn't have any family over here or, it seems, any friends. She hasn't got a job and she's been really sick with the pregnancy. She's keeping it all hush-hush from the family in the States so she can't talk to anyone about the wedding or the baby. And she wants to keep the all the plans for the wedding flowers as a surprise for her husband-to-be. I feel sorry for her. She seems quite lonely… and completely in the power of her fiancé. I suppose I've become her confidante – her confidante and her only friend in London.'

'That's all very well,' said Meghan. 'But remember she's your client at the end of the day. This is a business relationship.'

'Oh, if it's the money side – you don't need to worry,' said Celeste. 'She gave me another envelope today for the balance of the total cost. I put it in the safe. Sorry, I forgot to tell you. She's an excellent payer. I haven't even drawn up the invoices yet.'

It was three days before the wedding, and Celeste was now devoting every minute at Seventh Heaven to working on the final details and drawing up a plan of action for the next forty-eight hours when she, along with a former member of staff brought in especially to help, and two of the Saturday girls would be working full tilt on the Mia Madison wedding flowers. All the bouquets, buttonholes and arrangements were to be ready for collection at 10am on the Saturday morning, six hours in advance of the ceremony, scheduled for 4pm the same day.

Celeste got the padded envelope from the safe and handed it over to Meghan. 'I'm beginning to think she must be an heiress – or a fraudster! She's so free with her cash.'

'Perhaps you needn't bother with those invoices...' muttered Meghan, 'since she's paid in advance... unless she wants them for her records...'

While Meghan carefully counted the money and put it away in the safe, Celeste communicated her most recent fears about the welfare of Mia Madison.

'Seriously, I'm beginning to wonder about Mia's mental wellbeing,' said Celeste. 'That's why I'm trying to give her so much support. This mysterious bridegroom that she refuses to name, I can't decide whether he's subjecting her to coercion, which is why she's so desperately anxious about everything being perfect, or whether he's actually a figment of her imagination. The whole situation is so weird. Could she be one of those delusional fantasists who imagines she in a relationship with someone she scarcely knows? There's a word for it, isn't there? Erotomania. It's a type of paranoia, a recognised psychological condition.'

'Well she is pregnant, so there must have been a man on the scene at some point,' said Meghan wryly. 'Unless it's a phantom pregnancy! Thank goodness there's nothing imaginary about her money,' she continued, as she set the lock on the safe. 'That will pay for stock replenishment for the next six months. It's nice to receive a cash payment every once in a while.' Celeste knew from Meghan's tone that Mia's payment would not be recorded on the next Seventh Heaven tax return.

'There's certainly nothing imaginary about the injuries Mia showed me when she was here yesterday evening,' said Celeste, who was upset by Meghan's lack of empathy. 'She's got red marks and bruises all over her shoulders and chest and the tops of her arms. Either that bastard she's planning to marry hurt her badly or she's seriously messed up in the head and is self-harming. I don't know if I should be calling the police or a doctor.'

'You shouldn't get drawn in,' said Meghan sternly.

'I can't just turn a blind eye,' said Celeste. 'I've got to believe her. She said it wasn't the first time. I seem to be the only person in London she can talk to. She's been trying so hard to keep up a perfect front for this fantasy, fairy-tale wedding. But she let slip that in private things are a lot less rosy. He gambles and he drinks too much and when he loses or has a pint too many, he comes home angry and aggressive and takes it out on her. I think she's in love with him but scared of him too. She was making all sorts of excuses for him – pressure of work, anxiety about becoming a father et cetera, et cetera – all bullshit reasons, of course. You can't excuse the inexcusable.'

Meghan gave her a look. 'Celeste, don't forget this is a business. You can't allow yourself to get involved in the emotional hang-ups of our clients. So many people use our services at times of deep emotional need. We've talked about it before – the giving and receiving of flowers and floral tributes has so much psychological and cultural significance. People use us at every significant milestone in their lives. But you have to keep a professional distance. We're florists, remember, not social workers or psychiatrists!'

Meghan's patronising tone irritated Celeste. 'Well, I can't

help it!' she said. 'Mia's pregnant and she's away from her family, far from home with a partner who seems (from everything she's told me) to be excessively controlling and coercive. Someone has to watch over her. Someone has to call it out.'

PRESENT

32

*I*can't let it go. I'm bursting to break the news that your American bride is engaged to be married to the man from the club. I dress in my trendiest clothes – well it's just black drainpipe jeans and my black biker's jacket but when I glance at my reflection in the shop windows, I feel content that I blend in with the other shoppers strolling down the Kings Road. It's late-night opening tonight so the place is buzzing. I go into a café and pick up a handful of leaflets advertising some upcoming event and continue on to the garden square where the happy couple live. The leaflets will give me all the cover I need. I do a thorough job pushing the leaflets into the letterboxes of each address. All the properties are grand and imposing.

Like many others, the house where I saw Mia is divided into four apartments, one on each floor. I know that Mia and her partner occupy the first floor because I saw him carrying her into the flat the other night. I check the names on the buzzers as I push the leaflets through the door. 'B

Johnson' – that must be him. I click on my spyware tab and scroll back through your recent messages. I find what I'm looking for easily enough – a nonsensical message Anya sent You a few days ago. It's not the content I'm interested in. It's the names. 'BJ', 'Ben' – she mentions him about five times. Ben Johnson – he's my man. There's a light on in the living room but the place is very quiet. I sense that there's no one at home.

The basement flat is empty for sure – the estate agent's battered 'For Rent' sign fixed to the railings advertises the fact. Looks as if it's been empty for some time too, as the sign is discoloured and ragged. Metal steps lead to a separate entrance for the basement flat below the level of the pavement. I go down to post my leaflet into the dark. As I expected, the space between the steps and the concrete foundations provide a perfect hiding place to watch and to wait.

Celeste had worked so hard on the Madison Wedding that Meghan had released her from working on the set-up for the other two weddings booked in for the same weekend. Fortunately, for these two weddings, Seventh Heaven's involvement was more limited – in each case they were doing only the wedding flowers for the bridal party and the church, while the florist designated as 'preferred supplier' for the respective venues was taking care of the flower arrangements for the reception celebrations. In order to give Celeste a chance to catch up on her CelestialHeadstones. com orders, Meghan had decided to rope in her family to help her out. This meant using the services of her husband (who did the deliveries on a regular basis) and her eldest daughter who was back from university for a twenty-first birthday party over the May bank holiday weekend and was keen to earn some spare cash. Meghan's daughter had a natural gift for flower arranging – having learnt it at her mother's skirt.

Meghan had permitted Celeste to continue with her CelestialHeadstones.com business venture provided she was always accompanied by another member of staff on the graveyard trips. 'You can't take any risks. If anyone's got erotomania, it's that boy,' said Meghan. However, she had banned her from using the Seventh Heaven van until the repairs and the insurance had been sorted out. Celeste had received two confirmed orders to deliver memorial flowers to the Islington and St Pancras Cemetery, one of the large burial sites serving the north of London. So, it was agreed that she and Emily would travel together to the site on public transport, via tube and bus, to fulfil these orders, while the others dealt with all the wedding business of the day using the company van.

'If that kid has been tracking the Seventh Heaven van, he's less likely to see you leaving the shop or to have the gall to follow you on public transport, surely,' said Meghan confidently.

The girls had decided to make a day out of it and were both in high spirits when they met at Seventh Heaven on the Saturday morning. Celeste picked up her floristry workbox and her photographic bag containing cameras and tripod, while Emily carried baskets containing the two memorial bouquets. They called in to the deli to buy themselves a picnic lunch before setting off across the green leafy garden squares of Pimlico to the bus station at Victoria. It was a bright sunny day, which seemed to have lifted the mood of everyone out on the streets. Even once they reached the main roads, the pavements were less grey than usual. In contrast to the stony-faced, dark-suited commuter crowds, the people they passed today were dressed in bright weekend colours and were enjoying each other's company as they strolled by or sat chatting at outdoor café tables. London looked almost Mediterranean.

It was too nice a day to go down into the tube, like rats into a sewer, said Celeste melodramatically. Instead she decided they would take the scenic route by bus, and better still an open-top bus, at least for part of the journey. She found a 'hop on, hop off' tourist bus that was heading northwards, with a route passing close to Buckingham Palace, Pall Mall, Trafalgar Square and Covent Garden.

'Let's take this...' said Celeste, '...see a bit of London.

They found seats on the top deck, in among the tourists and day trippers.

'I feel like I'm on holiday.' Celeste laughed as they snapped selfies and pictures of the monuments along the way. She smiled at Emily. 'It's nice having company. I'm glad Meghan asked you to come along.'

They gathered up their bags and hopped off the bus at Trafalgar Square. There had been some kind of environmental demonstration going on in the square, so the tourists mingled with environmental protestors, a straggle of good-natured students, wearing sandals, cut-off jeans and faded T-shirts with gloomy slogans emblazoned across the front predicting the end of the world.

'Come on, let's get an ice cream,' said Celeste, as they

crossed the square. 'You wait here on the steps with all our stuff and I'll go and get us a cone each.'

They sat on the stone steps, licking their ice creams and watching a gang of shrieking Spanish schoolchildren who clambered up onto the vast bronze lions guarding the base of Nelson's Column, thereby incurring the wrath of their schoolteachers.

Leaving Emily to guard the other bags, Celeste then took out her tripod and camera and drifted along the wide terrace in front of the National Gallery, enjoying the street performers, the buskers and floating 'living statues' and the graffiti artists chalking up the flagstones. As she took in the scene she was filled with a sense of pride and solidarity with this great city. Only in London could you find such a juxtaposition between carnival festivity and ceremonious grandeur, street art and fine art – all co-existing so happily together.

Since it was such a beautiful bright sunny day, Celeste had brought along her camera with the intention of taking some pictures in central London and at the cemetery to freshen up her website. It felt good to be taking photographs of the living rather than monuments to the dead for a change. Some of these tourist attraction shots could go on her website. There was no reason why she shouldn't put up a few iconic images of London on CelestialHeadstones.com for clients who contacted her from overseas.

'We better get on,' said Celeste as she packed up her camera bag. They hopped on another tourist bus headed for the British Museum. There they would change to the regular service bus route, which would drop them outside the entrance to the cemetery. When they sat down on the bus,

Celeste told Emily (who seemed rather apprehensive about what lay ahead) all that she knew about the background to the orders. She glanced down at the baskets at Emily's feet. The first contained a heart-shaped wreath of delicate baby-blue and white flowers. It was made up of scented white oriental lilies, lilies of the Nile in the palest of blues, white avalanche roses, sky-blue iris, sweetly fragranced blue freesia and a sprinkling of tiny pale blue forget-me-nots.

Celeste had designed, and lovingly and painstakingly put together, this floral arrangement for the headstone of a baby who had died shortly after childbirth. The baby's mother lived in Pimlico and had come in to Seventh Heaven earlier in the week to select the flowers and write a card for the memorial tribute. This baby had been her first-born child, born with a life-limiting congenital disorder. Celeste had begun to realise that florists were like hairdressers – people found it easy to open up to them and tell them their deepest sorrows and most personal secrets along with the trivia of their lives, things they wouldn't discuss with their family or with their closest friends. There was an intimacy in these services, thought Celeste, whether it was arranging someone's flowers or arranging someone's hair – services performed by strangers but with love and care. Florists and hairdressers – they were the modern-day confessors – better than priests, as they didn't impose penances or pass judgement.

Anyway, Celeste had listened patiently and empathetically while the mother told the tale and she remembered every detail as she recounted it to Emily. The little boy had been born eight years ago. She now had three girls – the oldest aged seven, born almost a year to the day that their first-born had been born, and twin girls aged three and a half. Saturday was the eighth anniversary of the infant boy's death but there was a traditional May Day Fair taking place at her little girls' primary school – they even had a Maypole. Alice had been practising her dancing for weeks. She would be so upset if her mother didn't go to watch. And the following day they were celebrating Alice's seventh birthday party – fifteen little girls coming around. It was a nightmare – she couldn't bear to think of it. What with all the shopping for the party tea and the party bags, and thinking up party games, and keeping the twins entertained – the 'terrible twos' had been bad enough, but, 'let me tell you, the terrible twos are nothing compared to the "fearsome threes"! And I should know – I've got double trouble. I'm rushed off my feet.' The mother had finished up her tirade with a laugh.

To be fair, Celeste's new client did look dishevelled and overtired. The dark roots of her hair were coming through and she had big dark circles under her eyes.

The mother had continued to 'share' while Celeste wrote down the details of the order. She explained that the family had moved away from Islington before her second child was born partly to get a fresh start and leave behind all the sadness. She was so busy with her young girls that she didn't often get the chance to make the journey across town to visit her little boy's grave.

'I'm ashamed to say I haven't been to the cemetery for over four years,' she had said. 'I just can't spare the time this weekend to go and put flowers on his grave, but it would be such a blessing and a comfort to me to know that you will.'

Celeste had smiled at her sympathetically.

'It will be an honour and a pleasure,' she had said quietly.

Who am I to judge you? had been the words she really wanted to say.

As well as the blue heart wreath, the first basket contained a picture drawn by Alice as a gift to her brother, and two matching little blue bunnies from the twin girls. Celeste's client had been tearful when she handed these over. She'd also drawn a crude map of the cemetery on a page ripped from a notebook.

'I can visualise it so clearly,' the woman had said. 'The grave is in the corner of the Children's Memorial Garden, in front of an ivy-covered wall, a few feet from the gravel pathway.' Celeste had folded the map away safely in her purse.

Celeste had also felt moved as she took the drawing and the bunnies from her.

'I'll laminate Alice's picture for you,' she had said, her voice breaking, 'to make it last longer.' She had put it carefully into a folder, planning to take it into college on the Friday to use their laminating equipment.

The child's drawing had really got to her. As her client left the shop, she'd had to run into the back room to regain her composure, leaving a young man who had just come through the door fidgeting impatiently as he waited to be served.

As the bus came to a halt in the midday traffic, Celeste took the drawing out of the basket. It was of three little girls, of course – Alice and her twin sisters – and they were all standing in line holding hands. A round yellow sun in a blue cloudless sky sent its rays down over the children. (The sun always shone in these pictures.) On the left-hand side, Alice had drawn an apple tree with oversized red apples. And a boy was sitting in the tree with his legs hanging over a long branch. The boy figure was bigger than the girls and clearly represented the big brother she had never known. He had a Cheshire-cat smile on his face, and he was holding out a huge red apple to his sisters. Celeste handed the drawing to Emily wordlessly. Emily just smiled and nodded. The picture said it all.

The second basket contained a traditional classic white chrysanthemum-based cross with a scarlet ribbon edge, finished with a spray of red roses and foliage. It was the kind of arrangement that Celeste hated – particularly the conventional chrysanthemums – traditional funeral blooms that she felt lacked imagination and soul. But it was what the client had asked for. This type of tribute was popular with her older customers. Celeste had discovered from the notes on the order that it had been placed by an elderly woman who had previously lived in Highbury with her husband. When she became widowed, the client had moved out of London to live near her daughter and young grandchildren in the West Country. She rarely came into town now. She had apologised in advance for the state of her husband's grave.

'It's weird the way my clients feel they need to apologise to me for the neglect of their loved ones' graves,' said Celeste to Emily. 'After all, if they were taking proper care of them, I'd be out of job!'

As the bus came to a stop in front of the entrance to the Islington and St Pancras Cemetery, Celeste commented to Emily that she had enjoyed their bus trip across London.

It had been fun seeing the sights and mingling with the tourists. Her fears seemed irrational and disproportionate on this bright sunny day. She wouldn't let either of those men intimidate her. Ben – well, she'd already made up her mind what she was going to do about him, and Theo – Theo was just a kid with a crush. His infatuation with her now proving useful. She could handle him. She'd had to contend with a whole 'rugby fifteen' of alpha males in her friendship group as a teenager.

Having someone to chat to on the long journey had taken her mind off her concerns about stalking and stalkers. She was grateful to Emily for coming along – some uncomplicated female company was just what she needed. But it was more than just companionship that she needed today. For what was about to happen, she would need not only a companion, but also a witness.

PAST

33

She pounds up the muddy path, crying out as sharp stones and rough tree roots cut into the bare soles of her feet. Fear gives her wings. She hears him following, crashing through the undergrowth, still shouting, calling her a 'frigid bitch', commanding her to 'Stop! Wait!'

It's not him she's scared of anymore. Even the feeling of disgust is gone. All of her fear is concentrated in one horrific premonition – what she will see when she gets to the crest of the hill.

He comes up behind her just as she comes out of the trees on to the lawn. He grabs her arm to steady himself, more than to hold her back.

'Oh my God,' he shouts. And then louder, the same words, again and again, ringing with despair. While he stands rooted to the spot, she sprints ahead of him across the lawn, to where two fire engines are pulled up in front of the barn, with their hoses trained on a bonfire of flames coming from the windows on the upper level below a gaping hole in the roof.

She hasn't enough breath left to scream. As she crosses the grass, five or six girls, crying and dishevelled, in a state of drunken panic, run to meet her. The girls surround her babbling incoherently. 'Thank God, we couldn't find you...' 'You didn't answer your phone...' 'We thought you were inside...' They hug her and each other. 'It's OK, we're all accounted for now. Just you and Ben were missing...' 'We've done a head count. Everyone's out...' 'Everyone's safe...'

Ferociously, she shakes away their clinging hands and throws them to one side as she pushes past. Now she's found her voice – shouting at the top of her lungs as she runs towards the police officer keeping watch over the motley crew of teenage partygoers gathered on the lawn.

'Tom! Where's Tom? Tom... Has anyone seen Tom?' All she can see is a circle of dumb, shocked faces, looking at her. Why won't they tell her where he is? She screams, high-pitched yelping animal screams she didn't know she was capable of. 'My little brother's inside,' she cries hysterically, fearing the worst. The officer holds her in a vice, gripping her wrists firmly, to stop her beating him round the face, as she tries to break free and force her way into the barn.

'Calm down,' he shouts. 'If you want to help your brother, you've got to calm down.' The officer puts his face close to hers. 'Where was he? Where did you last see him?'

'In the bedroom,' she screams. 'At the top of the stairs. He's up there. Let me go.'

As the officer breaks away to alert the fire brigade, Harry steps in and folds Celeste firmly into his arms. Her shoulders are bare. She is trembling. All her strength is gone.

In a waking nightmare, she sees Ben crossing the lawn and closing in on them. She can't bear to look at him. He's become a monster. Her legs give way and she falls to the ground.

Ben heard the police officer's question and his instinct for self-preservation takes over. He runs after him.

'He's in my bedroom,' he says. 'We left him in my bedroom, playing with my Xbox.' His face is stricken. He nods back in her direction, collapsed on her knees in the grass holding her head in her hands. 'She locked him in,' he yells frantically. He stares at the officer with wild eyes, wide with terror. 'I told her not to... But he's only eleven. She locked him in to keep him away from any trouble at the party.'

She hears him but she can't speak. Her shock and horror at his words is unspeakable. Her senses are overwhelmed with the crackle and roar of the flames, and the beat of the music, belting out from the speakers in the living room that is unbelievably still untouched by the fire. Her head is filled with the sweet, smoky, voice of the pop singing goddess Roxhanna as the brutal lyrics resound and reverberate in the night sky like the soundtrack to the raging fire. '*Gonna lie here and watch you burn... Gonna die here as the flames climb higher...Can't hurt me with your cries...You choked me with your lies...Nothing left but smoke and fire...*' She chokes on the pungent smell of black smoke that's hurting her lungs... and the wine and the shots and the spliffs he made her smoke...

She leans forward and retches into the grass.

He stuffs his fist into his pocket and holds out his bedroom door key to the police officer... just like a small boy putting out his hand for the cane.

But the police officer has already charged past him, ignoring his injured outstretched hand, yelling at the top of his lungs to the fire crew and gesturing to the window of Ben's bedroom.

'There's a boy trapped inside – top of the spiral staircase, first door on the right-hand side of the landing. The child's in the bedroom.'

A key will only slow them down.

Ben's wild staring eyes are fixed on the officer's back as he runs towards the fire crew. He closes his fist on the key and after a moment's hesitation, he zips it into the interior pocket in the lining of his leather jacket.

PRESENT

34

I'*ve been waiting about twenty minutes when I hear his footsteps. I should be well camouflaged in this rat hole, which smells of men's urine. I shut my eyes, hold my breath and sit very still. I hear the key turning and the door closing behind him. Lights go on in the first-floor flat casting out the shadows and revealing the dead leaves, cigarette butts and used condoms that litter the floor. I don't know why it surprises me that even in this chic and exclusive part of Chelsea inhabited by the mega-rich, life's debris finds its way into unused underground stairways.*

She's wearing soft-heeled flats, so when she walks up to the front door above my head more than two hours later, I smell her before I hear her. As if in anticipation of things to come, she has that milky talcum powder smell of newborn babies.

Before her key is in the lock the door flies open and he sticks his head out. He grabs her roughly by the arm. 'Where the hell have you been? I've been trying to get hold of you for the last three hours.' She stumbles on the step and mumbles something I can't hear. Although the house looks solidly built, I can hear him ranting through the walls. On and on it goes. I decide it's time to leave my hiding place and relocate to the garden square. If one of the neighbours calls the police, I don't want them to find me here.

'Let's have our picnic first,' said Celeste, 'before we start on the headstones.' They found a grassy spot, in the partial shade of a cherry blossom tree. 'Oh, isn't this heavenly?' Celeste lay back and looked up at the branches shimmering overhead. She closed her eyes, relishing the soundtrack of birdsong and insects – if you only stopped to listen, the graveyard was teeming with life, an ecosystem of biodiversity in the heart of the city. It was like a chorus of renewal. The sap was rising in nature and the sap was rising in her. As the breeze rustled the branches, she felt cherry blossom petals dropping gently onto her face and her closed eyelids. *Like a kiss – cherish blossoms*, she thought sentimentally. *Someone is smiling down on me.*

'People always talk about looking for "peace and quiet" in green open spaces,' mused Celeste out loud. 'But listen, lie back and close your eyes. It's so peaceful here, but it's anything but quiet. If you really start to focus, you'll hear the cacophony of noise.' They lay there listening to the individual sounds – the cooing, chirping and tweeting and trilling of various species of birds, a dog barking in the distance, the buzz of an early wasp, the fluttering of wings, and from God knows where in this part of North London, a cockerel crowing for his mate – and that was just sixty seconds' worth of sound. Celeste sat up and started unpacking the picnic.

'Imagine if you went out one day into the countryside and you could hear absolutely nothing – now that would be scary.' She handed Emily a sandwich. 'Total silence would mean everything had died. It's kind of reassuring to hear that this garden of the dead is bursting with life.'

After the picnic Celeste was feeling sleepy.

'I feel in need of caffeine,' she said. 'I saw a café, on the other side of the road just opposite the entrance. Do you mind getting us drinks?' She handed Emily a ten-pound note. 'I'll have a latte with almond milk, if they've got it please, and get whatever you fancy for yourself. While you do that, I'll have a look around and try to find the plots.'

Emily was already back with the coffees and a chocolate bar to share when Celeste returned to their picnic spot.

'I started drinking mine. I hope you don't mind. It was getting cold,' said Emily.

'Of course,' said Celeste. She put down her floristry workbox. 'I found the husband's grave – it's over the other side of the wall, by that tree. I couldn't find the baby's one – the mother's map is very confusing. We can start with the husband, and then we'll look for the other one together.'

It didn't take them long to attend to Edward Mark Hunter's burial plot. The municipal cemetery was well kept, with the lawns mown short and small shrubs planted between the headstones, to soften and add colour to the landscape. Together, the young women fetched watering cans from the caretaker's hut and scrubbed the headstone until it shone, front and back, like an iceberg rising up out of the green grass.

'At least Edward lived to a decent old age,' said Emily, calculating the span of his life from the inscription. 'He was seventy-seven years old when he died.'

'That shows how young you are! Now that I've reached the ripe old age of twenty-four—' Celeste laughed '—seventy-seven sounds far too young to me.' She adjusted the viewfinder and snapped away with the camera. 'I want to live at least until I'm one hundred.'

She moved the tripod around to capture different viewpoints, then checked through the photos on her camera screen.

'OK. I'm happy with that,' she said. 'I've got some nice pictures for the client and I can put a couple on the website too. Let's go.'

They set off in the direction of The Children's Memorial Garden and Celeste handed Emily the hand-drawn map.

'Here, you see if you can work it out – I couldn't find it.'

It didn't take Emily long to identify some landmarks in this section of the cemetery graveyard and they followed the path leading towards the grave. It seemed that a new shelter housing water taps, dustbins, watering cans and the like had been erected recently as it didn't figure on the mother's map.

'Maybe that's why you couldn't find it earlier,' said Emily.

Emily walked ahead of Celeste and stopped beside a headstone a little way in from the path.

'This is the one,' she said. It was made of pale, grey marble, about half the height of a typical headstone with the short inscription,

George David Hartley
'Georgie'
7th April 2010

Held for a moment
Loved for a lifetime

'Oh my God! It's so sad,' mumbled Emily, her eyes fixed on the headstone. She stood there – lost in the moment. Eventually, she looked round to beckon over Celeste, then unexpectedly dropped down to her hands and knees to peer at what, from Celeste's viewpoint, looked like a group of little flags stuck into the grass in front of the headstone.

'This is really weird,' Emily called out to Celeste. 'Come and see.'

Celeste walked over briskly and sank down next to Emily.

It was Celeste's turn to exclaim, 'Oh my God!' Celeste changed her expression from sadness to horror.

The entire plot in front of the baby's headstone was decorated. But the squares of paper fluttering in the breeze were not flags. They were laminated photographs, each individually taped to a jumbo-sized, flat wooden lolly-stick, pushed into the turf.

'This is freaking me out,' said Emily. 'Every single one of these photographs is a picture of you.'

Emily pulled out one of the wooden sticks and passed the photograph to Celeste. 'What on earth is all this about?'

Celeste stared at the photographs, then manically, she began to tug them all up, glancing briefly at each image before throwing it on to the grass into a messy pile.

'Did Meghan tell you about my stalker?' she asked.

Emily began to look through the pile. 'They all seem to be taken in front of different graves, in different locations,' said Emily. 'Meghan told me someone's been following you around. Is this the work of that student?'

'I don't know,' said Celeste quietly. 'I suppose it must be him.'

'It looks as if whoever it is, has been stalking you for weeks,' said Emily. 'Different outfits, different times of the day, different seasons… in every photograph. This is scary. It's psycho. He's been following you everywhere. He must be absolutely obsessed with you.'

Suddenly, Celeste cried out urgently. 'Oh God, put them down. We shouldn't be touching them. If I go to the police with these now, they might be able to get fingerprints.'

Emily threw them to the grass as if they were on fire. Then she said, 'But Celeste it's too late. Your fingerprints will be on every one of them. You pulled out every photograph.'

'Oh God! What was I thinking of?' said Celeste. 'But still, his fingerprints may be on them too.'

It was too late but nevertheless, she put on her lightweight gardening gloves from her floristry workbox and gathered the photographs into a black bin liner.

'What confuses me,' said Emily, 'is why would the stalker want you to know? That he was stalking you, I mean. I would have thought a stalker would want to keep his spying secret from you – and would take pleasure in deceiving you.' She put her hand on Celeste's knee protectively.

Celeste looked at Emily and said solemnly, 'On the contrary, I think he wants me to know he's stalking me. He wants to intimidate me, to make me feel within his power.

It's all about coercion. That's how these people who are sick in the head operate.'

Emily stood up. Celeste's hand trembled a little as Emily helped her up to her feet, concerned that she was feeling faint from the shock of the discovery.

Celeste looked around the memorial garden with an anxious expression on her face. 'The frightening thing is that whoever took these photographs is probably here right now...'

She tailed off, and Emily completed the sentence for her. 'Watching you.'

'Shushh...' murmured Celeste, clutching on to Emily's arm. 'Listen...'

Emily stood stock-still, listening with bated breath.

'The sound of silence.' Celeste's voice was barely a whisper and there was fear in her eyes. 'It's absolutely still. Nothing... Even the birds have stopped singing.'

PRESENT

35

I pick a spot in among the bushes as my new watching post and take out a small pair of binoculars. In his temper Ben must have forgotten to pull down the blinds. I can see them in the open-plan kitchen. He is pacing the kitchen, alternating between scrolling through a mobile phone and jabbing his finger in her face as he berates her. I'm guessing the phone is hers and he doesn't like what he's reading on it. She turns her back on him and starts to stack the dishwasher. The breakfast bowls and mugs are still on the table. He blocks her way. Still yelling accusations, he picks up one of the bowls and smashes it to the floor. He does the same with the second and then with the mugs. She cowers away from him.

Suddenly he picks up a half-empty glass of orange juice and slings it straight at her head. The juice goes flying across the kitchen in an impressive orange arc. She ducks with lightning speed and the glass shatters against the tiles behind her head, sending shards ricocheting across the kitchen.

For a moment she is stunned and stares at him with rabbit-caught-in-the-headlights eyes. Then she sidesteps over the broken glass and lunges for the door. He gets there first. With one foot he jams the door to prevent her escaping from the room and traps her so that she is standing in front of him with her back to it. He stands head and shoulders above her. For a moment he puts his left hand to her throat and seems to hesitate between leaning in to embrace her or closing his fingers around her neck. Then he takes one step back, forms a fist and punches her pregnant belly with all his might.

Now it's my turn to be stunned. I can't believe my eyes. In all the hours I've spent watching people, it's the most disturbing thing I have ever witnessed.

He stands back and runs his hand through his hair while she crumples over and down on to her knees. I look on in horror. I would call the police, but I don't want them to trace me. I do the next best thing. I race for the front door and press all the buzzers. I tell the first neighbour to answer, that I have a delivery for him, and he buzzes me in. Once in the hallway, I scan the walls to find the break-glass unit that activates the fire alarm system for the building. I smash it. Then I run.

Because it was the May bank holiday weekend, it wasn't until the Tuesday morning that Meghan got a chance to grill Celeste about the photographs.

'What's all this about?' said Meghan. 'This is getting out of hand. You should report him to the police. He must have been following you everywhere. He must be seriously obsessed.'

The Saturday girl had blabbed. Celeste had known that she would, of course. Meghan was quick to pick up on the expression of annoyance that came over Celeste's face.

'There's no point getting angry with Emily,' said Meghan. 'She's very worried about you. This guy sounds like a freak.'

'I told her not to bother you with that,' said Celeste. 'It's probably just some stupid prank.'

But, of course, Meghan wouldn't leave it alone. 'This is more than a teenage crush, Celeste,' she lectured. 'He's behaving as if he's seriously mentally disturbed. He could be dangerous. He goes to the same class as you at college. Other than that, you know nothing about him.'

Celeste appeared to waver. In the end she said, 'Please don't put pressure on me to go to the police. It's got to be my own decision. There'll be no going back – it will set in motion a whole process. Right now, I can't face the thought of being questioned and writing statements and giving evidence in court. Besides what would they charge him with? He hasn't actually done me any harm. I'm not even one hundred per cent certain it was him who placed that order or took these photographs. I need to be sure before going to the police.' She reached into her floristry workbox and took out the black bin liner in which she had wrapped the photographs. 'Look, why don't you put these in the safe? That way we know the fingerprint evidence is preserved, if I decide to make a complaint against him later.'

Meghan would probably have pressed Celeste harder but there was another 'situation' that needed to be dealt with first. She'd never faced anything like this before – in sixteen years of being in business as a florist. She was hoping that Celeste might be able to provide the clue to the mystery.

'Come with me,' said Meghan. 'I really don't know what to do about this.' The door of the cold room was closed. As Meghan opened it, a great wave of mingled fragrances surged over Celeste, making it almost hard to breathe.

'They've been here all weekend. Nobody came to collect them.'

The expression of shock registered on Celeste's face was so graphic it was almost comical.

All of the flower arrangements for the Mia Madison wedding that she had slaved over for the past three weeks were sitting there in the cold room in exactly the positions she had left them ready for collection, still looking gorgeous but not as pristine and fresh as when she painstakingly put them together.

'What on earth...' said Celeste. 'What happened?'

'She never showed up,' said Meghan.

PAST

36

She's flanked by police officers on either side, like a criminal. She's under restraint, but that is to stop her from running into the flames. One of the rescue team has thrown a survival blanket round her shoulders. She's shaking and whimpering like a puppy in pain, and her face is stained with smoke and tears. The thundering jets of water have dampened down the blaze. Her eyes are riveted on the point of entry to the smouldering barn – the back door, which leads to the spiral staircase, which leads to Ben's bedroom where Tom was locked in – the black hole that swallowed up two firefighters each clothed in full personal protection equipment with breathing apparatus and tools, entering the premises in search of her brother.

Ben is crying too. A third officer has taken him to one side. A firefighter is with them. The woman is speaking into a radio – relaying information about the layout of the barn from Ben's incoherent answers that she's trying to make sense of.

It can't be more than five minutes but feels like an eternity before the firefighters emerge from the black hole. The biggest man is carrying Tom. He must have lifted and dragged him down the spiral stairs. The other firefighter is supporting Tom's upper body and holding a breathing apparatus to his face. As soon as they reach the grass, the paramedics who were waiting on standby wheel over the stretcher and Tom is laid out, and strapped on and trundled into the ambulance that's parked up on the lawn.

She's beside herself now, desperate to reach him, tears streaming down her face, beating her hands against the police officer's chest. She begs to go with him to the hospital, promises to calm down. Once Tom's secured inside, the police officer releases her and she runs to the ambulance. She grabs his hand. She gives thanks to God. He's here, his body is whole, untouched by the fire.

A paramedic leans over his chest, adjusting dials and tubes. Her euphoria turns to despair. His hand is warm but limp and lifeless in hers. His beautiful brown eyes are closed, and she fixes her gaze on his long dark lashes (wasted on a boy, her mother always said) watching for the slightest flicker or twitch. She'd like to kiss him, but his lips are hidden by the oxygen mask covering the lower part of his face. She remembers the fire safety lessons they gave them in school. 'It's the smoke that kills, not the flames.'

Ben stays behind, his back turned, while the ambulance pulls away. He didn't watch her go. He didn't even come over to check on Tom. He's got more pressing things to do. He's trying to contact his parents. They're not picking up. He shouts desperate, tearful messages into their mobile phones… He knows they are somewhere in Majorca… He can't remember the name of the hotel.

And what happened down in the woods (whatever it was – lovemaking, seduction, rape?) has nothing to do with him anymore. He's just a child in a man's body. Did it even happen?

All his focus now, is on how the hell he's going to face his mum and dad when they come home to find that half their house has been burnt down.

PRESENT

37

*B*y force of habit I find myself haunting the backyard of Seventh Heaven. I feel lost. Of course, You are not in the Bridal Room because there is nothing more to talk about with Mia. The wedding flowers are done. Instead I see your boss. She looks agitated and tense. The 'Madison Mystery' has left her feeling on edge and perplexed. I zoom in to scrutinise her expression while she studies your photographs. She notices the Seventh Heaven logo on the plant markers but if I'm not mistaken, she draws the wrong conclusion, which is why she is so jumpy, checking over her shoulder, deadlocking the doors. I know what she's thinking. Could there be any connection between Celeste's stalker and the disappearance of Mia Madison? She's thinks I must have broken into the storeroom to steal the green tape and the plant markers. She would be even more confused and disturbed if she discovered the true identity of the thief.

*

Celeste kept her eyes firmly fixed on the roomful of fading flowers as Meghan filled her in on what had happened. She couldn't bring herself to look at her boss.

'We were all dashing around on Saturday as you know, doing the deliveries for the other two weddings – and you and Emily went off early to do the cemetery run – so Mum was here, holding the fort for me in the shop. I'd told her all the Madison flowers were ready to be picked up, all wrapped and prepared. I'd left the back door to the cold room unlocked, so that the wedding planner could get the delivery guys to drive into the yard and load up the flowers without coming through the shop floor.

'Anyway, Mum was distracted and busy with customers in the shop. She lost track of time and it wasn't until lunchtime that she remembered the wedding flowers. She'd been expecting the wedding planner to at least pop her head round to let her know they'd arrived. She couldn't believe her eyes when she saw that all the flowers were still there.' Meghan went on to explain that her mum wasn't too good with mobile phones and had been stressed and rushed off her feet for the rest of the day with people coming in to buy flowers for special events and family gatherings on the May bank holiday weekend. So, the long and the short of it was that Meghan hadn't found out there was a problem until she got back late in the afternoon. Her immediate thought had been that there'd been a mix-up with the dates. But she had checked, and rechecked Celeste's function sheet and notes and the date was correct.

'Of course, I wanted to call the wedding planner, but I realised I didn't know her name or her number. So, then

I tried to get hold of the chief bridesmaid, but I kept getting the message *number unavailable* again and again. And then I tried Mia's mobile, but she's not answering her phone or returning her messages. Every time I ring, it goes straight to voicemail, and then I get the message to try again later because her voicemail is full. I've tried emailing her too but no response.'

Meghan pulled the door shut impatiently and went into the office to pull out Celeste's file on the Madison wedding.

'I've been through the whole file and couldn't find any other contact details. Didn't you take an address?'

Celeste flipped through the pages, for a couple of minutes and then said, 'No, I don't think I ever did get an address. She gave me her phone number and her email. She doesn't have an address in the UK. I guess she was staying with her in-laws or with friends or in a hotel. I have no idea. *No fixed abode*, I guess. Because she paid in cash, I didn't need her address for a card payment, so I don't even have her US address.' Meghan didn't make any attempt to hide her annoyance with Celeste.

'It's so unprofessional,' she muttered.

But Celeste's tone was defensive. 'It didn't seem necessary getting her postal address. We had the address of the venues. Sorry I just didn't think about it. Everything is done online these days.'

Meghan blamed herself for not being stricter with Celeste about following the proper procedures. She understood that the younger generation were less focused on geographical and physical locations since so much took place in 'cyberspace' these days. But still, the Madison bride must have an address, she thought crossly. A woman of her standing would have a roof over her head.

Meghan was getting herself more and more worked up. 'Do you have any idea why she could have done this?' she said in exasperation. Celeste shrugged, and carried on turning the pages of her notebook.

'Do you have any other way of contacting her?' asked Meghan. 'What about the bridegroom? Do you have any contact details for him?'

Celeste closed her notebook and put it back in her workbox. 'No... No contact details for the bridegroom,' she said flatly. 'I could search for her on Facebook,' said Celeste, in an effort to sound amenable 'but if she's broken up with her fiancé or he's stood her up at the last minute or there's been some other crisis, the last thing she'll want is to have gossip and rumours flying around on social media. This wedding was supposed to be kept a secret from her parents, remember.' Suddenly, Celeste blurted out. 'Maybe it's something to do with the baby... a miscarriage or something... some kind of emergency? That would explain why she hasn't been in touch and why we can't get hold of her.'

Celeste noticed that Meghan had put on her 'business manager' face, with pinched lips and furrowed brow. 'Think about it, Celeste. It doesn't look good for us. I know that we're not in any way to blame for this situation, but we don't want the name of Seventh Heaven to be linked to some kind of drama or calamity. That kind of bad association creates adverse publicity. More importantly, we don't want to be seen out there on social media platforms as breaching the bride's confidence by not respecting her privacy if she has had some sort of life crisis. It is paramount that we keep up our reputation for absolute discretion and respect for our clients' privacy.'

Celeste understood why Meghan was paranoid about this. As florists, they were often involved in delivering flowers to hotel rooms or unusual addresses when it was patently obvious that the gifts were being delivered to a mistress or in the course of an illicit affair. Before Celeste's time there had been a mishap in which a bouquet of flowers intended for his mistress had mistakenly been delivered to an important business client's billing address (which was also his home address) instead of a hotel address in London, and he (and his wife) had had a huge row over it. Needless to say, that business account had been lost for good.

'I'll keep trying her numbers,' said Celeste briskly. She took out her phone and dialled. Once again, the calls went to voicemail. 'I guess there's not much more we can do at this stage.'

'Perhaps the woman's a fantasist with a wild imagination?' mused Meghan. 'Maybe the wedding was all in her head? I always thought she had more money than sense.'

At that point, Meghan's reflections were cut short by a van pulling into the yard bringing weekly deliveries of fresh flower stock from one of the Seventh Heaven suppliers. Meghan's bewilderment and concern turned to annoyance as her practical business instincts resurfaced.

'Well, thank goodness Mia Madison paid in advance! Let's just hope she gets in touch soon to let us know what to do with all these flowers – it's such a waste. At least they could be given to a hospital or care home if she doesn't want them anymore… In the meantime, you better push them all over to the side of the room to create some floor space for these deliveries.'

Later that afternoon, Celeste loaded up the panniers on her bicycle with two bedside arrangements of 'get well' flowers for delivery to in-patients at the nearby Lister Hospital in the heart of Chelsea. She had been tempted to use blooms from the abandoned Madison wedding flowers, but in the end, she thought better of it. It felt disloyal – like a betrayal of their friendship. It was an easy fifteen-minute bike ride through attractive residential backstreets.

Celeste was glad to get out of the shop into the fresh air and away from Meghan, who had been distracted and bad-tempered all day. Celeste had the uncomfortable feeling that Meghan blamed her for the mystery and embarrassment surrounding Mia Madison's wedding flowers. Meghan had more or less said as much, thought Celeste, as she unloaded the panniers and carried the flowers up to the hospital reception desk. They had almost had an argument over it as she was preparing to leave. Celeste had made a show of defending herself vigorously.

'It wasn't my fault that the woman did a runner!' Celeste had said. 'I went out of my way to give her excellent client care and support. What more could I have done?'

It's a quiet afternoon in Seventh Heaven after the bank holiday weekend so Meghan tells Celeste she can go straight home after the two hospital deliveries. While Celeste cycles back to her apartment, Meghan decides to call it a day. She flips the sign on the door to 'CLOSED.' There are so few sales that it doesn't take her long to transfer the takings from the till and cash up.

When Meghan puts the cashbox into the overnight safe, her fingers brush against the plastic bag containing Celeste's photographs. She is suddenly curious to look at the images Celeste brought back from the North London cemetery. She has set herself the task of getting through her inbox and up to date with her invoicing this evening, so she puts the bag to one side on her desk. The photographs will be her incentive to get through her work. She concentrates so hard that she doesn't notice the light fading as the sun goes down. Every now and then she looks up from her paperwork to glance at the plastic bag, positioned on her desk like a smoking gun.

The office window faces onto a side street. Her attention is drawn by the sound of a car pulling up outside. The beams from its headlights are like searchlights on the other side of the glass. It is dark outside, and she jumps at her own reflection in the windowpane. She walks over briskly to close the blind. A few seconds later, she hears a car door closing and the sound of footsteps. 'Pull yourself together,' she says out loud as she switches on all the lights. The business with Mia has upset and unsettled her.

She goes into the cold room (where the smell of the open blooms is now so overpowering as to be almost nauseating) to collect a pair of disposable surgical gloves from the store cupboard. Florists use these routinely for precision handling certain varieties of blooms that are staining or harsh on the hands. These gloves are also ideal for the purpose of looking through photographs without leaving behind the marks of one's own fingerprints.

She takes the photographs into the office and spreads them out on her desk. There are about thirty of them – all of Celeste, taken from various different angles, and positions, some face-on, some from behind or to the side, some wide-angle and some zoomed in, at different times of the day, on different days, in front of different graves. Meghan will insist that Celeste takes this up with the police. This ridiculous situation cannot be allowed to continue. Her hands tremble slightly as goes through the photographs. Then abruptly they stop moving altogether.

She pulls out a photograph and holds it under her desk lamp. It isn't the image that has caught her attention but the fixings – the flat wooden stick and the tape attaching it to the paper. Gently she pulls away the green tape, so familiar in her fingers because she works with this green tape almost every day. Removing the wooden stick from the photographic paper, it comes as no surprise when she turns it over to see the words 'Seventh Heaven' printed on the back.

Hastily, she puts the photographs back into the bag, all the while glancing towards the windows where every passing shadow makes her stiffen. She closes the safe then puts on her coat, locks the back doors and makes her way to the front door. She avoids exiting through the backyard – just in case the driver of the car parked in the side street is still lurking around somewhere in the vicinity of the shop.

Slowly the chilling realisation dawns on her – whoever took those photographs of Celeste must have broken into the premises at Seventh Heaven to steal a roll of floristry tape and a handful of plant markers.

It's time to go.

PAST

38

Celeste is in the garden with Tom at their old family home. Tom is about three years old and she's about ten. They're playing on the swing – or rather Celeste is pushing Tom on the swing because their mother is 'resting' on the sofa in the sitting room with a splitting migraine and an empty bottle of gin and has sent them out 'for some fresh air'.

Celeste knows the score. She's not stupid. But she plays along in an unspoken conspiracy with her mother to protect her little brother's innocence.

'Mummy's been working very hard. She's very tired,' she tells Tom (almost believing in her own lies). 'She'll be feeling better soon and then she'll take us to the park.'

Tom's having fun. He doesn't need his mum when Celeste is here.

'Up, up, up,' he shouts. He giggles and yelps at the thrill of going higher and higher 'up to the sky' as Celeste pushes him, again and again, harder and harder, swinging him up to the height of the branches until Toms yells at the top of his voice, 'I'm flying.'

And Celeste fears that the rope will break.

The weeks after the fire are like a black hole – as dark and charred and desolate and devastated as the black hole that the flames left in Ben's barn. Celeste cannot sleep or eat or speak. She can barely think – she's falling deeper and deeper into the black hole and she never wants to climb out. She wants to die.

Celeste tries to kill herself. But she can't do it. She takes sleeping pills, but at the last minute some instinct for self-preservation makes her go to the bathroom and put two fingers down her throat. She cuts herself, but never too deep. She walks out of the house in the middle of the night through the woods and over the fields and down to the river. She stands looking down into the water while a cloud shadows the moon and the cold and the damp seeps into her soul. But a rustle and a crack in the branches behind her back, fills her with fear and sets her running home.

She can't kill herself. So, she settles for second best. She hates herself.

Her mother makes things even worse – of course, she's in pieces – and she blames Celeste.

'If Celeste hadn't taken Tom to the party... If she hadn't lock...' (she can't even bring herself to say it out loud) '...he would still be alive.'

Celeste has lost count of the number of times she's heard her mother say those words. It's a self-evident truth – a facile statement – yet no less poisonous.

Celeste hates her mother too.

As for her father, well, Celeste can't even bring herself to look at him. If he hadn't abandoned them when she was only thirteen and Tom was only seven, then none of this would have happened. She can't even put a name to the way she feels about him.

But the person she hates and despises the most is herself. She can blame her father for abandoning his children with an alcoholic and opioid-addicted mother; she can blame her mother's sleazy boyfriend for distracting his girlfriend from her maternal responsibilities; she can blame her selfish, egotistical mother for years of neglect (and for making her babysit on a Saturday night); she can blame Ben for forcing her to go to the party and for plying her with drink (and God knows what else), and for doing what he did to her in the boathouse...

But at the end of the day and through the sheet-twisting terrors of every sleepless night she tortures herself with the thought she was the one who locked Tom inside Ben's bedroom. For that Celeste has only herself to blame. And for that, there is no forgiveness.

Each time her eyes close, her mind conjures images of her hand turning a key.

Every night, without a rope, she hangs herself.

PRESENT

39

I had no idea You were such a good actress, Celeste.

I know You are lying to Meghan about the photographs because I watched You planting those photographs at the grave.

This makes me wonder what else You are lying about and more importantly, why?

I get that uneasy yet peculiarly arousing feeling that You are framing me as your fall guy. You are becoming the mistress of deception.

Well, Celeste, I stand ready. If I can't be your lover, I will be your accomplice.

Things had been stressful in Seventh Heaven all week. Meghan was reacting badly to the business with the Madison bride. She was tetchy and short-tempered with Celeste. Almost a week had passed since the scheduled date of Mia's wedding and so far, there had been no word as to why the wedding had not gone ahead and no instruction as to what should be done with the flowers.

The cold room was beginning to reek with the pungent, sickly-sweet stink of decomposing vegetation as the blooms began to rot. Meghan was getting more and more vocal in her complaints. Celeste could barely bring herself to step inside the room. Smells were so evocative, and this smell reminded her of the flowers on her little brother's grave. She was transported to the evening of Tom's burial when she had gone back to the churchyard alone as the sun was setting. There had been no headstone as yet but the mound of earth covering Tom's fresh grave had been heaped with floral tributes. Every inch of soil was covered with blooms. It had been a mild evening and the smell of flowers in the evening air was intoxicating and overpowering.

Celeste remembered falling to the ground and lying there sobbing into the grass and crushing the petals into her hands in desperation. It was the first time she had been able to cry since the night of the fire.

Finally, on the Thursday lunchtime, Meghan lost patience.

'This lot has got to go,' she announced. 'I want my cold room back. We're going to have to bite the bullet and throw them away. Can you bag up all the flowers and take them out to the bins?' Celeste understood that Meghan couldn't help feeling there was something vaguely shameful and disturbing about getting rid of the flowers, without having heard a word from Mia. 'Do you think we should notify the police?' she wondered out loud to Celeste for about the hundredth time as she handed her a roll of large black bin liners. For all the reasons spoken and unspoken (bad publicity, tax avoidance, not wanting to be caught up in a domestic scandal or the personal affairs of clients), Meghan was averse to the idea of calling in the police but there was a sense of unfinished business that held her back from disposing of the flowers entirely.

In the end, Celeste came up with a solution. There was a skip just outside the entrance to the backyard that was being used for the debris from some building work that Meghan was getting done in the flat above the shop to update the kitchen and the bathroom.

'Look there are too many flower arrangements to fit in the bins anyway. Keep the bags. I'll just carry out them out to the skip. It's going to be there for a few weeks. That way, (if you insist on being melodramatic about this), we won't be accused of "destroying the evidence" or anything like that, if the police come calling!' She put on a mock dramatic voice to show Meghan that she was being ironic. 'And also, if Mia turns up this afternoon asking for her flowers, we've still got them. She can help herself.' There was no doubt that she was being disingenuous now.

The next day was Friday so Celeste went into college for her regular digital design and marketing course. When Meghan unlocked the premises at just after six o'clock in the morning, she found an envelope lying on the doormat. It was a plain white A3 envelope with just one word written on it. 'Celeste.'

Meghan was burning with curiosity but resisted the urge to rip it open. She tried texting Celeste to let her know a missive had arrived for her, but the message wouldn't go through. Then she remembered that it was college policy to require students to switch off their phones during classes.

'I'll just have to wait until she gets here this afternoon,' Meghan muttered to herself crossly.

The minute Celeste stepped through the door that afternoon, Meghan handed her the envelope.

'This arrived for you overnight. It was posted through the door before I got here this morning – hand delivered – there's no stamp,' said Meghan.

Celeste turned the envelope over in her hand uncertainly.

'Well come on then, open it!' urged Meghan. 'It must be from Mia.'

'Let me get through the door, at least,' said Celeste.

She hung up her jacket and put her handbag on the shelf in the office. Meghan followed her in and stood by her side expectantly. Celeste unsealed the envelope and pulled the letter partly out so that only the opening few lines were visible.

'It's not from Mia,' she said. Meghan was hovering in anticipation of some revelation.

> *Hello,*
>
> *I'm in London for the next few days. Just got your deets from Jessi who also tells me you are now an award-winning florist. Many congratulations! Joe, Ed, and I and no doubt others are going to Surrey Grammar School old boys' drinks at the RAC Epsom early evening on 27th May. Why not come too? Deets on their website. It would be good to catch up... it's been almost seven years!*

Celeste couldn't help smiling at the word 'deets'. He must have been in touch with her mother. Still the same old 'try-hard' Harry exaggerating her minor achievements

– winning a couple of medals in a Surrey flower show! Even before she glanced at the signature, she could guess who it was from.

At that moment the bell above the door rang as a client entered the shop.

'I'll get it,' she said hastily, keen to get away from Meghan's questioning eyes. She stuffed the note into the front pocket of her Seventh Heaven apron and went through to the shop to serve.

'How can I help you?' she said, with a bright smile.

When she got back to the flat that evening Celeste tapped on Jessi's door.

'You didn't tell me Harry was in London,' she said. Jessi looked sheepish. 'Yes, I didn't want to upset you, stir things up, you know...'

Celeste shrugged. 'I've got to move on from that,' she said. 'Put the ghosts to rest.' There was a steely edge to her voice and a new intensity in her eyes. She walked into Jessi's room and sat on her bed.

'He's asked me to meet him,' she said.

'That's so exciting. You should go,' said Jessi. 'I heard he always had a bit of thing about you when we were at school... if Ben hadn't muscled in...'

'Let's look him up then.' Jessi's phone was on the bed. 'I've deleted my Facebook – you do it,' said Celeste throwing the phone across to Jessi.

Celeste looked over Jess's shoulder as she scrolled through Harry's Facebook feed. As Celeste was vaguely aware, Harry had been seconded to New York a couple of years previously to work for the US office of one of the UK investment banks. Being a fellow 'Englishman in New York' it seemed from his Facebook posts as if Harry and Ben hung out quite a bit together in the bars and the clubs around Tribeca and trendy eateries in Chelsea Market, Greenwich Village and SoHo.

'I thought they'd had a big falling out after...' Celeste couldn't bring herself to finish the sentence. 'After he was expelled, he told me he never wanted anything more to do with...' She couldn't bring herself to mention Ben's name either.

It felt like a betrayal to Celeste, seeing all those pictures on Harry's Facebook feed of the pair of them downing beers and propping up the bars of fashionable establishments in every corner of NYC. Harry was the one boy in Ben's macho gang who had broken ranks and been a good friend to Celeste when she had begun to re-emerge from the wreckage of her life wrought by the fire.

'Well, they're big buddies now,' said Jessi. 'I guess all the expats hang together. It's good to see a familiar face when you're far from home.' Jessi continued flicking through the feed at great pace until suddenly her finger stopped dead on one of the posts.

'Oh my God!' she squealed. 'Look at this.' Jessi tapped the screen.

The picture was of a group of guys, all looking the worse for wear, sitting round a table in a sleazy pole-dancing venue (judging by the glittery poles and podiums in the background). Harry and Ben were in the front of the shot – arms around each other's shoulders, flanked by a 'hostess' on each side, a big leery grin on Ben's face and a slightly pained look on Harry's.

Celeste read out the comments to the post Jessi was pointing at.

'#bestman'   '#bridegroomBen'   '#legend'   '@polecatslondon'

'So, Ben's getting married,' said Celeste slowly. 'This must be his stag night and Harry must be his best man.' She said the words out loud, mechanically and without betraying her emotions. But a different tag word for her old friend Harry seared inside her head, as if written with a red-hot poker:

'#traitor'

When Celeste stood up to leave Jessi's room, she was struck with a thought that drained the blood from her head, leaving her dizzy and faint.

'Oh my God! I've been such an idiot,' she said. 'I can't believe I didn't put two and two together. But now it all makes perfect horrible sense… What's the date on that post?'

'What are you talking about?' said Jessi while Celeste dropped back down onto the bed. 'Now you're not making any sense.'

'My American bride, Mia Madison – that poor girl, she got herself in such a state about the wedding flowers. Her fiancé seemed to exert so much emotional control over her. I think she was terrified of doing anything wrong. Now I feel almost certain that Ben Johnson is the man she was supposed to marry last week – at the Chelsea Register office. No one turned up to collect her flowers. I think maybe she finally worked up the courage to run away from him.'

'My God,' said Jessi. 'That's such a bizarre coincidence. How come you didn't make the connection before?'

'Mia never told me his name,' said Celeste, 'It didn't even cross my mind it could be him. Meghan was taking Mia's money "off balance sheet" so we didn't write anything up in the company books – that's partly why she got me to deal with it all so informally, writing up all the details in my notebooks instead of, as usual, in the Seventh Heaven Wedding Bookings Ledger.'

'When did you find out her fiancé was treating her badly?' said Jessi, eager to find out every detail.

'I've known that for weeks, though she refused point blank to reveal his identity and swore me to secrecy about what he was doing to her. Mia was always trying to make excuses for him,' said Celeste. 'She told me he was he was going through a period of stress at work and had problems with "anger management". She blamed herself for everything. But then the last time I saw her the other night, things had got even worse. It wasn't just coercive control. He was abusing her physically. I tried to persuade her to go to the police. She let me take pictures of her bruises but then she changed her mind and started back tracking. She said it was 'rough sex' that had got a bit rougher than she expected. She was still determined to go ahead with the wedding. I think she didn't want her family to know that her marriage was broken before it had even begun. They had been so against the relationship in the first place that she didn't want to prove them right. She still thought she could fix him. She was in love with him. She thought he would change... once the baby arrived... once they were married... He had promised to go to therapy for his anger issues and never to force her into rough sex again. The control that he exerted over her was so absolute that I think she had lost all agency and objectivity. She kept trying to rationalise his behaviour… just couldn't see that the way he was treating her was an outrage.'

Jessi was busy scrolling back through Ben's feed while she listened to Celeste.

Suddenly she stopped. It was a post, several months back, with a selfie photograph taken in New York from the top of the Empire State Building. The woman standing beside him was pretty and blonde.

Celeste looked at the screen.

'That's Mia Madison.'

Ben hadn't given her name in the post, only the hashtag:

#SheSaidYes

PAST

40

Perversely, just when she is most in need of support from her friends, Celeste's personal tragedy makes her a social pariah. Nobody wants to be tainted by it, nobody wants to be implicated in it, nobody knows what to say. They circle away and close ranks.

At school Celeste has no one she can turn to for comfort or support. Her so-called 'friends' feel awkward in her presence. They are all devastated and shocked into silence about what happened to Tom but on the topic of what happened in the boathouse, they all have something to say. They take sides. Of course, they pick Ben. He's more powerful than her. They 'slut-shame' her for the nudes – even the girls – who should know better. The online 'chats' are on fire with comments from both the boys and the girls. Instead of calling out Ben, they call out Celeste for the way she behaved at the party. 'She was drunk…' 'She was stoned…' 'She was bouncing off the walls…' 'She jumped on him...' 'She had her tits out all night...' (Yes, she was wearing a low-cut bodycon, but 'tits out'? Really?)

One girl ventures to use the term 'date rape' but only to minimise what happened in the woods. All the others close her down anyway. 'What did she expect when she went down to the boathouse...?' 'She took off his shirt...' 'She undid his belt...' 'She could have said no...' 'She was gagging for it...' (That's a direct quote from Ben.)

Everyone seems to have a better recollection of what happened in the boathouse than Celeste herself! They all seem to have forgotten that she is still in on the chats. It's only weeks later that she scrolls back and reads through the poison and then she deletes herself from them all.

Ben's parents put up a huge great solid wall in front of Ben to prevent him from any contact with Celeste. When he's not at school, he's grounded at home. They take away his phone and lock up the car keys. Ben's mum, Miranda, used to act like she was Celeste's surrogate mum, but Miranda hasn't offered her a word of condolence or sympathy since the fire. She blames Celeste for burning down her house.

When the police liaison officer gets involved, Miranda goes on the attack – a ferocious animal guarding her pup. She knows how to shape the narrative, just like Ben. She already found the nudes Celeste sent to Ben a week before the fire. She's in the habit of checking his phone. She also knows that within thirty minutes of receiving them, he forwarded every image to every member of the rugby team. Of course, Miranda keeps that information to herself. But she decides it's better to discredit Celeste before Stacey starts making accusations against her adored youngest son.

In a pre-emptive strike she discloses the images to the police officer and to the school. Three weeks after the fire, the headmaster calls a meeting. Celeste's mother is no match for Ben's mother. A broken heart and alcohol and opioids have addled Stacey's brain.

'Sexting' is still in its infancy (provoking shock waves in the school community – not partially normalised as it is today). The headmaster is all condescension and benevolence. Celeste's transgressions would in any normal situation have led to her expulsion from the school, he explains, but given the tragic circumstances, he is prepared to exercise his discretion to modify the school policy in this case. In his wisdom, the headmaster pronounces that it would be in the best interests of Celeste and of all concerned if she is 'voluntarily suspended' from the school for the remainder of the summer term on compassionate leave.

What hope is there for Celeste to challenge Ben's abusive behaviour towards her, when she has been hung out to dry even among the adults as a sexual deviant who distributed teenage porn, got paralytically drunk and threw herself at Ben at the party? 'He's an eighteen-year-old boy, not a monk!' 'She was asking for it!' say Celeste's grown-up detractors. 'He was just being a lad.' 'That's what happens at parties.' The language is (marginally) more measured but the message is the same.

The fact that Ben's father is a school governor and one of the biggest charitable donors to the school fundraising project for a new science block probably goes some way to explaining why Ben gets off scot-free.

Eventually word gets out that one of the boys circulated the nudes. Of course, Ben denies that it was him. Miranda has already taken care to delete all the evidence from his mobile phone. All the students know from their relationship and sex education lessons that Ben is the guilty party who should be disciplined or reported to the police: Celeste has not committed a criminal offence in sending him intimate images of herself whereas he has committed a criminal offence in sharing them with his mates without her consent. Ben knows this too. Ben needs a fall guy, so Ben blames Harry. The headmaster wants to rebuild the reputation of the school. Harry wants an easy life. The headmaster calls another meeting and Harry gets expelled.

PRESENT

41

*L*ondon is like a ghost town without You.

I think You must have gone away for the weekend because your curtains are shut when I ride by at lunchtime on Saturday and still shut when I do a second tour at 5pm in the afternoon – and You didn't go to work at Seventh Heaven – I checked.

To be honest, when I come by the second time, what I feel is mainly relief because then I feel confident it's not a long night of passion that has kept You between the sheets – I don't believe You'd be debauched enough to spend the whole day in bed with a new lover.

The person I have in mind when I say 'new lover' is that creep who put the letter through the door at Seventh Heaven. From my usual vantage point across the street the other day, I watched when he delivered it and then later I watched when You opened it, and I didn't appreciate the way your face lit up as you read his letter. You made a show of indifference for the manager's benefit, but I could tell that *was a mask. You were engaged – engaged and excited. It was obvious – even through the medium of a long-distance lens.*

Anyway, my mind is put to rest when, thanks to my Spyware, I see You get a text message from 'Stacey Mum' at 17.07 saying:

'Please buy low cal tonic water and bag of ice from the co-op. will give you cash when you get back and pay for your diet cokes too. c u xx'

I can live with the idea of You spending a night or two in the country at your family home. Out there, I guess you're safe from other men. In fact, I could use some time off. Where do You get the energy from – running around all day long? It's exhausting watching over You.

Examining the lining of your curtains night after night has given me a good idea – so good that I can't understand why I never thought of it before. Maybe because your bedroom is on the second floor, You never bother to close your curtains fully. There's always a gap of five or six inches or more where they should meet in the middle. I'm going to spend the rest of my weekend researching for a purchase that is long overdue – a piece of kit that will make my life a whole lot easier.

I'm too big to be climbing trees. I'll get myself arrested, falling out of branches in the middle of the night. No. I've had enough of that. I'm going to buy me a drone.

Celeste had asked Meghan for the Saturday off because her mother had finally decided to 'get her shit together' (her mother's words) and move in with 'The Boyfriend', selling up the house where she had lived with Celeste and Tom after the divorce. Estate agents were coming in the following week to value the place before it was put on the market. Although it was a decent little semi-detached property on one of the village estates, the place was an absolute pigsty as Stacey was a slovenly layabout whose day started and ended with an alcoholic drink and a fag. Celeste had cautioned her mother against the move because she knew that her loser of a partner was not a nice guy and had knocked her around on more than one occasion after his bouts of drinking. But Stacey had made up her mind. There was no talking her out of it.

For her own part, Celeste had mixed feelings. On the one hand, the house had never felt like home and was steeped in sadness and heartache. On the other hand, it was the place where she felt the strongest connection with Tom.

Tom's room was the only room in the house that had escaped the ravages of Stacey's domestic incompetence. Her mother kept it like a shrine. Not a fragment of his clothing, or a piece of his Lego had been removed. Celeste would never forget the night about a year after the tragedy when she had slept in Tom's bed while two of her girlfriends used her own bed for a sleepover. Stacey had been so angry (and distraught) when she bumped into Celeste coming out of Tom's bedroom on her way to the bathroom in the middle of the night, that she had almost smashed the glass of gin she was taking up to her own bedroom for a nightcap, over Celeste's head.

But Celeste shared her mother's reverence for the room. On the rare occasions when Celeste went to visit, she would open the door to Tom's bedroom and stand in the doorway, holding very still. For a second or two she could lose herself in the sensory throwback to her childhood and imagine that he was still alive and would come bounding up the stairs any second.

Celeste was absolutely determined that 'The Loser' would not be allowed to play any part in dismantling Tom's room. She didn't want Tom's treasured books and toys being desecrated by that man putting his hands all over them and stuffing them into charity bags. She would take care of going through and sorting out Tom's things as well as packing up her own few childhood remnants that were locked in a cupboard in the faded 'guestroom' that had been her bedroom.

Anya had reluctantly lent Celeste her Mini Coupé for the weekend task ahead and despite the emotional baggage she carried on her journey, Celeste was happy to be driving out of London, with the sun in her eyes and the wind in her hair, into the green Surrey countryside. Thank God, for once Stacey was sober when Celeste arrived early on the Saturday morning. Driving the last few miles of the trip along the country lanes had unleashed a wave of homesickness that could not be assuaged by stepping across the threshold into her old family home. Celeste hugged her mother and breathed in that familiar mix, at once comforting and repellent, of cigarettes and Chanel No 5 that was her mother's signature scent.

They sat in the kitchen for a coffee and Stacey asked Celeste how work was going and regaled her with snippets of village gossip about which her daughter had no interest, concerning people whose names and faces she could not recollect.

It was safer to keep to these trivial topics of conversation, as any deeper level of interaction led inevitably to confrontation and distress. Their mother-and-daughter relationship was now forever intimately bound up with the trauma of losing Tom and the blame and recrimination that went with that, which could never be resolved or healed. Stacey could never forgive Celeste for having taken Tom to the party and everything that followed. Celeste could never forgive Stacey for all those years of neglect and for all her failings, past and present, as a mother.

Celeste finished her coffee and left her mug by the sink. She would have rinsed it out, but the sink was already full of dirty dishes and burnt pans.

'Right, let's get to it!' she said, to herself, more than to her mother. 'If you make a start in the kitchen, I'll take care of Tom's room and then I'll clear out my old bedroom as well.'

Celeste knew that although her mother would never admit it, she would be thankful that she was being spared the task of going through Tom's things. Beneath the hard exterior, Stacey was so fractured and fragile that any renewed trauma could smash her into pieces.

Celeste walked up the stairs, registering the sensations of the rough bannister against her palm and the creaking of the seventh step, which were ingrained in her sensory memory.

She paused outside Tom's door and took a deep breath.

His bedroom remained unchanged.

Celeste lay down on his pale blue duvet cover (that she knew her mother religiously washed and ironed and replaced once a week) and looked up at the vintage airplane mobile hanging from the ceiling. She was always the one who would turn out the light and kiss him goodnight. This view of Tom's airplane mobile sent her reeling into a time warp. The mobile had travelled with them, originally installed above his cot and then his first bed at their old family home. All at once, she was back there, lying next to her little brother under the covers, cuddling him to sleep or singing nursery rhymes to drown out her mother and father screaming and shouting at each other down in the hallway.

It was always Celeste that he would cry out for if he woke up in the night afraid of the dark.

'This won't do,' said Celeste out loud. She got up and went over to the bookcase. It was as good a place to start as any. Even though he hadn't been a big reader himself, somehow, she seemed to feel Tom's presence most closely in his books, perhaps because she was the one who always read him his bedtime stories when he was little. She pulled one of her favourites off the shelf. It was a picture book version of *The Wizard of Oz*. The book was smudged with her own writing on the inside cover.

'*Dear ToTo*, (that was her pet name for him then)
Happy 4th Birthday
Lots of love from your
Big Sis Celeste'

She reflected that she would have been about ten years old when she gave that picture book to Tom. She'd read the original version of the classic children's tale, which she had borrowed from the school library after a rare family outing to London to see the musical *Wicked*, which she had fallen in love with. She leafed through the pages of the dog-eared picture book, relishing the vivid illustrations that had so captivated Tom's attention as a young boy.

There's no way this book is going to a charity shop, she thought defiantly. She wrapped it carefully in Tom's pale blue pillowcase and put it in her shoulder bag.

By lunchtime Celeste had been through most of Tom's room. There was very little she could bring herself to give away to charity – some of the old puzzles and games that he'd never been interested in and a few of the soft toys that he'd grown out of long before he died. But certainly not Toto – a small fluffy brown toy dog named after Dorothy's dog in *The Wonderful Wizard of Oz* (and the source of Celeste's nickname for Tom). Toto had been Tom's Christmas present from Celeste that same year.

Toto joined the picture book in her shoulder bag. They would both be finding a new home on her bedside table. She packed up another box with Tom's Nintendo, his football and his prized Chelsea shirt. That was destined for her flat too – even if it sat in the back of a cupboard. She wanted to keep his favoured possessions close to her. Most of Tom's other baby toys, along with his bedding and his clothes, she packed into plastic storage boxes. Stacey had hired a storage unit. That way Celeste's mother could defer the painful time when she would have to dispose of his stuff altogether.

It was around lunchtime by the time Celeste was loading the boxes from Tom's room into the Mini. At the end of the day there was not much to salvage from his short life. The boxes didn't even fill the boot. In contrast, Celeste's heart was full to bursting. Although the task had not been physically arduous, she felt emotionally exhausted.

Washed by a few late spring showers the sky was now a Photoshop blue and the air so beautifully clear you could cut it with a knife – every outline was sharp, and every plant and tree perfectly in focus. Celeste decided to allow herself a lunch break out in the garden. There wasn't much food in the house to make lunch, which came as no surprise, since Stacey had never been one to keep her cupboards well stocked or to put a meal on the table for her children when they came home from school. It had often been Celeste who would scavenge for food in the kitchen of an evening and put together a meal for herself and Tom from the past-their-sell-by-date packages and tins that she found in amongst her mother's stash of vodka and gin.

Celeste found a Diet Coke, an apple and a sachet of peanuts and headed out to the garden to sit under the apple tree. When they first moved in after the divorce, Stacey, who had undergone a brief resurgence of her interest in gardening, had got both the children involved in choosing and planting a young apple tree. Celeste had understood at the time that there was something symbolic about this action – the three of them were embarking on a new life together. The mythology of Adam and Eve, the tree of life and the knowledge of good and evil had perhaps been lost on her, but she had grasped something of the significance that it held for her mother.

The white apple blossoms were gone but still it was relaxing sitting with her back against the rough bark of the trunk, looking up at the fresh greens of the young leaves. This spot in the garden had been a place of refuge on summer days for her and Tom to get away from their mother's drinking and to look up to the sky. She watched the cool breeze swaying the slender new branches on the tree. Before, she was like a new branch on a tree, flexible and bending, she reflected. Now she was like a dry old twig, rendered tough and brittle by the storms of life, which would not bend in the breeze – flex it too far and it would snap.

She would have loved to dig up this tree and take it with her. But unlike her, it had put down its roots in this place, finding sustenance in the black soil. It could not be wrenched away. Where she sat, she was also surrounded by the dying foliage of the daffodils she had planted with Tom's 'help' the autumn that they had moved into their new 'home' after the divorce. Celeste's interest in growing flowers had flourished even after Stacey's enthusiasm for the new garden had waned. Now in early summer all the yellow blooms were gone and the leaves had turned brown and crinkled. Celeste knew from her horticultural training that after the narcissi had flowered and the foliage had died down was the perfect time to dig the bulbs and store them, ready for replanting in the autumn.

She went back to the house and shouted upstairs to Stacey who was banging around in her bedroom pulling open drawers and slamming cupboard doors.

'Do you still have that old garden fork? I want to dig up some of the bulbs to take away with me.'

'I haven't used it for years,' she shouted back. 'Look in the garage.'

She found the garden fork (the handle was loose and one of its prongs was bent but it would do the job) and an old hessian sack in a corner of the garage. It was better than any mindfulness exercise from a self-help manual – the physical effort of driving the steel prongs into the turf (she was pleased at the ease with which she could do this, now that her body was toned and strengthened by her regime of running and exercise), followed by the tactile pleasure of gently shaking loose the soil from the newly dug bulbs.

When the sack was full, she felt a quiet satisfaction. She would store the bulbs in a cool place until the autumn. Then she would plant most of them around Tom's grave. The remainder she would keep for herself to fill the window boxes she had installed outside her bedroom window at the flat.

In the springtime she would wake every morning to a blaze of golden daffodils, and she would know that the ground above where Tom was sleeping was crowned with a blaze of golden daffodils too.

PAST

42

In the weeks and months following the fire, Celeste runs through the events of that night again and again in her head. Her memories spool like a psychedelic horror film. But there are blanks in the sequence. She can remember nothing from the moment when she was dancing with Ben in his cavernous drawing room (the music is pounding, the lights are flashing, and she is spinning, and all around her everyone is spinning except for Ben who holds her up in his arms). Nothing, nothing until the time when she is in the boathouse with him on top of her, his pelvis grinding her to the ground – that instant when, her head reeling and stars falling from the sky, and sparks flying in the air, she smells the smoke from the fire, and senses that something is dreadfully wrong, and screams out in panic: 'Stop, stop, get off me.'

The time in between those two moments is a strip of empty black frames. So, Ben fills in the blanks, first for her, and then for his family, and for Celeste's mother, and their friends, and later for the coroner, and for the local press, and for everyone else at the inquest.

'She was very drunk,' he tells them all at the inquest. 'She brought along one of her mother's bottles of vodka. She drank most of it herself. She was drunk before she even got to the party... knocking it back as I drove her to my house.' He speaks of his recollection of dancing with her, and of her being so drunk that he had physically to hold her up to stop her falling over. 'God knows what other shit she took,' he says. 'She was bouncing off the walls.' In two minutes of evidence, he utters the word 'drunk' eleven times. Celeste is keeping count, her head bent low.

Then she looks as if she's going to be sick, he says. So, he helps her upstairs to the bathroom. The bathroom is occupied so he waits with her in the corridor outside the bathroom door. Was he smoking? No, he wasn't smoking. He was in training for rugby. He never smoked. Was she smoking? Yes, he thinks she was smoking a cigarette. She doesn't usually smoke. Only when she's drunk. What happened to the cigarette? He doesn't know. It's true, he can't remember. He says that while they stood outside the bathroom door, she asked him for a joint. He recalls rolling the joint and handing it over. Beyond that, he says he can't say. He starts to cry. A little boy in a grown man's body.

When pressed by the coroner he says that Celeste must have dropped the lighted joint in the upstairs corridor before he led her down the steps to the back door 'for some fresh air'.

Ben pauses as the coroner writes a note on the file, his scratchy nib audible throughout the silent courtroom.

When asked why his bedroom door was locked, Ben tells

the inquest that Celeste was worried that Tom would go downstairs to join the party – because Tom was only eleven years old, he says and, despite Ben's 'best efforts' his mates had smuggled in alcohol and drugs. 'Celeste didn't want him going down and drinking shots and sharing joints with the older kids,' he says. 'She insisted on locking the door.' He leans on the word 'insisted'. Her mother would go nuts if she brought him back drunk, he says, unconscious of the irony. 'Double standards!' he says. He gives an awkward, complicit grimace.

In her anguish, Celeste begins to doubt her sanity. She rakes through the ashes of her memories. She cannot imagine what could have possessed her to lock her little brother into Ben's bedroom? Given the anger and disgust she had felt towards her father for locking *her* in to her old bedroom at their former family home only the week before Ben's party, she finds it hard to comprehend why she would have done the same thing to Tom, even if she was 'off her head' at the time, as Ben told everyone. Why would she do that?

Celeste is called upon to give evidence at the inquest too. She is still in a state of numbness and shock. She speaks very quietly and like an automaton. In her evidence she testifies that she can't remember much of the events at the party leading up to the fire. She is questioned about how much vodka she'd drunk and if she'd been under the influence of drugs and whether she'd smoked weed.

Her account is vague and unconvincing. But where she can't remember the details, Ben's detailed testimony fills the gaps, completing the narrative. Unlike Celeste, his recollection seems remarkably clear. He has told her so many times about how she took the key from inside his door and locked it from the outside because she thought her little brother would be safer away from the older kids at the party, that now he is word-perfect. He describes the scene in the corridor to her so vividly that sometimes she wonders whether he may have created the memory in her head of her turning the key, and locking Tom in. The line between her imagination and memory has become blurred.

'Why do you have to keep repeating this to me again and again?' she wants to say. But instead, she says, 'I wish I were dead.'

At the inquest, fire investigators testify that since Ben's room is immediately opposite the top of the spiral staircase, and the forensic evidence shows that the fire started and took hold further along the corridor away from the top of the stairs, then if the door had not been locked, Tom would in all probability have had time to escape down the spiral staircase and out of the back door to the lawns. Celeste already knows this but to hear it confirmed by the experts twists her soul. The fire investigators hold up drawings and plans, complete with pin diagrams representing Tom, to illustrate their hypothesis. She is tortured by guilt and remorse.

And then there is the fire investigators' testimony concerning the cause of the fire, which seems to confirm Ben's story. The spark for the blaze that engulfed the upper floor of the barn does not appear to have been caused by defective wiring or any other electrical fault, say the experts. The fire's most likely cause is a discarded cigarette or match dropped by one of the partygoers. These expert findings are a further brutal blow.

The testimony of the firefighters is the most painful to hear. They confirm that Tom died in the ambulance on the way to the hospital at 02.48 as a result of smoke inhalation while trapped inside Ben's bedroom. The firefighters discovered him still alive, but unconscious, barely breathing. When they gained access by breaking down the locked door of Ben's room with a pry axe, they found Tom's unconscious body slumped on the floor on the other side. In a tragic twist of fate, the bedroom windows had recently been fitted with security locks following a spate of burglaries in the neighbourhood. Tom was a prisoner in the room.

Celeste's memories of what happened outside the bathroom door remain fragmentary and confused. But Ben's testimony leaves no room for doubt in her mind or the minds of all the others sitting in the courtroom, that it was her drunken carelessness that started the fire.

Stacey sits through all the harrowing testimony. Miraculously, she stops drinking for the duration of the inquest and is there every single day with notebook and pen, writing down each incriminating detail of the night. Ben is a convincing witness – he demonstrates ample contrition for his own stupidity. And he appears to have a lucid recollection of the details. He is a good performer. He is persuasive. *The same cannot be said for my daughter*, thinks Stacey.

There were police enquiries in the immediate aftermath of the fire. All the partygoers were interviewed and both Celeste and Ben were questioned intensively. The phrase 'involuntary manslaughter' was mentioned on more than one occasion. But the police decided not to pursue any prosecutions – perhaps in part out of compassion for

Celeste – who was so deeply and personally involved in the tragedy and so devastatingly affected by it. This inquest is not supposed to be about attributing judgement and blame but by the end of the process it is engraved on the hearts of both Stacey and her teenage daughter: Celeste is the guilty party. She killed her little brother. For that she will never in a million years forgive herself and neither will her mother.

Instead of providing any kind of resolution, the inquest simply serves to fan the flames of Celeste's despair.

PRESENT

43

That night outside B Johnson's flat, I fled the scene, but I didn't go far. I waited around the corner on the Kings Road and minutes later I watched two fire engines pulling into the square. All the residents of the flats had evacuated the building and were gathered on the lawn. I couldn't believe my eyes. Mia was there with him, sitting on a bench. She was crying. She sat huddled over, wrapped in a blanket, hanging her head. It was obvious to me that she was in severe pain and distress. She should have been sitting in an ambulance – that was my intention in setting off the fire alarm.

He sat very close to her supporting her in his arms looking for all the world like a solicitous husband concerned for the welfare of his pregnant partner. His performance was astonishing. The other residents give him little approving glances. Little did they know…

★

Celeste slept light that night. She had left her bedroom window wide open and woke to the sound of bells drifting on the air across the fields from the parish church on the village green.

There must be a christening today, she thought. No doubt, the bell-ringers were having a run-through in advance of the service later that morning, when they would ring again to herald the joyful ceremony. She knew the sound of those bells so well and they conjured up the world of her childhood. She noticed how the particular timbre of each bell was unique with its characteristic hues and tones. Those evocative chimes from the parish church were like voices calling to her from the past.

Celeste jumped out of bed with a new determination to get on with the task in hand. First, she would go for a run. She had made sure to pack her new black trainers and her running kit and was looking forward to a circular run along the public footpaths that criss-crossed the Surrey countryside linking one village settlement to another. It was unusual for her to feel this positive when she was at home and she wondered why. And then it occurred to her. This new sense of freedom had come about because for once she felt sure that she wasn't being watched. She didn't have to be on her guard. She didn't have to worry about going out running alone. The fact of having driven out of London in Anya's car gave her a sense of security that she hadn't been followed. Her stalker would not have been looking out for a Mini Coupé.

Celeste's escape to the countryside wasn't the only thing that was liberating. There was also the expectation that within a few months the house that had been the stage-set for so much tragedy would be sold, bringing down the curtain on that grim part of her life for the last time. This knowledge that it was all coming to an end motivated her to create some good memories of her last visit here so that she could in future look back in a more positive light. Perversely, it was only now that she could appreciate that her mother had tried to make this place a home – and that their life here as a threesome had not been all bad.

After digging up the bulbs the day before, Celeste had spent the rest of the afternoon helping out her mother because it was obvious that Stacey would never get the house cleared without someone giving her a hand. Unexpectedly, working together on this shared task had been the best 'relationship therapy' they had undergone since the fateful party, and for the first time in several years Celeste had felt close to her. As they filled rubbish bags and storage boxes, Stacey spoke candidly at last. Her mother had acknowledged and was trying to control her addictions, attending self-help groups and the like. Moreover, it seemed that the prospect of selling the house, if not giving her closure (which she did not seek or aspire to) had at least given her the resolve to move on with her life.

When they had finished in the sitting room (which Stacey had been using as her dumping ground for old newspapers and magazines, stacks of CDs, videos and DVDs, all her unopened mail and filing, and lots of other junk), Celeste had persuaded her mother to go out for a walk.

'It's such a beautiful evening,' she said. 'It's criminal to stay stuck inside. We've done enough for today.'

Celeste had suggested one of her old favourites (the same circuit that she intended to run on the Sunday morning), a pretty walk that looped between two picture-postcard villages, skirting riverbeds and winding through ancient woodlands whose undergrowth was carpeted with bluebells, before opening onto a hillside overlooking the vast sweeping curve of the river in the valley below. They had stopped at a country pub for their supper. Celeste had installed her mother at a table in the pub garden (to keep her away from the bar) and gone inside to order traditional pub fare of beer battered cod and homemade chips for them both. Celeste hadn't eaten this dish for years – but she remembered having it the one time they went out as a family for a pub lunch on her father's birthday.

'I got us each a Diet Coke,' Celeste had said pointedly as she plonked the drinks on to the table. 'We should do this more often... It's nice getting out of London. I'd forgotten how much I miss being in the countryside. I can breathe...'

After the walk, Celeste had thought about offering to drive her mother across to Shearham village church to visit Tom's grave. (Stacey was on a two-year driving ban for drink driving.) But in the end, she decided against it and said nothing. Their relationship was not sufficiently robust. Though seven years had passed, the trauma and pain associated with Tom's death was still too toxic and raw for that kind of intimacy.

Over breakfast on the Sunday morning, things were getting back to 'normal', and not in a good way. Celeste had come back from her early morning run feeling energised and refreshed but already the tension was beginning to rise. It didn't help that Stacey had shouted at Celeste to show some respect and leave your muddy trainers outside', before she had even stepped through the door, which was ironic since the floor looked as if it hadn't been washed in weeks!

'It would nice if you could at least say "good morning" before you started having a go at me!' Celeste shot back. She was carrying a small bunch of wildflowers she had picked along the hedgerows on her 'cool-down' back to the house. She walked over to the sink and filled an empty jam jar with water for the flowers.

Celeste had noticed that they could just about tolerate each other when they were out of the house on neutral territory but when they were back on home turf, they were conditioned to start bitching at each other like Pavlov's dogs. Being jointly engaged on the packing up yesterday had been a bonding experience but they could only maintain the peace for so long. The only way they could avoid fighting was by keeping interactions to a minimum.

'I need to get off to London soon,' said Celeste. 'Anya will be wanting her car back. I think she was planning to use it this afternoon.' The fresh breath of freedom she had experienced briefly out in the countryside was extinguished and the feeling of claustrophobia associated with the family home was closing in. She had to get away.

'I was hoping you would help me drive the boxes over to Mike's house,' said Stacey. 'And I thought we could look in at the cemetery after that. It doesn't seem right with you running that headstones business and visiting all those strangers' graves, not going to visit your own brother's grave.' Her mother looked angry.

'Stop trying to guilt-trip me,' Celeste snapped back. 'It's the least Mike can do to come over and shift the boxes for you. I don't see why I should break my back helping you with that.' Celeste clattered around the kitchen putting the dirty dishes that Stacey had left out the previous night into the dishwasher. 'And I'm going to pop into St Peter's on my way back to London – it's on the route home.' She nodded towards the sink. 'The flowers are for Tom. I'm sorry but you can go anytime. We don't need to do that together.' Her mother's face fell, and Celeste knew that she was being cruel. Stacey's suggestion of visiting Tom's grave together was perhaps her own clumsy way of trying to signal her willingness to forgive Celeste at last for her part in the tragic loss of her son.

While Stacey sipped a black coffee, Celeste finished stacking the dishwasher. Then she wiped the table, scoured the pans and rinsed out the sink. She'd had enough of acting like her mother's scullery maid.

'OK. I'm going upstairs for a shower before I clear out my room. Then I'll be off,' she said. 'I need to get back to London.' Stacey tried to persuade her to stay another night and drive back to London on the Monday morning. 'I'll be out for lunch,' she said. 'So, you can relax at home. Then this evening we could get a take-away and watch a movie. Just the two of us. For old times' sake.'

Celeste wondered what 'old times' her mother was imagining. That wasn't the way she remembered their evenings together. But she didn't challenge that. Nevertheless, her mind was made up.

'Sorry, Mum, I have to get back. One of my friends is in

hospital. She's had some complications with her pregnancy.' She was deliberately vague. 'I want to go and visit her this evening.'

Back in the guestroom, Celeste stripped the sheets and piled them up at the end of the bed. Then she turned to the wardrobe. It contained all the things that Celeste had left behind in her room when she moved into the flat in London. Stacey had unceremoniously stuffed them into the wardrobe and with that 'Celeste's bedroom' had become 'the guestroom' (though, God knows, Celeste doubted that Stacey ever had any guests to stay).

Out of sight, out of mind, thought Celeste. Back then, it seemed the main purpose of the 'rebranding' exercise had been to hide away anything that reminded Stacey of her daughter whom she blamed for Tom's death. For more than a year, Stacey had scarcely been able to look at her.

Stacey had tied the handles of wardrobe doors together with a length of rope to prevent them from swinging open under the weight of the things she had piled inside. When she touched the rope, Celeste remembered she had cut it from the broken garden swing. Her sensory memory of the feel of that prickly rope on the palm of her hands was so strong. The rope was tough and so tightly knotted that Celeste had to go down to the kitchen again in search of a sharp knife to cut it free. She was adept at using knives and other blades for her floristry work, so slicing through the fibrous rope was an easy task for her. As she did so, the doors swung open and all her stuff fell out onto the carpet.

'What a pile of old junk,' she said to herself as she spread it out on the floor. 'I can't believe I used to be so attached to all this old rubbish.'

It was far easier and quicker than dealing with Tom's things. The emotional connection had gone. She hated all these old clothes and ridiculous platform shoes and bits of trinket jewellery and dried-up make-up that reminded her of a miserable episode of her youth. There was no point trying to recycle any of it. She didn't want any of these despised possessions to have a new lease of life. She shoved almost all her stuff into the black trash bags – it would go into landfill, better still to an incinerator. She felt bad for the environment, but more important to her, was to get rid of it once and for all.

There were a few things she couldn't throw away, some old diaries and letters and photograph albums and school certificates and the like. She hadn't time to sort through them all now, but they formed part of her identity and she would keep them. She leafed through the pages of a photograph album that she had put together a year after the party displaying random family photographs that her parents had taken sporadically when she and Tom were little. The pictures were shot on an old camera owned by her father, which used photographic film. There were so few images compared to the multitude of photographs people now took with the advent of digital photography.

I guess every image cost money in those days, thought Celeste. *So they took care to compose every shot. Every photograph had to count.* But she reflected that although there were fewer of them, these photographs were perhaps more permanent than the hundreds of pictures taken by her generation in the digital age, since they were preserved on paper. How many of all those shots posted on Facebook and Instagram feeds would survive when the technology moved on? They would disappear into virtual cyberspace when the technology on which they were stored became obsolete.

Celeste squinted at the blurry images that had been stuck in the album. Some of them were of her and Tom – here she was pushing Tom on the swing, then the two of them licking ice creams, and another of them both jumping into the paddling pool.

'It wasn't all bad,' said Celeste out loud. '*She* wasn't all bad.' With maturity and distance, Celeste now understood that Stacey had tried to make their childhood happy – it was the alcoholism that had overwhelmed her and made her unable to cope.

She put the album carefully to one side and opened one of the exercise books that she had used for her diaries. On the front cover she had written, 'January to June 2009'. She would have been fifteen at the time. She opened the diary on a random page and read a few lines. How predictable, she thought, her teenage self was lamenting something about Ben.

Ben blanked me today. Made me cry. He was sitting next to Kate at lunch.
They walked out together laughing about some private joke. He stared right through me as I passed them in the corridor.
He's such a dick. Ali says I should forget about him.
Easier said than done.

She couldn't bear to read any more. It was all in the same vein. That boy had hammered her self-esteem throughout her formative years. She had been like one of those ever-hopeful, ever-grateful strays in search of a master and the occasional pat on the head. He had been the master – one minute throwing her scraps, the next minute kicking her out of the way.

She threw all the notebooks and papers into a cardboard box. Those would definitely be going in the back of a cupboard. They were part of her history, so she felt she had to keep them. But that didn't mean she had to look at them.

Her old wardrobe in the 'guestroom' was tall and deep. She got a chair to scoop everything out from the back and the corners of the top shelf. She leaned into the furthest corner to grab a red plastic bag containing something soft and squidgy. For some reason, this bag evoked a bad vibe and the ghost of a memory even though she couldn't remember what it contained. She jumped off the chair and looked inside. It was all coming back to her now. She lifted out the black leather jacket and put it up to her face. She wasn't imagining it. The slightly rancid smell of leather mingled with something else. Yes, it was there. After all these years she could still detect the smell of smoke. She kneaded the leather abstractedly in her hands, breathing in the familiar scent.

As her sensory memory conjured images of the night, a kind of horror and fascination took hold of her. She buried her face deeper into the folds of the jacket and breathed deeply. Just out of her reach, like something submerged in briny black water, she could sense the shape of her memories reforming. The mental effort of trying to touch those memories made her head throb.

Gradually she became conscious of another scent, just

a trace, lingering in the inner lining of the jacket, coming back to haunt her after all these years. It was the smell of Ben's aftershave cologne – Eau Sauvage (a present from his adoring mum for his seventeenth birthday). After he read somewhere that Eau Sauvage contained the chemical compound called hedione, which stimulates an area of the brain responsible for the release of sex hormones in females, he wore it religiously every day. He used to spray it so liberally – thought it made him so cool and seductive – and one up on the other boys who were still dousing themselves in Lynx Africa body spray. She tossed the jacket on to the bed in disgust.

Ben's jacket. She spread it out on the bed. Aside the smell, it was a quality item in soft Italian leather and still in pretty good condition – charity shop or trash? She was about to stuff it into a black bin bag when she noticed the name written in marker pen on the inside of the collar. The letters were faded but still legible.

Harry S

So, it wasn't Ben's jacket. It was Harry's. How on earth did Harry's leather jacket come to be stuffed in the back of her cupboard?

As Celeste cast her mind back, she remembered Ben wearing Harry's black leather jacket on a number of occasions. In fact, she had a picture in her head of him sporting it (along with tight jeans and slicked-back hair to complete the 'Saturday Night Fever' image), when he came to pick her up from her house in his Dad's MG on the night of the party. She'd made some lame joke about John Travolta, which hadn't gone down well.

'He fancied himself in it, of course,' mused Celeste. 'That's why he was always commandeering it from Harry.' He wore it so often that everyone assumed it was his. The girls had picked up on his vanity and sniggered about it, behind his back. They called it his 'pulling jacket', but perhaps that was why Celeste had been secretly flattered to see him wearing it when he knocked on her door!

'I guess I should give this back to Harry,' she said out loud. 'Though what would he care after all these years?' she thought bitterly.

Her fingers shook, as she went through the pockets, fearful yet morbidly fascinated to see what she might find. She searched the jacket methodically. She started with the breast pocket. This contained an old five-pound note, a few mouldy coins, two folded Rizla papers of the kind used for rolling cigarettes, three unopened condoms in their individual foil wrappers (*He was hopeful...* thought Celeste), as well as two empty ripped foil condom wrappings (*Two?* thought Celeste. *So maybe I wasn't his first conquest that night at the party?*).

Ben was so morally bankrupt in her eyes that these findings came as no surprise. Burning with curiosity, she unfolded the two Rizla papers, which she could see each had a few words written on them in black biro. The first read, 'the most boring girl,' and the second, 'the biggest slag.' She should have been horrified at the appalling sexism these small rectangles of paper revealed but she had known those boys too well to be shocked. She didn't need to be a detective to work out that the scribbled words related to some 'macho' challenge or contest they had set up among themselves all those years ago.

Next, she moved on to the side pockets. The left-hand pocket contained an empty plastic pouch (of the kind used to carry tobacco and weed), a carton of Rizla rolling papers and a small crushed matchbox. Celeste stood staring long and hard at these items that she'd laid out on the bed. She knew they told a story, and it wasn't the story that Ben had told at the inquest. She slid open the matchbox. There were only seven matches left. As if in a trance, she struck a match. She watched it flare and burn before her eyes until the flame scorched her fingers and she cried out in pain before hurriedly blowing it out. He had testified at the inquest that he wasn't smoking that night, that he never smoked. She had suspected it before but now she was more certain than ever. He had lied – at the very least, he had distorted the evidence. She had been painted as the villain, the person who carelessly dropped her cigarette and started the fire in the corridor outside Ben's room. But the contents of this pocket suggested something very different.

She cast her mind back to that moment in the corridor. The sensory familiarity of the leather and the aftershave and the smoke from the match seemed to work as a trigger, stirring her memories. As she sat with her eyes closed and her hands gripping the jacket, something began to emerge phoenix-like from the ashes of the night – fitting another, alternative narrative.

Were these real memories beginning to re-emerge or created memories? She couldn't be sure. She knew that Ben's parents imposed an absolute ban on smoking inside their house since it was a wooden barn. But Ben wasn't one to obey orders. In her mind's eye she could see Ben's hands, expertly rolling her a joint. He was good with his fingers – at least when it came to experimenting with recreational drugs! (His clumsy fingers when it came to experimental teenage sex had been something else...) She had been enthralled and aroused, watching him do it that night. It was the first time she had seen someone rolling a joint. And now she remembered him striking a match and lighting the joint before putting it up to her lips and saying, 'Try it. Breathe in deep. It's good. You'll like it.' The memory was so intense, she could feel the touch of his fingertips on her lips.

She had done as he said, breathing the acrid smoke deep into her lungs, and passed it back to his mouth, and so it had gone on, exchanging the joint, and it was good, and this had seemed like the most decadent and reckless and sensuous thing she had ever done in her entire life... until at last, unable to contain himself any longer, Ben had ripped the joint away from her lips and flung it to the floor to give her the most erotic kiss (was she imagining that or was it a true memory?) she had ever experienced.

All the romantic stuff was irrelevant. There was only one thing that mattered. She sat with her head bowed and her eyes screwed shut as a sweet, growing conviction gradually flowed through her body, releasing the tension and filling her with peace. It was like the feeling she had occasionally heard people describe in church when witnessing their conversion to the faith. She was convinced that the vivid images she could see in her head (as if from only yesterday) were real. These were not half-remembered scenes from some second-rate teenage rom-com. These were not figments of her imagination. These were recovered memories that had lain buried for years in the mire of her trauma and shame. But now, at last, she knew the truth:

It wasn't her who started the fire. It was him.

PAST

44

It's not until four years after the fire that Celeste refers herself for therapy. It's her twenty-first birthday present to herself. A session with Dr Sunita Kaul, a highly qualified trauma psychologist that she found online. She was too ashamed to speak to anyone before.

It's not like it is in the movies. Celeste doesn't get to lie on a couch. She sits in a chair and the chair is uncomfortable and the grey-haired, softly spoken woman on the other side of the table takes notes and offers her a cup of tea and forgets to take out the teabag. But none of that matters.

Slowly and painfully, the words come out. She tells the woman that she is too overwhelmed by the trauma of losing Tom to acknowledge the sexual abuse that she suffered at the hands of Ben that night... She defines herself as a killer... What Ben did to her is irrelevant and trivial in comparison to what happened to Tom... Her suffering is as nothing compared to his loss. She is locked in a pact of silence with her former schoolmate... They are both criminals...

To dwell on what Ben did to her in the boathouse seems like a gross self-indulgence and betrayal of Tom… Her little brother's death and what happened in the boathouse are inextricably linked in her head… Both she and Ben are stained with the shame and the guilt.

The woman on the other side of the desk doesn't say much. She lets Celeste speak. She doesn't prompt or fill the silence. She looks down at her notebook as she writes. She listens. And when Celeste gets to the end of her story and her time is almost up, the woman puts down her pen and looks at Celeste.

'You know, you were a victim that night too.'

It's against the rules but she reaches across the desk and puts her hand over Celeste's.

'That boy raped you…'

The woman's words feel like a gift.

At last, for someone acknowledge it… to affirm it… to say the words out loud… and with kindness and understanding. Dr Kaul isn't finished yet. She gives Celeste's hand a gentle squeeze and looks deep into her eyes.

'But you survived.'

From then on, Celeste redefines herself. She is a 'rape survivor'. Her mission is to work out what that means and what she should do about it.

PRESENT

45

Whens the light goes on in your window, my heart leaps. You are back in town. Although it's only been one night, it feels like you've been away for a two-week holiday. From a distance, I monitor your light and when it goes off again, I move closer to the house in time to see You at the bus stop getting on to a bus. I'm quick enough to run and catch the bus just before it moves away.

Our journey is slow through the Sunday afternoon traffic but I'm happy to sit here observing You from behind. When You get off, I follow and it's only a short walk to your destination, a private clinic in the heart of Chelsea. I follow You through the entrance, wait behind a stand while You enquire at the desk and then I follow You upstairs. The plaque on the door says 'Gynaecology'. When the door releases to let you in, I can go no further. But it doesn't take a genius to work this out. You are not bringing flowers, so this isn't a Seventh Heaven delivery. Something bad has happened to Mia and her baby. And that bastard caused it.

Celeste opened her eyes and sat staring down at the matchbox and the Rizla carton for a full five minutes. The sense of peace had gone. Now she was in a cold sweat, trembling all over. What was she to do with this? What good could it possibly serve to rake up all the embers again and set them blazing? At this remove, the police wouldn't be interested. What would anyone care which of the two of them, her or Ben, had started the fire? They had both been irresponsible and reckless. And in any case, if she spoke to the police, Ben would just deny it. It would be her word against his. 'He said. She said.'

Celeste picked up the matchbox and held it up to the light. She cared – even if no one else did. That was enough. On the back, she read the stark warning: 'DANGER! FIRE KILLS CHILDREN'. She guessed it would be too late to recover fingerprints but that didn't concern her. She had no intention of going to the police. She squeezed the box so hard that the matches cracked and splintered through the cardboard. She would find her own way of getting justice for herself and, more importantly, for Tom.

Impatient to get going, she started stuffing the jacket into a plastic bag and felt something else – small and hard concealed in an inside pocket sewn into the lining of the jacket. The zip was stiff and caught on the fabric but eventually she managed to yank it free and slip her hand inside the pocket. She pulled out a key. Now rusty and a little blackened with age, she knew immediately what it was...

...the key to Ben's bedroom.

This shocking new discovery threw her into fresh turmoil as she struggled to remember…

How the hell did this leather jacket and the key that seemed to brand her skin end up in her wardrobe anyway?

She wasn't sure how long she had been sitting there gripping the key so hard that her fingernails had gouged into the palm of her left-hand when she became aware of her mother yelling at her up the stairs. Getting no response, Stacey banged into the room, where Celeste was sitting rigid on the bed.

'What's wrong? I thought you were in a hurry to get away?' said Stacey. 'Mike's taking me out for lunch, so I've come to say goodbye. Just pull the door when you leave.'

She gave Celeste a quick hug and then she was gone.

Celeste heard her mother leaving the house and a car accelerating away (middle-aged Mike driving his 'pimped-up' Nissan Skyline like a boy racer as usual…) and got to her feet. There was no point moping around here on her own any longer.

'Crime and punishment,' she said to herself through gritted teeth, over and over, unable to get the words out of her head. The inquest had never got to the truth of what happened that night. Ben had dumped the blame squarely on her shoulders – in his account, she had dropped the cigarette and she had turned the key. Of course, no one had pressed charges against her because all acknowledged she had already been punished enough by the tragic outcome. But now it seemed that his testimony was all a pack of lies.

What if it was Ben's carelessness (throwing a flaring

match or the lighted joint to the floor) that had started the fire? And what if it was Ben who deliberately locked Tom into his bedroom making him prisoner to the fire? Who knows? That would have been a very different story. A hot tingling sensation rose up through Celeste's body until her cheeks began to burn and she registered the feeling as rage. She was beginning to grasp at the truth, and she wanted revenge.

Celeste's knowledge of the law was derived mainly from detective stories and murder mysteries, but Ben's conduct might surely, she reasoned, have amounted to the crime of 'involuntary manslaughter', which she understood from her law and politics reading to be the unintentional killing of another person as a result of criminally negligent or reckless conduct. Even though the investigation might not have led to a criminal conviction, at least if the truth had been known she wouldn't have been hung out to dry as the main culprit for the horrors of that dreadful night. Everyone's moral evaluation of the tragedy would have been very different and perhaps, her mother and all the others would have been able to find it in their hearts to forgive her for her part in it.

As for her, she would never forgive herself for taking Tom to the party and for getting herself drunk and for leaving him alone. But at least she might find it easier to live with herself if she knew that she was not the only one to blame for Tom's tragic death. She was tortured with doubts once again, frustrated by the confusion and incompleteness of her memories. Why was the jacket here? Had Ben asked her to hide the evidence? To be complicit in a cover up? In the knowledge that she would get off more lightly than him? Had that been his final act of domination over her?

Her mind was made up.

The black leather jacket should be returned to its rightful owner. She found and reread the handwritten note from Harry, which she'd folded into her wallet. He'd as good as asked her out on a date. Yes, she would go to the reunion and yes, she would find an opportunity to talk to Harry alone. She would insist that he told her everything he knew about Ben's actions that night. Once and for all she needed to find out the full truth of what had taken place. Her heart smouldered with a burning desire for retribution. But first she had to be sure. She tapped out the number that Harry had scrawled at the bottom of his letter and sent Harry a text – short and to the point:

'See you there.'

PRESENT

46

You are off to some fancy do tonight – high heels, hair-up, full face of make-up, and a floaty dress that looks almost as seductive as the body-hugging little numbers you usually go in for. Watching your taxi pull away, I'm tempted to follow. You are my vision of summer. But I have some self-control. You'll be out for the evening. And I'm in luck. You left your curtains open. This is the ideal opportunity to try out my latest gadget. Small, light, quiet, unobtrusive, responsive and easy to control. Delivered overnight – my quadcopter drone.

The drone comes equipped with camera live video and an adjustable wide angle/zoom lens Wi-Fi camera. It features GPS, Return to Home, Follow Me, Altitude Hold, Long Control Range, Night and Day Modes – all the functionality I require to hover outside your window with a bird's-eye view of the inside of your bedroom. I get hard just thinking about it.

Once darkness falls, I position myself between the skip

and the parked cars. All is quiet on the street. Judging by the British summertime smells of smoke and charred meat hanging in the air, all your neighbours have been busy barbecuing in their back gardens. Gently, I position the drone for take-off and adjust the controls. I take a deep breath – up, up, up it goes.

Believe it or not, I bought the drone on Amazon for less than one hundred and fifty pounds. It does the job to perfection. You are worth every penny.

Despite the dark purpose behind her coming, Celeste thought it might be nice to see Harry and the boys. Harry had assured her that Ben would not be at the event and with the passing of time, she felt fewer qualms about exchanging small talk and banter with the others. They had grown up. She had developed her social skills through dealings with the public at Seventh Heaven and she was happy speaking to just about anyone these days (with one or two notable exceptions) as long as the conversation remained on a superficial level.

The RAC Epsom, was a lovely venue for a reunion, an elegant country mansion, with magnificent gardens, wide green lawns, and far-reaching views of open countryside. They stood around for drinks and canapés and listened to dull speeches about projects undertaken by the school foundation. After the obligatory fundraising auction, Celeste took her opportunity to speak to Harry alone by suggesting a stroll around the grounds.

'It's such a beautiful evening,' she said. 'Let's take our drinks out to the garden. We can watch the sunset.'

They found a bench with a fabulous view over the fields and hills. As the sun sank below the tree line, they were treated to an impressionist tableau of clouds and sky lit up in a painter's palette of purples, pinks and greys. When the colours began to fade, Celeste jumped straight in. 'What do you remember about the night of the party?' she said. 'I've been thinking about it a lot recently and I want to find out exactly what happened.'

Harry was taken aback. 'It's a long time ago,' he said. 'It doesn't feel real anymore. I'm not sure I can be of much help to you.'

'Perhaps this will help to jog your memories,' said Celeste icily, taking the leather jacket from her shoulder bag. 'Remember this?' She threw the jacket at his head.

Harry recognised it immediately.

'What the f... My leather jacket.' He laughed. 'Where did you dig this up?' He stood up to try it on. 'God, I must have been slim.' Although Harry was still in pretty good shape, there was a three-inch gap at his torso when he went to do up the zip. 'I never got to wear this. Ben grabbed it off me for every party. He said it looked better on him than on me.' Suddenly the real significance of the jacket clicked.

'Ah shit... I'm so sorry.' He looked up at Celeste.

She brushed it aside.

'Typical Ben!' she said. 'So, you hooked up with him again? I saw your Facebook. I thought you'd fallen out?'

'Yes, we went our separate ways. To be honest, after I was kicked out of school, I wanted nothing more to do with him... well, you know why...'

Harry was guarded despite being on his fifth glass of Champagne.

'As I'm sure you heard, he abandoned his place at Cambridge that he'd grafted so hard for and went off to an American uni. Left the shit-storm behind. His parents wanted to get him as far away as possible from home. He told me they had been worried that the police would decide to investigate further and perhaps launch a prosecution. "Out of sight, out of mind". I guess his parents thought the police wouldn't go to the trouble of issuing proceedings to bring him back from America to stand trial.'

'*I thought* we were friends,' said Celeste. 'You knew all this, and you said nothing?'

'I know this sounds bad. But it was all in the past by the time he told me about it,' he said.

Celeste shrank away from him. For him it might be in the past but for her it was in the searing present. She knew she would have to control her anger and act a part in order to get the information she craved out of him, so she steeled herself. She said nothing while he continued: 'Don't forget I was expelled,' he said. 'To be honest it was the best thing that could have happened to me. Being in that gang of boys was toxic. I was shell-shocked by what had happened – felt somehow contaminated. Anyway, I moved on. I made new friends at my new school and then at Exeter university and cut ties with my Surrey Grammar School friends.' Harry tipped back his Champagne. 'So, I lost touch with Ben for years. But then he looked me up two years ago when I started work in New York. He stalked me online until I agreed to have a drink with him.' He smiled apologetically. 'He's matured a lot,' he said. 'A changed man.' He tailed off. 'That's enough about me... What about you?'

Celeste ignored the question. She was determined to get to the truth.

'What happened that night?' she said passionately. 'I've been torturing myself for the last seven years, trying to work out what happened the night of the party... how my little brother got killed.' She turned to Harry and gripped his arm. 'I've got so many blackouts from that night. And then I find this.' Losing her cool, she shook the jacket violently. 'And what I find in the pockets makes me think that bastard lied to me and to everyone else all along. I need your help...'

Harry kept his eyes on the horizon, which was now a bank of dark grey clouds.

'It's a long time ago,' he repeated with a sigh.

But having made up her mind, Celeste was not going to be deterred.

'I left the jacket as I found it,' she said. 'Look in the pockets.' Harry began to go through the pockets one by one without saying a word.

'I want you to tell me everything,' she said. 'And I mean *everything* that you remember about that night.' Harry unfolded the Rizla papers and gave her a pained look.

'I can't believe we were such sexist pigs,' he said, going off at a tangent again. He shook his head.

'I guess I was "the most boring girl",' said Celeste in a matter-of-fact voice as she watched Harry reading the scraps of paper.

Harry grimaced. 'Well it's true, until then you'd had a reputation among the boys for being a girly swot and a bit of a prude,' he said, reverting to the teenage lingo. 'But then there was that thing with the nudes that caused such a scandal at the time. You'd gone up in our collective estimation because of that. Of course, Ben, (being Ben), had circulated every one of the nudes you had sent him to all of us boys. Suddenly you shot up in the popularity stakes.'

Celeste faked a smile. She knew she'd have to rein in her disapproval of the group's appallingly sexist behaviour in order to get full disclosure. The important thing was to keep Harry talking.

'God it's all coming back to me now. How did you girls put up with us?'

Harry told Celeste how one of the boys had come up with the idea of the dares, and they had all drawn lots out of a beer mug before the girls arrived at Ben's house.

'It was so cruel,' said Celeste.

'We were only seventeen,' said Harry. 'It was just schoolboy pranks.'

'Eighteen,' said Celeste. 'Anyway seventeen, eighteen? What difference does it make? You were all old enough to know better.'

'For most of us it was just a quick kiss and a fondle in a dark corner. You know what those parties were like,' said Harry. 'Ben took it more seriously. He was always the ringleader... Everything was a competition. Had to win every time.'

'I know exactly what Ben was like. I pretty much lived round his house between the ages of five and ten, don't forget,' said Celeste. 'I blame his parents in part. They put such impossible expectations on him. Rugby. Cambridge. Whether it was on the pitch or in the classroom, he had to be the best at everything. Selection for the county wasn't good enough. It had to be the nationals. A place at university wasn't good enough. It had to be Cambridge. They were the sort of parents who, if you came home and told them you got ninety-four per cent in an exam, would turn around and say, "Well that's good, darling, but what happened to the last six per cent?" Anyway, the upshot is he was always a deceitful coward and a bully. But we can't blame his parents for the fact he became a sexual predator.'

Forcing herself to stay calm, Celeste pressed Harry to carry on with his account of his memories of the night. Once the party got going, Harry told her, Ben hadn't wasted much time in getting his first dare (who was not 'officially' in their friendship group as the boys considered her a bit frumpy and fat) over and done with, after which the poor girl (who had been plied with drink to facilitate the challenge) was sick, and he sent her home in a taxi to get rid of her. Having successfully disposed of 'dare number one', he turned his attentions to 'dare number two'.

'He'd always secretly fancied you,' said Harry. 'I think he'd always been a bit in love with you since you spent all that time together as little kids. But he kept it quiet – because you were special to him...' Harry hesitated. 'And also, because, well... you weren't cool... you know what I mean... a bit awkward and shy... until the nudes, of course.'

'It's hardly surprising I was socially awkward,' said Celeste bitterly. 'He was always doing me down and ordering me around. He destroyed my self-confidence.'

'Well anyway,' continued Harry. 'That night, he was determined. He wanted you and nothing was going to stand in his way. He knew we'd all been drooling over your pictures and I think that fired his determination to hook up with you – to bolster his position as pack leader, make us all jealous... You get my drift... As you know to your cost, Ben wasn't the kind of boy to take no for an answer.' Celeste gave a hollow laugh while Harry took another slug of Champagne. 'We tried to talk him out of taking his father's car. He'd already been drinking. But we couldn't stop him. You arrived with Tom. You were looking bloody fit and you were on everyone's radar after the pics so all the boys were trying to chat you up.' Celeste sat in silence, gazing at the rising moon. Her face shone white in the moonlight. Harry glanced across at her, and suddenly lost his thread.

'You know, you're very beautiful,' he said. 'Did anyone ever tell you that?'

'Stop trying to change the subject,' she said. Then she tried to lighten the tone. 'You've been in the US for too long. Are you going all gushy and sentimental on me?'

Harry touched her hand. 'Are you sure you want me to carry on?' She nodded and moved her hand away.

'You were in a flirtatious mood and Ben was getting really rattled because Tom kept bugging him. Ben had installed Tom upstairs in his bedroom to keep him entertained with his vast Xbox collection but Tom kept coming downstairs and asking him stuff about changing channels or setting up the games. He wanted some attention from him mainly, I think – you know how Tom hero-worshipped Ben.'

Harry paused, shifted closer along the bench to Celeste and took her hand.

'Do we have to talk about this now? It all happened so long ago.'

'I've got to know,' said Celeste grimly.

'OK. So, Tom kept coming downstairs asking Ben for help, and bothering you too, saying he was tired and asking when you'd be going home and the like. Obviously, this was cramping Ben's style and his efforts to make progress with "dare number two".' In his discomfort, Harry got up from the bench and stood with his back to her. 'In the end Ben got really exasperated with Tom,' he said, 'and he must have worked out what he was going to do. The last time I saw them going off together, he turned around to me... I'll never forget these words because his look was hard as nails...' Harry turned around, and Celeste shrank from the look in his eyes too as she hung on *his* every word. '"This time I'm going to lock the little bugger in." That's what he said.'

When Harry glanced across again at Celeste, this time her eyes were lit with an icy sheen that had nothing to do with the moonlight.

'I didn't think he would do it, of course,' he said hastily.

'Look in the inside pocket,' ordered Celeste. Harry yanked open the zip and pulled out the key. While Harry sat silently staring at the key, Celeste's hands gripped her Champagne glass so hard that it shattered, spraying liquid and shards of glass all over her dress. Blood streamed from the palm of her hand. Harry jumped up to help her.

'Now what do you think?' she hissed through gritted teeth. She clasped his arm, careless of the bloodstains on his white shirt. 'I need to know everything.'

'Oh my God, we need to get your hand sorted out.'

'If you don't tell me everything, I'm going to scream my head off and tell everyone you tried to rape me.' She glared wildly at Harry.

There was nothing for it but to plough on.

'I was about to go after Ben,' said Harry, 'to tell him to stop being a bloody idiot. But as he walked off, you came up to me. And actually, you seemed to be coming on to me.

I didn't want to break away.' Harry put his arm around Celeste's shoulders and this time she didn't resist as she sat rigid on the bench. 'You're shivering,' he said. 'If you must know, I had pulled the dare, *the hottest girl at the party*, and you were my target. I was going to give it my best shot for a quick snog in the corner while Ben was distracted by Tom.' Harry looked long and hard at Celeste. 'Now, of course, those words are etched into my brain – *This time I'm going to lock the little bugger in* – and I can never forgive my crass teenage self for just standing by.'

Celeste had no interest in Harry's futile and belated self-recriminations. But now a clear picture seemed to be emerging. Ben had locked Tom in his bedroom to keep her little brother out of the way; put the key in the pocket of his leather jacket – Harry's leather jacket; plied her with alcohol (possibly spiked with other blackout-inducing illegal substances such as ecstasy or cocaine that temporarily set her bouncing off the walls and stripped away her inhibitions); got her away from the other boys; and then taken her upstairs with the intention of having sex with her. He had been unable to use his own bedroom because he had locked Tom in there; couldn't use the bathroom because it was otherwise occupied; and couldn't use his parents' room or his older brother's room because they had taken the sensible precaution of locking them too before leaving Ben alone in the house for the weekend. So, in the end he had taken her off to the lake... And finally, got down to the serious business of notching up his second sexual conquest of the night, down and dirty on the earthen floor of the boathouse.

It wasn't a pretty tale, but it was plausible. As she processed all this, Celeste felt as if the grey mists of confusion that shrouded her memories were gradually melting away only to be replaced with a red mist of impotent rage – seven years too late.

But there was one piece of the jigsaw still missing.

'How did your jacket end up in my wardrobe?' The key was in the jacket and the jacket had been in *her* wardrobe. She was still tortured with the horrible thought. Could she have been the one to turn the key as Ben had claimed all along? What if Harry was wrong?

'I remember the scene very clearly,' he said. 'It comes back to me in dreams.' Harry was looking away from her now, staring at the moon. 'The sight of the barn in flames, and a group of us, refugees from the party (many drunk and dishevelled) huddled on the lawn. Someone was trying to do a headcount. And some of the girls were screaming for you and Ben. We'd all forgotten about Tom. And then suddenly you appeared out of the trees, barefoot, in your red dress, like some kind of wild woodland nymph, sprinting for the house, heading for the flames. I ran across the grass to intercept you. You were hysterical. Out of your mind. I remember grabbing your arms to restrain you. Your dress was ripped at the chest and your arms were bare.' He turned to her and said pointedly, 'I remember that – bare, so slender and pale. I just held you.'

He knocked back the rest of his Champagne. 'The next thing, Ben appeared out of the trees, yelling and waving his arms like a lunatic. He was wearing my leather jacket. I watched him running over to the police officer. He was out of control. At one point it looked as if he was going to punch him. Then he came over to us. You were trembling in my arms. He took off his leather jacket – my jacket – and put it around you. It seemed a thoughtful, gentlemanly gesture putting the jacket over your shoulders. But now I think he already had an agenda – hiding his guilt and shifting the blame. Maybe he was trying to cover up the rip in your dress. And maybe he was trying to plant all the incriminating evidence on you. Even in the heat of the moment, he was always one step ahead… watching his back.'

Celeste sat silently for more than a minute, taking it all in. 'Why the fuck didn't you say something?' she said very quietly, shifting away from Harry.

'It's complicated,' said Harry. 'I was scared, and I was weak, and I was stupid. What else can I say? When the police spoke to us on the night, I was drunk and in shock, like everyone else. But yes, you're right. Later, I should have spoken up. There's no excuse. I knew that he lied at the inquest. But I got caught up in his lie. And then I got caught up in other things. It was easier that way. He had so much power over us. It wasn't only the girls who were afraid of him. All of us boys were in awe of him and scared of becoming the next object of his ridicule.'

Harry couldn't look at Celeste. 'He was our God and I think I was a little in love with him, in the way that teenage boys crush on their heroes. A few weeks after the fire, before I got expelled, I wanted to tell our teacher – that was the only person I could think of – because I was appalled by your pain. But Ben blackmailed me to keep quiet. There was a thing that had happened between him and me and another boy a year before. Ben had instigated it – you know, just a one-off locker-room sexual experiment between teenage boys after a rugby match. It meant nothing. He had forced me into it. But that gave him power over me. I was confused.

He said that if I didn't have his back, he would make me suffer for it. I wasn't man enough to run the prospect of him making out to the whole world that I was gay.'

Harry bundled up the jacket. 'And then there was the fact the key was in the pocket of my jacket. Ben said the police would never take any action against you as you were Tom's sister and it was such a terrible family tragedy. But if they thought it was him or me, it would be a different story. That could lead to a criminal prosecution. Ben told me that if I told the truth, he would swear blind that I was the one who had locked Tom up in Ben's bedroom. It would be his word against mine. I would be locked up myself. I admit it, Celeste, I'm a coward. I was terrified.'

Celeste sat dumbfounded for a few minutes, gazing at the stars, while the blood seeped into her dress. Then she stood up.

'Thank you for having the courage to tell me the truth at last,' she said and began to walk along the pathway to the exit of the club. She turned once. 'I never want to set eyes on you again.'

And then she disappeared into the dark.

PRESENT

47

*T*he 'XYX'. I've no idea what the letters stand for, but it
sounds extreme – painful and sexually deviant, if the
website's anything to go by. No, it's not a reincarnation of
an extremist right-wing clan. XYX is the hottest new gym
north of the river in London town, and You just joined it.

Not content with wearing out your Nike trainers
running me ragged circling the garden squares and parks
and manicured residential streets of The Royal Borough of
Kensington and Chelsea (in the end I had to buy myself
some running shoes too), now You decide that not only do
you want to be fit, but you also want to be strong! For me,
that's a step too far.

When I see You registered as a member (I'm still checking
your devices remotely every day), I google the XYX. Their
promotional video is terrifying – I've overheard some
people saying I'm 'a bit weird', but this lot are lunatics.
Their studios are torture chambers of weights and pulleys
and ropes and chains and psychedelic bicycles that don't

take you anywhere. Their classes have names that sound like criminal offences – 'HIIT and Run', 'TRX Suspension', 'Sweat and Burn'. Whatever possessed You to give these gangsters your credit card details?

Tonight, You are signed up for the 'Meta-XYX 4X4 class' with 'Niklaus' and 'Juan'. I read the description.

'This class is not just a status symbol. It's powerfully built, as hard as a rock, and it's going off-road. Total body workout incorporating power, speed and endurance – 4 stations X 4 exercises make this the ultimate smash HIIT'ing, fender-bending extra to your weekly workout programme.

'Buckle up, Biatches, and sign up for your test drive.'

Biatches…?! Call me old-fashioned – but honestly, have You lost your self-respect? Those suffragettes who died for You would be turning in their graves.

I can't follow you into that house of horrors. I can see from the photographs of 'Niklaus' and 'Juan' and 'Nikita' and 'Kym' that you need a body beautiful before darkening its doors. So now I have a new class of rival: the up-close and personal gym instructor – Fake tan, bulging muscles, reeking of testosterone and Paco Rabanne (I can tell just by looking at the pictures), glistening hairless chest (yes, man-waxing's all the rage these days). That's just not fair competition.

No wonder You deleted your Tinder account. It's all there for the taking at XYX.

Jessi and Anya wanted to hear all about Celeste's school reunion at the RAC Club when she got back to the flat late that night. Celeste was giving nothing away.

'It was fun,' she said. 'None of my old girlfriends were there but the boys were on good form. I spent most of the evening with Harry.'

Although Celeste's flatmates had been in the year below her at school, they knew many of Celeste's peer group socially and the three girls had many 'mutual friends' on social media.

'Ben didn't show his face, of course,' said Celeste, 'now that the wedding's off. Thank God, Mia came to her senses and bailed at the very last minute!' The girls were all ears but Celeste didn't want to get drawn into a deep discussion about it. 'Harry didn't seem to know the reasons for the break-up,' said Celeste evasively. 'Ben's been putting around his own version of the story. Something about a former boyfriend turning up and rocking the boat. The bride got cold feet and is going back to the US. I'm sure you've seen it on the chats.'

Although she knew it not to be true, Celeste referred to the rumour that was doing the rounds in an effort to close down the conversation. There were things Mia had told her in confidence about her relationship with Ben that she had no intention of sharing with her friends. A lot had happened in the time between Celeste's visit to see Mia in the hospital and her reunion with Harry. Celeste knew only too well that Mia's safety and security depended on her absolute discretion. Anya and Jessi were lovely girls, but they couldn't keep a secret to save their lives.

She had discussed Mia and Ben's affairs only briefly at the club with Harry before she managed to get him away from the group to speak to him privately about his memories of the night of the fire. Re Mia's last-minute non-appearance,

Harry had told her that Ben 'wouldn't give me the intel, but seemed pretty cut up about it'. Ben had told Harry that his fiancée had told him she was 'going back to her teenage sweetheart.' Ben had refused to elaborate, said Harry.

'That's surprising. I thought she was pregnant and that he was the father,' Celeste had said, trying to test how much Harry knew.

Harry had looked at her strangely. 'How did you know that? I thought it was a secret.'

Celeste had frowned. That was a careless slip on her part. She didn't want Harry to guess at the extent of her involvement with Mia.

'Oh, just idle gossip,' she had said. 'You know Chelsea, it's like a big village.' She spoke lightly. 'Anyways, I'm glad that woman dumped him. He doesn't deserve a wife or a child.'

Celeste's conversations with Harry at the RAC had stirred up the embers of so much heartache and pain about the death of her little brother that she couldn't get to sleep when she retired to her room long after midnight. She felt anxious and agitated, almost scared to be alone in her room, even though she knew that Anya and Jessi were only next door. Raking up those memories had left her feeling violated and exposed. She lay in her bed shivering. The headlights of passing cars flickered in the corner of her room. A nearby streetlight lit up the back of her curtains with a dim grey glow. Normally these things didn't bother her. But in her sleep-deprived purgatory of 3am, she was alert to noises and shadows outside her open window.

Although it was stuffy in her room, she got up to close the window and pulled the curtains all the way until the fabric overlapped and the gap was closed. Had she turned her head she would have known that she wasn't being paranoid. Her fears were justified. A small black object, something like a mini spacecraft, not more than a few inches in diameter, hovered almost soundlessly above the branches of the tree, only a few feet away from where she stood at the window.

As Celeste stood at the open window, looking up at the stars and the moon, an almost spiritual feeling of lucidity, strength and determination seemed to flood into her being. At last the smoky 'fume of sighs' had lifted, and her eyes sparkled with a fiery passion for justice. Things had to burn, to make a light. She had seen the light. Now she knew for sure what she had suspected for some time: for the last seven years she had been suffering from false memory syndrome. Ben's lies and manipulations had embedded false memories in her brain of what had happened on the night of the fire. Now that she knew the truth, it was time to have it out with him. Better late than never. She still had her whole life ahead of her. She couldn't put off this confrontation any longer. Only once she had put the past to rest could she could she move forward with rebuilding her life.

PRESENT

48

You are a very busy lady these days, Celeste. When you're not in class or serving in the shop, You go out for a run or work out in the gym. And when you're not working on your strength and fitness regime – what are You doing? Sightseeing!

All that effort I made designing the software and setting up your website, is going to waste. Your clients are falling away. CelestialHeadstones.com is dying a slow death.

I miss spending my weekends mirroring your website on my screens. I miss our Sunday excursions by motorbike to country graveyards. Instead, I have to take public transport, which I hate – so crowded, and sweaty and claustrophobic – as You lead me from one tourist attraction to another.

What is your game? Five minutes in the Tate, ten minutes at the National Gallery… At Tower Bridge You queue for a ticket but turn away at the gate. In the Food Hall at Harrods, You stop at each display counter, but You don't buy a thing.

In the tearoom at Fortnum's, You eat a mouthful of cake before pushing your plate away.

Late in the afternoon, it clicks – or rather, You click – again (one of the great bronze lions guarding the base of Nelson's Column) and then I click: it's not the experiences you're interested in, it's the photographs.

My homework this evening confirms my hunch was right.

You're not as sweet and innocent as You look, Celeste.

What is your secret purpose in setting up the @ MiaMadisonMemories fake Instagram account?

Almost a month later, Celeste was locking her bike to a railing outside Seventh Heaven when she noticed something unusual. Meghan always arrived an hour before the others to bring out the buckets of flowers that would be displayed on the pavement and to open up the shop. This morning, the flowers were set up as usual outside the shop window, but the sign on the door had been flipped over to read *CLOSED*. A police car was parked about thirty metres further up the street. She felt her stomach flutter and put on her brightest smile as she stepped through the door.

Inside the shop, three people were bent over the counter, examining some paperwork. Three faces turned to look at her as she came in – Meghan, looking sombre and concerned, and two police officers, a man and a woman, each with a face as blank as a mask.

Meghan made the introductions and explained stiffly that the local police were following up some missing person enquiries received from overseas. A woman, who identified herself as Officer Whiteley, stepped forward to confirm that it was not a formal investigation as such, but that they had been contacted by a family member in the state of New York on behalf of Mia's parents who were concerned about the whereabouts of their adult daughter.

Officer Whiteley was as tall and as broad as a man. Celeste skirted around the counter to put down her jacket and bag, as much to give herself some time to compose herself, as to put some space between herself and this giant of a woman.

Sensing Celeste's discomfort Meghan spoke up. 'You remember Mia Madison, the American woman who asked us to do her wedding flowers and then never collected them? Well, apparently, she's gone missing, or not missing exactly, but her family are worried about her.'

It was unusual for Celeste to see Meghan sounding so flustered – she usually took all interactions, whether with officials or members of the public, within her stride. Celeste had anticipated that sooner or later she would have to answer questions about the bizarre behaviour of their client, the 'phantom bride' and had resolved to reveal as little as possible about the true reasons for which Mia had bailed on the wedding. She was playing for time. The police could do their own legwork.

'I remember,' said Celeste. 'How could I forget? I spent hours in meetings with her.'

Officer Whiteley explained that Mia had told her family that she was coming over to London for a three-week holiday with her new English boyfriend but this had extended into a three-month holiday and for the last two weeks they had had no direct communication with her. Before Mia's departure for the UK there had been a family dispute because her parents disapproved of the new boyfriend whom they held responsible for the break-up of Mia's long-standing relationship with her American partner (held in high esteem by Mia's parents both for the large family fortune that he stood to inherit and for the fact that he came from a family of devout Catholics). In their eyes, the English boyfriend was a bad influence (new money, not old money, and more money than sense) who had turned her head and would leave her discredited and damaged as well as taking her away from the faith.

'What an old-fashioned view of the world,' commented Celeste.

Officer Whiteley ignored Celeste's aside. 'They were expecting her back a week ago,' said the officer, 'but she didn't turn up. She's been in contact by text and email. But she won't answer her phone. She's also been posting on social media – pictures of tourist sites around London, Carnaby Street, Harrods and the like. The usual thing...'

'Well, perhaps she's just too busy having a good time to keep in touch,' said Celeste brightly. Making show of her willingness to cooperate, she reached for the shelf to get down the file containing the invoices for the Madison Wedding.

'What the family find strange,' the officer went on, ignoring Celeste's intervention, 'is that there are no images of her in any of the posts. Apparently, this is out of character for her. She's in the habit of posting lots of selfies.'

Meghan had made a pot of coffee and Celeste handed round the mugs.

'We're not unduly concerned,' the officer concluded. 'Our

hunch is that maybe Mia Madison doesn't want to go home or wants to keep a low profile for some personal reason. It will probably turn out that she's had a perfectly reasonable change of plan or that she doesn't want to be found because she's got the hump with her family. But we've agreed to look into it and ask some questions of anyone we can find who's been in contact with her since she arrived in London.'

'Mia kept the planned wedding a secret from her family' said Celeste. 'She's pregnant. She didn't want her family to know. She thought they would be scandalised, especially as she knew how much they disliked her new boyfriend.'

The atmosphere had changed for the better after this pronouncement. At last a rational explanation for Mia's inexplicable behaviour seemed to be emerging. Celeste had removed her notebooks from the safe and handed them to the officers.

'Here are all my notebooks from my meetings with Mia,' she had said. 'It's mostly about the flowers and designs but you're welcome to take them away if you want to.' They all sat down to drink their coffee. Meghan seemed relieved as if she had been let off the hook for not reporting Mia's disappearance earlier. The police officers speculated unguardedly with the jaded air of professionals who had seen it all before. When they got up to leave, Officer Fairway, who had taken the back seat so far, but appeared to be the senior of the two, chipped in with a new line of questioning.

'We haven't had the opportunity to speak to the bridegroom as yet because he's been away on company business in Asia for the last two weeks. Benedict Johnson.

I believe you went to the same school. Is that right?' He spoke casually.

'Yes. It's a small world, isn't it?' There was no point in denying it. She gave him her sweetest smile.

'We're hoping he can shed some light on the mystery when we speak to him on his return to London next week.' Officer Fairway thanked both Meghan and Celeste for their time with studied formality. 'You've been very helpful,' he said. 'As my colleague mentioned, at this stage, we haven't launched an official enquiry, we're simply asking around in the hope of being able to provide some reassurance to the family.' He looked pointedly at Celeste. 'Do please let us know if Mia Madison makes any contact with you or if anything else occurs to you – our door is always open.'

Celeste was about to close the door to the safe, when suddenly she hesitated. *This could be the moment*, she thought to herself. *This is my opportunity to put up the smoke-screen.*

She handed Officer Fairway the black bin liner containing all the photographs of herself, which had been displayed in front of the headstone in the North London cemetery.

'It's probably completely unconnected,' she said, preparing to sow the seeds of suspicion. 'But in the interests of full disclosure, I should give you these. I think I'm being followed by a stalker. We spent a lot of time together, Mia and I, over a period of several weeks. He could have been watching her too... so... well... I think you should see them... just in case...'

★

When the police had finally left Seventh Heaven it was almost lunchtime. The disclosure of the photographs had led to another hour of 'conversations', which had ended with Celeste giving the police officers the address details of Theo's college and accommodation. She had been careful not to overplay her hand. She had repeated what she had said to Meghan. Theo was a young kid. He had a crush on her. He was socially awkward. He was probably completely harmless. But the police had taken it seriously. If the unexplained disappearance (or social disengagement of Mia) turned into something more sinister, it was sensible for the police to have him on their radar in case Theo's behaviour towards Celeste could be indicative of a more generalised dangerous and predatory disposition.

As soon as she had closed the door on the officers, Meghan announced that she was feeling emotionally drained and intended to keep Seventh Heaven shut for the rest of the day.

'What's the point of running your own business and being your own boss if you can't occasionally have an afternoon off?' she declared. 'We've lost all the morning's business anyway and I can't face dealing with the fall-out from the clients today. I'm just going to write this day off.' It seemed Meghan's compassion for the 'phantom bride' was wearing thin. 'I knew that woman was bad news the minute she stepped into the shop,' she said. 'This is all so distressing.'

Since Celeste had been given the afternoon off too, she decided to use it to attend to a matter that was long overdue. She had been planning to go to the gym at XYX on her way home from Seventh Heaven, so she had brought her sports kit in to work in a small rucksack. It was unseasonably rainy and dull this afternoon, but that would not deter her, in fact it could work to her advantage. She was going on a run. She went into the bathroom to change into her black Nike trainers, black leggings and a black T-shirt. It was that kind of day. Not a day for fluorescent Lycra or bright pink T-shirts. She would be in harmony with the weather, camouflaged by the stormy skies.

Celeste had a particular destination in mind. It had become one of her running routes in recent weeks and she had also got in the habit of walking there with Mia as an alternative to sitting in the office during their interminable discussions about the wedding flowers and other things. In the first days of their acquaintance, Celeste had made a point of befriending Mia who seemed isolated and bored, left to her own devices for the long hours that her fiancé was working in his firm's London headquarters during his stay in London. As she and Mia had become closer, the walks had turned into informal sessions for mutual counselling and support.

So, on this dreary, wet afternoon, Celeste set off through the residential streets as far as the Tate Britain art gallery, an elegant white building on the banks of the Thames where she had taken Mia on one of their walks. Mia had marvelled at the striking architecture ('*You English people are so lucky having all this history right on your doorstep*'), comprising a grand porticoed entranceway and a vast central dome that resembled a Byzantine temple (notwithstanding the statue of Britannia with a lion and a unicorn on top of the pediment that proudly symbolised its 'Britishness'). Mia had also sung the praises of the '*awesome*' collection of art housed inside the gallery, which laid claim to be 'the home of the greatest collection of British art' and whose treasures included a stupendous collection of paintings by the celebrated seventeenth-century British romantic painter and watercolourist, J.M.W.Turner, famous for his scenes of Venice and ships in stormy seas.

From that point, getting into her stride, Celeste headed westwards along the Thames towards the Chelsea embankment and the Chelsea Bridge, passing en route, the Chelsea Tea Rooms, where she had introduced Mia to the delights of English 'cream tea' consisting of Earl Grey tea served in a china Victoriana teapot, homemade English scones, strawberry jam and Devonshire clotted cream. Leaving that behind, she picked up her pace as she ran onto the Chelsea Bridge, which she had walked across in leisurely fashion with Mia. They had stopped to admire the far-reaching views downstream of bridges, The Houses of Parliament, the London Eye and imposing bulk of the Battersea Power Station on the south bank of the river (all of which had set Mia gushing with enthusiasm for this great city).

Continuing on, Celeste strode out over the Chelsea Bridge until she reached The Battersea Park. There the ground was soggy after recent rains, so she slowed her pace to walk over lawns alongside the river until she reached The Albert Bridge ('the most beautiful bridge in London especially at night time when it is all lit up' she had said to Mia, feeling very much the tourist guide).

Back on a firm surface, Celeste picked up her pace again and ran along the historic suspension bridge, heading back towards the north bank of the river on her circular tour. But at the midway point on The Albert Bridge, she stopped and went over to the edge of the pedestrian walkway. She looked down into the dark, swirling waters below. Perhaps on account of the wind and the rain, there were no pedestrians on the bridge, which was, no doubt, fortunate for her. Celeste cut a mournful figure, leaning over the bridge in her black exercise gear. If any passers-by had seen the intensity and sadness on her face at that moment when she stared down into the water, they might have feared for her safety and sought to intervene.

But Celeste had no intention of throwing herself off the bridge. Instead, she unzipped the pocket of her tracksuit top and took out Mia's mobile phone. The social media posts had served their purpose but now it was time to get rid of it. The police were on Mia's trail. Celeste smashed the handset three times on the metalwork of the bridge and then she flung it as far as she could into the black torrent below.

PRESENT

49

You are pretty as a picture this morning, skipping down the steps of the building in a strappy bright little sundress paired with kitten heels and your new Versace designer shades (I've been following your purchases online and know almost as much about women's fashion as floristry these days!) It's Sunday morning but I can bet You're not going to church. You look far too happy for that.

Meghan's Fiat 500 is parked in the street. You jump in, open the roof and you're off.

I follow at a distance. The traffic is light, and we make good progress, heading west out of town. Once You get to the motorway, You really put your foot down and I struggle to keep up. That little car is taking a hammering. Some fifty miles later, beyond the Oxford exit, You turn off the motorway, onto a busy A-road and then a scenic B-road and then a country lane twisting through open farmland and ancient woodlands, and then a rough stony track that leads to a farmhouse in the middle of nowhere – which is where *you stop. I'm glad You knew where you were going, because I am completely lost.*

I wheel my motorbike a little way along a footpath that leads into the trees giving me a vantage point over the farmhouse. You open the car door and the dogs go crazy. Two black Labradors and a Jack Russell run out into the yard from an open back door. There's shouting from inside, a woman's voice, calling back the dogs. But you're not afraid. The dogs jump up at You, tails wagging, and the woman (middle-aged, big and jolly) gives You a hug. You chat for a minute or two and then walk in together.

About twenty minutes later, just as my eyes are beginning to close from the early start and the long hard ride on the open road, the back door opens again, and You walk down the path with two other women.

From a distance, one of the women looks like Mia – slim, long blonde hair and petite. But when she gets closer, I can see it's not her. The other woman, from a distance, looks nothing like Mia. But when she gets closer, I can see – it is Mia, though even at close range she looks very different. She's put on weight and she's cut her hair and dyed it brown and tied it back into a short sleek ponytail. Her face is flat and pale without make-up. She's dressed in black leggings and a loose black T-shirt – and now she just looks dumpy and plain, like any other girl.

The older woman (hauling a big suitcase – Mia's?) and the dogs follow the three of you to the car. You open the front passenger seat of the Fiat for Mia, then with a lot of pushing and shoving, You wedge the suitcase upright into the back seat. The blonde Mia look-alike squeezes in beside it. More hugs all round and then you're off.

I follow at a distance, back along the track and the country lanes and the B-road and the A-road and the motorways until I see You take the turn-off signposted for Heathrow Airport.

Something tells me that's the last we're going to see of Mia Madison.

Celeste got back to her London flat late that evening. Instead of driving straight back to London after dropping off Mia and her friend at the airport, she had decided to pay an unannounced visit to her mother. Now that Mia was on a plane to Paris, a safe distance from Ben, she felt free to break the silence. A heart-to-heart was long overdue. They had spent the day talking and walking and visiting Tom's grave. Although nothing could heal the hurt between mother and daughter, it had been good for Celeste finally to open up about Ben's lies and the psychological damage he had inflicted on her over a number of years culminating in her rape. In the past, Ben had done everything to flip the narrative. Everything Celeste had discovered in recent weeks about his actions on the night of the party and his treatment of Mia, gave her the courage to speak out.

When Celeste walked through the door, Anya was sitting at the kitchen table with her laptop open, working on a legal document. 'Why didn't you answer my texts?' she asked Celeste, without looking up. 'I've been trying to get hold of you all evening.' Celeste took her phone out of her bag and plugged it in.

'I ran out of charge,' she said. When it lit up, Anya's texts took up the first three screens. 'What happened?' she said as she began to scroll down.

'Ben came around to the flat,' said Anya. 'He was demanding to know where you were, practically pushed his way in, literally kept his foot in the door when I told him you weren't here.' Celeste knew that Anya was not easily rattled but she could tell that Ben had upset her. 'He was very aggressive,' said Anya. 'But also, very distressed. One minute he was shouting at me, the next he was practically in tears. I think he'd been drinking.' Anya had never met Ben in the flesh before but knew him from his social media accounts. 'You better talk to him,' she said. 'He's making ridiculous threats about reporting you to the police, saying you've abducted Mia, that you're sick in the head. He said if you don't contact him by tomorrow morning, he's going to get you arrested.'

Jessi had wandered out of her bedroom and stood hovering next to Celeste, looking concerned.' Celeste laughed. 'That sounds like Ben. Charming as ever!'

Anya slammed the lid of her laptop shut and looked at Celeste. 'What's going on?' she said. 'I think you owe us an explanation.'

Celeste went to the fridge and poured out three large glasses of rosé. 'I'm so sorry you had to deal with him. I'll text him right now and tell him that if he ever sets foot in this building again, I'm the one who's going to call the police to let them know them exactly what he's been doing to Mia. He deserves to be locked up.'

The friends sat at the table over their drinks while Celeste filled them in on what had happened.

'I'm sorry I had to keep it all secret from you,' said Celeste.

'Mia made me promise not to tell anyone where she was. She was scared for her safety if Ben tracked her down. She's left England now. She's gone to stay with her closest friend in Paris until the baby is born. Then she'll probably go back to America. She never wants to see him again.' Celeste took a sip of wine. 'You know, she almost lost the baby as a result of being assaulted by Ben. He was rough with her many times throughout the relationship, usually when they were having sex. But just before the wedding there was one night when he all-out attacked her, punched her in the stomach. She didn't get immediate medical help, and a few days later things got serious, some kind of internal haemorrhage, and she was hospitalised for days. That's why the wedding was off. That social media story about a former boyfriend turning up in London was fake, just a smokescreen. Ben didn't want the world to know he'd beaten up his bride and nor did she. I'm sorry I couldn't let you know the truth sooner.'

Celeste explained that when Mia became seriously ill and ran away from Ben after the attack, she had taken a taxi straight to Seventh Heaven. Together with Meghan and Mia's best friend who came over from Paris to be with her, Celeste had come up with a plan. When Mia was admitted to the private clinic, she gave false contact details – 'borrowing' the identity of her best friend who was to have been her chief bridesmaid. The private clinic in Chelsea had refrained from asking any searching questions in accordance with an unspoken understanding (between Mia and Celeste and the consultant gynaecologist and Mia's best friend) that in cases of domestic violence, discretion (or deception) may save lives. Thanks to the care and expertise of the medical staff, both the mother and her unborn child had made a full recovery. When she came out of hospital, Celeste had arranged for Mia to have a period of recuperation in a women's refuge out in the countryside run by a woman that Meghan knew from years back and now, restored to health, she was safely arrived at her friend's apartment in Paris looking forward to making a new life with her baby.

'It's so ironic that you ended up doing the wedding flowers for Ben's bride,' said Jessi. 'Such a strange coincidence.'

'Not really,' said Celeste. 'I talked to Mia about that. Seventh Heaven was in Ben's search history. She found us when she went on his laptop because Ben had been looking for the place where I worked. We came up top of the list when she googled florists near his rented flat in Chelsea. As you know, I figured out quite early on that Mia was in a troubled relationship, but at first, I had no idea that the bridegroom was Ben. Because she was desperate to talk to someone, Mia had opened up to me without mentioning Ben's name and, in turn, I had shared my own experiences of trauma and abuse with her, also without naming names. Anyway, it turns out that very soon she made the connection between me and the shocking events in Ben's past. That made her all the more curious to find out everything she could about Ben as a person. By the time I found out that the person she was engaged to was Ben, things had reached a crisis in their relationship, with Ben becoming increasingly aggressive and physical in his abuse, until the night he attacked her in his kitchen and she almost lost the baby. I couldn't turn my back on her.' Celeste drained her wine and almost shouted, 'I can't bear to think of Ben out there, having learnt nothing, inflicting his violence and abuse on a vulnerable woman.' Then she seemed to take a hold of herself and continued calmly. 'Mia was desperate to get away from him and feared what he might do if he came after her. So, I agreed to help her. After she came out of hospital, and went into hiding at the refuge, I used Mia's phone to post lots of pictures of her sightseeing in London. She was out of touch with her family but didn't want them to get alarmed if she suddenly went off the radar. It bought her a few weeks to get some respite before the police started taking an interest in her as a missing person.'

Celeste tailed off and looked up to see both Anya and Jessi watching her intently.

'You are a very dark horse,' said Anya quietly. 'You should take care. Ben's out to get you.'

PRESENT

50

Y*ou may have heard me riding the motorbike up to the church, but I can't be sure. Sometimes I think You sense I'm here and that You get a secret thrill from knowing I'm watching over You. I leave the bike behind the wall and make my way to my old lair in among the trees from where I watched You on Valentine's Day. It seems like a lifetime ago. I lose track of time watching You stripping the thorns from the stems and placing the roses tenderly around your brother's grave. And when You lie down in the bed of roses, well, that tears me apart. I could die for You.*

Then he arrives and breaks the spell. He's not driving the red Ferrari this time – he's keeping that pretty baby well away from You now – 'twice bitten thrice shy…' Or perhaps, he had to hand it back to his employer – now that he's going away. Anyway, today he's driving a respectable metallic grey, VW Golf – a few years old, nothing too flashy. It belongs to his mother.

Downgrading his car has not diminished his high opinion of himself. He walks into the churchyard as if he owns the place and I creep closer under cover of the trees until I reach a point where the stone wall is some distance from the public footpath and separated by a hedge. Here I should be well hidden from any latecomers for the fireworks (the crowd is already assembled on the village green but there are bound to be some stragglers) and I'm hoping it's too late for dog walkers. I don't want some dog sniffing me out.

It was Midsummer's Eve, 21st June, the longest day of the year. Too early in the season to plant the daffodil bulbs, which she was saving for the autumn – but Celeste had another reason for going to visit Tom's grave. The head-to-head with Ben couldn't wait any longer. Ben was leaving town. She couldn't pass by this opportunity to confront him directly before he was out of her life forever. She had decided it was finally time to have that 'heart-to-heart' with Ben that she had been dodging ever since his return to the UK.

It seemed fitting for the meeting to take place in this churchyard on this day – the day when the sun was farthest north in the northern hemisphere and had travelled the longest path through the sky giving the most hours of daylight. She knew something of the pagan rites and ceremonies associated with Midsummer's Eve, which related to fertility and bountiful harvests. She had heard of the Midsummer bonfires, which were believed to ward off evil spirits, and the focus on nature, which harkened back to when plants and water were thought to have magical healing powers on the longest day of the year.

Besides the symbolic significance of Midsummer's Eve, Celeste had chosen 21st June for the date of the meeting out of expedience. She had seen on her social chats that Ben's time back at the London headquarters of his hedge fund was drawing to a close. He was about to take up his new overseas posting as a senior manager within their Singapore branch. The gossip was that Ben had hoped to settle in London with his new bride. But that had all turned sour. He had asked for another overseas posting. He couldn't wait to get away. The chats revealed only a watered-down and distorted version of the truth. Thanks in part to Celeste's actions in helping Mia to hide away from him for her own protection and that of her unborn child, Ben had managed to conceal the shameful reality of his abusive relationship with his pregnant bride from his social network both in the real world and in the cyberspace. Mia had chosen not to speak out and expose him. Instead she had gone to ground.

Of course, Ben had put a different spin on it. The pictures splashed on his Instagram account showed a riotous, glorious send-off from the London office as he prepared to jet off to new triumphs in the Far East. For Celeste, there was only one thing that mattered: Ben was booked on a Singapore Airlines flight the following day from London Heathrow to Changi Airport in Singapore. She might never see him again. As far as she was concerned, it was now or never.

'He really should be more careful of his security,' Celeste had said to herself wryly, when she looked at his latest Instagram post giving chapter and verse about his travel plans.

In these last months, Ben had been the one trying to track

her down and confront her. First, his appearance at Heavana, then the message on Tinder, and his attempt to get her number from her friends, and pitching up at Seventh Heaven, and tailing the Seventh Heaven van almost all the way to Birmingham. There would have been plenty of evidence of harassment there if she had taken it upon herself to go to the police. It was too late for that now. However, it seemed from what Harry had told her when they spoke at the RAC school reunion, that Ben claimed he was seeking her out in order to make his peace. He had told Harry he was hoping for some kind of reconciliation so that he could move on with his life as a married man. It was way too late. That ship had sailed. Celeste wasn't naïve enough to buy that. The real reason he had pursued her at first, she believed, was because he wanted to intimidate her into stopping her relentless social media campaign against him that was blackening his name and putting his reputation, his job and his future marriage at risk. The reason he had agreed to see her now was because he was determined to find out where Mia had gone and whether Celeste had had any part in her escape.

Celeste had placed the Seventh Heaven condolences card (on the back of which he had scribbled his number), in her purse, next to her credit cards, keeping it safe for the day when she would feel strong enough to confront him. Her agenda was very clear, motivated by the desire for retribution. Now she had worked out exactly what she was going to say and do. She reviewed the events of the past few weeks in her mind. She had made one failed attempt already to have it out with him but had bailed at the last in the doorway of the pub. They had come close to a face-to-face confrontation when he stalked her to one of the CelestialHeadstones.com deliveries and almost cornered her in the church. But she had been too smart for him and made a quick getaway. He had paid with his windscreen for that mistake.

In all these near encounters, they hadn't actually spoken. This time she had orchestrated the meeting herself. She intended to call him out. This time she was going to do the talking. For once he would listen, and she would make him understand that the way he behaved towards women was intolerable.

Neither she, nor Mia, nor any other woman was ever going to suffer his abuse again.

#MeToo

But in truth the real reason she had lured Ben to this final encounter, was because she was determined to punish him once and for all for having selfishly and recklessly locked Tom into his bedroom and then maliciously lied about it. She had spent seven years torturing herself with the thought that it was she who was solely responsible for her little brother's death. Ben's behaviour was unforgiveable, beyond redemption. Now it was time for him to pay.

#ForTom

The churchyard was quiet when she parked the van in the parking area. No one else was visiting the graves that early evening. Everyone had gravitated to the other side of the village where final arrangements were being made for the village Midsummer firework display being held on an area of common land just beyond the perimeter of the houses. An occasional dog walker passed by on the public footpath that ran alongside the brick wall leading to the fields. The church wall was festooned with climbing roses and jasmine and she caught the delicate scents on the air as she approached Tom's headstone. She put down her floristry workbox and then went back to the van for the blooms.

This time she was surrounded by her own heady aura of summer fragrance as she carried out armfuls of red roses from the van to the grave. There must have been two hundred blooms or more by the time she was done. Leaving at 4am that morning, Celeste had made a special trip to the New Covent Garden flower market and purchased three whole cartons of flowers, which she had specially selected – a perpetual rose called 'Stolen Hearts' with deep crimson velvety double blooms, dark green foliage and a strong, sweet fragrance. She had designed a special memorial for this Midsummer's Eve – a swathe of roses to encircle Tom's headstone.

She sat down on the grass and began to prepare the stems – stripping away the thorns and trimming the ends. She couldn't bear the thought of Tom's bed of roses being punctured with thorns. It was to be as soft and inviting as a feather mattress. Her design had been inspired by the art installation of 888,246 blood-red ceramic poppies that had progressively filled the famous moat of the Tower of London in the autumn leading up to Remembrance Day 2014, the hundred-year anniversary of the start of the First World War. Each poppy represented a British soldier killed in the war. Like so many Londoners she had queued to view the installation and been moved to tears at the sight.

With the fading of the light, nature's evensong was in full

swing – there was the clicking and cackling of toads and ducks from the pond on the village green, and even a barn owl joined in with the chorus of song birds calling softly from the trees. She knew these sounds so well, from having slept as a child with her windows open on balmy summer evenings in the Surrey countryside, that they scarcely registered. But then she was startled by a different jarring sound. She looked up. A motorbike engine. It could have been one of the punters for the fireworks. But it wasn't. She recognised the particular sound of that engine and she knew exactly who it was. She knelt down on the grass and carried on stripping away the thorns without a second glance.

By seven o'clock in the evening, Celeste had finished arranging the flowers. The roses glowed like fire in the warm rays of the setting sun. Unlike the ceramic poppies at the Tower of London, these blooms would not last long. But they were living, and they were real. Their transience represented the transience of life itself – from bud, to bloom, to blown – the short life cycle of the rose. It brought to mind that Shakespearean love sonnet she had committed to memory as a teenager for her English A level, *Shall I compare thee to a summer's day?* She could still remember most of the lines. 'Summer's lease hath all too short a date,' she said out loud.

By eight o'clock in the evening, the vast disc of the red Midsummer sun had sunk behind the church tower, stretching long, cool shadows across the churchyard, and Celeste began to wonder whether Ben had stood her up. He was supposed to have arrived at 8.30pm.

While Celeste was engrossed in creating her flower

installation, a few people had stopped to look over the wall and see what she was doing. Others had glanced across quickly, and moved on, respecting her privacy and understanding that this was a private and emotional tribute and that she might prefer not to be disturbed by the intrusions of a stranger. Just one woman walking her Labrador tried to strike up a conversation.

'Those look pretty,' she said. 'Are you going along to the fireworks later?' The woman was trying to be friendly. Nevertheless, Celeste was struck by how stupid she was to ask such a question to someone in the middle of preparing a memorial for a grave! Celeste looked at her blankly, but the woman didn't give up. 'Fireworks on the village green,' she said. 'Fun starts at 9pm, to celebrate Midsummer's Eve. There'll be a big crowd. The first firework goes off as the sun sets. It's become a big event. People come from miles away.'

Celeste stooped to gather together her tools as the woman went on her way. The sun was now so low in the sky that she couldn't see the disc, only its light reflected in the pink, dappled clouds above. Still Ben wasn't here. She began to feel edgy. As the time for the fireworks approached, a steady stream of people walked along the path towards the village green. But the churchyard was now so shadowy that no one seemed to notice her sitting quietly on the grass beside Tom's headstone. She was so tired from waking in the early hours to buy the roses that at last her fatigue overcame the slow anger that had burned in the pit of her stomach all through the spring and summer, leaving a strange emptiness and peace.

She lay down in the bed of roses that she had created. She turned her head into the pillow of soft, velvety petals, and she breathed in their sweet perfume, which seemed to intensify as darkness fell. Face down, she stretched out towards Tom's headstone, and crushed the rose heads and petals in the palms of her hands then pressed her fingers against the cold stone. She shut her eyes, and breathed deeply, and at last felt close to Tom.

Then, for the first time in many months, Tom came to her in a dream...

There is a road winding through the trees, and Tom (as a small boy) is running ahead of her with a little brown dog yapping at his heels.

She runs after him, in red stilettos.

She can't keep up because of her heels, and he shouts out to her from a distance.

'I'm going home. There's no place like home.'

She calls after him: 'Wait, you forgot your heart.'

She holds a beating heart cupped in her hands and there's blood everywhere.

Then she trips over a stone and falls down.

And he disappears around the curve in the road into the trees.

He is gone.

Tom's heart is lost.

She's lying face down in the dust on the road crying for her own broken heart.

She feels Tom tapping on her shoulder and his little boy voice saying, 'It's OK, stop crying, I found my heart. I'm here, I'm home.'

She looks at her hands and they are white: all the blood is gone.

He taps on her shoulder again.

She turns her head, and she sees Tom's face smiling down at her...

In her dream it was such a good feeling, like sinking into a warm bath, a sense of relief flooding through her body as she saw Tom happy and whole and unharmed. But now she felt the tapping on her shoulder, more insistent, and the voice, not a little boy's voice this time, a brusque man's voice, saying loudly, 'I'm here, I'm here. Are you OK?'

The dream melted away, along with all the good, warm feelings with which it ended, making way for a surge of flustered panic.

It was Ben.

'I'm sorry I'm late,' he said – though he didn't sound it.

She rolled over and looked up. It was almost dark in the shadow of the church. His face was sinister in the moonlight. She stifled a scream. Suddenly she was back in that damned boathouse, lying on the bare compacted earth, with the grit and the gravel digging into her spine. It was like stepping into a time warp. He towered above her, looking down, but now his features were set into hard lines, all the more mature, confident, domineering and cruel. She leapt to her feet and straightened her hair.

'This is such bad timing... I got held up at work. I had so much to finish off before my transfer to Singapore. I only got the chance to look in on my farewell drinks. And then the traffic... There was a crash on the A3... I've been trying to call you. You're not answering your phone.' Same old Ben. So quick to come up with excuses. So quick to shift the blame.

'What time is it?' she said. 'I must have fallen asleep.'

He looked at his phone. 'Twenty-one, twenty-one,' he said. 'Sunset.'

No sooner had he said the words than a burst of rockets exploded in the air above the village green.

The fireworks had started.

PRESENT

51

Like a dog, I feel my own hackles rise as I watch him go up to You, a menacing, looming shadow in the light of the moon. It's all I can do to keep still and stop myself charging in for the kill. You are face down in the flowers. Unlike Sleeping Beauty, You have no forest of thorns to keep you safe. You turn over and slowly get to your feet. I can't make out the words, but You don't sound happy when You engage with him. Your features are in shadow, but I can see from the set of your shoulders and your chin, that you're facing up to him, even though he stands more than a head above You.

Now You are waving your hands while he turns away and lights a cigarette and perches on the bottom step of a large stone cross. That seems to make You even more mad. It's almost dark but his arrogant expression is lit up as he strikes a match. You march over and grab the cigarette from his mouth and grind it into the turf under the heel of your black trainer. You are right to be angry. It's Midsummer. It hasn't rained for weeks. Everything is dry. The grass is like tinder. It only takes one spark to start a fire.

Now careless of any passers-by, Theo creeps along to a position behind the wall less than two metres distant from Tom's headstone. Shielded by a statue of St Peter he is able to watch and hear. Ben stands up. He towers over Celeste. He exudes power. He grabs her by the upper arm so hard it will leave bruises and shouts down at her and wags his fingers in her face.

From his new hide in the churchyard, Theo hears everything. Celeste unleashes seven years of bitterness and pent-up rage and lets rip with the accusations – *coercive, abusive, an ego-maniac, entitled, he lied, he betrayed her, goddammit, he sexually assaulted her, he's a brute, Mia's better off without him, he doesn't deserve happiness, he's always been a bully, he's not fit to be a husband, he's certainly not fit to have a child...*

'You killed Tom... rapist and murderer... I wish you were dead...'

It's fierce and it's loud. Ben counters every accusation. Discredits every claim. He accuses Celeste of interference in his marriage. He accuses her of poisoning his fiancée's mind against him. He accuses Celeste of kidnapping his future wife and his unborn child. He tries to force Celeste to tell him where Mia is hidden. 'What have you done with her?' he yells, as if Mia is an object who has been mislaid.

Ben is a fighter, but he's not used to people fighting back. Theo knows he should intervene to protect Celeste in her hour of need but is rooted to the spot, a silent witness to the fight. Surely someone else will overhear the row and have the sense to call the police? He doesn't want to be exposed for what he is, a stalker, but what holds him back is more primal than that – he's scared. Theo's never been a fighter. He's been the target of too many bullies. He cowers away from all forms of confrontation. There's something else, too, that stops him from jumping in between Ben and Celeste. He's spellbound and enthralled, mesmerised by Celeste. In her anger, she is radiant, superb, sublime… He's never been more in love.

Perhaps, because it's Midsummer's Eve with a party and music on the village green and fireworks exploding in the night, the fireworks in the churchyard go unnoticed. There's a firestorm overhead and all the eyes and ears in the village are focused on the rockets, fountains and Catherine wheels, whistling and banging in the air, lighting up the sky.

All except Theo's. His eyes and ears are still trained on ground zero. He watches with a morbid fascination. What started as a verbal confrontation becomes physical. Ben grabs Celeste's arms and shouts in her face. This time she won't be his chattel or his conquest. Those boxercise classes she did at XYX come into good use. Her muscles are toned and firm. Her technique is good. The aggression that Niklaus and Juan taught her to channel into punching a stuffed leather ball is aimed at Ben – she pummels his chest, dodges to avoid the retaliation then punches him in the face – once – hard. He stumbles back and cries out in pain. And that's when he lets rip. An eye for an eye, a fist for a fist. He takes back his arm and forms a fist, and he whacks the side of her face with a force that knocks her to the ground.

Celeste lands in a quivering heap among the roses. She looks up. He stands there panting, staring down at her with the same manic expression he wore on his face that night in the boathouse when he pinned her body to the ground under his. At the end of the day he's a man and she's just a woman. He's stronger than her. No amount of motivational training in the gym can combat biology. When it comes down to brute strength, he's her superior.

But XYX taught her something else. Resilience. Never give up. When you hit the floor, you regroup, you stand up, you summon all your strength and stamina, and you fight on.

When Ben knocks Celeste to the ground, she lands next to her workbox. She reaches in and grabs the first thing that comes to hand. As if by chance, her fingers fall on the floristry knife that she had been using to strip the thorns and trim the stems of Tom's roses. By now, Ben has turned away from her in contempt and is walking away down the path towards the woods, his shadowy bulk merging into the darkness. She leaps to her feet, her muscles, springy and strong. She holds the knife like a baton in a relay race, punching forwards at her side, and she sprints. He doesn't reach out to take the baton, he doesn't turn, and she doesn't slow.

For once in his life, Ben is not watching his back.

She hits him at full speed below the ribs. He crumples to the ground at the side of the path and she stumbles on top of him. Groaning with pain, he rolls over and grapples with her, crushing her in his arms. Weakened by the blow, he can't get to his feet and she is like an Amazon, writhing and struggling to get away. She frees her torso, but her legs are trapped under his body while the blood seeps from his side onto her trainer. She scrambles to her hands and knees, preparing for another sprint start into the woods. But he catches her by the ankle and won't let go – as if hanging on for dear life. She pulls away on all fours, dragging him behind. His bloodied hands slide over her ankle.

Her trainer comes off. At last she is free.

Like wildfire, she is gone.

Theo remains hidden in the shadows of the trees, appalled and terrified by what he has seen. He takes out his phone to make a call to the emergency services, then he stops. He can't help thinking that Ben *had it coming*. But he can't leave him lying there like a wounded animal bleeding into the soil. He counts the seconds, ten... twenty... fifty... until he hears the Seventh Heaven van being driven away, and then he calls 999. Before the ambulance arrives, he puts on his leather biker's gloves and picks up the knife that lies covered in blood at the foot of Tom's grave and Celeste's floristry workbox that stands abandoned among the blood-red roses that circle his headstone. He deposits them in the panniers of his motorbike.

As he puts on his helmet, the sirens get louder and louder until flashing blue beams bounce over the stone facade of the church.

He knows his time is running out. It's time to go.

It's only when Theo is accelerating away down the country lane leading from the village to the main road that it occurs to him: he forgot to pick up Celeste's black Nike trainer and Celeste's black Nike trainer is soaked in Ben's blood.

AFTER

52

I watch You walking up the hospital corridor that leads to *his private room. You have a bunch of red roses in one hand and your new wicker floristry box in the other. There's a bounce in your hair and a spring in your step as You clip along the polished floor in the sparkly red shoes that You wore that night at Heavana – the night of my fall. The night we fell in love.*

Until yesterday, I used to listen out for the squeak of your trainers. I wasn't expecting the click-click of stilettos, so You caught me unawares. Today your hips swing, and your stride is shorter, faster, purposeful. You're wearing the same clingy red dress that You wore the night I first set eyes on You at the club. It's a strange outfit for a hospital visit. But I guess You have your reasons.

There's a police officer standing outside the door of his private room. Is that why You wore the dress? The officer won't give You any trouble. I saw him flirting with the nurses earlier on. One sweet smile from those rosy red lips and he'll stand aside and let You in.

The flowers are a special delivery – compliments of CelestialHeadstones.com – an armful of blood-red blooms from the bed of roses strewn across Tom's grave. Your floristry box contains more than just ribbons and twine – though You may put those to good use too. I know this because I watched You through the glass frontage of Seventh Heaven taking the secateurs and the floristry scissors from the shelf and placing them in your box before You picked up the keys to the van.

I thought I knew You so well, but today I cannot say if You come in the name of redemption or revenge. I shall give You the benefit of the doubt. Those implements could be to strip the leaves and trim the stems of the roses. You are a perfectionist when it comes to flower arranging, after all.

You don't look in my direction. I don't mind. I am your fall guy waiting in the shadows. The police officer will find me here when You are gone.

And then the story of Us will begin.

Celeste concludes her course and hands in her project at the end of August. She receives a commendation for her website. The examiner's comment reads as follows:

Candidate 697 is awarded a commendation for the originality and creativity of her website 'CelestialHeadstones.com' combining sophisticated software solutions, an innovative business idea, aesthetic website design and impressive artistic content.

Despite this accolade, Celeste has decided that she will close her website at the end of the year. She will take her last new order on Christmas Eve. The business is not financially viable. The costs of delivering to churchyards and cemeteries make it unsustainable as a business model. What's more, she's had enough of visiting graveyards. She wants to get back to the land of the living. She wants to enjoy life and make a fresh start. She's had enough of living in the UK.

Celeste is in contact with Mia who moved back to the United States in time to enjoy the fall in New York and is getting her life back together again. Mia reconciled with her family and has been living at home working as associate manager in a family-owned art gallery on the Upper East Side. Her baby is due any day. She intends to go back to work a few months after the baby is born.

Mia has offered Celeste a temporary position working in the gallery while she takes time out with the baby. Mia is deeply grateful to Celeste for helping her to escape from her coercive and aggressive partner. All those hours Celeste gave up for her, listening and counselling, helping her to understand that she didn't have to put up with his abuse, that however much she may have once thought she loved him, she had to get away. 'It won't get better. He won't change,' Celeste had said. 'I know him. It's in his DNA. If he treats you like this when you are his fiancée, imagine what he will be like when you are married!'

Celeste hands in her three months' notice to Meghan on

1st December and she tells Jessi and Anya that she will be moving out of the flat at the end of February. She gets a rush of late orders for the Christmas and New Year period in the few days leading up to Christmas Eve. She is so busy prepping flowers for the Christmas Day deliveries that she asks one of the Christmas temps to process the last orders on her website on Christmas Eve, and when she gets back to her flat after the Midnight Service, she takes CelestialHeadstones.com offline. She spends Christmas Day and New Year's Day delivering floral tributes to graveyards in London and the suburbs. She is glad to have an excuse not to visit her mother and the ghastly Mike. She is happy to skip the festive celebrations and lose herself in work.

She goes back to Seventh Heaven when the florist's shop reopens after the Christmas break. Now she is busy planning her departure, applying for visas and work permits, and putting her stuff into storage and the like. She is thrilled to have the opportunity of spending the spring in New York. Who knows? Perhaps she will make that great city her new home. There is one cloud on the horizon. She knows that at some point in the not too distant future she will be called as a witness in Theo's trial. She has given an undertaking to fly back from America to attend the trial. She will testify against him for the prosecution. Her story is all worked out. Her statement was drawn up weeks ago. Her testimony contains it all: evidence of his stalking; his obsession with her; his fantasy that they are in a relationship together (his psychological disorder named as 'erotomania' in her statement); details of the photographs of her taken at so many different graves in locations all around the south east of England (powerful tangible evidence of his obsession, said her solicitor); his violent jealousy towards imagined rivals; the break-in and vandalism at Steve's place; the smashed windscreen on Ben's car; Theo's attempt to rape her in the cemetery in front of Tom's grave interrupted only by the arrival of Ben, and culminating in Theo's assault on Ben with her own floristry knife, which Theo grabbed from her workbox and used to stab Ben in the back in a frenzied and intentional attempt to kill him... This damning testimony is all neatly typed in black on white in the solicitor's file.

Some of it is true but her evidence is riddled with appalling lies. It would be easy for him to tear it apart and discredit her. But she knows he will not break faith with her. All along, he was ready to make the sacrifice. He resolved long ago to be her fall guy. Because he is in love.

However, there are blatant inconsistencies between Theo's fabricated statement and that of Celeste. Theo was willing to confess to attempted murder, but he drew the line at attempted rape, which he denies. His false confession states that he was watching Celeste in the cemetery when Ben turned up and got into an argument with her in which Ben became violent and assaulted her verbally and physically before attempting to rape her. Theo confesses to stabbing Ben in the back with Celeste's floristry knife *after* she managed to escape her attacker and run into the woods. Looking back, Theo can only think that he said this because he wanted to situate Celeste as far away from the stabbing as possible. He cannot forgive himself for being such an idiot. The minute he uttered the words, he knew his false confession was blatantly at odds with the physical evidence. The police have Celeste's black Nike trainer and Celeste's black Nike trainer is stained with Ben's blood. He cannot forgive himself for this schoolboy mistake. Maybe it is this that tips him over the edge.

AFTER

53

Theo does not cope well with prison. Care for the mentally ill should be therapeutic and in surroundings conducive to peace and recovery – not the barred, noisy, stressful and windowless prison where he is incarcerated in a cell for sixteen hours of the day.

A remand prisoner held in custody awaiting trial has certain privileges in accordance with the fundamental principle of English law that an individual is innocent until proven guilty. But in HMP Shadwell prisoners on remand for crimes of attempted rape and attempted murder are not treated well by the other inmates. The only place Theo can get some respite from the claustrophobia of his cell or the callous and casual aggression of the corridors and the dinner hall, is in the computer room.

Despite the gravity of the allegations against him, due to his compliant demeanour, he's classified as a 'low risk' prisoner so the prison officers don't monitor him too closely. He keeps his internal agony to himself. His conduct is exemplary. He volunteers for extra duties. He is the quiet one who doesn't cause trouble. He is always docile, respectful and polite. He has a plan.

Theo joins the prison computing club and becomes a useful member of it. Because he knows so much about information technology and computer programming, he forms a rapport with the prison officer who runs the sessions. Prison regulations are relaxed in the computer room and Theo is able to show the tutor some things he didn't know. Sometimes he stays behind when the other prisoners have returned to their cells to help the officer shut down after class.

On Christmas Eve, the prison officer breaks the rules. Alarm bells and a commotion in the corridor give the officer a reason to leave the classroom. Theo is left unsupervised alone. Five minutes to hack into the computer. That's all the prisoner needs.

The classroom will be closed over Christmas and all the equipment must be cleared. The officer asks Theo to pack up all the printers and carry them to the storeroom. Theo gets his second lucky break. Down in the storeroom, he helps himself to a three-metre USB cable. When the clearing job is done, he wishes the officer a Happy Christmas and walks back to his room with the cable wrapped around his middle concealed by the waistband of his tracksuit bottoms.

Back in his cell, Theo makes a small hole in the seam of his mattress cover and pushes the USB cable deep into the padding. Like the Princess and her Pea, he tosses and turns for the next eight nights, feeling as if the cable is digging into his bones and his soul. But come 1st January he is prepared.

There are special rules for remand prisoners relating

to sending and receiving letters and phone calls and engaging in reasonable activity to maintain their business outside the prison. Theo has made use of these to sort out his affairs. Now all his things are in order and his New Year's resolution is made. He chooses New Year's Day because on this day he will be alone in his cell. His 'roomie' is in solitary confinement in the punishment block for punching a prison officer on Christmas Day. Also, he knows this is a shift when there will be fewer officers on duty and the ones who are here will be sluggish and bleary-eyed the morning after the festivities of New Year's Eve. Today of all days, they won't want to be here any more than he does.

The cells are designed to be 'ligature resistant' but he judges that the metal bedpost and a loose metal protrusion on his door will do the job. It wouldn't hold the weight of a man but is strong enough to hold the tension of the cable for his purpose. He wedges the bed against the ceramic toilet pan. Then he twists the cable round his neck like a scarf and ties one end to the metal bedpost. Just before 'unlock' for breakfast he jams the other end of the cable into the gap behind the metal protrusion on the door. The door opens outwards. The cable is taut. He sits on the floor with his legs outstretched, his head held high, his back against the cold cell door... and waits.

In his right hand he holds a photograph of Celeste in her red dress.

Technically, it is the prison officer who strangles him in forcing open the door and tightening the noose about his neck. But in the Government statistics it will go down as suicide.

AFTER

54

The flowers are delicate with bright yellow centres and small radial sky-blue petals that set off the colour of her eyes and match the soft woollen jacket that she wears over a simple fitted black dress. The order specified this wildflower variety, *Myosotis scorpioides*, of the genus *Boraginaceae*. She had some trouble sourcing the variety through her wholesalers this early in the season but she persisted and has put together a lovely arrangement of long stems loaded with the *Myosotis* flowers in coiled, elongated clusters that gradually unfurl as the flowers bloom, their luminous petals set off by long deep-green leaves.

This order feels significant because it's her last. Her website is now archived and she's moving on. In two weeks, she'll be on a plane to New York. She walks straight up to the grave – fearless and assured. This time she is without her floristry workbox. The bouquet is ready, arranged to perfection.

The headstone is new, made in white stone, square-cut,

plain, nothing ostentatious. She glances in passing at the inscription on the back:

Greater love hath no man

She is not moved. She's seen these biblical words so many times before that they seem almost trite. But as she walks round to the front of the headstone her eyes fall on the name. She stumbles and almost drops the bouquet.

It's a simple inscription. He wanted it that way. Suspecting nothing, the prison chaplain passed on Theo's letter setting out his instructions unopened, as requested.

Theodore Petwick
6th July 2000 to 1st January 2019

Theo placed the order for his memorial flowers anonymously on CelestialHeadstones.com when he hacked-in to the prison computer on Christmas Eve. She had no idea. She followed it to the letter, as he knew she would. It's his parting gift. He chose Valentine's Day for this order to be fulfilled because his last wish was to make her understand what she meant to him.

She feels his presence here – the way she has felt his presence in every churchyard and cemetery she has visited in the past year. She glances over her shoulder, as if expecting someone to join her at the graveside. The churchyard is empty. She sinks on to her knees to place the bouquet carefully at the base of the headstone. When she is done, she covers her face with her hands and allows herself to cry.

While her head is bowed and her eyes are closed, he sets her free. He takes his leave silently, melting away into the shadows of the trees.

Perhaps tomorrow she will feel remorse, but for now, what she feels is an overwhelming sense of release. She breathes in quietly, soothed by the intense, sweet fragrance of the pretty blue wildflowers whose common name appears below his on the headstone. When she looks up, his chosen epitaph is the first thing she sees, right before her eyes, as he must have intended.

Forget-Me-Not

Acknowledgements

Thank you to my wonderful publishers, Aria, such a friendly, fun-loving, dynamic and committed team of professionals! – and to all in the wider Head of Zeus community. I feel so very lucky to be one of your authors. Thank you especially to my brilliant editor, Hannah Smith, for your wise advice, your transformative editorial suggestions and your cheerful patience with my missed deadlines! Thank you also to Rhea Kurien, for your work on the audio book of *She's Mine* and to Vicky Joss, for your wizardry with all things marketing and social media. Many thanks for the meticulous work of proof-readers and copy-editors dedicated to making the text as good as it can be and, of course, to the talented artists who have lit the flame of *No Smoke Without Fire* with such an eye-catching and intriguing cover design.

A big thank you to my fabulous agent, Hayley Steed, and to all at the Madeleine Milburn agency. You get the prize for the best Christmas parties (and the coolest new premises!) and it's been lovely getting to know everyone and meet other authors over the Champagne and mince pies! Particular thanks to MM author Lesley Sanderson for so generously taking time out from her own writing to read and review my first novel, *She's Mine*.

If anyone thinks writing is a solitary business, think again. It's a real pleasure staying connected with my hugely talented Faber writing group friends and making new friends in the writing world. I had a perfect time socialising and researching *No Smoke Without Fire* in peaceful country churchyards in the idyllic English countryside on a Blue Pencil retreat – thank you – and I can't wait for another spell away with fellow writers thanks to Sophie Hannah's wonderful Dream Author programme. Thank you, Kerry Fisher, for the intros to local authors and for being such a wonderful friend – I'm looking forward to dog walks and coffee in the Surrey hills! It's also been so nice reconnecting with old university friends I had lost touch with when our paths happen to cross in the cyberspace!

I am so grateful for the support I've received from friends and family. Thank you so much to my lovely loyal early readers, especially Sara (who has a gift for these things) who read an early draft (again) and gave me such insightful and helpful suggestions, to Sam for her input and thumbs up on the first few chapters, and to Carol for reading and passing on her expertise on all things botanical. Christine - thank you for those long transatlantic phone calls plotting the story and for reading and correcting and spreading the word among your friends in Texas over tea and cakes and crochet! Thank you to so many family, friends and neighbours who have lifted my days by contacting me with such nice and positive comments about my first book – this has given me the courage to keep going with the second.

I'm sure I've gone way over word count on this, but I

must include my love and thanks to my long-suffering husband Nigel (who reads nothing but military history) for indulging my 'vocation' and my paranoid musings about florists and stalkers; to Clara and Louisa for always being my most honest, perceptive, inspiring and creative critics and early readers; and to Jack (what can I say?) – well to Jack, for providing an endless fount of entertaining material for a future novel and for smashing only the mouse and not my screen when his Minecraft glitched! Of course, heartfelt thanks also to my father, Graham, for his invaluable help and support as ever, and to Anne, and to Peter and green-fingered Sylvia who taught me the names of so many flowers while I photographed every bloom in her beautiful garden.

And now I'm truly out of time (sorry Hannah!), so lastly thank you so much to all the bloggers and book reviewers and readers who are so kind and generous with reading and reviewing and commenting and tweeting. I read every review with great interest and love to hear all your thoughts – good or bad! I really mean it – keep posting. Thank you!!

About the Author

CLAIRE S. LEWIS studied Philosophy, French Literature and International Relations at the universities of Oxford and Cambridge before starting her career in aviation law with a City law firm and later as an in-house lawyer at Virgin Atlantic Airways. More recently, she turned to writing psychological suspense, taking courses in creative writing at the Faber Academy and story writing for screen at the Professional Writers Academy. Born in Paris, she's bilingual and lives in Surrey with her family.

Hello from Aria

We hope you enjoyed this book! If you did let us know, we'd love to hear from you.

We are Aria, a dynamic digital-first fiction imprint from award-winning independent publishers Head of Zeus. At heart, we're committed to publishing fantastic commercial fiction – from romance and sagas to crime, thrillers and historical fiction. Visit us online and discover a community of like-minded fiction fans!

We're also on the look out for tomorrow's superstar authors. So, if you're a budding writer looking for a publisher, we'd love to hear from you. You can submit your book online at ariafiction.com/we-want-read-your-book

You can find us at:
Email: aria@headofzeus.com
Website: www.ariafiction.com
Submissions: www.ariafiction.com/we-want-read-your-book

 @ariafiction
 @Aria_Fiction
 @ariafiction

Printed in Great Britain
by Amazon